# OUTLAW HEART

The solitude of the night pressed in on Jake, and an uneasy sensation settled in the middle of his back. "I don't like being out on these roads at night without a weapon, ma'am."

Katherine laughed, and Jake glanced at her questioningly.

"When have you ever known me to be without a weapon?" She pulled the derringer out of her pocket.

Jake stared at the bit of iron in her palm and struggled to withhold his amusement. Unable to do so, he threw back his head and his laughter echoed into the night. "That's not a weapon. It's a conversation piece."

Katherine frowned. "It's better than nothing. You can't expect me to bring my rifle to a party, can you?"

"I suppose not, but I'd be a happier man if you had."

Katherine leaned down and reached under the wooden seat, dragging her rifle from its hiding place beneath.

Jake nodded. "That's my girl."

# SECOND CHANCE

# LORI HANDELAND

LOVE SPELL  NEW YORK CITY

LOVE SPELL®

July 1994

Published by

Dorchester Publishing Co., Inc.
276 Fifth Avenue
New York, NY 10001

If you purchased this book without a cover you should be aware that this book is stolen property. It was reported as "unsold and destroyed" to the publisher and neither the author nor the publisher has received any payment for this "stripped book."

Copyright © 1994 by Lori Handeland

All rights reserved. No part of this book may be reproduced or transmitted in any form or by any electronic or mechanical means, including photocopying, recording or by any information storage and retrieval system, without the written permission of the Publisher, except where permitted by law.

The name "Love Spell" and its logo are trademarks of Dorchester Publishing Co., Inc.

Printed in the United States of America.

*To the Tuesday night ladies:*
*Ana, Ann, Georgann, Leslie, Mary, Peggy, Rasma, Sue,*
*Susie, and my Madison connection, Pam and Peggy.*

Enjoy the book!
Best Wishes,
Lori Handeland

# Chapter One

*Dear Lord, deliver me from a hanging on a Missouri summer day.*

Sweat trickled slowly down Katherine Logan's temple.

She was caught, with no way out of the crowd surrounding her short of scattering the people like flies before the horses. Stamping her foot on the wood floor of her wagon, she sighed in frustration. Patience was not one of her virtues.

She knew nearly everyone in the crowd packing the street. Not on a friendly basis—but she knew them. The Mandels, the nearest neighbors to the Circle A, stood a few feet from her along with several other ranchers from the area. The crowd emitted a festive air. Women, dressed in their Sunday best for the outing, held picnic baskets with brightly colored ribbons threaded through the handles. As Katherine glanced down the street, she saw the shops were closing. Owners and clerks had set up chairs on their front porches to watch the show. At the far edge of town, Katherine spied a group of children in the schoolyard. Attracted by the noise of the crowd, they peered in fascination down the long, dusty street. *What the devil is Ruth thinking to let them watch something like this?*

But even as the thought crossed Katherine's mind, Ruth Sanderson, the schoolteacher, came out to bustle around the children and herd them back inside. Reflecting on her own teaching days in Williamsburg, Katherine recalled how she had often raised her voice to its loudest level to command the attention of her pupils; Ruth accomplished the same result with a whispered word.

Sighing, Katherine remembered how she and her foreman, Dillon Swade, had come into town that morning for supplies. Once there, they separated to collect the necessities. It had been unusually busy in the shops and it wasn't until an hour later that Katherine made her last purchase at the general store.

"It certainly is busy in town today," she remarked idly.

The clerk looked at her oddly. "Always is when there's a hanging."

"Oh no, not today," she cried, then grabbed her purchases out of the startled man's hands and ran for the door.

## Second Chance

She came to an abrupt stop on the porch. Her wagon, stationed to the left of the jail, was surrounded by the milling crowd. Peering further, she stared in disgust at the hastily constructed hanging platform near the center of the town square. It must have been there that morning, but she, as usual, had been too preoccupied to notice. Had she known a hanging was to take place, nothing could have enticed her into town.

Katherine's lips thinned in irritation as she pushed through the crowd. She did not speak to anyone but moved silently and efficiently back to her wagon. Being short had some advantages when it came to moving through such a herd. Upon reaching her destination, she threw the packages in the back and climbed onto the wooden seat.

Accepting that she was in for a long wait, Katherine settled back against the wagon seat. Despite the fact that her calendar read mid-May, the stifling weather reminded her of an eastern July. At least she'd had the forethought to dress for the heat that morning. Her faded blue day dress covered only a chemise instead of the usual corset, petticoats, and hoop needed to produce a fashionable bell shape. She had bound her thick, pale blonde hair into a braid and confined the mass under her late husband's Union cavalry hat. The broad brim shaded her face as effectively as a sunbonnet without restricting her vision the way a woman's head covering would. The townspeople thought her a scandal in this attire, but she no longer cared. Even as a child, she had spent more time climbing trees than practicing ladylike pursuits. She'd carried her precocious ways into adulthood. This had driven her husband, Sam, who had expected her to live up to her frail, angelic appearance, to distraction.

The slam of a door returned her to the present, and her attention turned toward the jail. She squinted and saw two men step into the bright sunlight. Sheriff Jessup held the arm of his prisoner tightly, though such vigilance was unnecessary since the man was handcuffed, his feet hobbled.

Katherine had heard about the uniform of the Confederate guerilla, but she had never actually seen the ensemble until now. She recognized Confederate cavalry pants—gray with a yellow stripe on each side—tucked into black boots extending to the knee. The most fascinating piece of clothing on the man, however, was the infamous "guerilla shirt." Composed of several different colors of cloth, the shirt was cut low in front with a slit narrowing to a point above the belt. The slit was bound shut with lightweight fabric of a brilliant red. Four large pockets of bright yellow graced the light blue fabric covering the prisoner's chest, and a long shirt tail hung to the middle of his thighs. The outfit was a patchwork of confiscated clothing and remnant materials.

"Got the camera set up?" The sheriff's booming voice made Katherine start. She glanced

## Second Chance

toward him as he gestured to a ratlike little man standing nearby.

"Yessir." The photographer scurried toward the sheriff. "If you'll just step over here, I'll get started."

A flurry of activity ensued as a series of men posed for a photograph with the dangerous criminal. The photographer's wagon next to the jail provided the necessary darkness needed to prepare the materials. Katherine watched as the photographer took the plates coated with silver nitrate from his assistant, replaced the holders on the large camera, and refilled the gunpowder for the flash after taking each photograph. He would then disappear beneath a black cloth for several minutes to compose a picture on the plate before reappearing to instruct, "Don't move, please." The process was time-consuming but fascinating in its novelty.

The criminal ignored the men and the photographer as he avidly surveyed the crowd and the open area beyond. He appeared to be searching for someone, and Katherine turned her head quickly to study the outskirts of town, expecting the Coltrain Gang of guerillas to ride in for a rescue. But nothing out of the ordinary met her gaze, and no dust arose from the land surrounding them to indicate an incoming group of riders. Unless the Coltrain Gang could fly, and there were those superstitious enough to believe they could, there would be no daring rescue for this man.

## Lori Handeland

Glancing back at the jail, Katherine was startled to find the prisoner watching her. As the photographer and the men from town moved around him, he stared directly at her. Under his steady gaze Katherine grew warm in a way that had nothing to do with the sweltering sun, but she found she could not look away. He was handsome for a criminal, with hair so dark it glinted blue under the sun and light eyes the color of which she could not distinguish over the distance. The lower half of his face was shadowed by several days' growth of dark beard, but the skin over his high cheekbones glistened bronze and supple in the merciless sunshine. As he continued to stare into her eyes, a lump formed in Katherine's throat. No man had a right to be that beautiful.

Suddenly the prisoner narrowed his eyes and turned away to glare at the man in black climbing the jail's steps. The town undertaker, tall and sallow, was nonplussed by the evil looks he received from his quarry. Going about his business, he measured the prisoner for a coffin. The men on the porch were too busy with the photographer and each other to notice the anger on the criminal's face. Before anyone could stop him, the man raised his handcuffed wrists and shoved the undertaker down the steps.

The thud of the undertaker as he hit the ground caught Sheriff Jessup's attention. He whirled toward the prisoner, his hand going for his gun, but he hesitated at the sight greeting him. The criminal leaned against the porch

## Second Chance

rail, his gaze calmly focused on the undertaker, who was entangled in his measuring string and unable to get up from the dirt.

Jessup relaxed and dropped his gun hand to his side. "What're you pickin' on old Marley for, Banner? The man's just doin' his job."

"Seems to me he could do it just as well after I'm dead. It's not polite to measure a man for a coffin when he's still around to be offended by the gesture."

Katherine found herself smiling at Banner's observation. Not only was he a handsome criminal, but he was polite. He had a soft, deep voice with a slight trace of the South. That voice brought back memories of home and treasured male relatives. Katherine blinked away the uncharacteristic wetness in her eyes. Those men were as dead as the South these past five years since Appomattox Courthouse.

When Katherine glanced back at the jail, the sheriff was motioning for one of the men to help the undertaker up from the dirt. Then he bent to remove the chains from Banner's legs and led the prisoner down the steps.

A path opened before them as they walked through the crowd. The men came directly toward Katherine, but she barely glanced at the sheriff. For some reason she felt the need to know the color of Banner's eyes. Katherine drew in her breath as eyes of emerald green met her gaze. The prisoner stopped next to her wagon and seemed about to speak, but the lawman roughly jerked him away.

## Lori Handeland

As the sheriff and his companion climbed the wooden stairs to the hanging platform, their steps echoed dully in the heavy air. Banner towered over Sheriff Jessup who, at six feet, was previously the tallest man in town. Katherine stared at Banner's wide shoulders and strong legs. The man was obviously not a stranger to physical labor. With the sad lack of ranch hands in their area of Missouri, it seemed a shame to waste a firm set of muscles that could be used for honest work if only given the chance.

Suddenly, the moment arrived. Death hovered in the air. Katherine heard its approach in the shuffle of the crowd. They were there to watch the end of a life, and Katherine was disgusted. She wished herself anywhere but in Second Chance, Missouri, for a hanging. But her wish went unanswered as the sheriff took a deep breath in preparation for his customary speech to the crowd.

"Good people, our ancestors founded this settlement on the principle of second chances. The oath of my office requires me to ask: Will anyone give this criminal, Jake Banner, a second chance after he took part in the robbery of our bank?"

The prisoner's gaze darted around the edge of the crowd, and his jaw flexed with anger as he turned his eyes to the sheriff. A flash of insight struck Katherine. The man's cavalier attitude toward impending death had been based on his expectation of rescue—an expectation that faded quickly as the clock ticked

## Second Chance

resolutely onward toward his demise.

The noise of the crowd faded to a murmur, and Katherine's eyes met the stranger's. As bright green meshed with pale gray, she felt an affinity she could not define. The noise, the heat, the crowd receded as everything moved slowly before her eyes. She watched Jessup wait his obligatory minute for an answer, and then he took the noose in his hand to proceed with the hanging. He placed the rope around Jake Banner's neck, and Katherine watched it tighten around his strong, brown throat.

"Stop!" Katherine did not realize she had shouted until all eyes in the crowd turned to her. She found herself standing on the seat of her wagon, towering over the crowd. The illusion of height created a sense of power. Katherine enjoyed the feeling.

"Did you say somethin', Mrs. Logan?" Sheriff Jessup shouted, as if she were hard of hearing, as well as a bit crazy.

Katherine sighed. She would have to brazen her way through this or the town would consider her more foolish than they already believed her to be.

"Cut him loose, and I'll take him back to the Circle A with me."

The sheriff gaped at her. No one had ever before answered his routine question. His reaction reminded Katherine of her marriage ceremony three years earlier. When the pastor asked if anyone there had a reason not to unite the couple in holy matrimony, he never actually expected an answer.

Katherine resisted the urge to giggle at the idiotic look on Jessup's face. Laughing at this point would not help her cause. Instead, she adopted the stern face she would have used with her most difficult student.

"Close your mouth, Harley, and cut him down as I asked. I don't intend to spend all day discussing this with you in the heat."

"But, Mrs. Logan, no one's ever been given a second chance in Second Chance." Jessup scratched his head. "Leastways, not since I can remember."

"Just because you've never seen a thing happen doesn't mean it can't. Cut the man down."

"What are you doing, Katherine?"

A voice from below made Katherine look down—directly into the angry gaze of Dillon Swade.

"None of your business," she hissed. "You work for me, remember?"

The dratted man was a nuisance. From the first day three years ago when she arrived at the Circle A, a twenty-five-year-old bride who had met her husband only a month before in Williamsburg, Dillon had grated on her nerves. He forever hovered over her, correcting her and telling her what to do, as though his superior age gave him that right. Even though she now owned the Circle A, he would not stop treating her like a child—a useless city child. If she had been a frail flower, desperately in need of his strength and wisdom, she had no doubt Dillon would be much happier and easier to get along with.

One of his few redeeming qualities was his talent with a gun. He had spent many hours with Katherine teaching her to shoot—hours for which she would always be grateful. Still, if he wasn't such a good manager she would have fired him the day her husband died while breaking a wild colt no one else would touch. But despite her need of his skills, the time had come to give Dillon Swade a set-down.

She glared at her foreman. Were it possible, his small, watery blue eyes narrowed further as he took in her look and the belligerent set of her chin. Embarrassed, he glanced at the crowd. The smirks on some of the ranchers' mouths caused a red flush to creep up his face and across his bald head. When he didn't respond, Katherine hoped she had won a small battle in her war.

"She wants to give the thief a second chance," a malicious voice yelled from the crowd.

Katherine frowned in the direction of the speaker and opened her mouth to reply. But before she could speak, Dillon announced, "Ignore her and do your job, Jessup."

Katherine was so angry at the easy way Dillon dismissed her, she wanted to kick his smug face. She drew back her boot, then stopped. Such an action would only make her seem more irrational to the sheriff. Instead, Katherine took a deep breath and, with a deceptively soft voice meant for Dillon alone, whispered, "I would worry about your own job if I were you, not Jessup's." Then she turned to the sheriff with a sweet smile. "Mr. Swade works for me, Sheriff. Ignore him and do as I asked."

Jessup scratched his beard. He was slow at the decision-making process. But his sense of fair play and an eagle eye with a gun enabled him to perform his job adequately if not well. Katherine held her breath while he pondered. If Jessup denied her request, the entire town, along with Dillon, would be laughing at her.

"Ma'am, I can't let you take him. He's a member of the Coltrain Gang. We've got to set an example or they'll be thievin' around here forever."

Katherine's heart sank in disappointment, but she had learned not to back down once she made up her mind. When she jumped down from the wagon seat and picked up the reins to her team, Dillon backed quickly into the crowd. Coward, she thought.

"Sheriff, cut him down now so we can all get out of this heat. I have work to do before the sun goes down today." The look she turned on the townspeople standing below her asked why they were watching a hanging on a Tuesday afternoon.

Throughout the entire discussion Banner listened patiently, his green eyes following the conversants, a smile on his face whenever Katherine spoke. His cool demeanor seemed to irritate both the sheriff and the crowd, though

## Second Chance

Katherine could see the outlaw still clenched his jaw convulsively. She observed several of the ranchers pointing at him angrily. Complaints of "cold bastard" and "laughing at us" filled the air, and Katherine's throat clenched at the hatred in the voices.

When Jessup shook his head, Katherine's heart lurched painfully. With a muttered, "Sorry, ma'am," he checked the tightness of the noose.

The crowd turned their attention back to the show they had come to watch, forgetting Katherine's existence.

"If you didn't mean what you said then you shouldn't have said it." Katherine's voice rang out above the crowd.

A woman screamed when Katherine put a rifle to her shoulder and pointed the barrel directly at the condemned man. The crowd scurried away from her wagon, and the sheriff made a move for his gun as she fired.

The bullet sliced through the rope above Banner's head as she knew it would. She noticed the stranger had closed his eyes. Had he thought she would shoot him instead of the noose?

Jessup still held his drawn gun, gaping at the now useless rope. Lucky for her and Banner that Harley was a bit slow. At the sharp crack of the reins against her team's flanks, the crowd scattered. When the horses raced past the platform, Banner leapt into the back of the wagon, and they disappeared into the cloud of dust rising from the earth of Second Chance.

# Chapter Two

A half mile out of town Katherine slowed the horses from their breakneck pace. The wagon rolled along the dirt road lined by fields and prairie grass. The seat dipped beside her, and she turned to meet the green eyes of the man she saved from the gallows.

"Thank you." He spoke low, his voice overlaid with a soft southern accent. The sound reminded Katherine of the warm maple syrup her Aunt Adelaide poured over their pancakes on cool Virginia mornings.

"Don't mention it, please. I seem to have a knack for getting myself into things I shouldn't. We'll just have to make the best of this situation."

He was silent. She could tell her heated tone and flippant words had not pleased him. A short

## Second Chance

temper had forever been her curse.

The realization seized her that she was alone with a criminal—a thief and, for all she knew, a murderer. Katherine stifled a groan. What had she done in the name of pride? Hadn't she learned by now that rash actions, more often than not, led to everlasting regret? Slowly, stealthily, she used her foot to pull the rifle closer to her across the floor of the wagon. As an added precaution, she kept her booted heel firmly on top of the weapon.

After a few moments of tense silence Jake asked, "What was that speech the sheriff spouted about second chances?"

Katherine slightly relaxed her white-knuckle grip on the reins and glanced at him from the corner of her eye. He seemed genuinely curious and she drew in a deep breath, telling herself that she had the gun, after all. What could it hurt to tell him about the small quirk of Second Chance that had helped her to save his life?—insane impulse though it was. She shrugged, then began to speak, keeping one eye on the road, the other on him.

"The original settlers of the town were minor criminals from England. Every so often the prisons there became overcrowded and convicts were released with the provision that they leave the country. Over a hundred years ago, several of them came to America and settled in Missouri." Katherine paused and urged the horses to pick up their pace before continuing. "The settlers named the town Second Chance because anyone in their jail could have a second chance provided someone took responsibility for them. The ex-convicts were alive because of their own second chance, so they wanted to offer the same benefit to others. The tradition continued over the years and finally became a law."

"Anyone could have a second chance?" Jake's face reflected his amazement.

"No. Murderers and . . ." Katherine was unsure of how to state the other exclusion. Finally she held her breath and plunged ahead. "Murderers and those who . . . who force women don't qualify."

"But bank robbers do?"

"There's nothing mentioned about robbery as far as I know. As you could tell, no one's taken advantage of the law in a long time. But it's still the law."

"Lucky for me," Jake muttered and shifted on the hard wooden seat.

The movement caused his leg to brush against Katherine's, and she stiffened, her hand reaching for the rifle without thinking. Jake glanced at her but said nothing, and after a few moments she relaxed again.

She felt breathless with him seated so close to her. Only because he's a criminal, Katherine assured herself. Now that she had succeeded in getting the man out of town, what should she do with him?

"Well, Mr. Banner, it seems we have an awkward situation on our hands. Now that I've

## Second Chance

got you, I have to find something to do with you." She paused for a moment. "Have you ever worked around horses?"

His eyes gleamed as he flashed her his dazzling smile. Katherine began to return the smile, then stopped and frowned. The man was a criminal, and now she was responsible for his life; she would have to keep that in mind or he would be charming her out of all she owned. Why, oh why, hadn't she kept her mouth shut in town?

As though from a long way off, Katherine heard Jake speaking. He probably had been for some time. Her face colored with the realization that she'd been staring at his mouth but not listening to his words.

"I'm sorry. What did you say?"

Jake smiled again. "Horses, ma'am, I love them. I was in a cavalry-like unit during the war." His voice reflected pride in the fact.

Something he said struck Katherine as odd. A cavalry-like unit? What was that? Then she remembered that the guerilla units of the Confederacy were a type of cavalry. They were the best armed fighting unit of their kind. The word around Second Chance was that the members of the Coltrain Gang had all ridden as guerillas.

Although Katherine hadn't lived in Second Chance during the war, she arrived shortly after and knew the guerillas were considered outlaws, even by the army they had once belonged to. They had their own officers, rules, and plans of attack that did not coincide with the Confederate or Union forces. Guerillas were bloodthirsty, vengeful, and excellent marksmen—a dangerous combination in a trained force. And she had just invited one of them to stay on her ranch.

"You can sleep in the barn." Katherine blurted out the words before realizing how they might sound.

Jake raised an eyebrow but remained silent.

"It's just . . . I've never known a bank robber, or any criminal for that matter." *You're babbling, Katherine,* she told herself.

"I appreciate your helping me, ma'am, but there's no reason to have me on your place if I make you uncomfortable. I'll just leave now, and you can say I escaped on the way to your ranch." Jake made a move as if to jump off the wagon.

"No!" Katherine grabbed his arm, then pulled her hand away quickly, like a child whose fingers have been slapped. She stared intently at the road even though they were now close to the Circle A and the horses knew the way.

"I already look foolish to everyone for taking you with me. I don't need to look more foolish by losing you before we get you home."

From the corner of her eye, Katherine saw him studying her face; then he looked longingly at the trees lining the road. With his attention focused elsewhere for the moment, Katherine retrieved her pistol from beneath the wagon seat. When he made a move toward the trees

## Second Chance

she cocked the gun. From the way Jake froze, he was as familiar with that sound as his own voice. She held the Army Colt casually in her right hand, the reins in her left.

"You're certainly a collector of firearms, ma'am," he said, then settled back on the seat.

Katherine lowered the pistol. She could tell that Jake had abandoned the idea of running for freedom. Still, she gripped the handle of the Colt. It was better to be safe now than sorry later.

They remained silent for the rest of the ride to the Circle A. When the horses turned into a rutted lane, Jake sat up straight and gazed at his temporary home. A whitewashed house, barn, and bunkhouse, as well as other smaller buildings, sat in a hollow at the base of the lane. Horses grazed in fields of flowing grass beyond. Katherine focused on Jake's intent face, and her heart grew warm. Seeing her admiration for the land reflected in another's eyes revealed a kindred spirit. She loved the Circle A with all the pent-up affection within her. She felt at home there, for once not pulled between her northern birth and her southern upbringing. The ranch was the first thing in her life that belonged solely to her, and she would mold it into something wonderful.

Katherine pulled the horses to a stop in front of the barn. "You said you're familiar with horses?" she asked.

"Yes. I was an officer in my unit." The flicker of pride in his soft southern drawl came again.

"Well, *sir*, you can start by cleaning the stable. In there." She pointed at the barn with the Colt, then retrieved the rifle from the wagon and jumped to the ground. Walking toward the house, she shook her head again at the situation her unaccustomed spontaneity had brought her.

Jake sat where Katherine had left him in the wagon and watched her walk up the porch steps. He had never met a woman so prickly. That and the odd habit she had of pulling out guns during every disagreement made it hard to like her. Why then did he find himself smiling at her retreating, ramrod-straight back? Why was he planning to stay and work for a gun-loving female?

Perhaps it was the sadness he recognized lurking behind the studied coolness of her gray eyes. He had buried pain of his own, and though he tried not to remember that pain, at odd moments it snuck up on him and threatened to take over. Continuing on with whatever job occupied him at the time was always a test of his strength, a test he had thus far always passed. A similar strength existed in Katherine. Though she might appear weak and fragile on the outside, he believed she had come through emotional fire just as he had, and had emerged stronger after surviving the agony of the flames. Since the war, he had seen many people whose eyes mirrored a hidden pain. But he had never been so intensely curious about the

## Second Chance

cause of their pain until he'd encountered Katherine.

Jake jumped down from the wagon and smacked his palms irritably against his thighs. He wouldn't be around long enough to worry about Katherine Logan's problems, past or present. And he should know better than to wonder or care. In his position such emotions could only get him, or her, killed. He was going soft and he could ill afford such a weakness. He had thrown his hat in with those who preyed on weakness, like coyotes after a motherless calf. In fact, he could feel the Coltrain Gang snapping at his heels already.

Entering the stable, he glanced around the interior. The building was already cleaner than any stable he had ever seen. Though the ranch seemed to be operating with very few workers, Katherine Logan obviously took care of what was hers. His father had always said you could tell a lot about a man from the way he kept his stable and treated his horses. Jake smiled as he stared at the well-kept interior. Dad would like Katherine.

Jake grabbed a pitchfork and tossed clean straw around the empty stalls. Purposefully he pushed any further thoughts of Katherine Logan from his mind and allowed the monotony of his chore to soothe him. As he relaxed from the high drama of the day, his mind wandered back over the events of the past weeks and his reasons for being in Second Chance.

## Lori Handeland

\* \* \*

"We've got to get a man into that gang." Alan Pinkerton paced back and forth behind his desk, his short legs moving quickly in agitation. "Our employers, the Addler Express Company, are losing a fortune to the Coltrains."

Jake smiled fondly at his boss. The slight paralytic stroke that Pinkerton had suffered last fall did not seem to hinder him, though he had retired from actual detective work. His mind remained sharp as ever, and he continued to oversee all facets of each operation.

"I'm sure you're right, sir," Jake said. "Just who did you have in mind?"

Jake waited patiently. Pinkerton had a reason for everything he did. Not only did the man know who to send on this mission, he already had the plan mapped out in specific detail. Apparently Jake was the man, or he wouldn't be sitting in Pinkerton's Chicago office wasting valuable time.

Pinkerton didn't answer directly. At Jake's question the detective stopped pacing and, spinning gracefully for such a stocky man, unlocked his desk drawer. Withdrawing an envelope, he glanced at Jake across the table; the light from the oil lamp sent flickering shadows across his face. Pinkerton looked sinister in the indistinct light, and Jake experienced a tremor of premonition.

"Superstition and unfounded fears have no place in an agent's mind," he recited quietly to himself.

## Second Chance

"What was that, Parker?" Pinkerton's ears were as sharp as his mind. "Something bother you about this assignment?"

"No, sir. I just wonder why you decided on me for this one. Isn't Matthew Ward the expert on the Coltrains?"

"He is, but he was also a banker before the war. He's already in position at the bank in Second Chance under the name Matthew Rolland. He'll be expecting you to use the alias Jake Banner." Pinkerton slammed his fist onto the desk and his slight Scottish burr became more pronounced. "There's a leak at that bank somewhere, I'm sure of it. The way those outlaws know where the railroad payroll is at any given moment is too uncanny to be a coincidence. I've had two operatives check out the express company on this end, and they report no leak. I can't understand how Charlie Coltrain is getting his information since no one in Second Chance is party to Addler's plans regarding the shipment of the payroll until the last minute. I need you to infiltrate the gang and see if you can learn anything from that end."

"The Coltrain Gang's pretty rough. Are they going to welcome an outsider?"

Pinkerton smiled in satisfaction. "That's why you're perfect for this, Parker. The year you spent on that mission in the South gave you an understanding of their minds and motives, not to mention a command of the accent. I've also got to send someone who can ride as well as them, and shoot a tick off a dog's back from a moving horse. That's you, Jake."

"You know the town where they hole up isn't too far from St. Louis where I'm from?"

Pinkerton only stared at him, disgruntled. Of course he knew. Pinkerton knew everything about all of his agents. That's what made him an excellent manager and tactician.

"Something wrong with working in Missouri, Parker? Do you think someone might recognize you?"

"No, sir. I haven't been home much since I left for the war."

*And when I was, folks said they barely recognized me. Though I hope I've learned how to hide the haunted look that made my mother cry, and I have put back all the weight I lost since . . .*

Jake glanced up to see Pinkerton watching him closely. He cleared his throat. "I doubt if anyone I know will show up in a small town like Second Chance. What are the Coltrains bothering with it for anyway?"

"Though the town's small, it sits on a main stage route and the train passes nearby as well. Not to mention a honeycomb of caves just outside of town that make a perfect hideout. Charlie Coltrain knows the area as well as he knows his dead mother's name. Being from the state yourself, you know how divided it was in the war." At Jake's nod Pinkerton continued. "Well, Second Chance was very vocal about its Union support, then and now. Charlie hates

## Second Chance

Yankees, always has, and he's having a roaring good time terrorizing the town and everyone in it." Pinkerton looked at him closely, and Jake knew the man had caught his earlier momentary lapse into the past. "Can you handle this one, Parker?"

"Of course, sir. You know you can count on me."

His boss nodded with satisfaction. "That's why you're my number one agent, Parker. Now take this information, read it tonight, and then get out of town tomorrow."

So Jake had traveled from Chicago to Illinoistown on the train the very next day. As he stepped onto the ferry that crossed the Mississippi to St. Louis, he spoke with a soft southern drawl and became Jake Banner, former Confederate cavalry officer looking for work.

Now, as he continued to do the familiar chores in Katherine Logan's barn, he wondered what had gone wrong with the carefully laid plans of Alan Pinkerton.

He had been incredibly stupid to get caught on his very first job with the Coltrains. But he'd believed that Matt would arrange a way for him to escape, and then he would rejoin the gang. Today, trussed and led to his execution, he kept waiting for the eventual release, even wondering if the sheriff planned to let him escape in the mayhem of the crowd. When the noose went around his neck, he'd finally understood that something was terribly wrong.

But at certain times life had a way of working out for the best, and Katherine Logan was one of those times. At first he thought she had been sent to help him, but her obvious unease in the wagon after their escape proved that belief wrong. He had to smile as he recalled her drawing the rifle across the floor of the wagon, then leaving her foot on top of it. As though she could have stopped him if he really wanted that gun.

But he understood fear in all its forms, and if a gun in her hand made her feel better, that was fine with Jake Parker. What he couldn't understand was why she had saved him of her own free will, believing him a criminal. Jake shook his head and shrugged to himself.

Women.

This woman had given him the perfect opportunity to observe the town and its inhabitants. Pinkerton himself couldn't have devised a better cover. He would stay on the Circle A until he'd learned all he could from this angle, then return to the Coltrain Gang with no one any the wiser about his motives and identity.

One thing still bothered him, though. Just where the hell was Matt and what was he up to?

Katherine sent her housekeeper home when she learned her hired hands were camping overnight at the far boundaries of the ranch. After the woman left, Katherine decided to look in on her new worker.

## Second Chance

Pausing in the doorway of the barn, she saw Jake leaning on a pitchfork and seemingly lost in thought.

"You won't finish tonight if you continue to work at this rate," Katherine said.

Jake started at the sound of her voice. Nodding at her comment, he returned to his task without a word.

Katherine's eyes were drawn to the brown neck and chest exposed by the low collar of his shirt. The skin glistened with sweat, and dark hair curled around the ends of the faded blue cloth. As Jake lifted the pitchfork, the muscles in his arms strained the cloth across his chest. A patch of darker blue appeared in the center of his shirt as the material stuck to his damp skin. Katherine ran her tongue across her lower lip. Realizing guiltily the direction her mind had taken, she walked quickly into the barn and placed the blankets in her arms over one of the stalls.

"You can use these to make up your bed tonight." Discomfort at her wayward thoughts made her voice sharper than she meant it to be, and Jake eyed her strangely.

"I'm sorry if I upset you, ma'am. I'll have the stable done before dark. You'll see."

Katherine sighed. She was always too short, too angry, too brusque when dealing with people. She didn't know how to inspire the respect she sought, and her lack of confidence caused her to act remote. Her husband Sam had dubbed her "the ice queen" soon after her arrival in Second Chance. Originally he had meant the term to be complimentary, admiring her control. Later he used the words as an insult when the same control irritated him beyond measure. She had been taught as a child to keep her personal feelings to herself, in public and in private. Once she reached adulthood, she did not know how to change, and hadn't wanted to.

Katherine watched Jake work with renewed vigor, gratified to see the energy he applied to his task. She had a sudden urge to hear again his mellow southern tones. Anything to drown out the memories of her earlier life and her time with Sam that suddenly crowded her mind. Since she knew nothing about him beyond his name and crime, Katherine resolved to learn more about the man who called himself Jake Banner. After kicking over a bucket, she seated herself upon it and regarded him curiously.

The sharp, tinny clang caused Jake's head to jerk in Katherine's direction. Calmly seated on the makeshift stool, her arms around her knees, she looked like a young girl. The battered hat was gone, and a thick braid, the color of sun-ripened wheat, hung down her back. Jake never had a taste for small, petite women. His extreme height always made him feel awkward when paired with someone so delicate. But this woman's spirit almost blinded him to the fact that she was the most fragile-looking female he'd ever encountered.

## Second Chance

"You look like you can do a good day's work without difficulty," Katherine said.

"Don't worry, I'll carry my load. You won't be disappointed that you helped me."

"No, I'm sure you'll do fine. I'm wondering why a strong, able-bodied man takes the coward's way out by robbing people."

Though he knew how things looked to Katherine, it still sent a jolt of fury through Jake to hear the word "coward" used in connection to himself. Swallowing his anger, he prepared to weave a tale of lies. The false background Pinkerton gave him had satisfied the Coltrains' questions; he would soon find out how well the story satisfied Katherine.

He began, low and soft, to tell the story, and as Katherine leaned forward to catch the words, he became engrossed in his tale.

"I lost everything in the war: family, land, home. My place was in Georgia, between Sherman and the sea. When I returned from the hell of war, another hell waited for me: acres of burned crops and buildings, my parents and sister murdered. I tried to find work to stay alive, but the carpetbaggers and Reconstruction folk had taken everything. I wasn't good enough to work in my own town. Yankees overran the place. The minute I opened my mouth and they heard my accent, I was treated like dirt. I heard there was work in the West for an able man."

Jake stole a glance at Katherine and saw she was absorbed in his words.

"I came to St. Louis on a steamboat up the Mississippi, bought a horse and supplies with the last of my money, and headed farther west. Before long I discovered Missouri was still divided by the war, and in places my accent brought scorn from everyone I met.

"Then I came to Second Chance and found the Coltrains. They were guerillas and Confederates with the same background as me, giving back some of the terror and hate directed at them for so many years. I finally felt I belonged somewhere; so I joined them."

Silence descended over the barn when he finished his story. Jake went back to work without further comment as Katherine sat on the pail, deep in thought. Several moments passed before she spoke.

"I sympathize with the plight of the South. I lived there myself during the war. But how can you justify robbing innocent people?"

"The Pacific Railroad isn't innocent. It's owned by Yankees. They owe us something, and we're taking what we deserve."

"What about the men whose payroll you've stolen?"

"Yankees."

"After seeing all the death and destruction and hatred the war caused, don't you want to put all that behind you? Nothing either of us can do will change what happened. The South lost, and there's no going back to the way things were."

"I'll never put the war behind me, ma'am.

## Second Chance

Not now. Not ever. Not as long as I sleep at night and walk the day can I ever forget what happened to me while I fought for my country and my life."

Jake clenched his teeth to keep from saying any more. When had he stopped spinning a tale and started telling the truth? He couldn't remember. He could only hope Katherine couldn't tell the difference.

She sighed, a sorrowful release of breath, and he relaxed. She obviously believed his explanation and felt sorry for him, though his excuses for thievery irritated her. Guilt twisted inside him at his deception. Lies were easier to tell when spoken to thieves and murderers. Jake found feeding falsehoods to an angelic face extremely uncomfortable. This woman had saved his life, given him a job and a place to live. Jake opened his mouth to thank her, but before he could speak the silence between them was shattered.

"Mrs. Logan, why did you bring that filthy, thievin' Confederate onto our place?"

# Chapter Three

Katherine glanced at the door. The stocky, muscular silhouette proved as identifiable as the loud and blustering tone.

"I don't recall seeing your name on the deed to the Circle A, Dillon. The last time I looked I was the sole owner of this ranch. As such, I can employ anyone I wish."

"But a thief—and a Reb at that. We'll have to watch him all the time, or he'll be stealing us blind." Dillon removed his straw hat and wiped the sweat from his forehead.

"If so, he'll be stealing *me* blind. I think Mr. Banner will work out just fine here. We must make room for Christian charity in our lives, Dillon." Katherine held back a smile.

"Christian charity?" He snorted. "I didn't notice much Christian charity in the way you left me in town. How was I supposed to get back here without a horse? Maybe you were too interested in getting Mr. Southern Thief back here so you could have him all to yourself? If I'd known you were that desperate for a man, I'd a helped you out a long time ago."

Katherine gasped, shocked at the change in her foreman. He had always been insolent but never had he insulted her personally. Before she could retaliate for the affront, Jake grabbed Dillon by the collar of his shirt and lifted him off his feet.

"Apologize." The word was soft, but deadly.

Dillon sputtered and coughed, his face changing from dark red to mottled purple.

"Now."

"I don't think he'll be able to speak at all if you continue to cut off his air that way," Katherine remarked.

Jake loosened the hold but did not remove his face from its close proximity to Dillon's.

"The lady's waitin'."

Dillon rubbed his throat, stepping out of Jake's reach.

"I didn't know you liked your men rough. You don't need him. I can accommodate you."

Jake reached for Dillon before he could complete the sentence.

"Leave him be." Katherine's voice reflected her dejection, and Jake turned to her.

"Ma'am?" He remained within an arm's reach of Dillon.

## Lori Handeland

Katherine took a deep breath and eyed the two men. She had known there would be trouble, but she hadn't expected it this soon.

"Dillon, someday your filthy mind is going to get you into more trouble than you can handle. Jake is grateful to me for saving his life, and I'm sure there will be no problems where he's concerned. He's here to work. I want him treated like any other paid ranch hand." She started to walk away, then stopped. Dillon's insolence must be met head on—immediately. "Jake, go back to what you were doing. Dillon, come with me."

When they were out of Jake's hearing, Katherine turned to her foreman. "Just who did you think you were talking to back there? I'm your employer. I don't owe you any explanations about my behavior. If I want to bring Charlie Coltrain himself onto this ranch and have him wash my hair, I will. And I won't ask Dillon Swade for his approval of my actions, ever."

Dillon's eyes peered into Katherine's and he shook his head sadly. "You still don't see it, do you? If you'd stick to women's work and let me handle the ranch, I'd have this place running at a profit in no time." He reached out to take her hand, grasping her fingers painfully. "I'm sorry about what I said back there." He jerked his head toward the barn. "It makes me angry when any man looks at you. Especially a dirty Reb thief. You know I'd do anything for you, Katherine."

## Second Chance

Katherine carefully removed her hand from Dillon's damp clasp, stifling the desire to pull away quickly. Though still angry, she attempted to speak more calmly to the irate man. She needed him to help her with the ranch, much as she hated to admit that need. "I'm grateful for your help, Dillon, but the Circle A is my responsibility now and I intend to keep it that way. Your constant questioning of my orders has got to stop. I know you think Sam should have left you a share in the ranch, but he didn't. If you want to seek other employment, I can't stop you. Your expertise with the horses, however, would be greatly missed."

Katherine held her breath, knowing she would have a crisis on her hands if Swade chose to leave. But the time had come for him to work with her or quit.

Swade's face reddened. She had struck the intended nerve. He was unlikely to find a position of the same stature at any other ranch with his army record common knowledge in the area. Missouri may have had divided loyalties during the war, but those who supported an army were loyal to that army. Swade had made a small fortune selling horses to the Confederates before being caught red-handed by Katherine's late husband, Colonel Sam Logan. Fortunately for Dillon, Logan had recognized a man who could be of use to him after the war. He procured for Swade a court martial, with subsequent reduction in rank and loss of pay, instead of the hanging that Swade deserved. Since that day, Swade had been Logan's man, doing all the dirty work that needed doing and enjoying it. But Missourians didn't tolerate traitors, regardless of their politics, and Swade had endured their scorn enough times to know that word of his dishonor had spread. It infuriated him even more to realize he was still being blackmailed a year after Sam Logan had gone to his grave.

"You know I'll never leave the Circle A." Dillon narrowed his eyes and scowled at Katherine. "I work harder than anyone to make this ranch a success. It should be mine, as well as yours. Someday it will be, mark my words."

"I doubt that, Dillon." Katherine's voice sounded calm, but her heart skipped a beat at the thinly veiled violence she saw in Swade's eyes. She had come to realize over the past few months that Swade coveted her as much as the ranch. Though sometimes he almost tried to court her, at other times he treated her with a thinly veiled contempt reminiscent of her husband. Now he was angry and frustrated, a dangerous combination. She would need to handle him more carefully in the future. He would be dismissed, she vowed, as soon as the Circle A made a profit again.

"We can discuss this further tomorrow, after we've had time to calm ourselves," Katherine said.

Without replying, Dillon shouldered past Katherine and disappeared around the corner of the barn. She found herself staring at empty air and sighed deeply. Their arguments always ended the same way.

Glancing at the barn door, she saw Jake leaning against a pitchfork watching her. For some reason the look in his eyes made her shiver, and she hurried around the corner intent on seeking the safe haven of her office.

Rounding the side of the barn, she came to an abrupt halt at the sight of a familiar horse and buggy standing in front of the porch. Long, angry strides carried her to the house.

"You weasel!" Katherine pointed a long, slender finger at Dillon Swade. He turned from his position next to the buggy and looked at her in surprise. "I see you had no trouble finding a ride home. And I was feeling guilty for leaving you in town to walk. How could you bring that . . . that person onto my property when you know he's not welcome?"

Katherine marched up to the buggy and glared into the interior. An elegantly clad leg emerged from the carriage, followed by the rest of Harrison Foley, president of Second Chance Bank.

He was attired in the latest fashion. A dark brown, double-breasted frock coat neatly covered his immaculate white shirt. Loose-fitting trousers and shoes shined to a gloss were also dark brown. Foley's drooping mustache and bushy Dundreary sideburns only served to make his long face more pronounced.

*The man worries about his clothing more than*

*any woman in Second Chance.* Katherine wrinkled her nose in disdain.

For reasons she couldn't fathom, Foley seemed to think she was a displaced southern belle—a woman who needed his help and guidance for even the most trivial question. He made no secret of his proud Yankee heritage and took every opportunity to condescend to Katherine, the justly vanquished Confederate. It was no wonder the Coltrains had robbed his bank when he spouted outdated Union propaganda whenever the chance arose. Though she had tried to be civil in the past, she had finally lost her patience on his last visit and ordered him to leave.

"You better have a good reason to be here, Foley. When I threw you off the place last time I thought I made it clear I didn't need your help," she said.

Harrison ignored her as he climbed the porch steps. He removed a pristine white handkerchief from a coat pocket, wiped the seat, then lowered himself onto the chair. His movements were fluid, as though he placed each limb in a particular pattern of his own devising. Thin lips smiled in Katherine's direction before he spoke.

"My dear," he drawled in his exaggerated Boston twang, "you know I must keep an eye on my investment." Harrison's eyes swept Katherine from head to foot, lending a leer to the words that was not reflected on his proper face.

She was headed for another argument unless

she could get Harrison off her porch and off her ranch. He looked as though he planned to take up residence if she didn't act quickly. Realizing that Dillon was listening eagerly to every word, Katherine glared at her foreman and nodded toward the bunkhouse. Dillon returned the scowl, but he went, stamping his feet like a spoiled child the several yards' distance to his living quarters. The slam of a heavy door echoed in the still air.

"Now, why don't you come up here, and we'll have a little chat." Harrison's voice made Katherine wince. Oh, how she hated his affected, upper-class tone.

"I can hear you perfectly well from where I am. Since you won't be staying long, why don't you get back in your buggy while we 'chat'?"

Harrison laughed, though the sound held no mirth. "That's not a nice way to treat a guest. You've lost some of your southern manners out here in the wilds."

"I'm sure whatever I've lost wasn't worth keeping. What do you want?"

His smile revealed teeth in varying shades of yellow. "Just a little reminder that your mortgage payment is due soon."

"The end of the month is two weeks away. You'll get your money then and not a day before. Good-bye."

Katherine climbed the steps briskly, intending to breeze past him and into the house. She doubted that his uppity manners would allow him to barge into her home uninvited.

Harrison got up from the chair and blocked her retreat into the house. Not having counted on the speed he disguised with an affected lethargy, Katherine flinched at his nearness. Stifling any further show of weakness, she attempted to walk around him, but he moved with her, shaking his head as though gravely disappointed.

"Didn't your mama ever tell you it was rude to leave a guest alone?"

"According to my mother, guests are those we invite to visit our home. Now, if you'll excuse me . . ." Katherine raised her eyebrows expectantly.

Instead of taking her hint, Harrison reached for Katherine's hand, enveloping her fingers in his soft, damp palm. "If you invited me for dinner, I could discuss ways to improve the Circle A's profit with your foreman."

"If there's anything you want to discuss in regard to my ranch, you can discuss it with me." Katherine attempted to disengage her fingers from the banker's clasp but he held on diligently.

"I would never discuss business with a woman." Harrison's voice reflected his outrage at the suggestion.

"Then we have nothing further to say to each other. I'll see you at your office when I pay the mortgage in two weeks."

Katherine pulled her hand forcibly from Harrison's grasp, retreating a step despite her intentions when he walked past her and returned to his buggy. Picking up the reins, Harrison looked at Katherine thoughtfully. "I wish you'd allow me to help you, dear. When I left town, many of the men were planning to come out here and take that criminal back to his just reward. Things may get ugly unless you relent and return him to the sheriff."

Foley smirked and waited expectantly for Katherine to relent. When she merely stared at him impassively, his lips turned downward in irritation and he snorted dismissively. Then he flicked his whip over the horses and turned the team toward Second Chance.

Katherine watched him leave through narrowed eyes. The man was trouble wrapped up in a too pretty, condescending package. Somehow she would continue to get the money for the mortgage payments. She couldn't let the overbearing fop have her ranch.

Katherine wasn't the only one watching the banker's departure. Jake had observed the scene from the barn. He saw Katherine clench and unclench her fists reflexively in anger as she stared at the retreating buggy. Though he'd been unable to hear the conversation between Katherine and Foley, the raised tone of her voice proved that she didn't like the man. When Foley grabbed Katherine's hand and refused to relinquish it, Jake had been on his way out the door, prepared to push his fist through the man's arrogant nose. Seeing that Katherine was in control of the situation, he halted, but his fist still ached to make contact with Foley's smirking face.

He saw Katherine's shoulders slump in dejection, and she walked into the house as though her long skirt was weighted with lead. Jake's gaze followed Katherine until the closing door obscured his view. He could almost be glad Charlie and the boys had stolen from Harrison Foley. Hell, he was definitely glad he had been a part of the theft now that the fool had upset Katherine.

Aware that his anger was out of proportion to the situation, Jake forced his body back to work and turned his mind to his mission.

Where was Matt? The question had been nagging him since his first night in jail. Jake's fellow Pinkerton agent and partner in this operation should have made arrangements for an escape. Instead, Jake had narrowly missed being hanged as a thieving, Confederate guerilla. It was not the epitaph he envisioned for his tombstone—if a bank robber warranted a tombstone in the Second Chance scheme of life and death.

Jake stared into space, his worries foremost in his mind. Matt would never leave him to die if it could be helped. The fact that he had done so concerned Jake deeply. His partner should have been in town working at the bank as Pinkerton had promised. Matt should have known that Jake had been captured and arranged some kind of release, or at least contacted someone who could. The fact that Jake hadn't even seen his fellow agent since he'd arrived was very disturbing.

## Second Chance

Was his friend injured? Betrayed? Dead?

Jake and Matt had been friends since their days as Union cavalry officers during the war. They had both been recruited by Pinkerton, during the war as spies and afterward as agents. Their time as partners in nearly every situation imaginable had drawn them closer than brothers. The thought that Matt could be in desperate need of his help, as he had been in need of Matt's, had tied Jake's mind in so many knots he could barely think. He would have to find some way to learn the last known whereabouts of Matthew Rolland without arousing suspicion. Something was definitely wrong in Second Chance, and he planned to uncover the answers.

A movement caused Jake to glance in the direction of the doorway. Dillon Swade smiled at him. The smile puzzled Jake until he saw the pistol in Swade's right hand and a rope in his left. The man had come with trouble in mind.

"What do you want, Swade?" Jake asked, keeping a tight grip on the pitchfork as he uneasily eyed the gun.

"Drop it," Swade said and pointed at the pitchfork with his pistol.

Jake complied, knowing the farm implement was no match for a bullet. But he felt downright naked without his Colt.

"You and me are goin' to have a little talk, Mr. Southern Thief."

"About what?"

"About you. What you want here. When you're leavin'."

"I'm just helping Mrs. Logan. I'll leave when she tells me to leave."

Swade seemed to think Jake had an ulterior motive for staying at the Circle A. Why? Did the foreman know something about the Coltrains? And how was Jake going to find out if Dillon succeeded in hanging him as he obviously planned?

Swade continued to advance on Jake, then he motioned with the pistol toward the far end of the barn. "Down there. There's a storeroom where you can spend the night."

Jake started, then frowned at the rope. What did the man have in mind if not a hanging? "Does Mrs. Logan know about this?"

"Don't you worry about Mrs. Logan. I have her support. Now let's just mosey on down to the storeroom and have that little talk."

Jake considered refusing, insisting on Katherine's presence before he complied with Swade's orders. Then he looked into the foreman's eyes and swallowed his protests. He'd seen that look before. The man was waiting for his refusal and would be happy to shoot him at the slightest provocation.

# Chapter Four

Later that evening, as Katherine sat at the ancient desk in her office, she covered her face with her hands. When she lifted her head and returned her gaze to the open book in front of her, the numbers recorded in the ledger were still the same. The Circle A was in serious financial trouble.

The ranch had rarely turned a profit in years past, but Sam Logan had kept everyone clothed, fed, and paid. Planting extra crops and a small inheritance she'd received from her aunt had kept the Circle A going so far. But the added burden of the mortgage would soon become too much to handle. If only Sam had never seen and coveted the wild, black colt that must have escaped from hell itself.

## Lori Handeland

Katherine remembered the day her husband had brought home the mean-tempered beast. He would listen to no one when told the horse's temperament made it uncontrollable. Sam believed uncontrollable meant the animal had spirit—and spirit sired the best colts. Later, when Sam learned that not a single mare had been bred from the new stallion, he marched to the barn in a rage, vowing to take care of things himself. Katherine tried to stop him, pulling on his arm and imploring him to sell the horse. All she received for her concern was a swollen lip when the back of Sam's hand connected with her mouth. Minutes later, Sam Logan lay dead, his skull crushed by one kick from the powerful hooves.

Remembering the incident, Katherine felt the familiar weight of sadness. When she first met Sam in Williamsburg after the war, his charming manners and promises of the life they could build together in the West gave her high hopes for their marriage. To remain in Williamsburg would be to remain a spinster schoolteacher for the rest of her life. The teaching she could bear; the threat of a life alone once her aunt passed on goaded her into accepting Sam's proposal. She prepared herself to be a good wife to a good man. But what kind of wife could she be to a man who was far from good? A useless, barren, poor excuse for a woman was what Sam called her with increasing frequency as her monthly courses remained uninterrupted. She winced, remembering his hurtful accusations made all

## Second Chance

the more painful when added to her own crushed hopes for a child to love and nurture. By the time she realized that her husband's manners and promises were nothing but lies, she had been Mrs. Sam Logan for nearly a year.

A shadow passing near her office window ended Katherine's remembrances. Glancing up, she recognized the form of Dillon Swade headed toward the bunkhouse. Relief flooded through her at the sight. Over the past few months, Dillon had been making a nuisance of himself nearly every night, coming to the house like a gentleman caller. She did everything she could think of to discourage him, but he continued to arrive. Maybe he had finally decided to keep their relationship businesslike as she wished after their disagreements earlier that day.

Katherine returned to her work, though every few minutes her eyes were drawn to the window and the barn visible beyond. If Dillon hadn't been coming to the house, what was he doing wandering around at this time of night? After glancing toward the barn, Katherine shrugged and drew her gaze back to the task at hand.

But after an hour of trying to concentrate, Katherine finally stood and picked up the lantern on her desk. A persistent voice nagged in her ear that something wasn't as it should be, a voice which grew stronger whenever she remembered the way Dillon had crept past the house toward the bunkhouse. She wouldn't be able to work until she checked on things herself.

The house was quiet as Katherine made her way out the front door. As she walked toward the barn, the lantern cast eerie shadows in front of her and the sound of a dog howling in the distance drifted on the breeze. The low, mournful cry lifted the hairs on the back of her neck, and she covered the remaining distance to the barn as quickly as she could.

The lantern did little to alleviate the darkness of the barn's interior. Before she had gone a foot, a pained moan greeted her ears. Several more moans followed. Katherine listened intently. The sounds came from the storeroom near the rear of the barn. Quickly she walked to the door separating her from the source of the moans. Grasping the doorknob, she twisted her hand. The motion of her body carried her forward and she hit her head against the unmoving door.

Locked. *Damn*, she swore silently.

The moans grew louder, interspersed with mumbled words, and as the sounds echoed in the darkness, Katherine recognized Jake's voice. *What is he doing in there?* She lifted the lantern to peer upward, running her trembling fingers along the wall above the door. *Where is that key?* In frustration, Katherine slammed her fist against the door.

"Who's there?" Jake's voice sounded faint.

*What on earth was wrong with the man?*

"It's Mrs. Logan. As soon as I find the key, I'll get you out. Are you hurt?"

Silence.

## Second Chance

"Jake. Answer me. Are you hurt?"

Not a sound met Katherine's straining ears. When her searching fingers located the key, she shoved the metal into the lock and opened the door. Darkness and silence greeted her.

"Jake?" Katherine moved quickly to the center of the room and placed the lantern carefully on the floor. Her eyes swept the dark corners, coming to rest on what appeared to be a pile of clothes, flour sacks, and rope. Jake.

His eyes were closed and his breathing erratic. Sweat dotted his forehead and drenched his clothes. Jake's feet were tied to a wood pole supporting the ceiling. Katherine grimaced when she saw that the rope binding his wrists extended around his neck. As long as he didn't move his hands very far, the bonds wouldn't hurt. But further examination revealed red, raw skin under the unnaturally tight rope. Blood flowed in a trickle from his lower lip.

Katherine wasted no time in locating the knife used to slit the feed sacks and turning it on Jake's bonds. He still made no movement or sound. Next, she went to the horse trough and quickly doused her handkerchief with tepid water. Returning, she bathed Jake's face, and his eyelids fluttered.

He bolted upright, grabbing her forearms in a death grip, and the cloth flew out of her hands. His green eyes, wide and unseeing, bored into her own. The hands on her arms tightened and Katherine winced, fear flooding her at the strength of his grip. She had no idea what he was capable of in the midst of such a dream. For that matter, she had no idea what he was capable of when awake either. Perhaps she had not been wise to approach Jake alone. The isolation of the Circle A pressed on her, and she struggled against his restraining arms. But to no avail. She had to do something quick to calm him or risk having her arms wrenched from her body.

"Jake, what is it?" she asked, striving for a soothing tone and wincing when her voice cracked with tension.

He didn't hear her—probably couldn't hear her. His mind had retreated to another place. Anguish streaked Jake's face as the tortured man relived the horrors of some yesteryear. Compassion flooded her, and her fear receded just a little.

"I'm not dead."

Katherine leaned closer to hear Jake's muttered words.

"I'm not! Can't anyone hear me?"

The last words rose to a shout, and the flesh on Katherine's arms prickled at the hopelessness of the sound.

"Antietam," Jake groaned, then released her as he slumped to the floor.

The imprint of his fingers still burned into her arms. Remembering the horror of his words, she stifled the urge to run. There must be some explanation for what she had just witnessed. Katherine peered at his face

## Second Chance

in the semidarkness. Jake now slept deeply and peacefully. What manner of nightmare could cause such mutterings and moanings?

Without conscious thought, seeking only to comfort, Katherine extended her hand and smoothed a stray lock of black hair away from Jake's brow. The moment her fingers came into contact with his skin, Jake's hand sprang up, grasping her wrist in a crushing grip. Katherine gasped and found herself staring into an awake and aware green gaze.

"What do you think you're doing? A move like that on a sleeping man could get you killed." The calmness of Jake's tone did little to mask the anger in his eyes.

"And how do you propose to do the deed? With your bare hands?" Katherine wrenched her arm free from his grip.

"If you had done that in the dark, I might've at that." Jake raised himself to a sitting position and blinked at her in the flickering light. "What are you doing here?"

Katherine stood and moved to the middle of the room. As she looked back at him, she twisted the damp handkerchief in her fingers.

"Dillon was sneaking around outside and he made me anxious."

Jake snorted. "Nice right-hand man you got there, Mrs. Logan. A real prince. I see he takes no chances with you or the ranch. He made sure I couldn't breathe, let alone hurt his precious Katherine."

Katherine winced at his words. "Dillon does his job. He may have been a bit overanxious in this case."

"Overanxious? I'd say he was downright nasty. I haven't seen anyone in all my thirty-one years who enjoyed causing pain that much. Even in the war."

Katherine frowned and tilted her head in concentration. A thought pulled at the edge of her mind. The war. Antietam. Something was not right here.

Watching Jake closely, Katherine moved to sit on a sack of grain. Carefully weighing her words, she began, "When I came into the room, you seemed to be in the midst of a nightmare." Katherine saw Jake's shoulders tense, but she continued. "You said something that confused me."

"Ma'am?"

Was it her imagination, or did his southern accent suddenly seem more pronounced?

"Yes, you said 'Antietam.' In Virginia, we knew that battle as Sharpsburg, like everyone in the South. Only the Union army called that bloody mess Antietam."

Katherine studied Jake's features while she patiently waited for him to speak. She caught her breath when he looked into her eyes. The memories the dream had dredged from his mind were reflected in his gaze, and guilt flooded her for reminding him of such horror. She took a step toward Jake, her hand reaching down to him.

## Second Chance

The jagged sound of smashing glass startled them, and they both looked in the direction of the noise. Katherine hesitated, unsure of what to do about Jake, then she whirled and ran out the door.

Reaching the front of the barn, she peered out an opening in the partially closed door. From her vantage point, Katherine could see about twenty men with guns and torches filling the yard between the barn and the house. Her gaze went to the front window of her house, the site of the broken glass. Foley had not merely tried to frighten her earlier; the mob was real and howling for a hanging.

Katherine saw that most of the merchants from town and many of the ranchers and farmers in the crowd earlier that day were present. None of them could be counted on to see her point of view. A gasp of surprise escaped Katherine when she recognized the undertaker in the center of the mob. His long, black coat flapped as he waved a club, shouting louder than anyone. He looked like nothing other than a large, angry black crow.

Katherine still peered out the opening when Jake joined her. Turning, she noticed he absently rubbed his raw wrists, and guilt flashed through her. He moved closer, and Katherine put a finger to her lips in a gesture for silence.

"What is it?" he whispered.

"Town idiots. They've worked themselves into a mob over you and come out here to cause trouble."

As she watched, one of the men stepped forward and shouted, "Mrs. Logan, come on out now. We've got some talkin' to do."

Jake leaned past Katherine to view the scene. "Who's that?" he asked.

"George Simpson." Katherine's upper lip curled with dislike. "The man couldn't act on his own if he were the only person in the state."

Jake nodded. "I know the type. I suppose they've been milling around town working up to this since you wrecked their hanging party today."

"More than likely. I wonder . . ." She peered intently out the opening as Simpson strode up the porch steps and pounded his meaty fist on the front door.

"Come on out. None of your fancy shootin' will help tonight. We're all armed and ready for ya."

Katherine moved away from the door, bumping into Jake in her haste. "Pretty soon they'll search the house, and when they don't find me, they'll be coming here next," she said.

"Maybe we can hold them off."

"With what? Pitchforks and shovels? Besides, they're in a mood for a hanging. I don't think they'll listen to reason." Katherine took another look at the mob, then turned to Jake. "I don't see the sheriff, so I'm assuming they came on their own. But I'll bet Jessup knew about it. We can't expect any help from the law tonight."

"Welcome to the Circle A, gentlemen. What can I do for you this time of night?" Dillon

Swade's voice rang out clearly from the direction of the house.

Both Katherine and Jake jumped to look through the doorway, bumping their heads together for their effort. His lips twisted in a shadow of a smile as Jake rubbed his head and stepped back with a mocking bow so Katherine could see.

"Drat that man," she said as Dillon stepped up on the porch of her house. "He's nothing but a nuisance."

"My thoughts exactly, ma'am."

"You'd better quit worrying about Dillon and think of a way to get out of here. If we don't, you may feel a noose around that handsome neck of yours twice in one day."

The angry shouts of the mob calling her name forced Katherine to return to her post at the door. The men grew angrier as moments passed and she failed to appear. The fury on their faces made Katherine cringe, and her heart beat overtime with fear, though she would never allow such an emotion to show if she could help it. She'd learned the hard way that bullies thrived on fear.

Finally, when she didn't know if she could stand the tension much longer, Dillon spoke. "Mrs. Logan isn't well, so you'll have to deal with me. What do you want?"

"That she-wolf ain't never been unwell in her life," a voice yelled from the crowd. "Bring her out here."

The cry was taken up by the rest of the mob.

"Yeah, get her out here."

"We want the boss lady."

Katherine shivered. "I suppose I should go out there and see what I can do."

Jake placed a restraining hand on Katherine's arm. His warmth settled into her icy flesh and calmed her racing heart just a bit. "You said it yourself, that's a hanging mob. Let's see what Swade can do with them first."

Katherine nodded, then moved aside so Jake could see the yard. He leaned past her, and his hard, muscled shoulder brushed hers. She did not move away, taking comfort in his strength. Jake was in as much—no, more—trouble than she was, but his presence soothed her. He had lived by his wits for many years and so had she. Together they would find a way out of their latest dilemma. She studied his face as he concentrated on the scene playing before him, and an idea, totally out of place in their situation, struck her.

Jake Banner appealed to her as no other man had in her life. What a shame he had to be an outlaw. If he were a regular law-abiding citizen she might be tempted to . . .

Jake's muffled oath startled her and she looked up, her wayward thoughts disappearing as quickly as they had come.

"What is it?" She pushed futilely at Jake's hard shoulder in an attempt to see past him. When he moved away, her gaze went immediately to where Dillon stood on the porch. She gasped. Not only was Dillon pointing toward the barn, but every man in the mob had turned and seemed to be looking directly at her. Katherine pulled back from the door, her hand going to her mouth. She stared, wide-eyed, at Jake.

"I believe I've been thrown to the wolves, ma'am."

# Chapter Five

"Come on." Jake grabbed Katherine's wrist and yanked her in the direction of the storeroom.

"What are we going to do?"

"We've got to get out of here. Got a window in this place?"

"In back."

"Perfect. This is going to take timing, and a lot of luck, but we just might make it to the house." Jake smiled at her. "I assume you keep your firearm collection there."

Katherine frowned, then nodded. He seemed to be enjoying this.

They reached the door to the storeroom. Jake stepped inside, grabbed her lantern, and extinguished the flame in one fluid motion. Closing the door behind him, he held out an open palm to Katherine.

"Key?"

## *Second Chance*

Katherine pointed above the door. As Jake reached for the key, she listened closely to the sounds outside. Her heart thudded painfully in her chest. The mob was headed for the barn.

Returning her attention to Jake, she saw he'd already locked the storeroom door. Dropping the key onto the floor, he kicked dirt over it.

"That should buy us a little time," he murmured, then grabbed Katherine's hand in a bruising grip and dragged her toward the back of the barn.

Fortunately, it was summer, and the heavy canvas covering the window was not nailed down. Jake made a cradle of his hands and bent at the knees, looking at Katherine expectantly. When she heard the barn door creak open behind them, she hastily put her foot into the improvised stirrup and gripped the bottom of the window. Jake lifted her, and Katherine realized her skirt would impede her progress. She shifted her weight and sat on the windowsill, then hiked the material above her knees, drew her legs over the sill, and dropped neatly to the ground four feet below. Before she could straighten her skirt, Jake landed silently to her right.

"Let's move. We've only got a few minutes before they find that key and figure out I'm not where I'm supposed to be." As he spoke he slid along the side of the barn, his back pressed against the wood, keeping to the shadows. Katherine followed his lead, her hand in his.

"What if they left a guard outside?" she whispered.

Jake turned to look at her, and she saw the moonlight reflected in his eyes, turning them from emerald green to silver. He made a sound somewhere between a laugh and a sigh. "I'm hoping that they were too anxious for a hanging to think of it."

They reached the edge of the barn, and Jake glanced quickly around the side. His shoulders relaxed minutely, then he yanked her into the open yard.

Not a soul inhabited the open space between the barn and the house. They moved quickly toward their destination. Katherine grabbed a handful of her skirt and lifted it above her ankles so she could keep up with Jake's long-legged rush. Glancing over her shoulder at the barn, she saw the mob illuminated in the doorway by the light of their torches. Every man's attention was turned avidly away from the house.

They reached the porch without being detected, and Katherine hurried through the door, letting Jake close it quietly behind them. She was on her way up the staircase to her bedroom before his hand left the knob.

She burst through the door and grabbed her rifle from where it rested against the wall next to her bed. As Jake entered the room, she checked the gun, then loaded it. He held out his hand for the weapon, but she hesitated.

"They're after me," he said. "I think I'm entitled to save my own skin if I can."

## Second Chance

Angry shouts ruptured the stillness, and Katherine glanced out the window. The mob poured from the barn, streaming toward the house. She looked Jake in the eye, then slowly held out the rifle.

"There are more bullets on the dresser," was her only comment before she picked up her Army Colt from the nightstand and checked the ammunition.

Jake took up a position at the window but kept out of sight. The mob had reached the house and looked as though they planned to storm the front porch. He lifted the rifle quickly to his shoulder and shot into the dirt at the feet of the lead man. The entire mob halted in their tracks and looked at the window in unison.

Jake moved into view, but Katherine put a hand to his chest and shoved him out of sight.

"Are you crazy?" she hissed. "They'll start shooting up here if they see you."

Katherine knelt to one side of the window and rested the barrel of her Colt on the sill. From the corner of her eye she saw that Jake remained out of sight, but he focused his gaze intently on the crowd. A shout from the yard caused both of them to tense.

"Nice shot, Mrs. Logan. Now tell us where Banner's gone and we'll leave you be."

"Take the boys home now, George," Katherine called and sighted down the barrel of her pistol. "I've done enough fancy shooting for one day, my aim might be off next time."

"We'll go as soon as we take care of that Confederate thief."

"Now, I can't let you do that, George. I said I'd give him a second chance, and I don't mean to break my word."

George Simpson looked at the rest of the men, then smiled. "You can't take us all on, no matter how good a shot you are."

A bullet buried itself neatly in the dirt between his feet, and the smile froze on his face. "No, I can't take all of you, that's true. But I could do severe damage to a few favored parts of your anatomy. Should I start with you, George?"

Katherine cocked the pistol, smiling grimly when many of the men in the mob flinched at the deadly sound. Simpson swallowed convulsively and looked down at the torn ground. She waited, knowing that if the leader gave in, the rest would follow. Jake's tension was a tangible force beside her. He would be ready if things progressed to a fight. The one shot he'd fired had been a beauty. She hoped he could produce more of the same.

Simpson engaged in a heated discussion with a few of the other men. The mob had quieted during their conversation, and as she waited, some of the men glanced fearfully up at her window. She had them on the run.

"Since you're so fond of this criminal, Mrs. Logan, we'll have to let you keep him, I suspect." Simpson retreated into the protection of the crowd.

## Second Chance

"*Let* me keep him. That's a laugh," Katherine muttered, uncocking the Colt.

"We should have realized how attached you'd be to one of your own," a voice taunted, and Katherine's shoulders tensed. "I know how you Rebs like to stick together."

Katherine lifted her finger to cock the pistol again, but a sharp gesture from Jake halted her movement. When she looked at him, he frowned and shook his head sharply. But it wasn't his frown that caused her to lower her gun, it was the respect she saw in his eyes. She was used to seeing dislike, mistrust, and even fear in people's eyes when they looked at her—but never respect. Such an idea made her pause.

"Wise choice. One thing you need to learn, ma'am, is to quit when you're ahead." His smile softened the rebuke.

Katherine returned the smile. "That's something I've never been good at." She returned her attention to the mob in front of her house. All she saw were their backs as they retreated swiftly to the main road running in front of the Circle A.

"They must have left their horses on the road to keep the noise down. I'm sure they planned to surprise us," Jake said.

Katherine nodded absently, her gaze searching the yard below. What had happened to Dillon? Suddenly, a movement at the edge of her vision caught her attention and she turned her head, eyes straining to pierce the darkness. Dillon Swade exited quietly from his vantage point inside the barn where he'd remained after leading the mob to Jake's room.

Anger filled her, and her face flushed hotly. She turned quickly from the sight of Dillon slinking away in the night. Crossing to her dressing table, Katherine absently set down the pistol.

"I don't understand why you keep him on, ma'am."

Katherine clenched her teeth in frustration at Jake's quiet words. She had wondered the same thing quite often of late. But she had learned since coming to Second Chance that gratitude and loyalty were often the only things worth fighting for.

"You weren't here, Mr. Banner, when Dillon was the only person who treated me with any kindness." Katherine could see the skepticism on Jake's face.

"You think I shoot well? Dillon taught me everything I know. I came here a bride—a city-bred spinster schoolteacher from Williamsburg. I knew nothing about life on the frontier, but I was willing to learn. My husband . . ." she paused, weighing her words, then sat down heavily on her bed. "My husband was much older than me, close to fifty, and set in his ways. He had nothing but contempt for people he considered weak. He and Dillon were of an age and very close. When I noticed that Sam admired men who were good with a gun, I asked Dillon to teach me."

## Second Chance

"Is Swade as good as you are?" Jake's voice came sharply out of the darkness surrounding them.

She smiled. "No. I found that I had a natural aptitude for marksmanship. But Dillon's a skillful teacher—patient and articulate. I know he doesn't seem that way to you." Katherine moved her hands in a helpless gesture. "You have to know him as I do. He helped me when no one else would, and he took the brunt of Sam's anger without one word of reproach for me. I owe him."

"Sam? That's your husband?" At her nod he continued, "Why would he be angry? You're an expert shot."

"I was better than he was." Katherine laughed ruefully. "He wasn't amused."

Jake moved away from the window and came nearer. He watched as Katherine smoothed her palms over the green quilt. "I don't understand. Why wasn't he proud of you?"

She continued to look down at her hands as she spoke. "Sam was a Union cavalry officer. He prided himself on his shooting. I told you he admired men who could shoot well. His admiration didn't extend to women. I made the mistake of showing him what I could do in front of some of his cronies from town. He told me he never wanted to see me shoot a gun again. I didn't—as long as he lived."

Silence descended upon the room. After a few moments, Katherine rose briskly to her feet. "I'd be obliged if you'd lean that rifle back against the wall, Mr. Banner. We'd best get some sleep since there's a full day of work tomorrow."

Jake complied without comment while Katherine lit a lamp, then he followed her through the door. As they descended the stairs, he memorized the layout of the house. Being intimate with his surroundings had saved his life several times. It looked as though the parlor was to the right of the staircase and an office to the left. Jake assumed the kitchen lay down the hallway at the back of the house. Other than Katherine's room at the head of the stairway, the arrangement of the upper floor remained a mystery to him.

When they reached the foot of the stairs, Katherine turned to him. The golden light from the lamp fell on her face highlighting her fine bone structure and adding a luster to her wide gray eyes. She's beautiful, he thought. He had seen many beautiful women in his life. Most of them he had flirted with, danced with, maybe even bedded on an occasion, but few had ever affected him the way Katherine did. Deep within her lay something more important and lasting than beauty. Katherine Logan possessed strength and courage, two commodities which drew Jake to her despite his desire to remain uninvolved.

"It might be best if you slept in the house tonight," she said. "I don't think those cowards will be back now that they know we're on to them, but you never can tell with a mob. There's a room for the housekeeper back here."

## Second Chance

Katherine walked down the hallway and opened a door next to the kitchen. "The woman who works for me doesn't room in, so the place is yours tonight."

"Thank you, ma'am."

"They might have left some men to watch the house, so I wouldn't plan a night escape if I were you. Might get your head blown off."

"I wouldn't do that to you, ma'am. I owe you my life, twice over."

Katherine stared at him a moment longer, as though her calm, intelligent eyes could see his secrets. The thought made him decidedly uneasy, and he moved past her into the small room. The lantern's glow illuminated a small bed and nightstand against the far wall.

Katherine started to close the door but paused when she noticed Jake's longing glance at the lantern. "Should I leave the light?"

Jake continued to gaze into the flame for a moment, wondering if he dared deny his weakness. He sighed. What was the point? He had tried for the past several years to conquer his fear of darkness, but that one remnant of the war would not yield. He glanced at Katherine and twitched his lips in an attempt to smile. "If you don't mind; I'd appreciate it."

Katherine shrugged and held the lamp out to him. Jake's hand grasped the handle and their fingers touched. Startled by the ice-hot jolt between them, he nearly dropped the light. After a fumbling recovery, he looked into her face. No longer calm and collected, Katherine's eyes reflected her inner confusion. Had she ever experienced such an intense reaction to another person's touch before? For that matter, had he?

The temptation to touch her again was strong, if only to learn more about the strange sensations she aroused in him. She hadn't run from the room in fear. In fact, she continued to stare at him, holding herself very still, her eyes wide and her lips wet and slightly parted. Jake's gaze was drawn to those lips against his will. If he could be shocked to his boots by the mere brush of her fingers against his, what would happen if he kissed her?

Jake Parker wanted to find out. Jake Banner had no right to know. The sudden remembrance of his dual personality caused him to straighten and back away a step. He knew the exact moment Katherine registered his withdrawal. Her spine stiffened, her lips pressed tightly together, and her eyes changed from gray smoke to clouded ice.

She turned and walked to the door. Jake saw her inhale deeply, and he released a shaky breath of his own. They had been very close to taking a step that both of them would have regretted. From now on he would keep his guard raised against the new and unsettling reactions she engendered within him.

Katherine reached the door, and Jake relaxed, glad that he would soon be alone so he could think straight. But instead of leaving, Katherine turned, surprising him, and all memories of

## Second Chance

their shared sensations flew from his mind at her words.

"Tell me about Antietam." Her voice was curious, but her eyes reflected her suspicion of him. Despite the emotional reaction she had to his touch, her mind had not forgotten his earlier slip.

Jake did not allow his face to register any change in emotion at Katherine's sudden demand. He slowly and deliberately crossed the room to set the lamp on the nightstand. Then, as slowly, he seated himself on the wood floor and reclined against the wall. Katherine remained in the doorway.

"Sharpsburg? What do you want to know about that bloodbath?"

"Earlier, when I woke you from your nightmare, you distinctly said 'Antietam.' You know as well as I do that only northerners use that name; southerners call the battle Sharpsburg."

"Is that a law or something?" Jake's brain frantically scrambled for an excuse to explain his nightmare-induced mistake.

"No, but I'd think your Reb guerilla friends would take exception to Yankee battle names."

"We don't discuss the war."

"Why not?"

Jake closed his eyes, pushing away the memories threatening to overwhelm him at the mention of Antietam. The screams, the blood, the death were as real to him today as they had been when he lay on the field. He dreamed about the battle enough when he slept; talking about the place while awake would be too much.

"We all have our horror stories and we want to forget. Whether I call the battle An . . . An . . ." His tongue grew thick and he stumbled over the word. Drawing a deep breath he tried again. "Whether I call it Sharpsburg or—or—not, the memories are the same."

Jake didn't know when she had moved to stand next to him. Katherine touched his arm in sympathy, and he experienced another jolt of awareness before he looked down into her upturned face. The depth of concern he saw in her eyes mesmerized him.

"The war changed us all," she whispered.

Jake had been so caught up in the attempt to atone for his mistake, he had forgotten to pay attention to his accent. Since Katherine had voiced no questions, he must have done an adequate job of keeping his cover in place. But seeing the compassion in her eyes made him feel such guilt for his masquerade, he was at a loss for words. Luckily for him, she seemed to attribute his continuing silence to the after-effects of his memories. And, in that belief, she was partially right.

She looked so small and innocent standing near him, with her hand on his arm, obvious sympathy in her eyes. Petite women had never been his preference. But Katherine was different. There was an undercurrent of steel in her he had come to admire. She was such a contrast—so tiny and frail, yet she could fire a rifle without flinching at the recoil. Her hands,

## Second Chance

though elegant and tiny, exerted unbelievable strength when she touched him. Jake stared at her full lips, now slightly parted in an encouraging smile. Despite his earlier resolve not to touch her, he couldn't seem to keep from leaning toward her. His lips burned to touch hers, to soothe the memories of the hated war from his mind with the sweetness of her breath mingling with his.

Katherine must have guessed his intent, for her eyes widened in surprise, and the hand resting on his arm tightened convulsively. Was she drawing him closer or pushing him away? He couldn't tell, and he suddenly didn't care. He needed to lose himself if only for a moment in the heated mystery of her embrace. Before sanity returned and he changed his mind, Jake lowered his head and touched his lips to hers.

# Chapter Six

A sizzling arrow of heat flashed from Katherine's lips through her heart. The shock caused her to back away from Jake, nearly stumbling in her haste to remove herself from his nearness. She stopped when her back met the solid door frame, and she brought her fingers up to touch her tingling lips. She had never experienced such energy from another person's touch. Katherine didn't know whether her heart beat so fast from the feather-light caress itself or from her fear at the sudden and fascinating response of her body. She looked at Jake standing where she had left him, his face reflecting the same turmoil that raged within her.

Katherine backed slowly out the door and into the hall, feeling as though a trap had closed around her. After all, she was alone in the house

## Second Chance

with a common criminal. The men were camping at the far boundary of the ranch, and Dillon had probably slunk out to join them.

"I'm not going to hurt you." His voice, soft and warm as velvet, caused her to jump nevertheless.

She looked up and saw Jake lounging in the doorway, a grin lighting his face.

"I—I know you won't. It's time I got to sleep. Dawn will be here before we know it, and there's a full day's chores to be done." She babbled like a frightened schoolgirl, but for some unknown reason she didn't care. The sound of her own voice steadied her.

"You'd think no one had ever tried to kiss you, Katie."

Katherine frowned at the unfamiliar endearment. When Jake moved forward as if to kiss her again, she reached out and slammed the door in his face. She picked her way carefully, but quickly, upstairs without benefit of a lantern, Jake's deep chuckle following her into the darkness.

Banging the door to her room shut, she dragged the chair from her dressing table and, tilting it on two legs, braced the stiff back under the doorknob. She'd had enough surprises for one day.

A cool breeze blew through her open window, and Katherine welcomed the air gratefully. She removed her dress, wrinkling her nose in distaste at its stiffness—the result of sweat and dirt from an early summer day in Missouri. If she didn't have Mary around to wash clothes, how would she cope? Katherine debated sleeping in her chemise, but after a glance at the door she reached for her white cotton nightdress and pulled the garment over her head. She kicked off her shoes and drew off white stockings and garters, relishing cool air on heated skin. Picking up a hairbrush from the dressing table, Katherine pulled the rocking chair closer to the window and glanced around her room. As she sat down, a smile curved her lips.

She loved her room and the peace found there. The space was hers, and hers alone. She had decorated it in the blues and greens of the land she loved. Clearly visible from the window, horses drifted aimlessly in the paddock below and open pastures beyond waved gently with the breeze. The bedroom was peopled with her treasures: Mother's silver comb and brush set, Grandmother's rocker, Father's Bible. She had moved there the day after Sam died, and her mind held only good memories of the room. The bedroom she had shared with Sam had been cleaned, aired, and deserted. She had no desire to set foot in it ever again. The last year of her marriage had been spent learning the meaning of the word deception. But that year was a part of her past—a past she need never fear repeating now that she was once again in control of her life.

As Katherine ran her hand through her hair to loosen the braid, her mind turned to the topic she'd been avoiding—Jake Banner. She drew

## Second Chance

the brush through the long, golden strands seeking the solace this nightly ritual would bring. Suddenly, Katherine threw the brush to the floor and rose from the chair. She stalked to the window and glared into the distance. What was it about him that made her skin tingle and her nerves jump almost painfully?

"Drat the man," she muttered, then sat down heavily on her bed and began to re-braid her hair. What was she going to do about him? Not only had she backed herself into a corner by keeping him at the Circle A, but she found herself attracted to him. There, she'd admitted it. She was attracted to him. And the last time she'd been attracted to a man, she'd made the biggest mistake of her life.

Katherine sat up straight. Maybe that was why she became uneasy around Jake. Her interest in Sam, while mild when compared to the flashing jolt of awareness consuming her at Jake's slightest touch, had led indirectly to an existence of pure hell. The feelings she experienced whenever she came near her criminal houseguest must be a reaction to that earlier unpleasant experience with romance.

Feeling better now that she had an explanation for her nervousness, Katherine climbed into bed, leaving the simple lawn green quilt at her feet so she could enjoy the cooling breeze throughout the night. Despite her good intentions, it was a long time before she drifted off, and when she did, her dreams were filled with images of startling green eyes and the sound of the South.

The next day dawned bright and clear—another scorcher without the promise of a cloud to shade the sun. Katherine climbed from her bed as soon as she heard Mary rattle the stove in the kitchen. Her head felt stuffed with cotton, and she threw cold water on her face in an attempt to clear the mist from her eyes. Had she slept at all?

Yesterday had been wasted as far as work was concerned. She would have to make up for it today. Looking into her wardrobe, Katherine pulled out the Levi's she had bought from a young ranch hand several months previously. She had to roll up the cuffs at the bottom and use a rope around the waist to keep them from falling to her ankles. Other than that, they fit reasonably well. Paired with one of Sam's old red cotton shirts, she was ready to work. The men hated to see her dressed this way. Dillon had commented on the fact often. But she found it counterproductive to try to work with horses with yards and yards of material wound around her ankles. The hands would get used to her appearance eventually. Although they didn't seem to be coming around as quickly as she'd hoped.

Passing the guest bedroom, Katherine noticed the open door and glanced in. The room was empty, the bed made. She frowned, wondering if Jake had slept there at all. Could he have left, despite his promises?

## Second Chance

Ignoring Mary, her housekeeper and cook, Katherine strode through the kitchen to the window and peered out.

Jake stood at the horse trough near the barn washing up. Relief rushed through her, and the breath she'd held since she spied the empty bed in the guest room whistled out through her lips.

Mary handed her a cup of coffee and Katherine thanked her absently, her eyes remaining on Jake's bare back. He had quite an interesting back, she noted, strong, brown, smooth. How would his sun-warmed skin feel under her fingertips?

"Somethin' caught your eye out there?" Mary asked.

Katherine flushed guiltily at being caught staring at a half-clothed man. Turning quickly away from the window, she ran face first into Mary's frown. She pondered how to explain her avid interest in Jake Banner. But when she realized Mary's expression was directed at her attire, Katherine relaxed and decided to ignore the frown. Mary was an employee, though she insisted on behaving like Katherine's mother. The housekeeper would have to live with Katherine's eccentricities, even if she didn't like them. It was an attitude that had gotten Katherine through a lot in the year since Sam's death.

She took a gulp of the steaming black liquid, and the cobwebs parted in her head. "Mmm." She breathed in the aroma of fresh coffee and closed her eyes for a moment. The first cup of the morning tasted the best.

Mary's sniff of disapproval caused Katherine to open her eyes and focus again on the world around her. The older woman stood with her arms crossed over an ample bosom, her foot tapping impatiently on the wood floor. Katherine raised her eyebrows and continued to drink her coffee. There was no need to encourage Mary, she'd say her piece regardless. Katherine had learned to listen to what she agreed with and ignore what she didn't.

"I hear you were up to some tricks in town yesterday."

"No tricks that I know of. I got the supplies and came home." Katherine smiled behind her coffee cup.

"Now, missus, it's all over town how you helped that Reb thief to escape. Then I near run into him coming from the guest room this morning. Staying right in the house, mind you." She put her hand over her heart. "Land sakes, he gave me a start. What are you thinking of? You know everyone in Second Chance is already suspicious of you—being from Virginia and all."

Katherine frowned. Mary said the word "Virginia" as though the state existed in the pit of hell. The townspeople, being staunch Unionists in a former slave state filled with Confederate supporters, were very intolerant of anyone from the South. It had never helped to explain to any of them that she was originally from

## Second Chance

Boston, as Yankee a city as could be found. She hadn't moved to Virginia to live with her aunt until she was fifteen and nearly a woman grown. The year her parents died. The truth didn't matter to the townsfolk—a Reb was a Reb.

Katherine set her cup down on the table carefully, then turned to Mary. "I am not a Confederate sympathizer, no matter what those halfwits in town believe." Katherine softened her words with a tentative smile. "You should know me better by now than to make such a statement. I decided to give Jake Banner a second chance. Supposedly, that's what this town is all about—although I haven't seen the evidence of it myself. He slept in the house because there was a mob out here planning to hang him last night. I expect you to treat him as you would any of the other men."

"What are things coming to around here? Criminals in the house, mobs at the front door. Harumph," Mary grumbled and returned to the breakfast preparations. Katherine chose to take the cessation of sound as an agreement with her wishes and let herself out the back door.

Coming around the corner of the house, Katherine was surprised to see Jake in the paddock working a horse. She had planned to talk to him about his duties in a thoroughly businesslike manner. That should set whatever had happened between them last night into the proper perspective in Jake Banner's mind. But her plans were not to be realized.

Dillon stood at the fence with two of the hired hands. As Katherine drew closer, she heard them laughing and making bets as to how long Jake would last on the horse. Katherine glanced quickly past the men and into the paddock, then drew a deep breath.

Jake stood in the middle of the open space staring down a colt the color of a moonless midnight. It was the horse Dillon called Lucifer, and an animal with a nastier temper had not been born on the Circle A. Lucifer reminded Katherine of the horse that had killed Sam. She had decided just last night to sell the animal unbroken if only to be rid of him.

Jake already had the saddle and bridle on Lucifer, an impressive accomplishment in itself. Dillon was the only one who'd managed such a feat previously, and not without extreme effort. Katherine stepped forward to put a stop to the proceedings before Jake got hurt, but when she observed the confident way he handled the horse—making slow, deliberate movements, crooning nonsense words in his soft, beautiful voice, and showing no fear that might upset the animal—Katherine decided to see what he could accomplish without her interference. If Jake was as good as he professed to be with horses, she might be able to sell the animal broke and turn a higher profit. With the financial fix she was in, she couldn't afford not to

## Second Chance

make every cent she could on every animal she sold.

As Jake made his way to Lucifer's side, the horse skittered sideways to avoid him. Jake followed, patiently and slowly, talking the entire time. When the horse stopped its nervous sidestepping, Jake put his foot into the stirrup and swung himself onto Lucifer's back with a smooth motion born of years of practice.

Lucifer's eyes rolled back, showing large areas of white. Then the colt uttered a piercing shriek that sent chills down Katherine's spine. She'd never heard a horse make that sound in her life. Lucifer began to buck and shake in a desperate attempt to wrest the man from his back, but Jake held on. In fact, he seemed to be enjoying himself, if the smile of satisfaction on his face was any indication.

Katherine watched, breathless, as Lucifer continued to buck. The dust rose from the dry earth nearly obscuring the battling horse and rider. She squinted, then gasped when the cloud cleared and the two beings materialized. Lucifer raced toward the fence and attempted to smash his rider's leg against the wood. But Jake jerked the animal's head savagely in the other direction and the horse gave way. Lucifer galloped around the enclosed area, shaking his head against the bit, white foam flying from his mouth like a spring shower. Stopping suddenly, he reared and pawed the air, snorting in frustration. Jake clenched his knees into the animal's sides and remained securely in the saddle. The horse bucked and reared for several minutes, then he began to tire. Katherine glanced at the other men along the railing. They were silent, watching the confrontation in fascination.

When she returned her attention to the man and horse she gasped, then let out a cry of alarm and shouted, "Look out, he's going to roll."

But Jake had anticipated the horse's move and pulled up sharply on the reins. Lucifer's head jerked back. Katherine could see the corded muscles in the animal's neck strain against the pressure. All thoughts of rolling in the dirt in an attempt to wrench Jake from his back seemed to have left Lucifer's mind as he fought the pull on his mouth and neck. After a few more moments of half-hearted disobedience, the horse bowed its head in defeat and stood still. Jake dismounted and led the now docile animal into the barn.

Katherine let out the breath she'd been holding, then joined Dillon and the other men at the fence. The fury and hatred on Dillon's face made Katherine pause. She gestured for the other men to return to work before she spoke to her foreman. "I would think you'd be happy to have the colt broke. No one else could control the animal."

## Second Chance

Dillon glared at her, then spit on the ground at her feet. In a low, vicious voice he said, "I'd hoped the blasted colt would break both their necks, and I could have solved two of my problems in one day."

"Your attitude is deplorable. Not to mention your behavior last evening." She caught Dillon's look of surprise. "Yes, I saw you sneaking out of the barn like the weasel you are. Let's get one thing straight, Dillon. I'm in charge at the Circle A. You take orders from me, and if you don't like it you can leave. I've put up with your airs and bad temper long enough out of gratitude for your help in the past and your expertise with the horses. But now, I think I've found someone who could fill your shoes quite well." She glanced at the barn to make her point. "If you want to stay, you'll obey my orders."

Dillon's face darkened, and for a moment Katherine believed he might strike her. He made a visible effort to get himself under control, then walked away without a word.

She turned to find Jake standing at the barn door watching the exchange impassively. His gaze followed Dillon until the foreman was out of his sight. She knew instinctively he would have intervened had Dillon become physical. Though she believed she could take care of herself, Jake's protectiveness caused a warm glow deep inside her. No man had ever been her champion.

Jake turned back to her, and his grin of

triumph was infectious. She shook off her confrontation with Dillon to return his smile brightly as she joined him.

"Pretty fancy riding for so early in the day."

Jake shrugged, but she could tell that the results of his work pleased him. "The colt's not broke yet. I'm sure he'll think of some new tricks to try the next time we meet. But that's a fine animal. With some hard work he'll be a great stallion."

"I wouldn't have agreed with you before this morning. But I think we'll only have that result if you're the one to work with Lucifer. As I'm sure you've gathered, no one else on the Circle A can control him."

Jake laughed suddenly, a rich, vibrant sound that made Katherine want to laugh in return, although she didn't know what he found so funny.

"The colt's name is Lucifer?" he asked. "If I'd known that, I never would have made the attempt."

Katherine wrinkled her brow in confusion. "Whyever not? It's just a name."

Jake's green eyes searched her own before he replied softly, "I never deal with the devil—anymore."

His intense gaze, combined with the odd statement, made Katherine shiver. She gazed at him wide-eyed and hugged her arms tightly to her body. There were times when she felt totally at ease with this man. And then there was now—when she felt as though there were

## Second Chance

depths and secrets within him she could never hope to uncover.

Katherine frowned and mentally shook herself free of such foolishness. This man was a hired hand or, rather, a criminal working off his debt to her. Why should she care about his secrets or his troubled past?

"Breakfast is in fifteen minutes in the kitchen. Better wash up." Her confused feelings made her voice sound cold and remote. She saw Jake frown at her sudden change in mood, but Katherine headed toward the house. She turned back to him after only a few steps. "How did you learn to deal with horses like that?"

"When a man has stayed on his horse and kept alive in the midst of artillery, bullets, and bayonets, an unbroken colt is a romp in the meadow."

Katherine weighed his words, then nodded. "Yes, I suppose it would be at that. It's an admirable skill, Mr. Banner. We'll discuss it at breakfast." Katherine returned to the house, feeling Jake's gaze upon her back. Her self-consciousness did not ease until she rounded the corner out of his sight.

The four hired hands sat at the long table in the kitchen shoveling food into their mouths. Katherine took another cup of coffee from Mary, smiled her thanks, then sat at the head of the table. She noticed Dillon's chair was empty and asked Joe, the man nearest her, about his whereabouts.

"He's gone out to the south border to round up yearlings. We're supposed to meet him there after breakfast."

"It's unusual for him to miss a meal," Katherine mused.

"He said the company you're keeping these days turns his stomach. He won't eat with a thief, ma'am." Joe suddenly looked embarrassed and hurriedly returned to his meal.

The back door slammed, causing Katherine to jump. Jake stood in the doorway, his anger visible on his face. He'd heard the exchange.

Katherine motioned Jake to the empty chair next to her own before introducing him to the others. "Boys, this is Jake Banner. He'll be helping us for a spell. He seems to have a knack with the horses." Jake sat down and she smiled, hoping to ease the tension in the room.

The men stared at Jake as though he were in a side show at the county fair. Jake stared back belligerently, but before any confrontation could take place, Katherine intervened.

"If you've finished your meal, I think you'd all better get out to the south border. Dillon can't do much alone." The three younger men hesitated, then looked at Joe for support.

Katherine could tell they didn't like her telling them what to do. None of the men ever had. She'd lost a lot of workers before she understood that Dillon had to be the one to give the orders, even if she was their originator. Katherine smiled sweetly at the four men as

## Second Chance

they replaced their hats and left through the back door. A few moments later she heard them ride out to the south.

Jake ate his eggs and ham with a healthy appetite. The abundant food seemed to have improved his mood, for he smiled at Katherine through a mouthful when she turned to him.

"I haven't had food this good since before the war." He turned to Mary where she stood kneading bread at the counter. "Thank you, ma'am. I've always appreciated a good cook."

"Harumph," was Mary's only comment as she gave him a sour look and returned to her chore.

Jake looked at Katherine curiously, but she shrugged and waved her hand dismissively. "Mary's very protective of me. Don't worry, she'll warm up. I think we should talk about your duties while we have a minute."

Jake finished his last bite of ham and settled back in the chair with a cup of coffee. "I am yours to command, ma'am."

"You're very cheerful this morning."

Did his disposition have anything to do with the kiss they'd shared the previous evening? If anything, the gentle caress had made her mood less bright from the lack of sleep it caused.

"Nothing like a sunny day, a good meal, and a second chance at life to make a man feel like new again," Jake said.

Katherine started when Mary spoke from directly behind her. "If the two of you sit there mooning at each other over your coffee all day you'll never get any work done."

Glancing over her shoulder, Katherine saw Mary glaring at Jake, her bread-baking forgotten.

"Yes, well, let's go outside and look at the horses I want you to work with," Katherine said quickly.

Jake nodded, ignoring the evil looks emanating from the housekeeper. Katherine followed him out the door, pausing to give Mary a silencing glare of her own.

"No one seems to much care for me around here, do they?" Jake asked as they walked away from the ranch house.

"The people in this town have been terrorized by the Coltrains for the past year. I can't blame them for not liking anyone associated with the South. I've been here for three years and I'm still a Reb to most of them. And you—I doubt if they'll ever take to you." Katherine heard the bitterness in her voice, but there was no help for it. She was bitter. But once the Circle A was the profitable, thriving horse ranch she knew it could become, she hoped to make those who had scorned her regret their actions. Then all the townsfolk would see that being from Virginia didn't mean you were worthless—even if your own husband had believed it.

They reached the corral where the yearlings were kept, and Katherine pointed out the most spirited colts and fillies to Jake, telling him their names and temperaments. Jake nodded, listening carefully, saying little. She lost track of time as they talked of horses, but the sound of pounding hooves from the main road interrupted their discussion.

Katherine turned and began to run toward the house. If the mob had returned, it would be a close call with her guns upstairs. She had never needed to wear a gun on her own property. But times were changing. Katherine heard Jake behind her and she hissed over her shoulder, "Get out of sight."

"Not on your life. I'm tired of hiding."

Katherine didn't have time to argue. She neared the house, glanced over her shoulder to see how many riders were coming, then stopped short at the front steps. Jake bumped into her, nearly knocking her onto the wooden structure. He put his hands on her shoulders to steady her, then let them remain as he followed her rapt gaze.

"Dear God, he has the face of an angel."

Katherine didn't realize she'd said the words out loud until Jake answered, his voice low and rough with tension. "But a soul as black as hell."

The Coltrain Gang had come to call.

At the head of about a dozen riders galloped an immense white stallion. The group slowed, coming to a stop in front of Katherine and Jake. The animal reared and pawed the air before walking forward several steps on its hind legs and then returning the raised front hooves to the ground. Finally, the horse went down on one knee, bowing its head in a perfect bid for applause.

Despite all the theatrics, Katherine's attention was riveted to the man astride the performing stallion. She was reminded of a likeness of the angel Gabriel in a picture book she'd loved as a child. This man had the same pure, beautiful face—as though he could see a vision that normal humans could not. But he had a masculine air lacking in the picture of the angel. It could stem from the fact that, upon closer inspection, his nose had been broken at least once and a small scar over his right eye stood out brightly against tanned flesh. He was older than the other men, perhaps in his mid-thirties, but his hair was long and thick and golden with silver streaks shining in the sun. And there was nothing angelic about his body or his clothes. He wore a pieced guerilla shirt, much like Jake's, over worn Confederate gray pants. The muscles in his arms and legs bulged against the restriction of fabric. Six pistols, Navy Colts, were worn in various positions on his body, and a rifle rested across the saddle.

Katherine stared at the man in wonder, then blushed at her interest. When she met the outlaw's eyes she saw they were black and heavily lashed, but in their depths she saw a coldness that made her shiver. Jake's hands tightened on her shoulders, and she leaned back against the solid wall of his chest, glad she was not alone.

"It seems you've done all right for yourself, Banner." The sound issuing from the outlaw's throat was hoarse and broken. His ruined voice made Katherine gasp; something terrible must have happened to cause the rasping whisper.

"He took a rifle butt in the throat during the war. His voice has been that way ever since," Jake whispered in her ear, squeezing her shoulders once again before he moved to place himself between her and the outlaw gang.

"The lady saved my life, Charlie. More than I can say for the rest of you men." The sarcasm he put into his voice on the final word caused many of the rough-looking riders to growl and pat their guns in warning. Jake smiled.

"You know it's every man for himself in this gang. What did you expect from us?" Charlie Coltrain frowned at Jake.

"Nothing, Charlie. I know the rules. I was just funnin' with the boys."

"You ought to know better than to fun with these boys. They ain't got no sense of humor." A glimmer of a smile tilted Coltrain's mouth before he quickly controlled his features. "Get a horse and let's go, Banner." He turned his dark gaze on Katherine, and she moved closer to Jake. "I'm much obliged, ma'am. You'll never have to fear the Coltrain Gang on your place." He touched his forehead in a salute.

"I'm not leaving." The sound of horses' breathing and shifting seemed unnaturally loud in the stillness following Jake's words.

"I don't think I heard that right." The harsh voice made the words sound like a threat.

"This woman saved my life, and I promised I'd help out with the horses for a spell. I mean to keep my word." Jake stared Coltrain straight in the eye and did not look away.

The outlaw leader looked for a moment as though he would like to shoot Jake on the spot. Charlie studied him for several long moments, and Katherine wanted to squirm with unease.

How did Jake stand his ground in the face of that cold, blank stare?

Finally, Charlie shrugged. "When can we expect you back at camp?"

"A month at least."

"One month, no longer."

"I think we should shoot him now. He knows too much." A man moved his horse through the crowd to stand next to Charlie. This man was as ugly as the other was handsome. Greasy red hair hung past his ears. Scars of past battles marred his face and an evil sneer twisted his mouth. He held his gun at the ready, trained on Jake.

"Put it away, Bill." Coltrain's voice was low, deadly.

"Let me take care of him, Charlie. I never liked this Georgia boy anyway. Somethin' don't smell right about him." Bill cocked his pistol.

"Holster that gun or I'll shoot you myself. I don't care if you are my brother." Coltrain

## Second Chance

didn't bother to look at the other man. His eyes were still on Jake.

"Aw, you never let me have any fun." Bill returned the gun to its holster with a disgruntled grimace.

"One month, no more." Coltrain pulled back on the stallion's reins and the horse wheeled on strong back legs, galloping away. The other outlaws followed, except for Bill Coltrain.

"I'll be waiting for you, Banner. One month."

"I'll be looking forward to it, Billy Boy."

The outlaw narrowed his eyes at the diminutive nickname, but he yanked on his horse's reins and followed the others without further comment. Katherine continued to watch the riders until the dust settled and they could no longer be seen on the horizon.

"Nice bunch of boys you call friends," she said dryly.

Jake let out a startled hoot of laughter at her observation.

"I wouldn't call them boys or friends. But they understand me. We all come from the same horrors. Charlie's soul may be black, but it's no blacker than any of the others' or my own for that matter."

"I doubt if you're like them at all if you looked deep down."

Jake turned to her then, staring into her eyes. "Most people don't dig that deep."

His words sounded like a warning—or a threat. She took a step backward and came up against the porch steps.

The solid wood against her legs steadied her, and she tilted her chin upward and met his intense green eyes directly. "I appreciate your staying on the Circle A."

"I owe you my life. One month will hardly cover such a debt."

She cocked her head, curious. "Most outlaws don't boast about a sense of honor."

"You have just experienced the code of the southern outlaw. Kill, rob, and maim—but never, ever, break your word."

Despite herself, Katherine had to laugh. Then she walked up the stairs to the front door and turned to face him with a sterner face. "We'd best get back to work. I'll see you at supper. You can get something to eat from Mary if you're hungry this afternoon."

Jake nodded and strode off toward the corral. Katherine watched him for a moment, wondering about the mysteries of the man, then her eyes turned west where a haze of dust rose on the horizon, and she shivered at the memory of black, empty eyes.

# Chapter Seven

"Who on earth were those men?" Mary boomed.

The normal volume of the woman's voice always caused Katherine to wince. She had barely gotten in the front door before being set upon by the stout housekeeper. Obviously, Mary had watched the entire exchange from the parlor window.

"The Coltrain Gang." Katherine edged past Mary and headed up the stairs. The housekeeper's voice followed her all the way to her room.

"The Coltrain Gang! Heaven help us. Now we've got the whole gang riding in for a visit. She isn't content to have just one thief. No. She's got to have a dozen of them hanging around for tea. I wouldn't be surprised if . . ." The lament dwindled as Mary trailed toward the kitchen and Katherine shut her door.

Blessed silence reined in her sanctuary. Katherine leaned her forehead against the coolness of the wooden door and closed her eyes. It had been quite a morning.

After only a moment's rest, Katherine crossed the room to her nightstand, tugging her belt and holster off the bedpost when she passed. She fastened the leather around her waist, then checked her Colt carefully and settled the gun into place at her hip. She didn't plan to be caught without a weapon again after the events of last night and this morning. Until Jake Banner left her ranch, the gun would be near her hand at all times. Feeling more confident as she exited the house, Katherine's thoughts turned to the day's work.

Jake labored through the day without pause, needing to expend energy following his encounter with the Coltrains. Facing that bunch without a gun, with Katherine in the line of fire, had churned his insides more than he cared to think about. He found hard work the second-best cure for tension.

Throughout the day, Jake watched as Katherine moved about the ranch doing various chores. He noticed the addition of the gunbelt and smiled. She was a woman who took no chances; he liked that quality.

When the other men rode in at dusk, Jake ignored their curious looks and continued to work until they'd gone into the house. Only

## Second Chance

when all others had disappeared from sight did he return the horse to the corral. The dinner bell sounded and he went to the water trough to wash for supper.

Jake assumed his most humble posture, hoping to avoid conflict at the table. He stepped through the door and glanced quickly around the room, ignoring the openly hostile stares directed his way, then took a seat.

Katherine smiled at him warmly, then pointedly cleared her throat and folded her hands. The other men quickly folded their own hands and bowed their heads for grace. After Katherine finished the prayer, everyone began to fill their plates. They ate quietly until the arrival of Dillon Swade.

"What's this I hear about the Coltrain Gang riding in today?" His bellow put an end to the peaceful meal.

Katherine glanced over her shoulder to scowl at Mary, and Jake knew who had been talking to Dillon about the day's happenings. He would do well to remember the connection between the housekeeper and the foreman. Jake started to rise and face Dillon, but Katherine's hand on his arm urged him to remain seated.

Jake saw Dillon glance at Katherine's hand on his arm, and the stocky man's face reddened. Dillon looked into Jake's eyes with a scowl and Jake stared back unflinchingly. He would have to watch his back around the foreman more carefully in the future.

"It's all over, Dillon," Katherine said soothingly as she removed her hand. "The Coltrains wanted Jake to go with them, but he decided to stay with us for a month. We need his help to get this place running more smoothly. With his talent for breaking horses, we should improve our profits considerably."

Dillon took his place at the table with a grimace. "Why didn't you let him go? I can handle the Circle A. If we need more help, I'll find someone in town. We don't need his kind here stirring everyone up."

At the reminder of the previous evening, Katherine's eyes narrowed in anger. But, before answering, she glanced at the men and registered the interest on their faces. She took a deep breath, a forced smile appearing on her lips.

"Jake will be with us for a month." Katherine looked hard at each man in turn, then continued. "I don't think the Coltrains will come back. But, just in case, I think it would be wise to keep your guns handy and stay alert."

The men returned to their meals, seemingly content with the arrangements. Dillon glared at Jake for another moment, then followed their example. But the way he slapped the food onto his plate showed Jake that Dillon was far from content with life at the Circle A.

Katherine calmly ate her meal, ignoring Dillon's temper even when his energetic serving technique landed a clump of mashed potatoes on her cheek. Before she could wipe her

## Second Chance

face, Jake reached out and removed the food with his finger. He was struck by the softness of her skin, and the urge to touch her again was strong. As Jake continued to stare at the smooth expanse, a tinge of pink appeared in her cheeks. The warm hue reminded Jake of the roses his mother kept in their St. Louis garden. He looked into Katherine's eyes and saw his own desire reflected there. The pull between them he'd first noticed on the steps of the jail intensified.

Their gaze broke when a pitcher of milk slammed down between them.

"Who wants milk with dinner?"

Jake looked up into Mary's scowling face.

"Yes, thank you, ma'am." He reached for the pitcher only to have it snatched from his hands and handed to Dillon.

The foreman's scowl was matched by the scowls on the faces of the other men. Everyone had witnessed the exchange between Jake and Katherine, and no one but the two involved had enjoyed it. He would have to be careful or one of the men would jump him after dark in an attempt to preserve the honor of their employer.

Jake spent the rest of the meal observing the people at the table. The men obviously liked and respected Katherine. But he caught enough raised brows and puzzled shrugs between them to conclude that they found her a bit eccentric. Dillon was another story. The man professed to care about the Circle A and Katherine, yet he took every opportunity to alienate her and threaten his position. The looks Jake observed Dillon throwing Katherine's way were those of a man in the midst of a serious infatuation. In the past, Jake had found it best to steer clear of a man in that condition, and the woman involved also.

But when his attention turned to Katherine, Jake knew that that vow would be nearly impossible to keep. Her exertions throughout the day had loosened her braid and she lifted the stray hair from her neck. The cooling night breeze through the doorway wafted over the warm skin, and she smiled. Jake gazed at the curved lips, slightly parted and damp, remembering how they had tasted, if only for a moment, the previous evening. His response thickened and pulsed, and he looked quickly away only to encounter a pair of hate-filled ice blue eyes.

Dillon's attention had not wandered, contrary to Jake's own. Jake held the man's stare, knowing he could not give in. Dillon's lips thinned into a frown, then he pushed away from the table and left the house without a word.

The other men soon followed, excusing themselves politely, removing their hats from the pegs on the wall, and returning to the bunkhouse. Mary cleared the table silently and began to wash the dishes, preparatory to leaving for home.

## Second Chance

"Well, there's another long day ahead tomorrow, and I've got work to do in the office before I turn in . . ." Katherine stood, her voice drifting.

Jake recognized a dismissal when he heard one. Attempting to make peace with Mary, he carried his dishes to the sink. But his actions drew no thanks from the sullen housekeeper. With a quiet "Good night, ladies" in the direction of both women, he retired to the storeroom.

Once there, Jake assumed that sleep would quickly follow. He was used to riding horses, but he hadn't worked at breaking them for years. Muscles he didn't remember existed screamed for rest. The blankets Katherine had brought the previous day, combined with a cushion of straw, made the softest bed he'd known in years. Yet sleep eluded him. Each time his eyes closed, another question surfaced for him to ponder.

Who was the Coltrains' contact at the Second Chance Bank? Why hadn't Matthew sprung him from jail? Should he send word of Matt's disappearance to Pinkerton? What was there about Dillon Swade that had all his instincts warning of trouble?

Getting up from his bed, Jake uttered a sound of disgust. Maybe a walk would clear his head enough for sleep. When he reached for his hat he remembered it was still on a peg in the kitchen. Well, that would be his first stop.

## Lori Handeland

Jake crossed the yard with long strides, eager to walk in the pastures and find peace with himself. He opened the back door and strode into the kitchen, unaware of the lantern light in the room until too late.

Paralyzed, he stood in the doorway surveying the scene before him. The lamp's flame turned the glistening water droplets on Katherine's back to shades of golden fire. Intent on her bath, she hadn't heard the door open and continued, undisturbed, to wash her hair. Jake watched, barely breathing, as she lifted her hands to work soap through the long strands. The muscles in her back and upper arms flexed, contrasting with the visible bones in her petite shoulders. When the haunting scent of roses drifted to him, Jake knew he must make himself known or be lost to sensation.

He stepped inside and shut the door. The sudden sound made Katherine jump and reach for the towel on a chair close by. Her hair, wet and full of soap, fell past her shoulders and into the water, floating around her in a cloud of sunshine. Clutching the towel to her chest, she slowly glanced over her shoulder at Jake. At the sight of the intruder, relief washed over her face, quickly replaced by anger.

"What are you doing here?"

Jake held up his hat and shrugged.

Katherine grimaced. "That couldn't wait until morning? I could have shot you." She withdrew her pistol from behind the towel and placed it

## Second Chance

back on the chair. To Jake's chagrin, the towel remained firmly in place.

Though he knew he should leave, the scent of warmed roses drew him, and Jake walked further into the room. As he moved closer, he noticed her fingers tighten on the towel and her gaze darted toward the pistol.

"That won't be necessary, Katie." He leaned over and snatched the Colt out of her reach. He knew better than to let Katherine Logan have access to a gun.

Katherine's face held an expression of surprise, but she quickly recovered. "What do you think you're doing? Put that back and get out of here."

Jake continued to stand near the tub, staring at her. He should do as she asked, but somehow couldn't bring himself to leave.

"Get out before I scream."

The controlled tightness in Katherine's voice penetrated Jake's trance, and he looked into her eyes.

"You didn't lock the door." Jake uttered the first words that came to his mind while his gaze remained on hers. Had the air thickened with the heat from her bath water? He couldn't seem to draw an adequate breath.

"I've never had to lock the door," Katherine snapped. "All the men know that after supper the house is off limits. If anyone wants to talk to me, they knock on the front door."

"I'm not one of the men." Jake said the words quietly, a touch of resentment evident.

Katherine's tone softened. "No, you're not. And I suppose with all the excitement lately no one told you the rules."

"Are there any more I should know?"

"Any questions you have can be answered in my office later tonight or in the morning." Katherine paused, and the pinkening of her cheeks made her discomfort obvious. "Please go," she whispered.

Jake dragged his gaze from a detailed perusal of her delicate collarbone, and moved a step closer. He reached out, his finger tracing the path his eyes had wandered a moment before. Her bones were so fragile beneath her soft, white skin. He could crush her with the slightest effort. Her hair, heavy and slick, dampened his fingers. He picked up a pitcher from the floor next to the tub and used it to rinse the remaining soap from the strands. As he let the mass slip through his hands and back into the bath water, Katherine shivered. She held herself so still, so tense, that Jake ached to rub away the rigidness from her shoulders. He began to kneel, drawn to her as he'd been the night before, when Katherine's fingers whitened as her grip on the towel intensified.

Jake looked into her eyes and saw her fear. Did she fear him or the attraction hovering in the steamy air between them? Muttering an expletive, he straightened, wheeling away from Katherine and the temptation she presented. He slammed the pistol back onto the chair and walked quickly away.

## Second Chance

"Start locking the door." His throat was dry with the tension caused by Katherine's nearness. Opening the door a crack, he searched the darkness for any sign of movement. Finding none, he slipped out, leaving in silence.

Jake strode away from the house, his hat crushed tightly in his fist, his thoughts in a turmoil.

*What is it about her that makes me forget what I'm here for? I know better than to get involved when I'm on an assignment.*

His desire for a mind-clearing walk forgotten, Jake reflected on stories he'd heard of men brought down by their trust in the wrong woman. Absently he crossed the yard to the barn.

He had heard of agents who became involved with women while undercover. Their concentration shattered and they often ended up dead. One agent had revealed his true identity to his lover. The woman turned out to be a Rebel spy, and the man's unguarded words had lost the Union a key battle in the war.

Quietly entering the shadowed barn, Jake heard a movement in the storeroom. Stealthily he made his way to the door and listened. There it was again—a small kernel of sound that only a trained ear would notice. Without waiting for further confirmation, Jake pushed open the door and entered.

The intruder turned, creating enough movement for Jake to pinpoint his whereabouts. One leap later Jake wrestled in the dirt, attempting to immobilize his victim.

"Dammit, Parker. If this is the way you treat your friends, I'm not surprised you don't have many." The voice was muffled, but Jake instantly stopped his actions at the use of his real name by a familiar voice.

"Matt?"

"Who else? Now get off me, you big ox."

Jake released the stranglehold on his partner, and they got to their feet.

"What are you doing sneaking around, Matt? I could have killed you." Jake dropped the southern accent he took pains to use around all others.

"Do you think we could get some light in here, or is that an unreasonable request?"

"Hold on a minute." Jake quickly lit the lantern. Soft, warm light filled the room and illuminated Matthew Ward.

Matt's well-tailored brown tweed suit made him look the part of a respectable young banker. His reddish-blond hair had been recently washed and barbered, and the center part gleamed in the lamplight. Matt's short beard was trimmed neatly, nearly masking the scar along the left side of his jaw. Jake remembered well how his friend had received that scar—he would always regret he had been just a second too late to prevent a bayonet from slicing Matt's face. Still, as Matt often reminded him, Jake had managed to keep the scar from being around Matt's throat instead. His friend's laughing brown eyes never seemed to darken with remembrances as Jake's did, and his face

## Second Chance

resembled that of a cheery leprechaun. Matt, somewhat sensitive about his lack of height, never enjoyed that comparison. Though short of stature, he had a never-ending reservoir of strength and courage. In a tight spot, a better man could not be found.

Jake had to admit that Matt pleased the eye when he was cleaned up. Tonight he looked a far cry from the grizzly trail comrade Jake knew so well.

Matt leaned over to pick up his tan felt hat and spent a moment brushing dirt from the brim. Then he smiled, and Jake grinned back.

"It sure is good to see your ugly face, Matt. When you didn't turn up in Second Chance yesterday, I was sure something had happened to you."

"You didn't waste any time getting the town stirred up. The minute I got back I was regaled with tales of Jake Banner, notorious bank robber, saved from death by a lovely lady. I like the alias, by the way." At Jake's nod, Matt's teasing manner evaporated. "What the hell happened at that bank anyway?"

Jake rubbed his chin, feeling the thick stubble always evident on his face by three in the afternoon. He thought back to the day of the bank robbery and his capture.

"We were told to ride in, rob the bank, and leave. No one was supposed to get hurt, no one was supposed to shoot." Jake gave a rueful laugh. "Charlie must have forgotten to tell Bill the plan. The second we got the money,

## Lori Handeland

Bill started shooting off his gun at the ceiling, howling the Rebel yell, and scaring everyone in the place half to death. The people panicked and the sheriff came running. We got out of the bank with the money, even made it onto our horses, when Jeff Soames took a bullet in the shoulder." Jake shook his head ruefully. "He's just a kid now, Matt; he must have lied about his age to enlist during the war. Anyway, his horse reared and he couldn't stay on with his arm that way. All the others were on their way out of town—none of them ever looked back. I jumped down and got Jeff back on his horse, and he took off as if General Grant himself were on his heels. The next thing I knew there were ten guns pointed at my head and I was being marched off to jail. I thought about having them send a telegram to Pinkerton, but these folks really hate the Coltrains. I doubt if they'd have listened to me. Besides, I figured you'd get me out. My mistake."

"Sorry, buddy, couldn't be helped." Matt spread his hands and shrugged. "You're right about this town, though. No one would have listened to one of the Coltrain Gang if they could hang him first, especially the sheriff. Pinkerton sent me a coded message last week. We're not supposed to tell anyone here about our mission, even the local law. Seems like our boss man is mighty spooked about this town. According to him, anyone could be involved; trust no one."

Jake nodded his understanding of the message. He'd been right to keep his mouth

## Second Chance

shut when captured. Luckily, Katherine Logan hadn't done the same.

"Where were you, Matt?" Jake asked the question that had haunted him since his walk up the steps of a hanging platform.

"Cooling my heels in Danville, the next town south. I went to their bank to follow a lead. Turned out to be nothing, if you're interested." He grinned at Jake's frown, then continued. "My horse threw a shoe. That delayed me a day. I didn't expect you to come in, shoot up the town, and practically beg to be hung in my absence."

"No, I suppose not," Jake conceded. "Well, it's done, and I'm still around to do my job. What have you found out so far?"

"You got any place to sit in your humble abode?"

Jake pointed at a barrel in the corner of the storeroom, and Matt perched himself on top of it with a grimace.

"I'm definitely more suited to my role in this assignment." Matt glanced at the bedroll on the floor. "Clean clothes and my own room with a bed. No physical labor either. Yes, I'm a lucky man."

"Give it a rest, Matt. I'll see to it that on the next assignment you get a taste of the rough life. Now tell me what you know before someone decides to come in and check on their pet criminal."

Matt looked at him closely. "Is that how they treat you here?"

"Most of them. Not her—she's different." Jake's face took on a faraway look as he remembered Katherine's moist skin and tousled hair. His attention returned to Matt in time to catch the speculative look on his friend's face.

"Is she the reason you're still here rather than back with the Coltrains?"

"No. Well, yes."

"Which is it, man?"

Jake made an impatient sound and began to pace. "There's something about her hired man, Dillon Swade, that raises my hackles. Can you make a few tactful inquiries in town?" At Matt's affirmative nod, he continued. "Then there's the fact she saved my life. I feel I owe her, and this place could use my help." He paused and took a deep breath. "Charlie and the boys came to get me today."

Matt glanced up. "The Coltrains came for you?"

Jake nodded.

"That's great. They must trust you, Jake, if they want you back. Why didn't you go?"

"Charlie gave me a month to repay my debt to Katherine. I'll take it and keep my eye on Swade. This is a perfect opportunity to observe the folks around here. If nothing turns up, I can go back to the Coltrains with no one the wiser."

"But a month? I don't think you can wait that long. If another robbery takes place and you aren't with the gang, there'll be hell to pay with the boss."

## Second Chance

Jake frowned, wondering why Matt was so anxious for him to get out of town. Usually they were in complete agreement when they worked together, though they hadn't been on the same assignment for over a year. As far as he could see, the setup at the Circle A was a godsend.

Pushing suspicions of his friend from his mind for the moment, Jake conceded, "I shouldn't need a month to find out what I need to know. As soon as I do, I'll go back. Satisfied?"

Matt studied him silently, then nodded slowly in resignation.

The sound of the barn's outer door slowly opening froze both men, each listening intently. At Jake's nod, Matt ducked behind the barrel he'd been perching on, and Jake moved another barrel next to it. He barely had time to return to his lounging position on the other side of the room before Dillon Swade opened the door and entered.

"I see the way you look at her." Dillon focused on Jake in the dim light, his small eyes narrowing even further.

Jake decided not to answer the obvious taunt. Instead, he quickly studied the man as an opponent. Dillon wore a pistol at his hip. The gun looked Union issue from Jake's vantage point. Since his talk with Katherine he knew the man could use the weapon well. Swade was short and stocky but muscular from hard work. Still, Jake could take him in a fair fight. He'd just have to wait until a fair fight was offered.

"Aren't you going to answer me, Reb?"

Calmly Jake looked into Dillon's eyes. "What's there to say? Yes, I've looked at her. It's hard not to when I work and live on the same place."

"You know the kind of look I mean, Banner. And you're touching her too. I won't have it."

Dillon took a menacing step forward, his hand caressing the butt of his gun. Jake's gaze rested briefly on that hand, then returned to Dillon's face. The advantage was Jake's, though Dillon didn't know it. At that moment Matt had his pistol aimed at Dillon's back. But Jake didn't want to give away their cover if it wasn't necessary. He had to talk the man out of his rage.

"Listen, Swade, I plan to work here for a month, plain and simple. Mrs. Logan saved my life and I'm grateful. That's as far as it goes." Jake put all the sincerity into his voice and expression he could muster.

The angry mask on Dillon's face slipped, revealing confusion. Jake remained where he was, waiting to hear how Dillon would interpret his words.

"That better be all. She's mine, you know." The foreman's voice took on a conspiratorial tone.

"No, I didn't know. How's that?"

"I've wanted her since she came here." His eyes took on the distant gaze of remembrance. "So smart, so beautiful. And I'll have her too in the end, you'll see. Everyone will see. Most of all, Katherine will see. She just needs to learn

## Second Chance

how much she needs me." Then, as though realizing he'd said too much, Dillon turned and moved quickly to the door. He glanced back, fixing Jake with his burning stare. "I've got too much to risk now to let a Reb thief take it all away."

After Dillon slammed out of the room, Jake quietly went to the door. Opening it a crack, he watched the short figure disappear into the night.

"He's gone." Jake rolled one of the barrels to the side so Matt could crawl out. As he'd thought, Matt's gun was securely in hand, ready for use.

"Well, buddy, I think you might be right for a change. He's obviously into something he doesn't want anyone to know about, especially you. Haven't you ever heard anyone mention his name at the Coltrain camp?"

Jake shook his head. "I'm the new man there. I haven't been told anything more than where to go and when since I joined up. I need more time with them before they'll trust me."

"Exactly my point, Jake. If you're here, you're not gaining their trust."

Jake frowned then nodded. "Point taken. If I can't dig up anything about Swade in the next few weeks I'll rejoin Charlie and the boys." He paused, hating the thought of leaving Katherine with Dillon Swade. Perhaps he could think of a way to get rid of the odd foreman before he had to leave. Jake returned his attention to his partner. "When do you want to meet next?"

"At least a week. I'll come here again."

"Just be careful. Next time it might be Swade who jumps you."

"At least he'd be some competition." With a parting grin, Matt slipped out the door.

Jake threw himself down heavily on his bedroll. All the information he'd absorbed in the past few days raced through his brain. As he attempted to make sense of the myriad thoughts, exhaustion finally won out, and he fell asleep. His dreams remained undisturbed by images of the Coltrains and Dillon Swade. Instead, he was haunted by the scent of roses, the sound of splashing water, and the sight of an angel's hair cascading onto pale, smooth skin.

# Chapter Eight

Over a week passed, and life at the Circle A settled back into a routine. Katherine found she looked over her shoulder only once or twice a day instead of every few minutes. But her memory of Charlie and Bill Coltrain insured the placement of a gun on her hip whenever she ventured outside the house.

Both Dillon and Jake went out of their way to avoid each other. That suited Katherine fine. Worrying about the two of them fighting or killing each other was one problem she didn't need.

At least the money for next month's mortgage would be taken care of. Thanks to Jake, Lucifer would be ready for sale by the end of the following month. Katherine had believed the horse a total loss because of its temperament.

## Lori Handeland

Leaving the house one afternoon, Katherine smiled, feeling carefree for the first time since her arrival in Second Chance. She was confident she could make the Circle A into the prosperous ranch it was meant to be. Then she would be guaranteed the independence and stability she'd craved all her life. The Circle A was the first place on earth that was hers alone. On the ranch she could be Katherine—not southern, not northern, just herself.

Katherine walked toward the barn, intent on riding out to inspect the fence repairs. She glanced at the paddock where Jake worked the colts, and her steps slowed, then stopped as she stared at the sight before her.

The afternoon sun beat down mercilessly, and Jake had removed his shirt. He sat astride the prancing animal, his bronzed torso glistening with sweat. Muscles bulged in his arms when he pulled on the reins, teaching the colt the intricacies of a master's command. Katherine stared as his worn Levi's outlined the hardness of his thighs where they gripped the horse.

How long she stood near the barn and watched him, unknowingly moving closer and closer, was a mystery to her. But when Jake's green eyes looked directly into hers, Katherine realized she stood at the paddock rail, staring at him in fascination. Her face flamed at being caught admiring him so openly. His grin did nothing to alleviate the warmth of her face, not to mention the heat suffusing the rest of her body at his state of undress.

## Second Chance

"I don't suppose you brought any water with you, ma'am?"

"What?" Katherine started at the sound of his deep, mellow voice.

Jake was always careful to use the same respectful form of address if there was a chance someone was listening. He'd only dared to use her first name, or his version of it, when they were alone. He'd called her "Katie" after kissing her, then again when he'd intruded upon her bath. His intimate shortening of her name, a name no one else in her life had ever called her, always brought unwelcome shivers of awareness. Despite the reckless foolishness of the thought, God help her, she wanted to hear that name on his lips again.

Her reverie abruptly ended when Jake jumped down from the horse in an easy movement. He came to join her at the railing, allowing the animal to canter around the enclosed area unfettered.

"I asked for water, ma'am. Breaking colts is thirsty work, especially in this weather." He dragged the back of his hand across his forehead, then pushed work-roughened fingers through sweat-dampened hair in an impatient gesture.

Jake's nearness mesmerized Katherine. She could feel his increased body heat radiating outward, and she swayed toward the warmth. He smelled, not unpleasantly, of horse and man—an honest smell from hard work at a job well done. She could see the way his black hair stood up where he'd pushed it from his brow, and she longed to smooth the strands back into place.

"Ma'am?" Jake's voice, slightly husky as though he knew her desires and shared them, jolted Katherine back to reality.

"Yes, water. I'll fetch some straightaway." Turning quickly, she nearly tripped over her own feet in her haste to get away from Jake and the odd feelings he engendered in her.

As she returned with a dipper of water from the well near the house, Katherine vowed to be about her business before she could embarrass herself further. But when she handed him the dipper, their fingers touched. The minute contact jolted throughout her body, and an ache sprang up deep inside her.

Katherine attempted to snatch her hand away and retreat, but Jake's fingers closed over hers and she raised her eyes to his face. Mirrored in the green depths she saw the same hunger and longing that coursed through her. Katherine allowed her fingers to relax as Jake gripped them more tightly, drawing her near. She continued to look into his eyes, and he leaned toward her over the fence between them. Her breathing increased in tempo with his nearness. Jake whispered her name, and Katherine knew he was going to kiss her in plain sight of anyone who happened by. Amazingly, she didn't care.

The sound of a horse and buggy approaching from the main road caused Jake to glance over Katherine's shoulder. He straightened away from her and nodded in the direction of the house. "Company, ma'am."

Katherine whirled, a hand going for the gun at her hip, then dropping to her side upon recognizing the visitor. She took a deep breath and left Jake without a backward glance. But a prickling sensation in the middle of her back told her his gaze followed her to the house.

"Ruth, what are you doing out here this time of the afternoon? Weren't there any children to torment after school today?" Katherine teased lightheartedly as she approached the small buggy drawing to a stop at the front porch.

"On the last day of the school year? Not even I could be so dastardly as to make children stay late on such a holiday."

Katherine laughed, her face and voice reflecting her delight with the woman emerging from the vehicle.

Ruth Sanderson daintily placed her high-topped shoe on the ground next to Katherine. The rest of her slim, straight body followed. Of average height, Ruth nevertheless appeared tall next to Katherine's five-foot-four-inch frame. Although they had become the dearest of friends during the year since Sam's death, Katherine still felt awkward around Ruth's ever-present grace and refinement. Despite the humid heat and dust, not a strand of Ruth's auburn hair escaped from the bun at the back of her head. Her skin was white and soft—testament to her religious wearing of gloves and sunbonnets when venturing into the elements. Though she was not a classic beauty, Ruth's inner kindness made up for any lack of comeliness.

Jake watched them from the corral, and Katherine wondered if he found Ruth's ladylike mien appealing; southern men often did. She frowned at the realization that she was placing too much importance on the opinion of a man she hardly knew—a man who was a bank robber, no less. With an effort, she eased the line from her forehead and led Ruth into the house, determined not to let any opinion of Jake Banner matter to her one way or another.

Inside the house, Katherine seated her guest in the front parlor and went to the kitchen to request lemonade. Mary complied eagerly, always happy when Katherine had a visitor. At the Circle A, company was a rarity.

Katherine seated herself on the sofa near the window. "I suppose you've heard about the incident in town last week?" she asked.

"Ah yes, the outlaw. Is that him I saw hovering over you when I arrived?"

Katherine looked at Ruth sharply, wondering how much her friend had seen. "He's the man I was talking to when you arrived." Katherine picked up her lemonade and took a healthy gulp.

"It looked as though you were doing more than talking." At Katherine's frown Ruth took a small sip of her drink before continuing. "He's quite nice-looking from what I could see. Don't you think so?"

"I hadn't noticed."

## Second Chance

Ruth looked skeptical, and Katherine glanced out the window to avoid her friend's regard. She had always been honest with Ruth, even when it came to talking about Sam. Katherine found she always felt better after discussing a problem with her friend. But now she avoided speaking of her reactions to Jake and the feelings he aroused in her. She didn't want to bring them into the open for scrutiny—not yet.

"You didn't notice! Katherine, you've been working too long with the men. You're starting to lose your feminine instincts."

"It's just as well. I never used the few I had." Katherine turned to Ruth with a smile. The woman was forever trying to get her to dress up and be a lady. Ruth should have understood by now she was championing a lost cause.

"Well, we're going to have to work on you some more." At Katherine's groan, Ruth stood up and gracefully joined her friend on the sofa. Taking Katherine's hand in her own, Ruth looked into her eyes earnestly. "You need to get out among the people here. If they could just get to know you, they would all see the wonderful person I've found in Katherine Logan."

Katherine returned the pressure of Ruth's hand, then shook her head. "You know it's no use. I'm the Reb from Virginia—the state that housed the Confederate government, Bobby Lee's home. It'll be a long time before anyone forgets the war. But in Second Chance, the Coltrains will make sure the memories live on forever."

Katherine's own memories crowded to the forefront of her mind, and she recalled the day she had arrived at Aunt Adelaide's home in Richmond following her parents' death. Suddenly she had been thrust into an entirely different world, a world where the rules for women were strict and, to Katherine, unfathomable. In Boston she had always been admired for her Yankee bluntness. Richmond society viewed that same honesty as rudeness. She had never fit in there, just as she would never fit in in Second Chance.

Ruth's soft voice brought Katherine back to the present. "The wounds of the war have to heal sometime. Ignoring them never does anyone a bit of good."

"You know how hard I tried to fit in when I first came here, Ruth. No one gave me a chance except you. Now that Sam's dead, folks don't even attempt to be civil. I gave up long ago on becoming a member of society."

"It's been three years since you came to Second Chance. Maybe it's time you tried again."

Katherine burst out laughing. "After stealing Jake Banner out from under everyone's noses and denying them the entertainment of a hanging? I don't think they'd accept me now, Ruth."

"If you hide here like you're ashamed of what you did, you'll never have a moment's peace and you know it. You've got to be bold, walk right into the middle of those bigots and say, 'Look at me. I'm not afraid of you. It's your loss not to accept me.'"

## Second Chance

Ruth had a point about hiding at the Circle A. Things were difficult enough for her when she ventured into town for supplies. Storekeepers waited on everyone in their shop before turning to her. People snickered and whispered whenever she walked down the street. If she waited too long to face the townsfolk, they would think she was ashamed of her behavior.

Katherine sighed in resignation. "What do you think I should do?"

Ruth's smile lit up her face and she hurried to press the advantage. "There's a barn raising and then a dance tomorrow at the Varners'. Why don't you join me?"

"I don't know. Everyone in town will be there. Couldn't I go to a smaller event?" Katherine's throat tightened at the thought of facing so many people who disliked her. Sam had stopped taking her to any of the various picnics or parties held in the area once he decided she was barren. She remained at home and worked, never getting further acquainted with any of the women in or around town. The sudden change in Sam's behavior had contributed to the town's distrust of her.

"No. You'll make a better impression if you attend a large event, and soon. The barn raising's perfect." Ruth paused and cocked her head with a smile. "And you should bring your outlaw friend."

"What? Are you crazy, Ruth? I had a mob here last week wanting to hang the man in my front yard. I'll have to stand over him as though he were a two-year-old if I take him into the midst of those wolves."

"No, I don't think so. If you bring Jake along as though he belongs there as much as you do, I don't believe you'll have anyone coming out here causing trouble again. Robert E. Lee nearly won the war through his daring. You can win your war too. Be bold, Katherine."

Katherine remained silent for a moment, digesting Ruth's theory. Her friend knew people. Ruth's skill with the children she taught was legendary. Katherine got up and walked to the window, glancing out just as Jake strode across the space between the corral and the barn. He moved like a man with a purpose in life. Katherine knew from observing him for the past week that his strength, ability, and confidence would cow any man. If she kept alert and told Jake to do the same, Ruth's idea could work.

Katherine turned abruptly and nodded to her friend. "All right, I'll do it."

Ruth smiled calmly. "I had no doubt you'd come to see it my way."

Katherine sighed. The woman was unflappable. Did she have any weaknesses? If she did, Katherine had never witnessed them, and in all their talks Ruth never mentioned a fear of anything. Katherine knew she herself appeared cool and unemotional to most people, but she was familiar with her own failings. Ruth's remained a mystery.

## Second Chance

"Wouldn't you like to stay for supper?" Katherine asked as her friend prepared to leave.

"I can't, but thank you for asking. I promised to bring a few items for the picnic, and I need to prepare them tonight."

"I'm sure you'll have a line of young men waiting to dance with you."

Ruth laughed. "If there was just one I was interested in dancing with, I'd be a happy woman."

"Maybe you can shoo some of them my way so I won't look a total fool."

"You can count on it." They stepped out of the house, and Ruth took Katherine's hand again. "Relax, Katherine. After a few awkward moments at the outset, I'm sure you'll have a lovely time tomorrow."

"I'll hold you to that prediction. I suppose you'll be there bright and early."

"The work begins at seven. I'll look forward to seeing you and meeting Jake." Ruth gingerly ascended into her buggy and, once seated, took up the reins.

Katherine remained in front of the house until Ruth disappeared down the road toward Second Chance. Her gaze wandered to the barn and she hesitated. Then, with an exclamation of irritation at her indecision, she crossed the yard and entered the steamy heat of the barn.

"Jake?" Katherine called at the entrance to the storeroom.

"Ma'am?" Jake appeared in the opening, a fresh shirt buttoned over his torso. Katherine recognized it as one of Joe's older shirts, and it pleased her that the hired man had been open-minded enough to share with Jake. She would have to remember to thank him privately.

"Can I speak with you for a moment?"

Jake shrugged and motioned for her to enter. She moved past him in the doorway, and her skin tingled at their close proximity, combined with the enticing scent of man and soap. Katherine hurried to stand on the opposite side of the small room before turning to face Jake.

"What can I do for you, Mrs. Logan? Is there anything wrong with my work?"

"No, nothing. I'm very pleased that you have such a gift with horses. I don't know what we'll do once you've gone."

"Probably sleep a lot easier," Jake said, a wry smile twisting his mouth.

Katherine looked at him sharply, thinking of the lost sleep and tormented dreams she'd had since Jake arrived. But his face held nothing beyond a mild curiosity, and she saw he was waiting for her to speak.

"I've been persuaded to go to a barn raising and dance tomorrow." Katherine paused, uncertain of how to raise the next problem.

"You could use a little relaxation. I hope you have a good time."

"You're going with me." Katherine hadn't meant to state the case so bluntly, but tact had never been her strong suit.

## Second Chance

"I don't think so." Jake folded his arms across his chest and leaned his shoulder against the wall.

"Yes, you are. If we go there as though we belong, I think it will go a long way toward keeping you safe. We can't hide here for the next month. If we do, we'll have a mob at the Circle A every few days trying to take you in or hang you on the spot. We need to face them all."

"Might this brilliant idea have anything to do with your visitor this afternoon?"

"Well, Ruth did suggest it, but I feel she's made a good point. We've got to be bold like Bobby Lee."

Jake burst out laughing, but changed the sound to a cough at the serious look on Katherine's face. "You do realize that the South lost the war."

Katherine gave Jake a disgusted look. "Very funny. I merely thought that a show of bravado would calm down the troublemakers."

Jake remained silent a moment, then nodded. "You could be right. Anyway, it's worth a try. Just make sure you watch my back."

"Don't worry, I'd planned on it. But who'll be watching mine?"

"I'd be honored, ma'am."

Ruth Sanderson urged her horse to a trot on the dry dirt road into town. The countryside wasn't safe these days for a woman alone. Before the war, Second Chance had been as secure as any small town in America. But now the hatreds and strife of a civil war had torn Missouri as well as the country. At the border with Kansas, skirmishes continued to be fought every day. Former soldiers from both sides roamed the land stealing food, clothing, and shelter. In the coming darkness there could be any number of desperate vagrants waiting for a lone traveler.

Despite her worries, Ruth was pleased she had taken the time to drive out to Katherine's. Now her friend would be coming to the barn raising tomorrow. Katherine really did need to get out more, she mused. The poor girl had been positively stifled in this town. That old tyrant Sam Logan was a perfect example of a useless human being as far as Ruth was concerned. Imagine, coaxing the poor girl into marrying him, under false pretenses no doubt, then dragging her to Missouri and treating her like dirt when she failed to conceive. It was a shame he'd had a chance to damage Katherine's spirit before having the grace to die. But Ruth believed the responsibility of running the Circle A over the past year had brought about favorable changes in Katherine's demeanor. She no longer jumped at shadows or flinched at loud noises. The ownership of the ranch had soothed Katherine Logan's wounded soul.

The nicker of another horse on the road behind her buggy startled Ruth from her reverie. A touch of panic crept into her throat at

## Second Chance

the thought of meeting a desperate ex-soldier or outlaw while she traveled alone on the deserted path. Ruth's hand strayed to the pistol, partially obscured by a dust robe on the seat next to her. Though she had never been good at firing the weapon, at least its presence gave her confidence. The horse and rider drew next to her conveyance, and she calmly turned to face them.

A pleasant-looking young man sat astride a roan gelding. He was dressed prosperously, well groomed and obviously not a thief on the prowl. Ruth relaxed her grip on the pistol.

"How do you do, ma'am? Are you headed back to town?" The young man smiled, his eyes reflecting a cheery disposition.

"Yes, I am. And you, sir?" Ruth was surprised to find herself returning the stranger's smile.

"I am at that. Would you mind if I accompanied you?"

"Actually, I would appreciate your company. The roads are not as safe as they once were."

"How true. It's a shame that decent people must carry a weapon wherever they go." His gaze rested on the butt of Ruth's pistol visible at the edge of the dust robe.

Ruth shrugged and covered the gun completely. "One can never be too careful Mr. . . . ?"

"Rolland—Matthew Rolland. Might I inquire your name?"

"Ruth Sanderson."

"I've heard talk of the lovely and competent town teacher. I see now that they spoke the truth, though words do not do you justice."

"I believe you have the gift of gab, sir." Ruth found she enjoyed the lighthearted banter between herself and this man. All the other men of her acquaintance, young and old, seemed to believe she wanted to talk about nothing beyond books and children.

"Words fail me unless I'm in the presence of true inspiration. Tell me, Miss Sanderson, where are you coming from this fine evening?"

"I visited a friend at the Circle A ranch."

"The fascinating and talented Mrs. Logan, I presume."

Ruth peered at Matthew in the dusky light. "You seem to know a lot about the people of Second Chance for a stranger."

"I work at the bank. You hear many things during a day there. And your Mrs. Logan has been the talk of the town for the past week. I wish I could have seen her performance at the hanging."

"I missed it myself, but I've seen her shoot. Katherine's the best."

As they'd talked, their horses drew near the town. Ruth looked up in surprise when they passed the first house on the outskirts. Time had flown while she spoke with Matthew Rolland. She usually found herself counting the seconds until she could make a polite retreat whenever she conversed with a man. A thought occurred to her.

## Second Chance

"Mr. Rolland, since you're new in town, I feel it would only be neighborly of me to invite you to a barn raising tomorrow."

Matt glanced at her with a smile, and Ruth flushed. She felt brazen asking him to the working celebration, but she'd gone too far to turn back.

"That sounds like something I'd enjoy, and I have no plans tomorrow. You will be attending, of course."

"Of course." Her voice sounded breathless to her ears, but she rushed on. "The barn raising is at the Varners'. Afterward there will be dancing in the new barn."

Ruth pulled the buggy to a stop in front of her house, and Matt reined in his horse. "I'm afraid I'm not familiar with the Varners. Perhaps I could stop by in the morning and we could go together? Then you could show me the way."

"That would be a practical solution, Mr. Rolland. Shall we say six-thirty tomorrow morning?"

"I'll look forward to seeing you then." Matt touched the brim of his hat and turned the horse to trot up the main street of Second Chance.

Ruth continued to watch him until he entered Sue Ellen's Boarding House part of the way down Main Street. While she unharnessed her horse and returned it to the stable, she contemplated her conversation with the new banker. For the first time in several years, Ruth Sanderson looked forward to the coming day.

# Chapter Nine

Saturday morning dawned bright and clear with the promise of heat to come. Ruth had been up with the sun packing the basket of cold ham and bread she'd been asked to bring to the picnic. She found herself looking out the front window anxiously, wondering if Matthew Rolland would truly drive her to the Varners'. For the first time in her life Ruth cared if her escort arrived.

She had taken extra time with her hair, pinning it neatly into a chignon, then pulling soft tendrils loose to curl around her face. Ruth wore her best dress, a violet muslin accented with frothy, white lace at the throat and wrists. The tightly fitted bodice showed off her ample bust and slim waist to their best advantage. Despite the coming heat, she wore several petticoats over a hoop to add fullness.

## Second Chance

At exactly six-thirty, Matthew Rolland's buggy came to a stop in front of Ruth's house. She drew back quickly from the window before he could see her waiting. At his knock, she counted to ten, then smoothed her hands over her skirt and crossed the room to open the door.

"Good morning, Miss Sanderson. And a lovely morning it is." Matt bowed slightly, his brown eyes sparkling.

"Yes, Mr. Rolland, I quite agree. Won't you step inside a moment while I get my things?" Matt nodded and walked past her into the hall. Ruth disappeared into the kitchen at the back of the house, returning quickly with the basket of food and her sunbonnet.

"I'd be honored to carry that for you, ma'am," Matt said, taking the basket, then opening the door politely. "After you."

Today Matt wore loose-fitting gray trousers and a light brown shirt. Scuffed boots had replaced the shined shoes of the previous day, and a straw hat rested on his head. Though it was disguised well by Matt's neatly trimmed beard, Ruth noticed a thin scar running along his jaw. The small imperfection gave him a rakish air that intrigued her.

Their ride to the Varners' was filled with the pleasant banter Ruth had so enjoyed the previous evening. She found herself relaxing in Matt's company, smiling and laughing like a young girl instead of the twenty-six-year-old spinster schoolteacher she considered herself to be.

All too soon they reached the Varners', and Matt jumped nimbly from the buggy to assist her to the ground. Glancing around at those already assembled, Ruth breathed a sigh of relief that Katherine had not yet arrived. She wanted to be there for moral support during the undoubtedly stressful first moments. A searching look at the wagons and horses entering the yard revealed no sign of her friend. She hoped Katherine hadn't changed her mind about attending.

"Where should I put your basket?" Matt's voice close to her ear brought Ruth's attention back to her escort.

"Let's take it to Mrs. Varner. Then I'll introduce you to some of the men." Ruth smiled at Matt with happiness.

A few moments later, Matt was deep in conversation with Stig Varner and several other farmers. Ruth returned to the house where the women were preparing to piece together several quilts while the men built the barn. They would all take a rest at noon for a picnic and then continue working until the barn was completed. Then the music and dancing would commence.

As Ruth helped Mrs. Varner organize the dozens of baskets of food in the kitchen, a startled gasp from one of the women drew her attention.

"I don't believe she's here. The nerve. And she's brought that Reb outlaw with her."

## Second Chance

"No!"

"She wouldn't!"

As the women gathered around the window to peer in fascination at an arriving wagon, Ruth hurried through the door and into the bright sunshine.

Katherine had arisen with the first streaks of light, anxious to leave her bed after a nearly sleepless night. Donning her second-best dress, a green gingham that tied at the waist and flared into a full, fashionable skirt, she noted the white lace at the collar contributed to the air of respectability she hoped to project.

Having no desire to run into Mary and explain her decision to attend the day's festivities at the Varners', Katherine hurried through the kitchen, appreciating the uncommon silence in the house.

The quiet continued when she crossed the distance between the house and the barn. Since this was the last weekend of the month, the men had received their pay and two days off. They often slept late on Saturday, resting up for the revelry to follow. She would not likely see the men at the Varners'. With the lure of alcohol and women in town, they would more than likely spend the day at the tavern or brothel.

As Katherine neared the barn, Jake emerged leading a team of horses hitched to the wagon. His clean-shaven face and damp hair gave testament to the fact he had also been awake early.

"Morning, ma'am." Jake raised his hand in greeting. "I thought you'd want to take the wagon today rather than ride. I see I was right." He eyed her dress in appreciation, obviously preferring it to the pants she had worn almost every day since he'd been at the Circle A.

"My presence alone will undoubtedly irritate folks enough without antagonizing them with my odd preference in clothes." Katherine took Jake's proffered hand and allowed him to help her into the wagon. She picked up the reins and waited for Jake to join her on the wagon seat. After he settled next to her, he surprised her by reaching over and taking the reins from her fingers.

"I've seen how you drive." Jake's amused glance caused Katherine to smile in return, and she attempted to relax as they drove away from the ranch.

The Varner farm was located off the same road as the Circle A, but a mile farther from town. Several other wagons and riders were headed in the same direction. Jake and Katherine drew many curious stares, but no one greeted them.

As they pulled into the Varners' yard, Katherine wondered if anyone would talk to them that day. A silent circle of men stood near piles of lumber awaiting the start of the day's activities. Katherine could tell by their hostile stares that no welcome would be forthcoming from that quarter. Glancing toward the house, Katherine saw several women gathered at the

## Second Chance

window pointing in her direction and talking among themselves. Before she could decide whether to flee or fight, Ruth Sanderson emerged from the house and waved in greeting.

"Katherine, it's so good to see you," Ruth said loudly, acting as though the sight of Katherine completely surprised her. "And who have you brought with you to help out?"

Katherine hesitated for a moment, her eyes passing warily over the group of men observing their conversation. The hostile glares directed Jake's way made her happy she'd stowed a Derringer in the pocket of her dress. Katherine straightened her back and returned the men's stares with equal fervor before answering Ruth.

"This is Jake Banner. He'll be helping at the Circle A for a while. Jake, my dearest friend, Ruth Sanderson." Katherine watched as the two of them smiled and nodded. Suddenly her attention was drawn to a man as he disengaged himself from the watching group and strode rapidly toward them.

The man's manner was unthreatening, and, nearing them, he smiled. Katherine relaxed, but her hand remained at the ready in her lap in case of a sudden move on anyone's part.

She glanced quickly at Jake to see his reaction to the stranger and was surprised to find a wry smile on his lips, almost as if he recognized the man. But, as she looked closer, the smile disappeared and she would be hard put to say whether it had actually been there.

Katherine was amused when Ruth put her hand on the man's arm and smiled warmly into his face. Her friend was obviously acquainted with the stranger, and pleased with the acquaintance.

"Katherine, Jake—this is Matthew Rolland, my escort for the day. Mr. Rolland is a new clerk at the Second Chance Bank. I thought it would be a good idea for him to meet some people from the area."

Katherine frowned at the mention of the bank that held the mortgage on the Circle A. But this man was a clerk and not Harrison Foley, so she nodded and smiled at Matthew.

"Call me Matt," he said, offering his hand to Jake as he descended from the wagon.

The two men shook hands. Ruth beamed her approval, then turned to give Katherine a look which clearly said, I told you this was a good idea.

After nodding to Jake, Matt moved past him to assist Katherine from the wagon.

"Mrs. Logan, it's a pleasure. I've heard so much about you."

Katherine looked curiously at Matt, suspicious of his words. Searching his face, she saw nothing but kindness and admiration. She relaxed and smiled. It felt good to be near someone pleasant again.

One of the Varner boys unharnessed the team, leaving the wagon with others in the open yard. The horses were put to graze beyond the house.

## Second Chance

"Matt, since you know a few of the men now, why don't you take Jake and introduce him around?" Ruth suggested as the two couples walked toward the house.

"I don't think that would be a good idea," Katherine said, eying the group of men who were now talking among themselves, casting black looks over their shoulders at short intervals.

"Do you want Jake to come in the house and sew with us? He'll be fine, Katherine." Ruth tugged at her friend's arm.

"I'd prefer to stay out here. It's too lovely a day to sit inside."

"It's going to be hot as Hades soon enough. Come on, no one's going to shoot or hang him today. I'm sure Matt can calm the worst of the lot."

Matt looked as though he'd like to deny her faith in him but nodded instead. The two men turned and walked toward the others, Jake looking over his shoulder and raising his eyebrows at Katherine.

Katherine stood staring after them, twisting her dress in her hands. When the two men reached the group, she heard Matt introduce Jake to Varner and a few others. She noticed they were all civil, if not friendly, before they turned away to begin the work. Jake and Matt joined them without further discussion.

"I always get at least one mother like you a year," Ruth said. "They never want to let their babies out of their sight. I nearly have to push them out the schoolhouse door to get the day started." Ruth firmly clasped Katherine's hand and pulled her into the house.

Sudden silence greeted their entrance. Every pair of eyes in the room were trained on Katherine, and she was glad she had taken some pains with her appearance that morning. These women couldn't fault her on that count at least.

Ruth cleared her throat. "Ladies, Mrs. Logan has decided to join us today. I'm sure an extra pair of hands will be welcome."

No one answered Ruth's cheerful observation. Instead, all the women busied themselves about the room, ignoring the twosome in the doorway. With a shrug, Ruth led Katherine over to Mrs. Varner.

"Vesta, you know my friend Katherine, don't you?"

Vesta Varner glanced around the room uncertainly, then squared her shoulders and nodded. "I am glad to welcome you to my house. We have much work today."

Katherine's lips curved at the woman's bluntness. The Varners were from Norway and had recently moved to the area. Since Mrs. Varner's English was limited, Katherine merely smiled her thanks.

The wail of a baby rose above the sounds in the room, and Mrs. Varner hurried toward a basket in the corner of the kitchen. Katherine followed, peering over the woman's shoulder at the infant. Her heart contracted at the sight

## Second Chance

of the small fists beating the air and the angry little face.

"May I hold your baby?" Katherine asked softly.

Mrs. Varner started when she heard Katherine's voice so close behind her. Turning, she smiled and handed the child into Katherine's waiting arms.

"The first girl. Stig is not so pleased. But me—I am happy. She will be a help to me in the house once she is grown."

Katherine's gaze was focused on the baby's crumpled face. She was fascinated that such a tiny mouth could emit so much sound. The child smelled of sun and fresh air—of life. Katherine began to hum and sway, cuddling the screaming girl close. Immediately the baby quieted and turned wide blue eyes to Katherine's face. The mouth previously used for ear-splitting cries now turned up in a joyous, toothless baby smile, and a cooing gurgle poured forth.

Mrs. Varner smiled. "You have a way with the little ones. You will do well with your own."

The woman's words struck Katherine's deepest pain, and she flinched. She took a deep, calming breath. Vesta did not know what she had said. The woman only wanted to be friendly.

Katherine continued to stare raptly at the tiny being in her arms, her throat thick with the need for a joy she could never have. Sam had desired a son to carry on his name and inherit the legacy of the Circle A, but Katherine had wanted a baby to nurture and love, to teach and touch and watch grow to adulthood. She put the baby up to her shoulder and nuzzled the short, downy hair covering the tiny head. Her barrenness would always be her most painful regret. She would never know the joy of holding her own child this way. Throughout her life she would ache inside at the sight of other people's children.

Katherine blinked hard against the unaccustomed wetness in her eyes. She cleared her throat gruffly. What was, was. She was not a woman to dwell on things that could not be changed. Carefully she handed the baby back to her mother. "She's beautiful. You and your husband are blessed."

As Mrs. Varner smiled and cooed at the baby, the whispers reached Katherine's ears. She glanced around the room and saw that all the women had been watching her with the child and now discussed her behavior avidly. Heat suffused Katherine's face at being observed at such an emotional moment, but her preoccupation with the baby had made her forget the others in the room. Never had she felt more detached from the women of Second Chance than at that moment. To them she would never be a complete woman without a child. Her childless state would always make her an oddity in a way more personal and more painful than the difference of her heritage. The sadness within her translated to a scowl at the whispering, twittering women, and they hastily returned to ignoring her.

## Second Chance

When she was able to talk again without betraying her pain, Katherine joined Ruth in the kitchen. "This doesn't seem to be progressing very well."

"Give it time." Ruth patted her hand gently. "You can't expect everyone to come to you right away. We've got to show them what kind of person you are. They've all been fed on gossip and the men's prejudices." Ruth walked away, and Katherine had no choice but to follow or be left alone.

Ruth approached a group of women, their heads bowed together in conversation while they sewed, and drew a chair directly into their midst. Then she cheerily motioned for Katherine to do the same.

"How are you today, Mrs. Jenkins?" Ruth addressed the robust woman to her right. "Your son Tommy is a delight to have in school. Such a bright child."

The woman preened under Ruth's flattery, and Katherine stifled a smile. She knew Tommy Jenkins, and the child was a terror.

"Thank you, Miss Sanderson. I do my best with him. He is a might high-strung. But, as I've told his father, that's only because he's so much smarter than all the other children."

"Yes, that's often the case with prodigies." Ruth turned to Katherine. "My friend Katherine was a teacher also. Have you met Mrs. Logan?"

Mrs. Jenkins turned her gaze toward Katherine, and her smile froze. The matron's glance swept over her from head to toe, laying

Katherine bare. "No," the woman said shortly and removed herself from the group, taking a seat elsewhere in the room.

The same scene was played out several times throughout the morning with few variations. Ruth would engage a woman in a conversation, but at the attempt to introduce Katherine all pleasantries would cease and the two friends would find themselves alone.

"I told you it would be no use." Katherine sighed as she and Ruth stood by the window. Peering through, Katherine observed Jake and Matt hard at work and, apparently, being ignored by the men as thoroughly as she was being ignored by the women.

"We'll keep trying tonight. Maybe some of the younger men will be more willing to forgive at the dance." Ruth's eyes sparkled.

"I don't know. I think we'd better leave soon."

"Katherine Logan, you'll do no such thing! If you leave, they've won. We'll stay until the last dance!"

"You're not the one who's getting shunned, Ruth. Although you may get a taste of it after inviting me today."

"Not if we start to break the ice tonight. Just be patient."

"Not one of my virtues, but I can try."

"We should help Vesta carry the food outside. It looks as though the men are ready for dinner." Ruth touched Katherine's arm gently in support, then crossed the room to help their hostess.

## Second Chance

\* \* \*

Jake had worked hard all morning in an attempt to prove his worth to the others. For himself it didn't matter, but he wanted to help Katherine in any way he could. At the very least he didn't want her to suffer any further for helping him.

Jake and Matt worked side by side. No one spoke beyond the necessities associated with the job, which suited Jake fine. The work progressed well, and they were close to halfway through with the structure by noon when the women started to bring the food outside. The men put down their tools and conversation commenced.

"I can see why Katherine Logan brought along her boy. He's a good workhorse."

"Yeah, I'm almost sorry I didn't save the bastard myself. I could use a slave."

"So could I. She must miss her slaves now that the war's over and all the darkies are free."

Jake's jaw clenched at the insults and he spun to face the speakers, fists clenched. Matt grabbed his arm and jerked him roughly away from the other men.

"Let it go," Matt said.

"I don't take orders from you. They deserve a few licks." Jake glared over Matt's shoulder at the grinning group of tormentors.

"That's just what they're waiting for, you idiot. Take it easy, your time will come." Matt looked closely at Jake's angry face. "You've never been this quick to lose your temper. Might it be

Mrs. Logan's honor you're worried about this time?"

"What do you think? I couldn't care less what this bunch of halfwits thinks about me. I won't be here forever." Jake spotted Katherine emerging from the house carrying a heavy tray. He hurried forward to take it from her, ignoring Matt's snort of laughter from behind him.

"How was your morning, ma'am?"

Katherine's lips projected a shadow of her usual smile. "As I'd expected. No better or worse. And yours? There wasn't any trouble, was there?"

"No. Everyone pretty much did their work and left me to do the same. No need for you to worry over me." Jake placed the tray next to others on a blanket spread over the ground.

"I'm responsible since I insisted on this mess. I'm glad Matt Rolland is a fair man. You seem to have taken to each other," Katherine observed as they walked away from the crowd gathering to eat.

"Since he's new here I expect he hasn't had the chance to assume the town's hatreds," Jake said.

Before Katherine could reply to Jake's words, Matt spoke from behind them. "Shall the four of us picnic away from this crush?"

Turning, Jake noticed that Ruth's hand was nestled in the crook of Matt's elbow, and she was flushed from laughing.

"That's a lovely idea. Why don't Ruth and I spread a blanket over there." Katherine pointed

## Second Chance

at a grove of trees behind the house. "Would you two men get us all plates?"

Jake and Matt went to do her bidding. As they carried the plates of food toward the semi-secluded trees, Matt spoke so softly Jake had to lean closer to hear him. "I was going to come out to talk to you tonight. Later, when the barn's done and everyone's getting ready for the dance, meet me where they've tethered the horses."

Jake nodded, wondering what news Matt needed to impart so soon after their last meeting.

The two couples enjoyed a companionable meal. Jake was amused by the obvious courting techniques Matt practiced on the lovely Miss Sanderson. If he didn't watch himself, Matt would end up at the business end of her daddy's shotgun. He noticed Katherine watching the other couple with a wistful smile. When she saw him staring at her, she flushed and focused her attention on the clear blue sky. Jake wondered if she had ever been courted.

All too soon it was time to resume the day's chores. The men left the women to pick up the remains and quickly returned to the skeletal structure of the barn.

The other men were already hard at work. A few glanced their way, but no one mentioned the secluded picnic. Jake and Matt returned to their tasks undisturbed.

Darkness had just fallen when the barn was completed. The men stood back and surveyed their accomplishment, then separated to wash and dress in fresh clothes for the dance. Jake busied himself with the tools until everyone was occupied elsewhere, then slipped away to a nearby area reserved for the horses. The moon had not yet risen and the night was black. He did not have long to wait before Matt silently joined him.

"Quite a day." Matt rubbed the back of his neck and stretched. "I'm not used to working like this. If we don't finish this job soon I'll get soft sitting at a desk all day."

"You're already soft, Matt. Now, what did you find out?"

"Nothing."

"Nothing? What's so important about nothing that you had to tell me here?" Jake stared at his partner in exasperation.

"Just that. When Pinkerton sent the two of us down here, I figured he wanted this through in a hurry and we'd be in and out in no time. Hell, with me at the bank and you with the gang, we should have caught the weasel in the hen house easy." Matt kicked at the dirt in frustration, then looked up at Jake. "But I can't find anything suspicious at the bank. I'm beginning to wonder if our boss has finally slipped up."

Jake frowned. "Pinkerton believed the leak was in the bank. He could be mistaken, but I think we should check out every angle before we tell him that. His information is rarely wrong."

"He also said to trust no one in this town." Matt shrugged. "Maybe I'll start making some

## Second Chance

night visits to a few employees' homes. Couldn't hurt."

"The Coltrains' contact has to make a mistake sometime, Matt. When he does, we'll be here to catch him."

Matt hesitated, then replied. "Not if you aren't in the middle of the action." He hurried on despite Jake's warning frown. "You need to get back with the Coltrains, Jake. You've got to see that. The railroad office will send out another payroll soon since their men haven't been paid for two months. I'd think the contact should give Charlie the information any time now. If you're at the Circle A and we miss this chance, someone could get hurt. I know that's not what you want."

Jake sighed and turned to look at the rising full moon. Matt was right. He wasn't doing his job. But his duty to Pinkerton pulled in one direction, and Katherine's need of him tugged in the other. He could still see her calm, gray eyes looking at him in gratitude when he'd volunteered to stay. The warmth he'd felt then was something long absent from his life. Nevertheless, he was in Second Chance for a reason.

"I'll see what I can find out about this Swade character over the next few days and then I'll go." Jake did not turn around but continued to stare into the sky.

"What is it with Swade?" Matt asked. "If we plan to follow Pinkerton's directive, the leak is at the bank. How would Swade know anything?"

Jake's shoulders slumped. "I don't know," he said quietly.

"Remember what happened to Carleton?" Matt returned, mentioning the name of the agent who'd been betrayed through his dalliance. "Women and spies don't mix."

Jake was curiously irritated that his friend should bring up the exact situation he'd been berating himself with earlier in the week. Choosing to ignore the reference, Jake turned and walked back toward the barn, leaving Matt to return to the festivities by a different route.

The recently erected structure was alight with lanterns, and as Jake came closer he heard the sound of a fiddle, and the air sang with the strains of a lively tune. To please Katherine he'd brought along a change of clothes. But after the restrained hostility of the day, Jake had no desire to spend the evening hours with the people of Second Chance. He would sit outside and listen to the music until Katherine was ready to leave.

"Well, well. If it isn't Mrs. Logan's pet outlaw." The clipped nasal voice caused Jake to clench his teeth in irritation. Slowly he turned to face the speaker, recognizing Harrison Foley's exaggerated Boston twang even before he saw the banker lounging against a tree several feet away.

"Is there something I can do for you, Mr. Foley?" Jake kept his voice deceptively calm, though he could tell that the man was spoiling for an argument.

## Second Chance

"Since you seem to be the proverbial cat with nine lives, dying is out of the question, I suppose."

Jake sighed. He was in no mood for another argument. "You made it quite clear when you visited me in jail that you wanted me dead. Sorry I couldn't oblige you."

Foley straightened and moved with fluid grace through the silver-tinged darkness. He stopped several feet away from Jake. "I don't approve of the man who robbed my bank living in the midst of decent folks. The people of Second Chance won't stand for it much longer."

"From what I've seen, the people of Second Chance wouldn't know decent if it bit them on the . . ." He stopped and took a deep breath. He had promised himself he wouldn't make things more difficult for Katherine. "I'm helping Mrs. Logan," he continued in a calmer tone. "The townsfolk have nothing to fear from me."

Foley snorted rudely. "Helping? So that's what they're calling it these days."

Jake took a step toward the banker and was pleased when the other man moved quickly back. Harrison Foley might talk big but the man was a physical coward.

"Y-you're a fine one to talk about decent," Foley stuttered. "Stealing from innocent people and then taking advantage of Katherine Logan's southern sympathies."

"Mrs. Logan is as much of a southern sympathizer as General Sherman. This town is so full of people still fighting the war, no one can see past a person's birthplace."

"What would you know about the people here? You're a Reb just like her. You'd think the woman would have enough sense to let a man handle her business." Foley shrugged. "I often thought Sam Logan was a bit hard on her, but now I see what he meant when he said she was unnatural. Walking around, in pants mind you, pretending to run the Circle A herself. She's a disgrace, and your helping her will only make things worse."

"If by making things worse you mean getting the Circle A running at a profit again, she doesn't need me for that. From what I've seen, Katherine is doing a damn good job with the ranch on her own."

"Not for long." Foley smiled smugly.

Jake crossed the distance between them with two long strides and grabbed Foley by his pristine collar. "What do you mean by that?" When Foley pursed his thin lips and refused to answer, Jake shook him like a puppy with a scrap of cloth. "Talk before I make you wish you had."

Foley swallowed and opened his mouth to speak, then a voice came out of the darkness.

"What the hell is going on here?"

# Chapter Ten

Katherine had been on her way to join Ruth inside the barn when the sound of angry voices nearby made her stop and listen. Recognizing Jake's deep tones, she hurried in the direction of the sound, pulling the Derringer from her pocket as she ran.

The scene was outlined graphically in the bright moonlight. The men's shirts glimmered with silver rays, their faces cast in shadow. Since Jake obviously had control of the situation, Katherine hid the gun before announcing her presence.

"Which one of you would like to answer me?" Katherine's voice was hushed to avoid drawing attention to the confrontation.

As she watched, Jake slowly released Harrison and the banker retreated quickly beyond reach. She looked back and forth between the two men, neither of whom would look her in the eye.

After a moment Jake spoke. "Just man talk, ma'am."

"About what?"

"Nothing that concerns you."

Jake continued to look at the ground instead of at her, and Katherine doubted the truth of his words. He was obviously not going to say any more in Harrison's dour presence. Katherine turned to Foley. "Shouldn't you be joining the others inside?" she asked.

Harrison looked up at Katherine and nodded silently. Without a word he walked away.

"We aren't through yet, Foley," Jake called softly.

The sound of Jake's voice made Katherine shiver and she looked at him sharply, sensing the threat behind his words.

Harrison continued on as though he hadn't heard, but his words floated back on the night breeze. "You can count on it, Reb."

They watched in silence until he entered the barn and disappeared from sight in the crowd.

"What happened here?" she asked.

"Foley doesn't much care for me."

"Can you blame him after you robbed his bank?" Katherine asked incredulously.

"Suppose not."

"Would you care to tell me why you had him by the collar? Certainly not because he doesn't like you."

## Second Chance

"No. He hinted that you wouldn't be in charge of the Circle A for very long." Jake shrugged one broad shoulder. "I didn't care for the way he said it."

Katherine's heart sank painfully at the reminder of the heavy mortgage threatening her ranch. Would she never have a place of her own free of the worry that it might be taken away at any second?

"Mr. Foley holds the mortgage on the Circle A."

"So?" Jake asked "As long as you make the payments, you have nothing to worry about."

"I'm afraid money isn't so easy to come by for those of us who don't steal for a living."

At the hurt look on Jake's face, Katherine cursed her too-quick tongue. She remained silent for several minutes, her mind searching for a way to smooth over her words. Finally, in an attempt to make amends and change the subject she said, "You'd better clean up and change or you'll miss the dance."

"I think I will." Jake looked down at his sweat- and dirt-stained work clothes. "But I'll just wait out here for you, ma'am. You have a good time."

"You aren't going to come in?" Katherine heard the disappointment in her voice and inwardly winced at her transparency.

"Everyone would have a better time if I stayed out here."

"Why? Did you have a problem with anyone else today besides Harrison?"

"No. But I can tell when folks are uncomfortable." Jake smiled at her wryly. "I think they might take more kindly to you if I'm not there to remind them of the Coltrains."

Katherine tilted her head, studying him. He was probably right. Not that she expected anyone but Ruth to talk to her tonight. And dancing was out of the question. No man in the territory would come within three feet of her for the rest of her life. Poor Ruth, she'd had such high hopes of making the day go well.

Taking a deep breath and straightening her shoulders, Katherine turned toward the sounds of music and gaiety. "I doubt I'll be long."

As she hesitated a moment in the doorway, Katherine noticed the change in atmosphere inside. Not only was the air stifling without the benefit of the night breeze, but the silence that followed her as she crossed the floor to Ruth caused her breath to come in short gasps. Pasting a smile on her face, Katherine pushed onward.

It seemed to take an eternity to reach Ruth. When she did, her friend's smile was a welcome sight. Matt Rolland was also there, and his cheerful greeting took the edge off Katherine's tension.

"I was afraid you'd gone home," Ruth admitted.

"The thought crossed my mind. But I'm sure you're right, and I should at least make an appearance so it doesn't look like the day has upset me."

## Second Chance

Ruth looked at her searchingly. "But you are upset, aren't you?"

Katherine smiled reassuringly. "I know you meant well, Ruth. But I don't think anyone in Second Chance is going to accept me for a long time—if ever. There's too much hatred within them to heal overnight."

"She's right," Matt spoke up. "Maybe if the Coltrains would quit stirring people up there'd be a chance. Five years isn't long enough to forget a civil war." He looked over the crowd. "I wonder if fifty will be enough."

Ruth and Katherine quieted as the truth of Matt's words washed over them. Finally Ruth sighed. "Let's not think about that tonight. I invited Katherine here to have a good time."

Matt bowed his head slightly and offered Katherine his hand. "Mrs. Logan, would you do me the honor?"

Katherine looked quickly at Ruth, who nodded, smiling. Katherine shrugged, then accepted Matt's proffered hand and allowed him to lead her into the crowd of dancers. Dancing was a talent her aunt had insisted she learn, although there'd been precious little chance to use the skill. Matt had obviously mastered the art as well, and Katherine began to enjoy herself for the first time that day.

When the song ended, Matt bowed again and Katherine curtsied with a laugh. But, as they made their way back to Ruth, Katherine's smile faded. All around her townsfolk glowered, obviously unhappy at her enjoyment of what was considered their party. By the time she and Matt reached Ruth, Katherine's back prickled from the stares directed her way.

An hour later Katherine was hot, exhausted, and thoroughly sick of being examined as though she were a new insect arrived to blight the crops. She listened as the makeshift band of a fiddle and guitar began to play Mr. Foster's "Beautiful Dreamer." The song was a far cry from the jigs and reels played throughout the evening. When Matt and Ruth left to dance, Katherine slipped through the crowd and out the door, hurrying around the corner of the barn in her search for isolation.

Fresh air and silence were a balm to her overworked senses. Lifting her face to the night sky, she breathed deeply. She admired the clear blue-black expanse sprinkled with white pinpoints of light. Soon she would have to find Jake and leave for home in case Ruth decided to search for her. But, for the moment, Katherine leaned back against the barn, closing her eyes and allowing her tense shoulders to relax. The summer evening was too beautiful to waste on worries. Besides, she wouldn't have changed any of her actions in saving Jake regardless of the consequences.

She didn't know how much time passed as she leaned back, eyes closed peacefully. Feeling a presence, Katherine slowly opened her eyes and, as the moon went behind a stray cloud, she peered into the oppressive darkness. An unidentifiable shape moved in the shadows,

## Second Chance

and Katherine gasped, straightening from her relaxed position.

"Who's there?"

The hazy form materialized into Jake Banner.

"I didn't mean to frighten you, ma'am. I saw you come out of the dance. Are you ready to leave for the Circle A?"

Music drifted to them on the breeze, and Katherine glanced in the direction of the sound longingly. Her dancing days were over now that she was a widow with responsibilities—responsibilities that would be waiting for her at dawn the next morning.

Katherine nodded. "I suppose we should both get some sleep. If you aren't exhausted, I certainly am." Her eyes strayed again in the direction of the music and she murmured, "There's nothing for me here."

"I take it the townsfolk didn't make you feel any more welcome at the dance than they did all day."

"I've never been welcome in the social circle of Second Chance. Today was no more than what I expected." Katherine glanced down at her hands and discovered she had twisted them together so forcefully, her knuckles were white. Without looking up, she purposefully unclasped her fingers and placed them against her legs.

"I'm sorry." The quiet words drifted to her on the warm wind.

*Lord, I love his voice,* she thought, and raised her eyes to his.

Jake stood close enough to touch, his form a shadow in the darkness. She stared into his face, and the errant cloud released the moon to bathe them in shimmering light. Katherine found she wanted to touch him—she wanted to very much.

In answer to her unspoken desire, Jake took her hand. The contact tingled up her arm and settled at the base of her neck. She had no desire to break his hold.

As he moved closer, she raised her head for his kiss. Instead, his arm snaked around her waist. Jake drew her body against his own, and his hardness pressed to her slight form. Tilting her head back to see his face, she recognized the desire in his eyes and her lips parted. Jake lowered his mouth to hers and moved them in time to the strains of a waltz drifting on the wings of a Missouri night.

Dillon stood in the shadows, his fists clenched and pressing against his aching head. He watched Katherine and Jake dance, his fury growing when they kissed.

From that first day when Sam had brought her home, Dillon had coveted his best friend's wife. He harbored no guilt over his feelings, they simply existed, and he could not change them even if he had wanted to try.

Petite and fair, with a fragile look that made her everything he believed a woman should be, Dillon dreamed of Katherine night and day. Even later, when he discovered her strength,

## Second Chance

both the physical and the inner, and realized she was not the woman he had believed her to be, he could not get her out of his mind. Her independent attitude irritated Sam beyond reason, and Dillon could understand that. A man wanted his woman to need him. He wanted to feel that without him in her life she would be nothing. With Katherine and Sam, that just wasn't the case. Dillon had believed he could show her the error of her ways if only given the chance.

When Sam had died, Dillon expected Katherine to come to him for help. When he had taken over her husband's duties on the ranch, Katherine had usurped him, taking on Sam's work herself and allowing Dillon to continue in his position as manager as though he should be thankful for the job. She never said anything outright, but he thought she was biding her time, waiting until the Circle A was out from under the burden of the mortgage; then she would get rid of him. That knowledge made him anxious, and he often took his irritation out on the cause of all his problems—Katherine Logan. Though he still loved her in his secret fantasies, his love had become bound up with a festering hatred. He wanted her to love him. He needed her to love him. If she would just love him, he could make everything all right forever. But now, with the evidence of her perfidy directly in front of him, his hatred swelled and pulsed hotter than ever before, putting all thoughts of love from his mind.

He'd show her. When she had nowhere else to turn, Dillon Swade would be there to save her. By then Jake Banner would be long gone. And if he wasn't, well, Dillon would make sure he soon would be.

Dillon turned away from the scene in disgust and hurried through the night to a rendezvous point away from prying eyes. Were it not for an urgent message, he never would have come to the Varners' at all. What did the man want now? Dillon had made some extra money doing small jobs in the past, but this sounded like something bigger. Well, it was lucky he'd decided to answer the summons or he wouldn't have found out what a lying snake Jake Banner really was.

Nearing a grove of trees that lined a shallow creek, Dillon saw a figure outlined in the moonlight. The scent of smoke from a cigarillo drifted to him before the small, glowing tip illuminated a face.

"I thought you had decided not to answer my summons. I'm happy you're not so unwise."

A twinge of unease came to Dillon at the threat, but he relaxed when he remembered that this man depended upon him to take care of certain unpleasant tasks.

"What's so important I had to come out here and interrupt my card game?"

The man took a last pull on his cigarillo, then ground it into the dirt with the heel of his well polished shoe. "Things are not progressing as quickly as I'd hoped. Your employer needs to

## Second Chance

be taught a lesson. I know just the thing."

The man smiled and Dillon frowned. He knew from past experience that this smile boded ill for someone. His companion was happiest when others were miserable. Dillon waited patiently for him to continue.

"A fire in the barn would work well, I think."

Dillon blinked. "What barn?"

"The barn at the Circle A." The man spoke slowly as though to a young child.

"There's horses in there, and that Banner character sleeps in the storeroom."

"Excellent." The word came out in a long hiss of satisfaction. "We need to get rid of him. I'm sure he'll be trouble. If he won't leave on his own, killing him will do."

After a moment, Dillon smiled. This was the answer to his problems. He could get rid of Banner and have Katherine begging for his help to set the Circle A straight. The ranch was meant to belong to him—him and Katherine together.

Dillon accepted a wad of bills. Without looking at the amount, he stuffed them into his pocket. Before his eyes swam the image of Jake kissing Katherine. "I'll do it tonight."

"Excellent . . ."

For the few moments of their dance Jake allowed himself to forget the secrets binding his life. He was unable to resist kissing Katherine as they waltzed, and, instead of pulling away, she leaned forward to kiss him back. Her breath was sweet, her mouth soft and pliant beneath his own. Surprising himself, Jake kissed Katherine gently despite the near explosion occurring inside him whenever she was near. He wanted nothing more than to push her down onto the night-cooled grass and bury himself inside her. Instead he indulged his need to touch her—letting his fingers tangle in the soft, moonlit strands of hair and grazing the alabaster smoothness of her warm cheeks with aching fingertips. When Katherine's lips parted, it took all of his hard-won self-control to keep from taking what she offered. As the last notes of the waltz died on the breeze, Jake sighed in disappointment.

"We'd best get home before the others come out," Jake said reluctantly.

His breath brushed the loose hair at her temple, and Katherine started, then stepped back quickly and nodded. "You're right. I don't care to see anyone else tonight, especially Ruth. If we hurry, we'll be home before they're done gossiping."

Jake found one of the Varner boys and had the youth retrieve the horses. When he placed his palms on Katherine's waist to assist her into the wagon, heat flashed through him at her nearness. Quickly releasing her, he soon had the horses pointed in the direction of the Circle A. The solitude of the night pressed on Jake, and an uneasy sensation settled in the middle of his back.

"I don't like being out on these roads at night without a weapon, ma'am."

## Second Chance

Katherine laughed, and Jake glanced at her questioningly.

"When have you ever known me to be without a weapon?" She pulled the derringer out of her pocket.

Jake stared at the bit of iron in her palm and struggled to withhold his amusement. Unable to do so, he threw back his head and his laughter echoed into the night. "That's not a weapon. It's a conversation piece."

Katherine frowned. "It's better than nothing. You can't expect me to bring my rifle to a party, can you?"

"I suppose not. But I'd be a happier man if you had."

Katherine leaned down and reached under the wooden seat, dragging her rifle from its hiding place beneath.

Jake nodded. "That's my girl."

Katherine's face lit with pleasure at his words, and guilt stabbed him at the memory of all the lies he'd told her. She needed a man who could give her the security and love she deserved, as well as the truth. He turned away from her and concentrated on the road. When he glanced at her a short while later, Jake saw he'd hurt her with his reticence. Her face reflected the cold, faraway demeanor she used to keep others at a distance. He hated himself.

All was quiet when they arrived at the Circle A. Jake lifted Katherine from the wagon, but as soon as her feet touched the ground she pulled away from him and turned toward the house.

He should let her go, confused and angry though she was. It would be better to put some space between them for both their sakes. But he found he couldn't let her go to bed alone and hurting.

"Is there anything you need, ma'am?"

Without turning, Katherine answered him coldly. "Nothing further from you, Mr. Banner. I appreciate your escort to the Varners', but I don't think today is an experience we need ever repeat."

She left him then, walking into the house and closing the door quietly without once looking back. A few moments later her shadow played across the window of her bedroom when she lit the lamp. The curtains obscured his view but did not curtail his imagination.

As he stared at the backlit pane of glass, his thoughts drifted and he imagined Katherine releasing the small white buttons of her bodice one by one. He remembered the creamy flesh of her shoulders, wet from her bath, and saw them again as she shrugged the dress from her body. Jake heard the fabric slide in a rush over her hips to the floor, and Katherine stood in her chemise, slim and pale in the glow of the lamp's orange flames. Long, nimble fingers removed the pins from her hair, and the heavy mass melted into waves down her back.

One of the horses stamped impatiently, and Jake's attention returned abruptly to reality. He reached out and scratched the animal between the eyes, then glanced back at the window. The lantern had been extinguished and darkness reigned. Shaking his head at such foolishness, Jake unharnessed the team.

Dillon returned to the Circle A immediately after his meeting. A rush of excitement came over him at the thought of what he would soon accomplish. He had been unhappy for a long time, but the answer to his problems was so simple. After tonight, Katherine would see how much she needed him, how they'd been meant to be together from the beginning.

Dillon cocked his head at an approaching sound. They had returned. Silently he waited, lurking in the shadows of the bunkhouse. He licked his lips in anticipation when Katherine went into the house. Banner stood outside, staring upward. When Dillon followed the direction of the other man's stare, his fury returned. The scum was watching her window. Rage pulsed through him at the Reb's audacity.

A few moments later Banner unharnessed the horses and led them into the barn. Dillon shifted impatiently. The time was near. Since the other hands would be in town enjoying their whores until dawn, he had no fear of being seen.

The hour he waited seemed much longer, but Dillon knew well the rewards of patience. He moved silently toward his goal, no longer bothering to hide in the shadows. Slipping through the open double doors, he quickly strode to the back of the barn where the hay waited for winter. Calmly, he set fire to the loose fodder. He watched until it blazed potently, then he retreated. As he exited, he closed the doors firmly behind him, pausing to pick up a heavy wooden plank from its resting place against the wall. Dillon slid the bar through the handles of the doors, effectively locking them from the outside, then slipped away into the night.

When he reached the place where he'd left his horse, Dillon turned around to survey the damage. Only a slight orange tinge around the rear window of the barn indicated anything was amiss. He smiled with pleasure. Swinging into the saddle, Dillon walked his horse toward the main road without looking back. He would spend the rest of the night in town with no one the wiser. Upon his return tomorrow, he expected the Circle A and Katherine to be in desperate need of his authority.

After nearly an hour of tossing and turning, Jake fell into a fitful doze. Since the war, his sleep was often troubled by dreams. But over the past week those dreams were of a different nature, though none the less disturbing in their content. He awoke sweating, hazy images of Katherine hovering at the edge of his mind.

"Damn, I'll never get any sleep unless I bed the woman or get out of here," Jake muttered, running his hand through sweat-dampened hair.

Pulling himself into a sitting position, he realized his bared chest was slick to the touch. A dunk in the horse trough would be just the

## Second Chance

thing to take care of both his problems at the moment.

As Jake pulled on his boots, he suddenly lifted his head and sniffed the air. Smoke. His body stiffened, every sense attuned to the threat. But where was the acrid smell coming from? He slowly turned his head toward the back of the barn and heard the unmistakable crackle of fire. Jumping to his feet, Jake burst through the door of the storeroom. As he neared the sound, his eyes and throat began to burn from the thick smoke. Peering through the gray-black cloud, his eyes widened. The rear of the barn was engulfed in a wall of flame. Sparks danced in the air like lightning bugs on a summer night. As red and orange streaks of heat shot toward the ceiling, the intensity of the blaze scalded Jake's skin.

At the front of the barn, the horses smelled danger and shrieked. Jake ran toward the sound, the smoke tearing at his lungs. The air was so dense he couldn't see more than a foot ahead. Suddenly the double doors loomed in front of him, and he shoved his shoulder against them in an attempt to be free from the flames.

The impact jarred his clenched teeth and pain radiated from his bruised shoulder. *What the hell?*

Jake pushed at the doors with all his strength, then pounded with his fists. He turned to stare into the smoke-filled area behind him and saw nothing but swirling blackness. As the screams of the horses rang in his ears and the snapping of the fire intensified, the truth became clear.

Someone wanted him dead.

# Chapter Eleven

Katherine awoke with a start. Sitting up in bed, she glanced around the room. Nothing seemed amiss: a sky blue wrapper lay over the back of the rocking chair, her pistol was in place on the nightstand, the rifle leaned against the wall near the head of her bed.

Everything was in its place, but something nagged at the back of her mind causing her to think things were not as they should be. Had a dream awakened her? She frowned in concentration, trying to remember, but nothing came to mind.

The cry of a terrified horse pulled her attention to the window, and Katherine knew in that instant what was out of place. It was not the silver glow of moonlight streaming through the glass but the red and orange dancing light of flames.

Jumping from the bed, she raced to the window and peered out. Smoke hung in the air above the barn as if frozen in time. Flames crawled across the roof while another shrill scream split the night.

*The horses!*

Katherine caught her breath sharply.

*Jake.*

After stuffing her arms ruthlessly into the wrapper and pushing her feet into a pair of workboots, she sped through the darkened house and crashed the front door against the wall in careless haste. She paused on the porch, her breath coming fast and hard in her chest.

Why had no one else been awakened by the horses? Running across the yard, she noticed the empty wagon and remembered. It was Saturday. All the men had gone to town. More often than not they didn't return until morning. Katherine's heart lurched painfully. She and Jake were on their own.

Nearing the barn, she heard a muffled pounding and shouting. When she reached the door, Katherine gasped. The heavy wooden bar lay in place. Not stopping to reason why, she grabbed the thick plank with both hands and pulled with all her might. The slab of wood slid slowly out of the tight resting place, dropping to the ground with a thud. Immediately she yanked on the doors, and Jake stumbled out in a cloud of smoke and heat.

"Just in the nick of time." He coughed before continuing. "As usual. Next time you rescue

## Second Chance

me, could you make it sooner? My heart can't take your timing."

The fire roared higher, catching more of the roof in its grip. Jake grabbed Katherine's hand and attempted to drag her toward the house.

Katherine pulled away shaking her head. "The horses."

"Leave them."

"I can't." She removed her wrapper, revealing a virginal white nightdress, and began to tear the garment into strips. "We'll have to blindfold each one and lead them out."

"We can't go back in there! The roof's caught now. The whole place will go up in a minute."

"Then we'd better hurry." She held out some strips of cloth, then looked him straight in the eye.

"I'll carry you to the house," he threatened.

"I'd only come back out the minute you let me go. Please, Jake, I can't afford to lose any more."

The pleading tone that had crept into her voice made Katherine wince, but she stood her ground. She saw his face soften, then he pulled the cloths from her outstretched hand with an impatient tug and walked over to dunk two in the horse trough. Tying one around his nose and mouth, he held out the other as he glared at Katherine.

"You'd better do the same or you'll choke before you go three feet in there."

Katherine let out the breath she'd been holding and snatched the dampened cloth from his hand. When she finished tying the material over her face, Jake was gone. Glancing toward the barn, she saw his broad, bare shoulders disappearing into the smoke, and she hurried after him.

The horses reared and kicked their stalls. Katherine's ears ached from the sound of the terrified cries. It was impossible to calm them, and they threw back their heads in fear, shaking and snorting. The approaching fire only increased their terror, and a swell of panic flared deep in her chest. After several attempts, Jake succeeded in holding one of the horses still and applied the blindfold. Time slowed to a crawl as he struggled with the others. Once all the animals' eyes were covered, they gave in to the tugs on their hackamores, occasionally snorting and pawing in fear at the smell and sound of fire so near to them.

Katherine opened the door of a stall and grabbed onto the hackamore of the animal inside. Then she followed Jake as he led one of the other horses into a cloud of smoke. Once headed away from the fire, the animal she led must have sensed the entrance for it tried to bolt, lifting Katherine from the ground and carrying her along toward the fresh air. It took all of her strength, but Katherine was able to control the terrified animal.

Despite the dampened cloth over the lower half of her face, her lungs and nostrils were

## Second Chance

scorched. Searching the dense smog in front of her, she looked for a sign of Jake. Either he was already out, or the smoke was too thick to see him. Another surge of panic threatened to engulf her. Was she going in the right direction? The swirling grayness told her nothing, and Katherine gritted her teeth as she continued in the direction she hoped led to safety.

Just when she thought her throat could not stand another minute of the red hot air, the horse lunged forward, catching her off guard and dragging her into the startling freshness of the night.

Jake pulled her hand from its death grip on the horse's hackamore and the animal ran to join other horses in a pasture behind the house. Katherine leaned against Jake's broad chest, gasping. She heard the horses in the fields beyond calling to their comrades still trapped in the barn. Pushing away from the comfort Jake offered, Katherine turned and re-entered the inferno.

Fortunately, only five horses had been in the barn—the horses used with the wagon and a few needing medical attention. The second trip was easier than the first since the animals were already blindfolded. Stumbling from the barn once again, Katherine went to her knees, coughing. Jake was there immediately, lifting her into his embrace, pushing the damp hair from her forehead and removing her protective face cloth. Suddenly the back wall of the barn caved in, and Katherine jumped away from Jake to look at the burning structure.

Flames shot forward from the rear, catching the front wall in their grip. At a shrill whinny from the remaining horse, Katherine hurried toward the entrance. Jake's hand on her arm halted her in midstride.

"I'll get him." His voice was rough from the smoke and heat.

"No, this was my idea. I should be the one."

His hand tightened as he pulled her back. "I said I'd do it. Now, stay here."

Before she could protest further, Jake ran into the building once more. The previous trips into the barn had seemed to occur in slow motion, but at least she had been occupied. She found the waiting worse.

A sharp crack caused her to look up at the roof of the barn as it caved inward. Katherine cried out, running forward to peer into the hazy depths of the doorway. Nothing moved but the aimlessly swirling smoke and wavering flames. Quickly replacing the cloth around her mouth, she prepared to enter the barn just as Jake emerged leading the remaining horse. Katherine stumbled back quickly to avoid being run down.

After releasing the last horse, Jake tugged off the protective cloth and took several deep, gulping breaths of air before he could speak. "I told you to stay here. You don't take orders very well, do you?"

## Second Chance

Ignoring Jake's question, Katherine put her hand out and touched his arm lightly. "When the roof collapsed and you weren't out, I was afraid."

"It was a close call, but we were almost to the door when that happened. Some falling wood came near us, and I think some of the sparks nicked the horse. I had to use some persuasive techniques to get him to move after that." Jake looked down into Katherine's face. "You shouldn't worry about me. The devil takes care of his own."

Several hours later, Jake and Katherine surveyed the damage. The barn was a total loss. No help had arrived from the neighboring farms and there had been nothing two people could do against the blaze.

"At least we got the horses out," Jake said.

"Yes, at least there's that."

Katherine's knees shook with exhaustion. Her nightdress was smeared with soot and torn in several places. She could feel her hair, freed from the confines of a braid by the wind, tangling uncontrollably, as her eyes burned from the smoke and ash.

Jake attempted to pull Katherine out of her stupor. "The horses will be all right until winter. Maybe by then you can have a barn raising here."

Katherine looked at him and began to laugh. She heard her voice rising in volume and realized she sounded hysterical. Maybe she was.

She felt removed from the situation, almost as if the fire had happened to someone else. Taking a gulp of the smoke-tinged air, she coughed violently, then forced herself to focus on Jake's concerned face.

"I'm sorry," she said. "It's just that the thought of anyone in Second Chance building a barn for me is . . ."

Jake nodded and turned away as Katherine's voice trailed off.

"You'd better get back in the house and rest. There'll be a lot of cleaning up tomorrow, and you'll need to talk to the sheriff," Jake said.

"The sheriff? What can he do?"

"It's his job to find out who put a torch to your property. Next time they might destroy the house."

Katherine's head whirled. The question of how the fire began hadn't occurred to her. Since she'd first seen the flames, all her energy had been focused on ending the inferno.

"What makes you think someone set the fire?"

Jake looked at her as though the heat and smoke had affected her mind. "Katherine, the only lantern in the barn was in my room and the fire started in the hay. I'm sure there's never a flame of any kind near that part of the barn. It would be senseless. Not to mention that the door was barred. Someone set that fire, and that someone meant for me to fry in there."

Katherine looked up at Jake. The descending moon highlighted his face and she saw the anger, along with something else that made her shiver. These past few days she had begun to feel at ease with him, to rely on him—to want him. What she saw in his face in the shadows of the night frightened her. She must never forget that Jake was an outlaw—a murderer and a thief. Whatever she felt for him in the privacy of her mind and heart must remain hidden forever. He was dangerous and he was not hers to keep.

Abruptly Jake looked away from Katherine's gaze, and she started. "What is it?"

"Don't look at me like that." His voice was hoarse, whether from smoke or emotion she couldn't tell.

Katherine looked at the ground. "Like what?" she asked, her voice a whisper.

"As though you wanted me to kiss you but were terrified I might do just that." Jake turned away from her.

Katherine didn't answer. There was nothing to say when he'd struck the truth.

"Let's go inside." She sighed. "You can stay in the extra room again."

He merely nodded without turning. She stared for a moment at his stiff back, then hurried into the house and upstairs to her room.

She halted in the doorway as her eyes widened in amazement that everything could look the same, so safe and normal, after what she had just been through. Life was short and could be even shorter for the unlucky. She saw the flames and heard the screams of the horses again. Jake's shouts through the barred door echoed in her mind.

Stiffly she removed her soot-stained nightdress and washed as best she could with the water in her basin. The liquid turned black long before she finished her ministrations and clothed herself in a fresh gown. The clean, crisp cotton felt wonderfully cool on her heat-sensitized skin. Putting a hand to her tangled hair, Katherine sighed. She didn't have the energy to brush the long mass smooth. Tomorrow would be soon enough.

Crossing the room, she sat down heavily on the edge of her bed. After a few moments a clicking sound caught her attention. Her teeth chattered uncontrollably. Dragging the quilt from the end of the bed, Katherine wrapped it around her shoulders. The blanket did nothing to alleviate the bone-chilling tremors wracking her body.

A movement in the doorway made her look up. She recognized Jake's silhouette in the hazy morning light.

"I wanted to make sure you were all right before I went to bed."

"I can't—seem—to stop—sh—shivering, although I don't—f—feel cold," Katherine ground out between tremors, her jaw beginning to ache.

"Shock," Jake stated. "You'll need to stay warm until it passes. Can I get you anything?"

Katherine shook her head and hunched her shoulders to draw the quilt closer. Sensing

## Second Chance

movement, she looked up to see Jake standing in front of her.

"Maybe I can help," he said, then sat next to her on the bed and drew her onto his lap.

"What—what are—you doing?" Katherine's voice was muffled in the quilt as Jake pressed her against his chest.

"Getting you warm."

Katherine remained rigid for just a moment. Then she relaxed and allowed Jake to hold her. He began to rub her back through the material of the quilt, and she sighed. Eventually the shivering stopped, and Katherine drowsed. She awoke immediately when Jake laid her on the bed.

"What's wrong?"

"One of us was getting too warm." Jake smiled down at her.

"I feel fine."

"I wasn't talking about you." He turned to leave.

"Where are you going?"

"I need to get out of your bedroom before something happens we might both regret."

Katherine stared into Jake's eyes and saw the heat there to match the warmth that had been building inside her since she'd met him—a warmth she could no longer ignore or deny.

"Don't go." The words were out of her mouth before she could stop them.

Jake raised his eyebrows. "I think you need some rest, ma'am. I'll see you in the morning."

"No. Wait." Katherine got out of bed. She crossed the room to stand in front of him, struck by his height and breadth compared with her petiteness. She found the difference exciting.

Jake put his hands on her shoulders, holding her away from him. "You shouldn't be doing this."

"I don't care. Until last year I've always lived by the rules, and it only brought me pain. Since Sam died I've done what I wanted, and I'm happier than I've ever been. When I'm with you I feel things I've never felt before. I can't go through my life wondering what it would have been like between us. You could have died tonight. We both could have. Don't leave me now, Jake. I need to feel alive."

Katherine stood on her toes and pressed her lips against his. Jake's hands did not leave her shoulders, but he did not push her away. For a moment he did not respond. Then, just when she was about to pull back, he groaned and crushed her to him.

The shocking sensation of the kiss reminded her of the first time she'd felt his lips on hers after they'd chased off the mob. That night their attraction had frightened her and she had run from him. This kiss fulfilled the promise of the other without the fear.

She sighed with pleasure when his tongue grazed her lips. Opening her mouth, she used her tongue in the same manner. His hand came up to tangle in her loose hair, holding her head

## Second Chance

still as he kissed her more deeply.

When he removed his mouth from hers, she whimpered in protest. His lips moved lower and he captured her nipple through the material of her gown. Pulling the tightened bud into his mouth, he sucked in a rhythm that soon made her knees give way.

Jake caught her and crossed the room. Lowering her to the bed, he sank down beside her. As he looked into her eyes, she reached up to touch his face, her hand sliding around the back of his neck and drawing his head down for her kiss.

A few moments later he abruptly stood up.

"Did I do something wrong?" she whispered, memories of Sam's taunts about her inadequacy crowding her mind.

Jake frowned. "Wrong? No, I just want to get out of these pants. That is the way this is done as I recall."

She sighed in relief. He quickly removed his boots, tossing them carelessly into a corner. She watched in fascination as he unbuttoned his Levi's and shrugged them down lean hips. Beneath the coarse material he was naked and ready.

Her breath caught in her throat. She had never seen a man naked. Sam had always extinguished the lamp before undressing and climbing on top of her.

Jake's body was hard-muscled and brown, so different from hers. Even the paler skin beneath his Levi's was many shades darker than her own ivory complexion. Katherine's attention turned to the part of Jake that made him male, and her cheeks grew warm. Her gaze lifted to his face and she saw he was watching her hungrily, his eyes glittering in the lamplight. No one had ever looked at her like that.

She stood up to remove her gown, but Jake's hands stilled her. "Let me."

His large hands fumbled at the small buttons closing her nightdress. Impatient to feel him touch her flesh, she raised her hands to help. He pushed them away, firmly but gently, and soon had the gown unbuttoned to her waist. As Jake slid his hands along her collarbone to her shoulders, Katherine shivered at the work-roughened touch of his fingers. He let the garment fall to the floor at her feet, and they both stood naked, not yet touching. She reached up tentatively, stroking the crisp hair on his chest. She had wanted to touch him thus from the first time she had seen his skin glistening in the sun while he worked with the horses. His skin warmed her hands, which were ice cold and still shaking a bit—from the earlier disaster or the present excitement she could not tell. She explored in wonder his shoulders and then moved down to his buttocks, marveling at the solid muscle and the curves so very different from her own. Jake stood very still, as though he didn't want to startle her into ceasing, but when her fingers grazed his thighs he swore softly and pushed her back on the bed.

## Second Chance

As he kissed her his large hand slid over her hip and up to her small, firm breasts. She clenched her teeth at his touch, the inadequacy which had always haunted her—she was too tiny and thin, too bony to hold a man's interest—rising up and threatening to overwhelm all her newfound joy with a pressing shyness. Gathering her courage, she ended the kiss and searched his face for a sign of the revulsion she'd often seen on Sam's. Jake's clear green eyes met hers and he smiled. She gazed at that smile in wonder, and her fears eased somewhat.

"Katie, you're so beautiful."

She turned her head away, the endearment causing unaccustomed emotion to clog her throat. "I'm not, Jake. You don't have to say that."

He put his finger to her chin and pulled her gaze back to meet his. "I know I don't, but I can't help myself." His gaze traveled down her body and she flushed. "I think you're perfect."

She shook her head and began to protest, but his mouth silenced her as he kissed her again, harder than before. Their urgency was reflected in the dueling of tongues, the increased tempo of their breathing and the frenzied movement of hands over damp flesh. Jake was no longer gentle, but Katherine reveled in the sensations his strong touch created. She perceived the need in him, and that need matched her own.

They explored each other—lips and fingertips grazing sensitized skin. Jake's moans mingled with hers, and she lost track of the line between reality and sensation.

"Katie, I don't think I can wait." His voice seemed to come from far away.

She reached down, enfolding him, guiding him to her. She wanted this, she wanted him as she had wanted nothing or no one before in her life.

Damp and willing, she still experienced some discomfort as he entered her. Jake paused when she tensed and allowed her body to adjust to the sensation. When she relaxed once again, he began to move slowly, probing further with each thrust. She arched her back, pulling him deeper within her. He swallowed her cry of fulfillment with his kiss. The tempo of their lovemaking increased, and her body strained toward something unknown. Whispering her name, Jake plunged into her deeply, holding himself still within as he shuddered. In that instant she contracted around him, pulsing as he pulsed. The tension in her most intimate parts broke into waves of sensation as he cried out his own release.

Katherine lay still enjoying the languid, satisfied feeling invading her body. Suddenly Jake turned onto his side, pulling her with him. He touched her damp, tangled hair and stroked her face. Katherine's skin tingled at the sensation of their joined bodies. Though she enjoyed the feeling of closeness, of oneness, uncertainty over what to do next made her attempt to pull away from him. Jake held her in place, gently but firmly.

"I've wanted to do that since I first saw you sitting in your wagon in a crowd. You were so calm and cool in the midst of all the chaos and the heat. I didn't hurt you, did I?"

"No, not at all. It's just that . . ." Katherine hesitated, stroking his chest and tangling her fingers in the soft, black curls covering his skin. She reached up and brushed his hair back from his forehead, noticing for the first time a small white scar at his temple. Momentarily she wondered what past injury had caused the mark. Then her thoughts turned to the question uppermost in her mind.

What did he expect of her now? Sam had always rolled away immediately after he was through, even in the early months of their marriage when he'd at least attempted to be pleasant. Once he'd decided she was barren, he'd still used her, but his technique lost finesse as time went on. The passion she had just experienced was a new and beautiful gift she was unsure of how to handle.

"Well?" he asked.

Katherine looked into Jake's eyes, which were concerned and curious as he waited for her to continue.

"I've never had anything like that happen to me." Her voice quavered at the admission she hadn't meant to make.

"I don't understand." Jake raised himself onto his elbow to look down into her face. "You were a married woman."

"I know, but with Sam I didn't feel anything. This," she waved her hand aimlessly. "This was always something we did in the dark—never talking, barely touching. I hated it."

"Things between a man and a woman shouldn't be that way. I'm sorry, Katie." His callused finger ran down her cheek, then he leaned over to kiss her gently.

"He only wanted me in order to get a son. I felt like a brood mare." Her voice was cold and hard as she remembered the humiliation of her failure.

"And there were never any children?"

"I'm barren," Katherine stated dispassionately and turned her head to gaze out the window.

"Who told you that?"

"Sam. He had bastards all over the West in his cavalry days, so our lack of children must have been my fault."

Jake bent down and nuzzled her neck until she turned back to him again. Katherine's arms went around Jake's shoulders as she hugged him tightly.

"I take it Sam was not a very understanding man."

"Well, he was disappointed. The only reason he married at all was to have a son. I couldn't provide him with one, so I was useless. He let me know how he felt—every day of my life."

## Second Chance

When Jake said nothing, Katherine pulled away to look into his face. The anger she saw there caused a warm glow deep inside her. It had been a long time since anyone had cared how she felt.

She kissed him lightly on the lips. "It doesn't matter now. Sam's dead. He can't hurt me anymore."

"Why did you marry him?"

Katherine sighed and rolled away from Jake onto her back, though she continued to hold his hand. She made a low sound of enjoyment as his bare foot stroked up and down her calf.

"Sam could be charming. When he wanted something." Katherine closed her eyes and remembered. "I taught school in Williamsburg and lived with my aunt. I saw the years of teaching other people's children stretched out in front of me, with no hope of my own. I met Sam, he offered me a new, full life in the West. I thought he cared for me and he made me care for him. Or at least care for the man he pretended to be. Things didn't change between us until . . . until too late."

Jake remained silent, and unease flooded Katherine at the thought of the confidences she'd revealed. Glancing at him, she saw that his attention was focused on the window. Katherine was surprised to see the sun was up and shining brightly onto the bed where they lay. Jake cocked his head, listening intently, and a moment later Katherine also heard the sound of approaching horses. The men were back, and as soon as they saw the barn, they would head directly for the house.

"I'd better hightail it downstairs before you've got questions to answer you aren't ready for," Jake said.

Jake pulled his fingers from hers and quickly got up from the bed, shoving long legs into his discarded Levi's. Katherine eyed the room frantically for her wrapper, then remembered she had torn it into strips for blindfolds. Instead, she reached for her own blue jeans and shirt.

He kissed her once, hard, then left the room. Katherine heard his boots clatter down the stairs and fade toward the back of the house. Thank God it was Sunday, and Mary didn't come to work until after church. Katherine turned at the doorway, ignoring momentarily the pounding on the front door, and surveyed her bed. Crossing her arms and hugging herself, she stored the memories of her time there with Jake in her secret heart.

Jake sat in the kitchen listening to the increasing furor of the knocks on the door. After several minutes, he got up and walked down the hall toward the front of the house. But when he heard Katherine's footsteps on the stairs, he retreated to the kitchen doorway. He waited there until he heard her calm voice explaining the fire and giving orders for the clean-up. When he was sure all was proceeding smoothly, he slipped through the kitchen and out the back door. Leaning against the house in the early morning coolness, he mulled over his actions.

## Second Chance

Why had he gone to Katherine's room after the fire? It was a question he'd be asking himself often from now on. When he'd found her shivering in mild shock, he should have covered her with a second blanket and left. Instead, he'd let his emotions take over and ended up bedding her. Never mind that he'd been aching to do just that since the first time he'd seen Katherine Logan. Jake slammed his fist against the wall of the house in frustration. She wasn't a lightskirt to be lusted after and abandoned at will. He didn't want to leave her. And if he didn't leave, what happened to his mission? To Second Chance?

Katherine was a wonder. She had given herself to him freely and without restraint when she knew him to be an outlaw. And after what she'd told him sex had been like with Sam, he was surprised she could stomach the act at all. But she'd turned out to be everything a man could want: responsive, passionate, lovely. Jake slammed his palm against the side of the house in frustration. His very presence in Second Chance was a lie. How would Katherine react if he told her who he really was? Especially after she'd gone through years of pain with a man who'd pretended to be what he was not. Jake didn't think Katherine would take kindly to lies.

A movement near the bunkhouse caught Jake's attention. As Dillon Swade crept stealthily into the outbuilding, Jake followed to investigate. Looking around, he saw no one in the vicinity, so he went to the back of the bunkhouse and peered into the window.

As he watched, Dillon pulled a large amount of money from his pockets and stuffed most of it into a saddlebag. Replacing the bag under his bunk, he sat down on the bed as though waiting for someone. Moments later, Katherine's entrance surprised Jake. She looked tired and worried, but she smiled at Dillon while they spoke. Although Jake strained to hear the words, he could make out nothing but a murmur. Then Dillon placed the remaining money in her hands, and Katherine nodded at something the stocky man said before leaving.

The entire transaction baffled Jake. Where had Swade gotten all that money? And why was he giving some of it to Katherine? She hadn't acted surprised, so she must have been expecting the funds.

His need to know what was going on overpowered his usual caution. Before he could consider what he was doing, Jake strode around the bunkhouse and entered. Dillon looked up, his face registering shock, then anger, at Jake's presence. He began to say something, then thought better of it and snapped his mouth shut, a mutinous look on his swarthy face.

"Where were you last night, Swade?"

"In town."

"Can you prove it?"

Dillon stood up and pushed his face close to Jake's. "I don't have to prove anything to you, Reb."

## Second Chance

Jake remained silent, debating the wisdom of shaking the truth out of the man. Instead, he strode to the window and looked out.

"You're awful rich lately. Where'd you get the money?"

When there was no answer, Jake turned around. Dillon's face flushed red with murderous anger.

"You're a dirty spy. I suppose you want some of it, too."

"No. I'd just like to know where it came from and why you gave some to Mrs. Logan."

Dillon's face became sly, and his mouth parted in what Jake found to be a poor imitation of a smile.

"None of your damn business, Reb."

Jake stared at him for a moment. He considered several methods of making the man talk, then discarded them. Using force on Dillon in this case would only make everyone suspicious.

Jake turned to leave, but Dillon's parting words caused him to stop short in the doorway.

"Did you really think she saved your Rebel hide because she liked your looks? Her and me have an understanding, and we'll save this place no matter what we have to do."

"Does that include selling information to Charlie Coltrain?"

"Coltrain?" Dillon blinked, caught off guard. "What kind of information could I sell him? I'm just a rancher."

Jake raised his eyebrows. There were ways to find out any kind of information, if a person wanted that information badly enough. He was sure Dillon would do anything to save the Circle A—and so would Katherine.

Cursing under his breath, Jake left Dillon alone in the bunkhouse. He walked around the back of the building, searching for a quiet place to mull over his options. Head bent as he thought, Jake tripped over the object in his path before he realized it was there. Bending, he picked up the dusty felt hat and frowned.

Dangling Matt Rolland's favorite hat from his fingers, Jake gazed toward the bunkhouse speculatively.

"Just what are you up to, my friend?" he whispered.

# Chapter Twelve

Doubts plagued Jake for the rest of the day as he helped with the clean-up. The work was dirty and hot, the blackened wood radiating a heat that increased the temperature of the heavy, moist air.

His conversation with Dillon echoed in Jake's mind. Had the man been implying that Katherine was involved in something illegal to make money for the Circle A? Jake had seen no evidence of that.

But she was desperate to save her ranch. Could she be involved in some way with the robberies? The fastest and easiest way to make money illegally in Second Chance would be with his pal Charlie.

And Matt. Well, Matt had been acting very strange on this job. Though Jake couldn't believe that his partner would turn traitor, he'd seen stranger things happen in his lifetime.

By sunset, Jake had made up his mind. The only way to solve the mystery was to finish the mission he'd been sent to accomplish. That meant he could not reveal his identity to Katherine or his suspicions to Matt. While his heart believed in innocence, his mind doubted. He had seen too many men die because of misread instincts. When he discovered the truth, he would come back and settle things.

He had to leave today. Another night with Katherine and he might never be able to break away. For her sake as well as his own, he must return to the Coltrains as soon as possible.

Sheriff Jessup arrived just as the men were washing for supper. Jessup seemed to take his own sweet time going about the law enforcement duties in Second Chance; the man's lax attitude made Jake wonder what else was getting past the sheriff.

Katherine came out of the house, her hair tied back with a blue ribbon and her face freshly washed. She looked young, innocent, and beautiful. She smiled at Jake happily, and he turned away, guilt chewing at his stomach.

"I hear ya had some trouble last night." Jessup observed the pile of blackened lumber that had once been a barn. He frowned at Jake. "Wanna tell me what went on here?"

The sheriff obviously suspected that Jake had something to do with the fire. Well, he couldn't blame the man. Pinkerton always said, "Known

## Second Chance

criminals should be your first suspects."

Waiting until the other men had gone into the house for supper, Jake told Jessup what had transpired from the moment he awakened until the last horse was rescued.

When Jake finished, the lawman remained silent for several moments. Jake could see why Pinkerton didn't want the man involved in the investigation. His plodding thought processes might be fine for small-town law enforcement, but dealing with Charlie, Bill, and the boys required a much quicker frame of mind.

"You sayin' you didn't see or hear anything?" Jessup asked.

Jake gritted his teeth. That's exactly what he'd said, several times.

"Mighty convenient, I'd say," Jessup observed.

Katherine, who had been standing silently next to the sheriff, spoke up at once. "Sheriff, someone locked Jake in there. No man would set a barn on fire and then lock himself in to roast. You're looking in the wrong direction here."

"Mrs. Logan, I'm just looking at all the angles. Maybe he thought you'd let him go if he helped you save your stock."

Katherine cast a quick glance at Jake. "Mr. Banner's free to leave anytime he wants. He would have no reason to harm me or the Circle A."

"Who would?" Jake's quiet question caught their attention.

"What's that supposed to mean, Banner?" Sheriff Jessup asked impatiently.

"If you can find a person with a reason to harm Kat . . . Mrs. Logan or the Circle A, then you've found your man . . . or woman."

The sheriff looked thoughtful, then said gruffly, "Well, we'll have to see what turns up. I'll go talk to the other men now, Mrs. Logan." Jessup strode toward the house, his large belly leading the way.

Katherine continued to look after the sheriff long past his disappearance around the house toward the back door. "I do believe he thinks you set the fire," she said.

"He should if he's any kind of sheriff. I'm a known criminal."

Katherine looked at Jake, her gray eyes puzzled. "You have no reason to burn down my barn."

Jake pushed his hair out of his face with an impatient gesture. "A lot of things don't make sense in this world, Katherine."

Hating himself for his doubts, he left her standing in the yard alone. Katherine had again defended him with the sheriff while he was planning to sneak out in the night as though he had something to hide. He wouldn't blame her if, come tomorrow, she believed him guilty of any number of misdeeds.

Jake succeeded in avoiding Katherine for the rest of the evening, though he knew she would be hurt by such behavior after what they had shared the night before. But better to leave her angry than to leave her after another night of lovemaking.

Packing the few clothes he'd borrowed from Joe earlier in the day, Jake went into Katherine's office and placed a folded piece of paper on the desk. He couldn't leave without some explanation.

> *Katie,*
> *I have some unfinished business to take care of, but I'll be back to explain everything. Sorry I had to leave before the month was up. I'll pay you back for Lucifer. Darlin', I'd never hurt you.*
>                                                  *Jake*

As Jake left the office, he passed the stairs and looked up toward Katherine's room. After a moment, he sighed in resignation and climbed quietly to the second level. He stood in the doorway of the room, silently observing her.

Katherine looked like a princess from a legend who had fallen into a deep sleep. The light from the moon spilled across her face, turning her hair to silver. Asleep, she looked even younger and more fragile than she did awake. Jake resisted the urge to kiss her one last time before leaving. In the storybooks a kiss awoke the princess. He couldn't take that risk.

Backing away from the sight, Jake turned and hurried down the stairs and through the kitchen. He let himself out the back door and quickly covered the distance to a nearby pasture where he'd quartered Lucifer after the fire. The horse was still half-wild, but Jake could control him if he made the effort. And he'd need a fast mount to keep up with the Coltrains, who always stole the best available horseflesh.

A short time later, Jake was mounted bareback on the horse, all the saddles having been lost in the fire. He'd have to make do until he reached the hideout and found an extra saddle left by some dearly departed guerilla.

Jake turned the horse's head sharply to the west and held Lucifer at a walk until he was sure the hoofbeats would not be detected by anyone at the ranch. Once out of earshot, Jake let the colt gallop at full speed through the vast stretch of prairie grass. The horse's long gait ate up the miles, and Jake was amazed at Lucifer's stamina. When other animals would have become winded and lathered, the horse still ran as though he'd just begun.

All too soon he neared the Coltrains' hideout, and halted his mount. Charlie had stumbled upon the place while harassing Union sympathizers with his guerilla band. Throughout Missouri there were countless caves and caverns, but the hideout was unique. A small opening in the red-orange rock formations provided access. Hidden from view by a grove of trees, the entry would be difficult to find unless the searcher was aware of its existence. Riders had to travel through the entrance, leading their horses single file for several hundred feet until the narrow opening expanded and

## Second Chance

angled downward, eventually opening into a huge cavern. A guerilla always guarded the second entrance in case a lucky lawman found the secret hideaway.

Jake entered the tight passageway leading Lucifer, and the horse balked at the unfamiliar closeness. Jake whispered soothingly in the animal's ear and stroked his nose. Finally the horse relented, although he pawed the dirt and snorted his displeasure. Reaching the inner entry to the cavern, Jake paused and called a greeting. Charging into the open without a word was a sure way to get shot, since guerillas had quick, indiscriminate trigger fingers.

"Who's there?"

Jake swore when he heard the voice of Bill Coltrain, the last man he wanted to see.

"Jake Banner."

"Well, well. Get tired of your easy livin'?" Bill laughed, but Jake heard no humor in the sound. "Come on through, Banner. Been waitin' for ya."

"Anyone else around, Bill?"

"Keep talkin' like that and I'll get to thinkin' you don't trust me. My feelin's'll be hurt. Wouldn't want that to happen, wouldja?"

"Where's Charlie?" Jake purposely avoided responding to the other man's taunts.

"Right here, Banner." The rasping voice echoed eerily in the enclosed space. "Quit bein' an old woman and get inside."

Charlie's tall form appeared in silhouette at the opening of the cavern. Jake breathed easier at the sight of the outlaw leader. Bill would never dare anything with his brother nearby. However, what went on behind Charlie's back was an entirely different story.

Upon entering the cavern, Jake was struck once again by the beauty of the place. The cave's walls and ceiling showed rich mineral deposits of all different shapes, sizes, and colors. Jake had lived in Missouri for most of his life, but he had never seen anything like this.

"What're you doin' back so soon?" Charlie asked as he examined Lucifer.

The horse didn't appreciate the attention and stretched out its neck to taste Charlie's arm. Without so much as a blink, the outlaw slammed his fist onto the top of the animal's nose. Lucifer retreated in sullen silence.

Jake watched the byplay dispassionately. He glanced over at Bill and saw the man stroke the barrel of his gun lovingly. The smile on the outlaw's face made Jake think of a cat toying with a mouse, and in that instant Jake knew he'd been right not to come into the cavern without Charlie close at hand.

"Well, Banner?"

Coltrain's impatient tone drew Jake's attention away from Bill. Focusing on Charlie, Jake attempted to remember the question.

"Weren't you gonna stay with Katherine Logan for a month?"

Jake cast a sharp glance at Charlie. He had never mentioned Katherine's name to the outlaw leader. Unless Charlie had done some

## Second Chance

checking, or knew Katherine personally, why did Coltrain know her name?

Jake pushed aside the distracting thought to be dealt with later in privacy. "The lady got too bossy, and the sheriff was starting to hang around. Made me nervous."

Charlie merely nodded as he stroked Lucifer's nose. Apparently the animal had decided to be friends rather than enemies.

"Good horse. Didja steal 'im?"

"Of course. How else would I get one?" Jake said irritably, thinking of Katherine's probable reaction to the theft.

"'Pears like you ain't partial to stealin'. When did you get civilized?" Bill's sneering voice irritated Jake further.

"You want to settle this now, Billy Boy?" Jake began to remove his gunbelt in preparation for a fight.

Bill smirked as his fingers reached for the clasp on his own belt. The quiet yet arresting quality of Charlie's ruined tones stopped them both.

"Not now. You two need to fight this out, but I want to tell Banner about the next job. There's plans to be made." He turned and walked away, confident Jake would follow.

Charlie Coltrain rarely had to enforce his decisions. The few times he did, the consequences for the unfortunate dissenter spoke volumes. Word of his vicious treatment of anyone who denied his authority was widespread. Jake had yet to witness such retaliations and wondered if Charlie's brutality had been exaggerated, as was often the way in the West. Still, he thought it best to stay on the outlaw leader's good side and avoid the possibility of trouble.

Bill remained to guard the entrance while Jake followed Charlie. The other gang members were gathered around a cookfire savoring their coffee and smokes. Many of them looked curiously at Jake, but no one spoke.

"Banner's back," Charlie said without further explanation. Some of the men nodded to Jake in welcome. "Our friend in Second Chance has informed me that another shipment of the railroad payroll will be transported in two days. This time on the afternoon train."

Jake listened intently, but Coltrain gave no hint of the contact's identity. Observing the others, Jake doubted if anyone knew their "friend's" name except Charlie. He'd have to watch the outlaw, probably follow him whenever the opportunity presented itself. Since the next job was already planned, he'd have to wait until after the train robbery for his chance to discover the contact. He could only hope no one got killed this time.

"We'll loosen the ties on the track where it curves near the creek and hitch them to the saddlehorns of our strongest horses."

Charlie continued to explain the plan, his voice so low the men had to lean forward to hear the gravelly sound of his words. Did the man purposely exploit his damaged voice to

## Second Chance

command everyone's undivided attention?

"Then we'll hide in the brush around the creek bed until the train comes. The men on the horses will pull the ties out when the train's too close to stop. The rest will be easy."

Charlie smiled at his gang and they returned the expression. To them Charlie was a legend, a hero of the dead South. That's not to say any one of them wouldn't shoot him in the back if they could profit from the action. But, for now, Charlie was their path to riches and they adored him.

"Banner, that horse you brought in will be perfect for this job. You'll be one of the riders." Charlie never looked at Jake for confirmation but proceeded to assign tasks to the others.

When the meeting ended and the others were bedding down for the night, Jake fell into step beside Charlie. He accompanied the leader as he walked up the path to his private cave set in the rock above the open cavern. There were several such caves, but the other men preferred to sleep in the open area together as they were used to doing.

"You seem to get your information pretty regular," Jake observed, hoping to uncover a clue during the conversation.

Charlie glanced at Jake out of the corner of his eye, then answered slowly. "I do. Why are you interested?"

"I just like to know that the source is reliable before I risk my neck."

"It's reliable. Let me worry about the information. You worry about the job."

Jake hesitated before continuing. It wouldn't be a good idea to make Coltrain suspicious with too many questions. Then he'd have Charlie watching him as closely as he planned to watch Charlie.

"I admit I'm curious about your contact. The town's a hotbed of Yankees. Who'd help us?"

Coltrain stopped and fixed Jake with a cold, black stare. "Someone who needs money as much as we do. This town's ripe for pluckin' and I aim to take every advantage. That they're all a bunch of damn Yankees just makes the thievin' all the sweeter."

"The war's over, Charlie. We lost."

"My war'll never be over. Just because Lee surrendered doesn't mean I have to."

Jake frowned, surprised at the depth of the anger contained in the outlaw leader's voice. What could have made the man so full of hatred?

"You plan to keep fighting your own private little war right here in Second Chance, don't you?"

"Why not?"

"Because eventually you'll get killed, that's why. You know as well as I do that when you let emotions creep into things you make mistakes."

Jake stopped abruptly. Was he talking to Charlie or himself? And why was he giving advice to the man he was supposed to be

## Second Chance

bringing to justice? He had never had any problem keeping himself separate from the job he had to do. Until now.

Charlie had paused next to him and turned to fix Jake with a curious stare. "Speaking from experience?"

Jake shrugged. "If somethin' happens to you and no one else knows the workings of this operation, that would be the end of the money. I just want to make sure I'm not out in the cold in the midst of a Missouri winter."

"Don't worry. As long as there's money to be made here, my contact will make sure he's makin' it. That means he'll need the Coltrain Gang around." He continued to gaze at Jake for another moment and then said quietly, "I don't like questions, Banner, never did."

Jake looked into Charlie's eyes and saw the threat of danger inherent in the man. Though he had not found out what he wanted to know, he did know when to retreat and regroup. Jake nodded in understanding, tugging on the brim of his hat in farewell as he turned away.

Dillon was taking his final walk around the house and through the pastures, as he did most nights, when he saw Banner sneak out of the house. Following, Dillon watched in amazement as the Reb rode out on Lucifer. When dawn broke and Banner had not returned, Dillon couldn't believe his good fortune. It looked as if the man had left for good.

Dillon quietly entered the house, quickly making his way to the office. He checked the cash box and ledgers. Both items were undisturbed. As he rose from the chair behind the scarred oak desk, Dillon noticed the note addressed to Katherine. Snatching up the paper, he unfolded the square. As he read the contents, his face flushed with fury. The thief was too familiar by far. When he finished, Dillon ripped the note into tiny pieces, continuing to shred the parchment long after it was necessary.

He went outside and let the scraps drift through his fingers, grinning as the dawn breeze rolled the bits of paper across the dirt and grass. If Dillon Swade had anything to say about it, Jake Banner would never return to the Circle A alive.

Katherine awoke feeling well rested for the first time in days. After a night of fighting the fire and then loving Jake, she had been exhausted. A full day's work on top of that had made her sleep heavily despite her concern over Jake's behavior. But the new day, combined with the boundless energy of a well-rested body, made Katherine believe she could conquer any adversity. She would track down Jake this morning and have things out with him. Maybe he felt worthless since she owned a ranch and he wasn't even a paid hand. Well, they could work something out; she was sure of it.

## Second Chance

Jumping lightly out of bed, Katherine went to her closet and selected a dress the color of a pink rose. Today she wanted to feel like a lady. After braiding her hair, she wound it around the crown of her head and secured the plait with several pins. Since she usually tucked her tresses under Sam's hat, she'd probably have a headache by noon from the pins sticking into her head, but she wanted to look her best for her talk with Jake. Minutes later, Katherine ran quickly down the stairs and into the kitchen.

"Good morning, Mary." She took her coffee, then laughed as the housekeeper gaped at her.

"Land sakes, child, you're wearing a dress. And your hair. Why, you're pretty as a picture."

"I bet you didn't think it was possible."

The older woman gave her a wounded look. "Now I never said that, missus. You just don't make the attempt is all. Why, a young girl like you with such prospects, you should have men waitin' in line on the porch."

Katherine smiled but refrained from comment. It would be a cold day in July before the men of Second Chance beat a path to her door.

Katherine looked up expectantly, a smile on her face, at the sound of the back door opening. The smile faded as she saw the men, followed by Dillon, enter and take their places at the table. Jake did not join them.

Katherine went to the door and peered out, scanning the visible area, but there was no sign of Jake.

"He isn't coming." Dillon's sullen voice caused Katherine to tense. She hadn't meant to be so obvious.

"Oh, and where is *he*?"

"I suspect he's back at the Coltrain hideout by now, wherever that is." Dillon forked wheatcakes into his mouth without looking up.

Katherine noticed that the other men were watching her with curious looks and decided she should have a private conversation with her foreman.

"Dillon, please come to my office."

He glanced at her, his mouth full, maple syrup shining on his chin. With an impatient gesture, she motioned for him to follow her, then left the room.

Katherine sat behind her desk and faced Dillon as he entered, wiping his mouth with the back of his hand.

"I'd like you to explain your comments about Jake Banner."

"What's to explain? He's gone."

"Gone?" Katherine's throat tightened as she looked into Dillon's face. He was serious.

"I was making my check around the place last night and I saw him ride out on Lucifer."

"He took Lucifer," Katherine whispered.

Dillon nodded. "I watched for a while, and he met another rider a ways out. Big, yellow-haired man on a white horse."

Charlie Coltrain. The name branded itself on Katherine's mind. He'd left with Charlie Coltrain and taken her best colt. She had been depending on the sale of that animal to make the mortgage payment next month. But worse than that loss was the feeling of betrayal. Jake had spent a night in her arms and then left a trail of broken promises. Honor, truth, gratitude meant nothing to Jake Banner.

Dillon watched her closely, his mouth quirked into a snide smile. Quickly she schooled her features into a calm mask. She would have to sort out her feelings and beliefs regarding Jake Banner while alone.

"If he's gone, we'll just have to make do. The loss of Lucifer could be a problem, though." Katherine sighed and reached into her desk drawer to remove the cashbox. Unlocking it, she removed the money Dillon had given her the previous day.

"I'll be going into town to pay Mr. Foley his mortgage. I should congratulate you, Dillon. I never would have believed we'd get this much money from the army for those old mares. You must drive a hard bargain."

Dillon shrugged but remained silent. Katherine continued to regard him for a moment, thinking he was acting somewhat secretive about his latest sale. Usually he bragged and told her every detail, but this time he'd been uncharacteristically mute. Well, he would tell her when he was ready. She rose and came around the desk.

"Thank you for your loyalty to me and the Circle A, Dillon. I know we've had our disagreements, but I'm beginning to understand the value of a good manager."

Katherine held out her hand. Dillon stared at her for a moment, then placed his hand in hers. Reaching out, he covered her small hand with his free one. She looked at him in confusion and saw a jubilant smile light his face.

"I'd do anything for you, Katherine—anything."

On her way to town later that afternoon, Katherine's thoughts turned to Jake. She hated to condemn a person without hearing their explanation first. But, in this case, her resolve wavered. When she remembered how she'd lain in Jake's arms and confided her secret fears and humiliations, she wanted to raise her fists to the sky and scream in rage. Without a backward glance, Jake Banner had left her to return to his life of thievery and murder. Where had she ever gotten the idea that he was not the cold-hearted outlaw he professed to be? Just because he'd torn down her defenses with his words of respect, and then made love to her gently and passionately, didn't mean he wasn't low-down scum. In fact, since he'd snuck out in the night, she felt inclined to believe he'd been after just one thing all along. She wanted to crawl into bed and hide until the humiliation left her.

Katherine rode up to the Second Chance Bank and tied her horse. Making sure her face betrayed none of her inner turmoil, she opened the front door and entered the dark, cool interior of the building.

## Second Chance

When her eyes adjusted from the bright glare of the sunlight, she noticed she was the only customer in the bank. Most of the workers stared at her curiously, obviously aware of her involvement with the thief who'd robbed the bank. Relief washed over her when she spotted Matthew Rolland. His wide grin and friendly wave made Katherine smile before she walked over to his window.

"Mrs. Logan, it's a pleasure. How can I help you?"

"You can start by calling me Katherine."

"Katherine then. Can I be of service?"

"No, but thank you. I came to take care of some business with Mr. Foley. Is he in?" Katherine's voice betrayed her distaste of the errand.

"Yes. I'll tell him you're here." Matt came out from behind the counter to join her. "Did Jake come with you?"

The question so startled her that all thought fled from Katherine's mind. After a moment of silence, Matthew's soft voice penetrated her confusion. "Katherine? Is something wrong?"

"N—no. I'm sorry. Jake's gone."

"Gone?"

Matt's puzzled voice made Katherine glance at him. For a moment she could have sworn he looked pleased. But she dismissed such fancies as a trick of the dim interior.

"Yes. I assume he's rejoined his friends. Things'll be much calmer at the Circle A without him, I'm sure."

Katherine put all her energy into making the words sound convincing. She failed miserably, but Matt did not seem to notice. He smiled at her somewhat absently and went to Foley's office, disappearing inside.

Returning a short time later, Matt escorted her gallantly to Foley's door. He leaned toward her with a whisper. "He's not in the best of moods today. My suggestion is to do your business as fast as you're able and leave."

Since a quick meeting had been her intent all along, Katherine nodded. One thing she did not need was a confrontation with Harrison Foley. She was already tired and emotionally drained.

"Katherine, how nice to see you. Do come in and sit down." Harrison's stilted accent drifted out the door, drawing her into the room.

Before riding into town she had changed from her dress into Levi's and a worn blue shirt. Her hair was once again jammed under Sam's hat. Katherine could tell from Harrison's glance of disapproval that he did not appreciate her informal dress for their meeting. She smiled inwardly at her small victory.

Harrison leaned back in his chair, his long fingers folded across his chest as he studied her face. "I hope you haven't come to tell me you can't pay your debt this month. Since the robbery, I am not inclined to be lenient."

"No, I've got your money right here." Katherine pulled the cash from her pocket and tossed it across the desk. The greenbacks landed with a

## Second Chance

satisfying smack in front of Harrison. "If you'd write me a receipt, I'll be out of your way."

Harrison's face registered surprise, which he quickly covered with his usual polite mask. He grabbed a piece of paper, scribbled the required words, and tossed the paper across the desk.

"I would have thought with your recent loss you would be unable to meet your responsibilities."

"You have nothing to worry about."

"But I do worry about you. All alone out there on that big spread. I've told you before, I'll give you a fair price for the Circle A, and you can return to Virginia. By now things should have settled down in the South. With the money you could get yourself a nice new husband."

Katherine clenched her teeth to keep from screaming at the man to be silent. Her last husband had left her with no desire for a new one. The only thing she wanted now was her home, free and clear. In order to have that, she'd continue to be polite to this ingratiating bore as long as he held the mortgage on her dream.

Katherine rose and edged toward the door. "That's kind of you, but I'm managing just fine. Good day."

Reaching the door, Katherine yanked it open, hurriedly leaving the office and the building before Foley could get in another word. As she drove down the main street of Second Chance, she noticed Matt Rolland in deep conversation with one of the railroad employees. When she raised her hand in greeting, Matt did not acknowledge her, though she could have sworn he saw her clearly.

# Chapter Thirteen

With school dismissed for the summer, several of the town's children played at the edge of the dusty street. As Katherine rode past, a few nodded in greeting while most looked at the ground and ignored her. She was amazed how the prejudices of the parents filtered down so strongly to the children.

When she drew near the schoolhouse, Katherine recognized Ruth's horse tied to the hitching post and turned into the schoolyard on impulse. Maybe a short talk would lighten the gloom of her spirits.

Entering the building, Katherine found Ruth at her desk focusing intently on an open book. It wasn't until Katherine reached out and knocked on one of the wood benches filling the room that Ruth looked up.

"Katherine, are you all right?" Ruth jumped to her feet. "I worried so when I heard about your barn. I'd planned to come out to the ranch tonight and check on you."

Ruth's genuine concern warmed Katherine deeply.

"I'm fine, Ruth. The barn's a total loss, but at least no one was hurt." Katherine joined her friend at the front of the room.

"That's a relief." She sat in her chair again. "When can you start to rebuild?"

"There's no money for a new barn. We'll have to struggle along without one for now."

At Ruth's concerned look, Katherine sighed. The weight of the Circle A sat heavily on her shoulders today, and she had no desire to talk about her troubles, increasing her melancholy.

Attempting to change the subject, Katherine forced a smile. "You know, Ruth, you should worry about your hearing. When I came in here I could have been any one of your rejected suitors come to kidnap you. I would have had you bound and gagged before you even heard me."

Ruth laughed. "I never hear anything when I'm reading. But I doubt that anyone would be so desperate as to kidnap me. To what do I owe this visit?"

Katherine perched on the edge of the desk and absently looked out the window. The day was not as hot as usual, but lack of rain made the air heavy with dust. For a moment, Katherine watched as shifting patterns of dust and sunlight chased each other beyond the glass. Stifling a sigh, she turned to her friend.

"I was on my way home when I saw your horse outside. I couldn't resist the urge to say hello. What are you doing here anyway? School's out for the summer."

"I need to clean this place before closing it until autumn. As you can tell"— Ruth pointed at the open book in front of her —"I haven't progressed very well with the work. What made you venture into town today?"

Katherine remembered her encounter with Harrison, and a twinge of unease speared her as she answered Ruth. "I came to pay the mortgage."

Her voice must have betrayed anxiety, for Ruth watched her intently.

"Did you have a problem with Foley?" Ruth asked.

"Nothing I couldn't handle."

"Hmm." Ruth looked at her closely, then obviously decided to let the matter drop. "Where did you disappear to the night of the dance? Matt and I searched high and low until the Varner boy told us your horses and wagon were gone."

"Jake and I had enough of the folks from Second Chance. I appreciate your trying to help, but I don't think my presence there did anyone any good. I know I didn't feel any better about my status as a citizen." Her voice sounded petulant, although she was usually nonchalant about other people's opinions of her.

Ruth frowned at her. "What's the matter with you today? Are you sure there's not something you came here to tell me?"

When Katherine didn't answer immediately, Ruth shrugged and went on. "Well, I've been wanting to tell you about Matt. I've never met anyone like him. He came over last night and he'll be coming over tonight. Oh, Katherine, I never believed I'd find someone so right."

Ruth's happiness penetrated the angry, hurt fog in Katherine's mind. She smiled at her friend.

"I'm happy for you, Ruth. I always knew there was someone for you somewhere."

"I've never been able to talk to a man before him. Funny, I've only known Matt a few days, yet it feels like a lifetime. I wonder if that's what love is supposed to be like."

"Love? I wouldn't know about that. Really, Ruth, I think you should wait awhile before talking about love. Not everyone is what they seem to be on the surface."

"I can't imagine Matt lying. He's the most open, honest person I've ever met."

Katherine didn't answer as she looked out the window again, gazing at the distant hills and wondering, despite herself, what Jake was doing.

"How's Jake?"

Ruth's soft question, so close on the heels of her own thoughts, startled Katherine. Returning her attention to her friend, Katherine smiled sadly at the radiant expression on Ruth's face.

## Second Chance

Katherine hadn't the heart to burden Ruth with her own fears and doubts over Jake's disappearance.

"He's fine, Ruth," she lied. "I'd better get back or I'll be late for dinner. You know how Mary is."

Ruth nodded and laughed. "If anyone should be a mother, Mary should. Aren't you lucky she's decided to adopt you as the child she never had?"

"I wouldn't exactly call it lucky, but she means well." Katherine wove her way between the benches and toward the door.

As Katherine mounted her horse, Ruth stood on the porch, worry creasing her forehead. "I can't shake the feeling that something's bothering you, Katherine."

"I'll be fine once I get a little rest." Katherine clucked to her horse and began the trip homeward. "I get enough mothering from Mary, don't you start now," she called over her shoulder.

Ruth's happy laughter grated on Katherine's taut nerves. She kicked her horse and galloped away from her friend, riding hard all the way back to the Circle A.

Thundering into the front yard at top speed, Katherine reined up short. Mary, Dillon, and the men ran out of the kitchen to stare at her in amazement.

"What's wrong?" The volume of Mary's voice caused the horse to shy.

"Nothing." Katherine dismounted, her tone surly. "Why is everyone out here staring at me?" When no one answered, she threw the reins to Joe. "Cool him down," she ordered and entered the house without a backward glance.

Dinner was on the table and Katherine sat down, waiting impatiently until the rest of her crew filed in. Folding her hands, she said grace quickly and commenced eating before the others had picked up their forks.

"You've never ridden a horse that hard for no reason," Dillon said.

"No."

He gave an exasperated sigh. "Well, why was today special?"

"I felt like getting home in a hurry."

"Katherine, that's no excuse for pushing a horse that hard. When we heard you coming we thought the Coltrain Gang was back."

"They won't be back," Katherine snapped.

Dillon shrugged and turned his attention to his plate. The remainder of the meal passed in uncomfortable silence. Katherine was disgusted with herself for allowing her anger and frustration at Jake Banner's betrayal to influence her actions and cloud her judgment.

Attempting to work in the office that night, Katherine found her attention constantly diverted to the window where, in daylight, the distant hills would be visible. The Coltrain Gang had a hideout in those hills that no lawman had ever been able to find. The gang's knack for disappearing under a posse's nose was near legend in Missouri. Even if she wanted to search for

## *Second Chance*

Jake, which she would never do, it would be impossible to find him.

Katherine pushed away from the desk and picked up the lantern, then walked upstairs to her room. Exhaustion tugged at her. Maybe another good night's sleep would cure the inertia that had threatened to overwhelm her since Dillon had told her of Jake's departure. She would never get any work done with her mind and heart in such a turmoil anyway.

Despite the fact that her body was limp with fatigue, Katherine's mind refused to relax. Every time she closed her eyes she saw Jake's face, heard his beautiful voice, remembered something they'd shared. Finally, in desperation she threw back the light blanket and got out of bed. Maybe a walk would clear her head.

Since her wrapper had been lost in the fire, Katherine pulled on her Levi's, tore off her nightdress, and tossed the garment on the bed. She had removed her chemise in preparation for Mary to wash the next day, so Katherine selected one of Sam's old shirts to cover her nakedness. She slid into her boots and strapped on a gunbelt to complete the ensemble.

The night was fresh and clear, the heat from the day still evident but fading. The full moon present on the night of the dance had waned. Katherine walked slowly past the buildings, planning to walk through the near pasture and find the horse she'd abused that afternoon. A few soft words, some stroking along the nose, and she might be forgiven.

The horses were huddled together in the cooling grass. None moved as Katherine approached. Easily finding her quarry, Katherine apologized to the mare.

The murmur of voices broke the stillness of the night. She strained her ears to hear above the sounds of the horses' constant movement. Moving away from the animals, Katherine located the voices emanating from a grove of trees at the far end of the pasture. Who could be having a conversation on her land at this time of night?

Katherine walked softly to the end of the pasture, paused a few feet from the trees, and drew her pistol, listening intently for the sound to be repeated.

"You better have a good reason for sending me that message."

Katherine gasped. There could be no mistaking the hoarse croak of Charlie Coltrain. What was he doing on the Circle A, and who was he talking to? She didn't have long to wait for her answer.

"Course I had a good reason. I ain't stupid," Dillon Swade answered. "Our mutual friend wants you to know the railroad payroll's gonna be on the second train tomorrow, not the first. The trains'll be an hour apart, so let the first one pass. It's just a decoy."

"And how did our friend find this out?"

The sound of Katherine's pistol being cocked echoed in the darkness as she stepped from her hiding place.

## Second Chance

"I'd be interested in finding out a few things about your friend myself, Dillon."

Swade looked at Katherine in surprise, quickly followed by anger. He made a move toward her, but Katherine waved her pistol in warning. "I don't think that's a very good idea. You of all people should know I won't hesitate to use this."

Dillon stepped back, but he remained tense and ready to overpower her at the first opportunity. Katherine kept her eye on Swade while she spoke to Charlie.

"I distinctly recall you telling me I would never have to fear the Coltrain Gang on my place. What are you doing here?"

"You don't need to fear me, ma'am. I'm all alone. I just came to talk to old Swade here. Nothing to get yourself riled about." Although his voice was rough, Charlie made the words seem smooth as silk.

"It sounded to me as though Dillon knows more than he should about the railroad payroll. Would you like to explain how?"

Katherine noticed the two men exchange a glance at her words and knew a moment of unease. Maybe she shouldn't have let them know how much she'd heard. Well, there was no help for it now.

"Ma'am?" Katherine's attention was drawn back to Coltrain. "Jake Banner was telling us what an accommodating woman you are. Maybe you would like to make some extra money by helping the Confederate cause."

Charlie watched her closely to gauge her reaction. But the jolt of pure fury that went through her at the thought of Jake discussing her with the outlaw leader was too strong to be denied.

"Why, that . . ."

Katherine struggled to find a word to describe her feelings for Jake Banner, and in that instant Dillon made his move.

Her gun discharged harmlessly into the air as Dillon knocked her arm violently upward. Before Katherine could regain control of the pistol, Coltrain had jerked the weapon from her hand and pulled her arms behind her back. She heard the gun cock, and the cold muzzle was pressed to her temple. Katherine shivered and closed her eyes.

"No, I don't think so," Charlie whispered in her ear. "Killing women is so un-southern." He chuckled and uncocked the pistol, throwing the weapon to Dillon. "I'll have to take her with me; she knows too much."

Swade looked doubtful for a moment, then nodded his assent.

Katherine gasped in astonishment. "You're just going to let him take me? What about the ranch? Someone will notice I'm missing."

"I'll just tell them you ran off with your Reb thief. Everyone in town's talking about the way you two have been mooning over each other." Dillon's voice was harsh with anger.

"Dillon, that's not true," Katherine said desperately. She struggled against Coltrain until he pulled her arms upward in a vicious twist, causing her to cry out.

Dillon stepped forward uncertainly. "I don't want her hurt."

"I'll look after her myself," Coltrain said as he removed a rope from his saddle and efficiently tied Katherine's arms.

"After this next job is done, me and you'll go away." Dillon looked earnestly into Katherine's face. "Everything will work out for us, you'll see."

Katherine stared at him, amazed. The man actually believed she would go away with him. Hadn't she made it clear to Dillon that his feelings for her were not returned? Obviously she had not.

"You can come an' get her at the river crossing day after tomorrow, Swade. Then you two'd best be on your way west."

Coltrain punctuated the last sentence with a threatening look at Katherine and Dillon in turn. Katherine was amazed that a man whose face must send women swooning whenever he walked into a room could impart evil glances with such ease.

After Charlie mounted his white stallion, he reached down for Katherine, easily lifting her in front of him on the saddle. She did not appreciate the press of his strong thighs against her buttocks or the way his arms went around her to guide the horse. Stiffly, Katherine held her body away from him as far as she could.

Charlie laughed and kicked the horse into

a gallop, effectively throwing Katherine back against him. Dillon shouted something after them, but she could hear nothing over the pounding of hooves. Unable to straighten against the momentum of the horse, Katherine stopped trying and allowed her back to rest against Charlie's broad chest. She flinched away when Charlie's breath stirred the loose hair near her ear.

"I'll have to blindfold you before we get to the hideout."

"Why?" She shouted in an effort to be heard.

"I don't like to kill women. I will, but I don't like it. No one knows where the hideout is except me and the boys. I mean to keep it that way."

She didn't answer, realizing Coltrain was not just trying to frighten her. There was something about his voice, ruined as it was, that made her believe every word he said without knowing him at all.

They continued on in silence, and then Charlie slowed the massive horse. When they stopped, he reached into his pocket and pulled out a bandana. Katherine shuddered as he placed the worn material over her eyes.

"Don't worry, it's clean. I only use this cloth for prisoners." He snorted at his own wit, but Katherine remained silent.

Soon she would be face to face with Jake Banner. A thrill of excitement shot through her before she forced the emotion away and concentrated on anger instead. He had left her secretly, silently, and she would not show him that she cared by word or deed.

The horse began to move again, slowly this time, as they neared their destination. Charlie dismounted and the animal began to carefully pick its way downward. Katherine sensed a feeling of closeness, as though they'd entered a cave.

"It's Charlie."

The words, spoken so close to her in the blind darkness, made Katherine cry out. A hand clamped onto her ankle, and she snapped her mouth shut obediently.

"Who else you got with ya, Charlie?" a suspicious voice shouted from ahead.

"Just a woman who got in the way. We're comin' in."

The horse moved forward, and the closed-in feeling ended, replaced by a humid warmth and the sound of low, rumbling voices.

Suddenly the blindfold was removed, and Katherine blinked in the glare of several lanterns. When her vision had cleared, she saw they were surrounded by nearly a dozen rough-looking men, all of whom stared at her intently. She wasn't so naïve that she didn't realize what those stares meant, and she glanced around frantically for Charlie in the hope he would not throw her to the rabble.

"What the hell is she doin' here, Charlie?"

There was no mistaking the smooth beauty of that voice. Katherine searched the crowd for Jake and found him pushing aside the leering figures until he reached the horse.

"She heard too much while I was talkin' to a friend at her ranch. We'll keep her here until he picks her up after the job tomorrow."

"Did you have to kidnap her?"

"No." Charlie paused long enough to lift Katherine from the horse. "I could have shot her, but I heard she was a Reb. Hate to shoot women, especially when they're Rebs."

Katherine could only stare at Coltrain in astonishment at the casual way he discussed killing women. He noticed her watching him and grinned, then winked before unsheathing a long, wicked knife. Katherine swallowed convulsively and started to back away. But he grabbed her arm and spun her around, cutting her bonds with a single swipe. He pushed her toward Jake and she stumbled into his arms.

"Here, you can watch her." Charlie turned to the others with a stern look. "No one touches her. I gave my word she wouldn't be harmed."

The crowd of outlaws grumbled but began to drift away. Suddenly Bill Coltrain pushed his way through them and blocked his brother's retreat.

"I can touch her and not hurt a hair on her head, brother. Why does Georgia get 'er?"

Katherine's throat went dry when Bill turned his black, snakelike eyes on her. He would never live up to his boast. In the depths of those black pools she saw his need to cause pain. Her hand fumbled for Jake's, clinging desperately.

Charlie looked at both men as though re-

## Second Chance

considering. When he spoke, his gravelly voice shattered the tense air.

"You two have been spoilin' for a fight since Banner first got here. Fight over her then, but I don't want either of you killed. I need you both." He turned to the closest man and shoved him forward. "Make sure neither of them has any weapons." Then he turned and left without a backward glance, obviously uninterested in the outcome of the battle.

Jake removed his hand from Katherine's tense grip and began to unbutton his shirt as Bill did the same. The outlaw chosen by Charlie took each man's gunbelt and ran his hands over them to check for knives. Satisfied, he stepped back and motioned for the fight to commence.

Katherine clenched her fingers as she watched the men circle each other warily. She'd kill herself before she let Bill Coltrain touch her. Just looking at the man made her want to gag. She eyed the two combatants. Jake was the taller of the two, but Coltrain was heavier. Both men were muscular from their rugged outdoor way of life. Katherine prayed Jake knew how to fight. From the scars on Bill's face and chest, he'd obviously had plenty of experience.

Coltrain lunged for Jake's legs, connecting and bringing both men heavily to the ground. They rolled in the dirt, loose rocks cutting into bare flesh, as each grappled for the upper hand. Several punches landed with the sickening thud of flesh striking flesh. Suddenly Jake straddled Bill's chest. He viciously used his hands on Coltrain's face several times before being thrown to the ground. Bill jumped up, kicking Jake in the ribs before his quarry was able to roll away and stand.

The shouts of the other gang members were deafening as they yelled encouragement to the two men. Katherine was disgusted as she watched them bet on the outcome. She returned her attention to the fight as the wagering continued.

The combatants circled each other again, and Jake landed several hard punches before Bill backed off. Coltrain seemed to be tiring: his shoulders slumped and he lowered his fists, shaking his head slowly as though to clear it. Then, with a swift movement reminiscent of a rattler's strike, he reached for one of the bystander's knives and ripped the weapon from its sheath. Dropping to a crouch, knife in hand, Bill crept toward Jake.

Jake backed away slowly, his eyes riveted on Bill. Looking around desperately for a weapon, Katherine's gaze lit on another man with a sheathed knife. Quickly she crossed the distance between them and snatched the weapon. The outlaw turned, making an attempt to retrieve the knife, but Katherine warned him away by brandishing the weapon. He raised his hands in defeat and returned his attention to the fight.

Katherine maneuvered herself closer to Jake.

## Second Chance

When he was far enough from Bill to avoid a lucky swipe, she called out, "Jake, here," and threw the knife in his direction.

Jake looked up and caught the weapon in one hand, spinning quickly to avoid Bill's lunge.

"I said no weapons." The grating voice whispered through the cavern, causing everyone to look up.

Charlie stood on the ledge above them, naked to the waist, golden skin gleaming in the reflected light from the campfire. The sheer physical presence of the man commanded attention, and Katherine drew in her breath at his beauty. Charlie drew his pistol and aimed it first at Jake and then at Bill.

"No," he said as if to himself, "I can't shoot you now. Maybe in a few days." He holstered the gun. "Fight's over. Banner wins."

"I don't think so, Charlie."

Coltrain looked at his brother as though he'd admitted to being a secret Yankee.

"What was that, Bill?"

"I'm not done with him yet."

"You were the first one to take a weapon. You lose the woman since you broke my rule. Bill, you know how I hate it when someone breaks one of my rules." Charlie sounded as though he were speaking to a small child.

"To hell with your rules. I want to finish him." Bill moved toward Jake menacingly.

"Boys." The softly spoken word barely left Coltrain's mouth before ten pairs of guns were cocked and trained on Bill. It was obvious where the loyalty of the gang lay.

Bill's face grew even uglier with anger and frustration. He threw down his knife and glared at Jake.

"I'll finish you, Banner."

"Or I'll finish you," Jake answered.

Bill stalked away, leaving the cavern. The rest of the men holstered their weapons, then dispersed to argue about their bets.

Katherine looked at Jake and saw his attention focused upward toward Charlie. As she watched, Jake nodded to the outlaw leader, who returned the salute and then disappeared into his cave.

"What are you doing here?" Jake asked without turning.

Katherine frowned at the accusing tone. "Charlie kidnapped me."

Jake turned and truly looked at Katherine for the first time that evening. She was startled by the doubt she recognized in his eyes. Why on earth didn't he believe her?

Suddenly he grabbed her by the wrist and dragged her up the steep path at the far wall of the cavern. Katherine saw the other outlaws watching and grinning, a few pointed and laughed. Her face burned in humiliation. They all thought he was about to . . . Well, if that's what Jake planned, he would find another fight on his hands. She began to struggle against his hold, but he only gripped her arm more tightly and yanked her along.

They reached an opening in the cavern wall

# Second Chance

next to the path, and Jake shoved her inside. The interior was illuminated by a lantern; only a bedroll and pack were visible on the floor.

"What's this?"

"My place. Like it?"

"No. I like my own, thank you. Why don't you sleep with the others?"

"I want my privacy." Jake lay on the bedroll, putting his hands behind his head.

"Don't they think you're odd?"

"That bunch? They don't know the meaning of the word. Here, every man lives his own way and takes care of his own hide."

Neither spoke for several minutes. Katherine found herself thinking how handsome he was as he reclined, shirtless, before her. Her gaze wandered over his chest, resting for a moment on the smooth, hard muscles of his stomach. Katherine let out the breath she held and wet dry lips with her tongue. When she realized the direction of her thoughts, she raised her eyes to his. Jake smiled slowly, knowingly.

"Oh, no. You can forget that." Katherine turned away and stood as far from Jake as the small cave would allow.

"What?"

"Get another bedroll. I won't sleep anywhere near you."

"Who said anything about sleep?"

She could hear the amusement in his voice and gritted her teeth.

"If you think I'd let you touch me again after the way you've used me, you're crazy."

"I can understand your being mad that I left in the middle of the night, but I said I'd be back. Why are you acting like this?" Jake's voice sounded genuinely puzzled.

He sat up suddenly, and Katherine flinched but refused to back down from the glare in his green eyes. She had been waiting to talk to him. Now was the time. Katherine took a step forward, hands on her hips.

"Let's see. You sleep with me and lead me to believe you care. Then, the next day, you barely speak to me before sneaking away in the night with my best horse." Katherine ground a loose stone into the dirt with the heel of her boot. "I should have let them hang you."

"I'd hoped that after what we'd shared you would try to be understanding when you read my note. Maybe give me a chance to explain and make things up to you."

She froze at his words, confusion washing over her. What was he talking about? Katherine crossed the dirt floor and stood in front of Jake, searching his face for an answer. His steady gaze made her drop to her knees beside him and look deeply into his eyes.

"What note?"

# *Chapter Fourteen*

As Jake sat up he smelled the scent of roses that always clung to Katherine's skin. His body responded instantly, but he attempted to ignore the reaction and focus on the meaning of her question.

"I left a note on your desk. I said I'd explain everything and pay you back for Lucifer."

Jake reached out to cup Katherine's cheek, reveling in the smooth coolness of her skin. When she didn't respond, he withdrew his hand and searched her face. He saw disbelief and distrust in her eyes.

"Katie, I wouldn't leave you without a word, and I'd never steal your best horse. Someone must have taken the note."

"Who could have been in my office?"

Jake shrugged. "Anyone."

Katherine shook her head vigorously.

"What about Swade?"

"He wouldn't..." Katherine began, then paused. "You might be right. He's gotten it into his head I'm going to go away with him after the next job. I caught him with Coltrain. That's why I'm here."

Jake stood up suddenly and began to pace. "He was talking to Coltrain? What did you hear?"

Katherine looked at him oddly before answering. "Dillon had a message. From a friend, he said. Something about the railroad payroll being on the second train and not the first." She stopped and thought a moment. "I never put things together with all the excitement. Dillon is working with the Coltrains."

"Looks that way."

"And all the time you two acted as if you hated each other." Katherine stared at Jake as though he'd betrayed her all over again. "I was actually worried he might hurt you, and all along you were working with him."

"Now hold on. No one knows who Charlie's contact is, least of all me—the new man. In fact..." Jake hesitated, then went with his instincts, deciding to lay some of his cards on the table. "Swade hinted you two were both working together with Coltrain."

"What?" Katherine's voice squeaked with surprise.

Jake watched her closely as he told her the rest. "I caught Swade with a lot of money one day, and he all but told me you were willing to help anyone if you could make a profit. Then, later, I saw him give you some of the money."

"You were spying on us?"

"Well, yes, I guess I was. Things were so suspicious."

"Dillon gave me the money because he sold some horses, and I paid the mortgage for the month. But you say he had more than what he gave me?"

Jake nodded.

"He must have gotten it from Coltrain." She sighed. "I thought he received an amazing price for those old mares. I wonder if he even bothered to sell them."

Suddenly Jake began to laugh.

"What's so funny about my foreman being a criminal?" Katherine asked.

"I was just thinking about Foley. You paid him his mortgage with money stolen from his own bank." Jake continued to chuckle until Katherine joined him.

"I shouldn't be laughing. What if Harrison figures it out?" she said.

"How could he?"

"I don't like the idea of using stolen money," Katherine said, "even if I wasn't the one doing the stealing." Defiantly she looked up at Jake. "How could you think I'd be involved with a band of outlaws?"

"I don't know. Let's forget it."

"What I can't understand is why you'd care. If I were involved, wouldn't that make me one of you?".

The pieces of the puzzle had begun to fall into place for Katherine. That was the last thing Jake wanted. He believed she wasn't selling information to Charlie to save her ranch, but he still needed to find out who was feeding Dillon the information. An image of Matt arose in his mind, but he pushed the thought away to be dealt with later. Until he learned the whole truth, his mission wasn't over, and Katherine could not be told his identity. The knowledge would be too dangerous now that she was in the midst of the action. Diversionary tactics were called for.

Jake crossed to the bedroll and dropped down next to Katherine, taking her in his arms. He ignored her startled gasp as he pressed his lips to hers. She resisted at first, but as he continued to tease and pull on her lips she relented and opened her mouth in a sigh of satisfaction.

Jake's mouth moved, pressing hot kisses over Katherine's cheek, then on toward her ear. He continued to kiss her, his mind working frantically for a way to keep her thoughts from his interest in Charlie's contact. Tomorrow he'd be riding out to take part in the train robbery; then he'd return Katherine to the Circle A. When he had seen her ride in blindfolded and tied in front of Charlie, he realized how much she meant to him. When this assignment was over he wanted to confess all his secrets and find a place in Katherine's life. Jake only hoped the lies had not gone too deep for his redemption when the time came. If he could stay away from her until the mission was over, he would tell her the entire truth afterward.

"Ahem."

The sound at the cave entrance made Katherine pull away from him sharply. Jake sighed in irritation and turned to face the intruder.

Jeff Soames, the young gang member Jake had aided at the bank robbery, stood sheepishly at the entrance. He looked pointedly in the opposite direction. Jake smiled at the youth's embarrassment, so incongruous in a guerilla raider.

"Something you wanted, Jeff?"

"Charlie wants everyone below. There's been a change in the plan for tomorrow."

"Tell him I'll be right down. Thanks, Jeff."

The youth turned to smile at Jake, admiration plain on his face. Then he tipped his hat and nodded to Katherine before silently retreating.

Jake looked at Katherine and shrugged, then reached out to run his hand through her hair. Her braid had loosened during the ride to the cavern, and the lantern light glistened in the golden strands hanging past her hips. Jake lifted the heavy mass in both hands, enjoying the sensation of the soft, silky texture as it slid through his fingers.

He groaned and forced himself to stand up. "I'm sorry, but I have to go down there."

Katherine gazed up at him, her smoky eyes wide and dark with passion. "He'll only tell you what I overheard about the second train."

"I know, but he may have changed the plan. If anything is even a second off tomorrow, someone could get killed." He walked to the entrance of the cave, then turned with a smile. "I have too much to live for now. I'll be back as quick as I can."

Jake walked down the steep path to the floor of the cave. The image of Katherine remained in his mind—hair unbound, lips swollen from his kisses as she sat on his bedroll, her legs drawn up to her chin. He ached with the desire to return and finish what he had begun.

The gang members stood or sat in a circle around Charlie, but Bill Coltrain was not among them. The meeting turned out to be exactly as Katherine had predicted. Jake ground his teeth in frustration as Charlie informed them of the decoy train and then went over each minute detail of the plan once again. Jake's desire to get back to Katherine became a pressing problem.

"That's enough for now, boys. Get to sleep."

Jake sighed in relief and wasted no time retracing his steps to the cave.

He stopped in the entrance to admire the sight greeting him. Katherine lay asleep on his bedroll, hair spread out in a shining curtain about her head. She'd removed her boots, and the sight of her tiny feet curled toward her buttocks made Jake swallow with difficulty, his throat suddenly thick with emotion. His manhood continued to pulse painfully, but he ignored it, removing his own boots and lying down next to her. He pulled her close, molding his

## Second Chance

body to her curves. Leaving the lantern alight, he too fell asleep.

He dreamed again of Antietam—always Antietam.

The battle raged around him. Men died, loudly, silently—it didn't matter, they were still just as dead. He had learned to ignore the bodies, ignore the terror, ignore the sound, the smell, the horrible heat.

His company tried to overrun the sunken road as unit after unit fell back from the deadly southern fire. Finally some New Yorkers found a place where they could shoot down upon the entrenched Confederates. From then onward, the blood flowed into Bloody Lane. The southern bodies piled up, two then three deep. The enemy ran for survival and their line broke. As he followed his comrades into the Lane, kneeling on top of the ghastly flooring to discharge his weapon at the fleeing men, a stray bullet grazed his head, then blackness descended.

He awoke in the dark to the smell of death. Attempting to rise, he found he could not. Disoriented, he tried again. Something heavy lay on top of him. He tried to roll from beneath the weight, first in one direction and then in another, but a soft, unyielding mass penned him in on either side. The metallic stench of blood filled his nostrils as the memory of where he'd been before he lost consciousness came to him with frightening clarity. Sudden and horrified understanding dawned. Jake struggled violently, pushing with all his strength against the heavy objects weighing him down.

Bodies. Hundreds, no thousands, of dead bodies in the sunken road. Opening his mouth to scream, he found the sound muffled by the body on top of him.

Dark, it was so dark. He had never feared the dark, but he did now. In a last valiant effort to escape from being buried alive, he pushed away the body above him. Immediately another slid onto his chest, pinning him firmly in his grave.

"No!"

Jake sat up, his eyes wide open and staring into . . .

Nothing. Pitch-black nothingness. His ever present nightmare.

But this time he was truly there—in the midst of the bodies at Antietam. He could hear the sound of the shovel throwing dirt over him and the rest of the dead in ever increasing piles.

He took a deep breath and smelled again the death and the blood and the despair. "Let me out," he shouted. "I'm alive!"

"Jake!"

From out of the darkness a hand clasped his shoulder, and he flailed about wildly at his attacker.

"Stop that, Jake. It's Katherine."

The urgent female voice caused Jake to go still. Another dream. Thank God, only a dream this time. He reached out blindly in the blackness of the cave and found her, drawing the

## Second Chance

warmth of Katherine to him. For a moment she resisted and he paused.

He had frightened her with his wild ravings and thrashings. Gently he stroked her, caressing her face lightly and tangling his fingers in her hair until she relaxed. Katherine's arms slid around his waist, hugging him tightly and offering comfort. In her embrace, his thundering heart returned to a normal, steady beat quicker than it ever had on the countless occasions when he'd recovered from the nightmare alone. In the silence that followed, Jake recalled the truth about the night he'd awakened in a Confederate grave.

In his dreams, he could never manage to get past the bodies. In reality he'd pushed them away in disgust and climbed over more dead men to reach the side of Bloody Lane. Night had fallen and the battle was over. He crawled toward the sound of voices and soon found his army, and received medical aid. He told no one of the horror he'd experienced in the sunken road, burying his terror deep within his mind until it only reappeared to haunt him in the dead of night.

The Union Army had waited for daylight and the opportunity to attack and crush the rebellion once and for all. While they waited, the Confederates slipped back across the Potomac, and though the battle was won for the Union, the war continued for three more years.

As for himself, he'd been left with a cursed fear of dark, closed places—not a productive fear for a spy, he'd learned. Only by keeping a lantern burning could he manage to endure his cavern home.

"Did you have another dream?"

Katherine's concerned voice brought Jake back to the present.

"Yes," he answered shortly, tangling his hand in her loosened hair as she nestled under his chin. "What happened to the lamp?"

"I woke up and saw the flame flickering, so I put it out. I'm sorry. I didn't think you'd have a nightmare if I were here."

Katherine snuggled closer, sliding her hand over his chest and stroking him soothingly. His tense muscles relaxed, and the memory of the dream began to fade.

They sat in companionable silence, and Jake found that he didn't mind the darkness with Katherine beside him. The spirits of those dead Confederates didn't haunt him while she lay near. Once his eyes adjusted, he was able to see the doorway of the cave as a lighter shade of black, illuminated by the flickering firelight in the cavern beyond. The closed-in feeling that had grabbed his throat upon waking disappeared.

"Do you want to tell me about your dream?"

Jake hesitated. He wanted desperately to share the horror of his nightmare and exorcise it from his mind, but he could not reveal the truth about Antietam without disclosing his presence in the Union Army. Those revelations would topple the fragile structure upon which all his lies were built. He needed the protection of those lies for himself as well as her. If something happened to him during the robbery the next day, it would be better for Katherine if he died a thief rather than a hero. She could get on with her life more easily if she didn't carry the burden of his secrets. The decision made, Jake leaned over and kissed Katherine's forehead.

"I don't think I can talk about it yet."

"Oh—I understand."

Jake heard the disappointment in her voice, but that was for the best. Her soft palm began to stroke his chest again, and his breathing quickened as she ran her fingers across his stomach. She meant to soothe him, but her fingers worked another sort of magic.

Pulling her head gently away from his chest, Jake lowered his mouth and found her lips. She leaned into the kiss, opening her mouth and making soft noises of encouragement at the back of her throat. He groaned as her quick response sent heat shooting throughout his body.

"Why do you have this effect on me? I can't seem to stay away from you, no matter how hard I try."

"Why try?" Her voice mellowed to a husky whisper as her breath stirred his hair. The sensation caused a shiver to run down his spine.

She kissed his ear, her pointed tongue darting into the cavern; then her mouth trailed a path of hot fire to his neck.

He loosened the buttons of her shirt, pleased to encounter bare skin beneath his touch. The feel of her small, unbound breasts made his shaft thicken and press uncomfortably against his pants. Quickly he slipped the shirt from her shoulders and pushed her back on the bedroll. He caught her hand where it stroked his side and drew her fingers to the buttons he wanted desperately to be free of.

"Help me," he ground out between clenched teeth.

She hesitated, but at the insistence of his hand on hers, Katherine unbuttoned the straining fabric, freeing him to her touch.

He thought he would burst as her small, shy hands stroked him. He could tell she had never touched a man in this way, and the knowledge drove him wild. Controlling his desire to immediately bury himself deep within her, he allowed Katherine to continue her tentative caresses. She drew a fingertip up the length of him, then stroked a circle around his pulsing tip. As she grew more bold, his control wavered. Hastily he removed the rest of their clothing and leaned over her, his aching shaft pressed to the warm juncture of her thighs while he kissed and suckled her breasts, delighting in the way her nipples hardened at the first stroke of his tongue to their rosy tips. When she reached between them, cupping him and urging him forward, Jake lifted his hips and sheathed himself in her softness with a single thrust.

## *Second Chance*

The contact brought a cry of relief from both of them. As they began to move together, he kissed her cheeks, her eyelids, her chin, her nose. Her strong hands clasped his buttocks and pulled him back to her whenever he withdrew. She wrapped her legs around his back and strained toward him. He claimed her mouth as they climbed toward the exquisite ending they both desired.

They climaxed together, each drinking in the other's cries of release and fulfillment.

Afterward, Katherine whispered his name and fell asleep trustingly in his arms. Jake lay awake listening to her steady breathing, hoping that soon there would be truth between them and they could plan a life in which another lie would never be necessary.

They awoke to the shouts of the men in the cavern below. With an appreciative eye, Jake watched Katherine's slow, catlike stretch. That she did not attempt to cover her nakedness was not lost on him. He relished her artlessness, even though her trust was based on untruths.

"We'd better get dressed before someone comes up here looking for us."

Katherine smiled and obeyed Jake's suggestion, picking up his discarded shirt and holding the garment out to him. Jake returned her smile and couldn't resist giving her a chaste peck on the mouth. He didn't dare do anything more or they would end up back on the bedroll.

"Should we leave now or wait until they've gone?"

Jake looked at her in confusion. "What are you talking about?"

"Leaving. We can go back to the Circle A now. You don't have to be a thief. I have a horse ranch, and you're a genius with horses. We'll be a great team." Her face shone with happiness.

Jake gaped at her. His mind searched frantically for a way to tell her he wouldn't be leaving, without wiping the beauty from her features. The task was impossible.

Frustration roughened his voice, making him sound gruffer than he intended. "I have a train to rob. You'll be staying here."

The smile left Katherine's face instantly as her brows drew together in confusion. "But— you don't have to do that anymore."

"Yes, I do. I'm committed to help them. It's too late to back out now."

"You mean there's honor among thieves? I need you at the Circle A."

"And they need me at the train tracks." Jake sighed, then crossed the distance between them to put a hand on her shoulder. "Did you ever wonder why I left the Circle A in the first place?"

Katherine lowered her head before answering. "I thought you'd gotten what you wanted from me and left."

"You know that's not true." Jake swore silently at the pain she must have endured believing he'd used her like a whore. He wouldn't blame her if she never trusted another man. "I care about you, Katie. Too much to let you tie yourself to someone like me. You're a lady. You shouldn't be involved with a criminal."

"Half the men in this country are criminals in one way or another. Don't I get a right to choose who I want to be with?"

Jake admired her strength of will. How could this woman care for him even though she believed him a murderer and a thief? She could teach him many things about the meaning of love and loyalty.

"I don't think it would be right for me to take advantage of your property for myself."

"You can't take from the woman who loves you, but it's all right to steal?"

*Love? She loves me?*

Jake sighed. As much as he wanted to sweep her into his arms and declare his own feelings, such revelations would have to wait. Someday soon she would understand. But, for now, he would have to be blunt.

"I'm staying with the gang. I'm an outlaw. You need to face that fact. I don't know where you've gotten the notion that I'm different from the others. I'm not. I've killed and I've robbed. There're a lot of things I'm not proud of, but I don't lose sleep over any of them."

Jake stared Katherine straight in the eye, daring her to deny the truth of his words. When she faced him defiantly, he knew she did not believe him. He turned from her in exasperation. "I'll take you back to the Circle A after the job's over." Then he left the cave to join the others gathered below. When he reached the cavern floor, he couldn't resist glancing upward.

Framed in the doorway of the cave, Katherine raised her arms behind her head as she braided her hair. The top buttons of her shirt hung open, and he could see pale skin gleaming beneath. She wore nothing under that shirt, and the thought stirred him deeply. Swallowing hard, Jake turned back to the men.

"Rough night, Banner?"

Bill Coltrain's leer in the direction of Katherine made Jake take a step toward him. Infuriated that everyone believed Katherine his private doxy, Jake's hands curled into fists. Before he could take out his fury on Bill, Charlie stepped between them and held up his hand for attention.

"I assume you all know your jobs today." He looked each man in the eye. When no one voiced a doubt, Charlie waved his hand toward the entrance to the cavern. "Mount up."

Jake glowered at Bill Coltrain's retreating back. But now was not the time to deal with the man. He had to focus all his attention on the job. As he went to get his horse, Charlie reached out and grabbed Jake's arm to detain him.

"I told Soames to stay and guard our guest. We don't need her warning the sheriff."

Jake looked up at his cave and saw the sullen-faced young outlaw sitting outside the entrance.

## Second Chance

"He doesn't look too happy about the assignment."

"He's not." Charlie grinned. "But he'd never tell me that."

"Shoulder still botherin' him?"

Charlie nodded. "Don't have time to nursemaid the boy during a job. He'll be more useful here."

Jake agreed, glad someone would be with Katherine. The thought had entered his mind that she might attempt some mischief once they left.

They retrieved the tethered horses from the far side of the cavern, and Jake accompanied Charlie up the narrow passageway into the bright heat of the day.

The others were mounted and ready, the horses dancing with the excitement generated by their riders. Charlie urged his white stallion to the front of the group and spurred the animal into a gallop. Soon a cloud of dust rose from the hooves of the thundering horses and enveloped the riders. Jake glanced back for one final look at the entrance to the cavern and hoped he would return safely to Katherine. With a soft word to Lucifer, he maneuvered the horse forward into the dusty cloud and followed the Coltrain Gang toward destiny.

"Thirteen—fourteen—fifteen—turn. One—two—three," Katherine mumbled as she paced the cave.

She was frustrated and furious. How dare he so casually dismiss her offer of an honest life and then calmly leave to rob a train? The urge to ride after Jake and force him to stop his thieving ways was strong. Unfortunately, that scheming Charlie Coltrain had left a guard. Damn them all!

She needed a plan. "Ten—eleven—twelve." Katherine stopped pacing and slowly walked to the entrance of the cave. The Soames boy still sat dejectedly on the path outside. An idea crept into her mind, and she smiled.

"Jeff?"

"Ma'am?" The startled boy jumped to his feet.

"Do we have to stay in the cave all day?" Katherine offered her sweetest smile and even tried fluttering her eyelashes. She felt utterly stupid, but her crude attempt at flirtation worked.

Jeff gaped at her, then flushed red. "I—I don't think so, ma'am. Charlie just said I was to watch you. He didn't say nothin' 'bout stayin' inside."

"Well, let's go for a ride. I can't stand this place a moment longer."

"Um, I don't know, ma'am."

She stepped close to the boy and put her hand on his arm. "Oh, please. We can just go a little ways and then come back." Katherine paused as if an idea had just occurred to her. "Say, I could show you some fancy shooting tricks I know. Would you like that?"

## Second Chance

Jeff's face lit up so much a shard of guilt pierced her at the duplicity. But when he nodded eagerly and led the way down the path, the guilt faded with the excitement of her victory.

After saddling two horses, Jeff joined Katherine at the entrance to the passageway. He drew a bandana from his pocket and glanced at her sheepishly.

"I'm sorry, ma'am. Charlie's rules. I wouldn't want him to shoot ya because you knew about the entrance."

Katherine nodded, grimacing at the dirt on the cloth. She much preferred Charlie's bandana to Jeff's, but she stifled her distaste and stood still as the boy tied the cloth about her eyes. He fumbled with the knot, and Katherine smiled at his nervousness. The young outlaw was really very sweet, and she wondered at his presence with the roughened riders.

A short while later they were riding toward a clump of trees several miles from the hideout. Upon reaching the grove, Katherine dismounted and waited for Jeff to follow. She pointed at the farthest tree.

"Do you think you can hit that?"

Jeff took out his pistol, aimed, and missed by several inches.

"Here, let me help."

Katherine went behind the boy and placed her hand over his, guiding his aim until he could hit the tree dead center. Jeff was so excited at the prospect of showing the gang his newfound skill, he didn't hear the deadly click by his ear until seconds after it happened. Stiffening, he dropped his pistol.

"Sorry about this, Jeff, but I've got a date with a train. Hope you understand."

# Chapter Fifteen

After binding Jeff securely to a tree, Katherine mounted her horse and raced toward the area where she thought the robbery would take place. There was only one spot where the track curved near a small stream hidden by dense cover. She couldn't think of any other place where a dozen men could hide.

For a moment while she worked with Jeff, she considered heading for town to enlist the aid of the sheriff. But she discarded that plan almost immediately. Jake could get killed, or at the very least, captured again. She didn't think the folks of Second Chance would give him a third chance. If she could only get there ahead of the train, she'd make sure Jake wasn't involved in this robbery if she had to remove him from the gang at gunpoint.

Katherine pushed her horse hard. As she neared the stream, nothing stirred but the hot breeze. Sweat trickled between her breasts, and the sun beat on her bare head. Tomorrow her skin would pay for this folly. Katherine slowed the horse and searched the low bank for any sign of movement. Could she have guessed wrong?

Not a bird twittered. Things were too quiet, unnaturally so. She urged her mount forward. It pushed through the dense brush and, coming upon a stream on the other side, paused to drink. Katherine glanced around the area uneasily, the feeling of being watched increasing with every moment she and the horse stood in the open.

The animal's head jerked upward. Water dripped from the horse's muzzle as its ears pricked forward. Katherine strained her ears to hear what had startled the animal. Several seconds later, the low, steady rumble of an approaching train sounded in the distance.

Suddenly a figure pulled her from the horse and threw her to the ground behind a bush. The gun she'd stolen from Jeff and stuffed into the waist of her pants dug into her stomach as a heavy body pinned her to the earth. Katherine struggled, but a strong arm crushed the air from her lungs and a large hand smothered her mouth.

"Don't even think about screaming."

Katherine knew that rasping whisper as well as her own voice. She had found the Coltrains. Forcing her body to go limp, she nodded to

## Second Chance

indicate her cooperation. Charlie obliged by freeing her mouth but not her body.

"What the hell do you think you're doing here?" he growled in her ear.

"I don't like being left home like a naughty little girl." It was best not to mention her desire to stop the train robbery or let him know she had a gun. She'd look for her chance and take it—if one ever came.

Charlie's arm tightened on her ribs, and Katherine coughed. He eased up on the pressure slightly, though not enough for her to breathe normally.

"I don't like being disobeyed."

"Too late, I've done it."

A heavy silence descended, and Katherine feared she had at last gone too far. When a low chuckle tickled her neck, she turned her head to look at him. He lay next to her, his beautiful face only inches from hers. Thick and soft, his silver-gold hair brushed her cheek, but she did not draw away from him. Instead, she met his gaze levelly, despite the shiver of apprehension gripping her when she looked into his black, emotionless eyes.

"You aren't afraid of me at all, are you?"

Katherine hesitated, then answered truthfully. "Yes, I am. But I won't let fear stop me from doing what I have to do—not anymore."

The whistle of a train caused Coltrain to tense. Then he reached out, parted the brush in front of them, and peered through the dense foliage. Katherine followed his gaze to where the others waited. Two lines of concealing brush grew near the tracks, one close to the stream and another several yards beyond. She had been unable to see past the first level as she watered her horse. Now, as she peered through the brush along with Charlie Coltrain, her gaze sought out Jake.

Not seeing him immediately, she experienced a moment of panic. But as she observed more closely, she saw him mounted on Lucifer. Two other outlaws were also mounted nearby. But why were they on horses when everyone else lay hidden? She did not have long to ponder.

As the train drew closer, Jake gave a whoop. Lucifer and the two other horses surged forward dragging heavy objects behind them. Katherine squinted into the sun, then caught her breath. Railroad ties. The track was now ruined, a wreck imminent, and she turned her horrified gaze toward the oncoming train.

She wanted to jump up and shout for someone to put the ties back, to stop that train, to do something, anything. But it was too late to change the inevitable. Despite the hopelessness of the situation, Katherine must have made some kind of movement toward the tracks, because Charlie grasped her more tightly and shifted his body closer to make sure she couldn't get away.

The engine driver saw the disaster ahead, and the train jerked suddenly, brakes screeching in protest. The locomotive slowed quickly, but not quickly enough. Reaching the portion

## Second Chance

of mutilated track, the engine stopped with a jerk, then toppled sideways like a barn pushed over in a strong wind. The attached cars bumped into each other with a resounding crash—a few slid onto their sides, others remained upright. In a matter of seconds, the Coltrain Gang had reduced the train to a useless heap of metal. Deafening silence followed the wreck.

Charlie must have released her while she watched the train destruct, for when a whirlwind of movement surrounded her she was able to jump to her feet unhindered. The gang members ran to their horses, and, with the Rebel yell, crashed through the brush toward the disabled train. Everyone moved too quickly for Katherine to stop them.

She gasped when Charlie twisted her arm sharply behind her back. "Stay here and keep out of the way. I want as little bloodshed as possible."

Katherine fell when Charlie released her with a shove. She searched for Jake and almost immediately encountered his intense stare. From the look on his face, he was not pleased to see her in the midst of his domain. After a scowl in her direction, Jake cut the ropes and released the railroad ties. Then, wheeling Lucifer toward the train, he joined the others without a backward glance.

The uninjured passengers had climbed out of the wrecked train as best they could and stood in a group with several outlaw guns trained on them. Katherine heard moans and cries from inside the train and stifled the urge to run from the concealing cover of the brush to help the injured. She feared that any more trouble from her would only make the situation worse. And she knew next to nothing about medicine anyway.

The sight of the dazed and frightened people, some with blood trickling down their faces and others with torn clothes, a young woman holding a baby, her face drawn and pale, her eyes round and frightened as she tried to shush her shrieking child, made Katherine cringe with remorse. She should have tried harder to stop this train robbery. Until now, she had merely been trying to keep Jake from getting into more trouble. The reality of the wreck shocked her to her toes.

Charlie walked his stallion close to the passengers, and the horse reared, pawing the air theatrically. The people cringed back and then moved closer together. When the animal's front legs connected with the earth, Coltrain backed him away, then pulled his gun and cocked it. The sound echoed in the forced stillness engendered by fright.

"You folks just stay out of the way and no one gets hurt," he told them. After waiting a moment for his threat to sink in, Coltrain turned his attention to the third car of the train.

Moving close enough so his ruined voice could be heard, Charlie called, "We know the

## Second Chance

money's in the safe. Just throw it out and we'll be on our way."

The third car had tipped onto its side and the door gaped partially open. A man's face appeared through the slit, fear etched on his features as he gazed at the wreck and then at Charlie Coltrain.

"It—it'll take me a minute to open the safe." The clerk withdrew quickly, and no further sound issued from the car.

Katherine glanced toward the rest of the gang and saw they were robbing the passengers. Men's watches, women's jewelry, gold and silver coins, and greenbacks were all tossed into a burlap sack held by one of the outlaws. Jake stood back, watching the passengers closely but not taking part in the robbery itself.

"Do you need help with that safe?" Charlie growled impatiently and motioned for Jake to join him.

Lucifer snorted and pawed when brought near the white stallion. The black beast's teeth flashed, and, cursing, Jake jerked its head away from the other stallion's neck. Charlie's attention was diverted from the train as he also attempted to keep the two horses from tearing each other apart.

From the corner of her eye, Katherine saw the sun flash on the barrel of a gun within the car. Instinctively she reached down and yanked the stolen gun from the waistband of her blue jeans. She fired, thinking only that Jake was in danger.

The clerk cried out, clutched his wounded hand, and dropped the gun. Jake and Charlie turned toward the spot where Katherine lay concealed, their faces reflecting their astonishment. Then, realizing they had a job to complete, the two dismounted quickly and entered the car to collect the money.

Katherine stared at the gun in her hand until Jake rode up next to her. "Get on that horse and ride," he hissed.

The lash of his voice forced her to move, and she caught the reins of her horse as he threw them into her face. Mounting the horse in a swift motion, Katherine followed Jake and the rest of the gang across the rolling hills. When they were well away, she remembered her bare head and knew that every person on the train had seen her pale blonde braid waving like a flag in the sultry summer breeze.

Jake was so furious he didn't trust himself to speak. What was she doing at the robbery? When he'd seen her there it had taken all his control not to grab her and ride away, never looking back.

He could tell that Charlie found the situation amusing. In fact, knowing Charlie, he thought the outlaw would probably offer her a position in the gang since she had saved their lives. Jake looked over at Katherine as she rode next to him and grimaced. How could she look so damned innocent after taking part in a train robbery?

## Second Chance

As they neared the hideout, Jake quickly blindfolded Katherine at Charlie's nod. Once safely inside, he removed the cloth and they unsaddled their mounts without speaking. Both lingered near the horses after the others had gone to divide the spoils.

"I hope you have a good explanation for being out there."

Katherine looked at him, her eyes wide with innocence. "You should be thanking me about now."

"Thanking you? You're the one who ruined my concentration. I would have been fine without you."

"Yes, it looked as though you were just fine."

"I don't need you following me around and watching my back. You're a great shot, I'll admit, but I can take care of myself."

"That's a nice way to treat someone who keeps saving your hide."

"I'm takin' you back to the Circle A, right now," Jake growled then went in search of Charlie.

"Go ahead," the outlaw replied after Jake told him his plans. "I won't say I'm sorry she came, but she's better off at home. The boys won't leave her alone for long."

"I can take care of myself."

The softly spoken words came from behind Jake, and he turned to find Katherine had joined them. She was looking at Charlie with guileless gray eyes, but he was a tough customer.

"I know, ma'am. But sooner or later my boys would start killin' each other over you. I don't have enough men to spare."

Jake took Katherine's arm and tried to lead her away, but she resisted. He stubbornly dragged her toward the horses.

Charlie's broken voice stopped them. "I hope Soames had the brains to blindfold you before he took you outta here."

"Yes, he did. You don't have to worry about your precious secret hideout. I didn't see a thing," Katherine said irritably.

Charlie's eyes narrowed as he stared at her face searchingly. "Well, I suppose I know where to find you if you're lyin'. What did you do with Jeff?"

"Oh, the poor boy," Katherine exclaimed, then bit her lip contritely. "He's tied to a tree about two miles south. Will you send someone to get him?"

Charlie looked at her, and Jake could have sworn he saw the outlaw's face soften. But when Coltrain noticed Jake observing him, the outlaw turned away abruptly. "I should let the young whelp rot. He couldn't even guard a woman."

Katherine opened her mouth to protest, but Jake pulled her away. "Leave it be before you do any more damage," he growled in her ear.

For a moment Jake feared she might fight him, but after a final glance at Charlie, Katherine changed her mind and followed without further comment.

## Second Chance

They rode to the Circle A in silence. Jake wanted to ease the tension between them. He hadn't meant to sound ungrateful, but seeing her at the robbery had struck fear straight through him. He was used to taking care of himself and, maybe, watching a partner's back. He'd never had to fear for a woman he cared about. He found the feeling miserable.

They rode into the yard near dusk as the men were washing for dinner. All eyes stared at them as Jake dismounted and moved to help Katherine. She jumped down without assistance, ignoring his outstretched hand.

"Land sakes, child! We thought you were gone for good. Praise be you're back." Mary's voice echoed in the silent air, then she descended the porch and enveloped Katherine with a motherly hug. She eyed Jake over Katherine's shoulder. "I suppose we have you to thank for this?"

"I wanted her safely home, ma'am. Now I'll be going."

Mary looked puzzled and pulled back to look into Katherine's face. "You mean you didn't run away with him, girl?"

"No, I did not." Katherine looked around the yard. "Where's Dillon?"

"Right here."

Dillon emerged from the house and stood at the top of the stairs. Katherine extricated herself from Mary's embrace, then smiled at the woman reassuringly. "You'd best get inside while I talk to Dillon. Take the others with you and feed them." She waved her hand at the small crowd. "Go on now."

Mary and the ranch hands walked toward the house, looking over their shoulders warily. Katherine smiled and nodded until they had all disappeared around the corner on their way to the kitchen. She faced Dillon with her hands on her hips.

"Why would you tell people such a thing? We both know where I was and how I got there."

Dillon shrugged, his gaze remaining on Jake as he spoke to Katherine. "It was a good explanation since you were both gone. That way no one would come looking for us when we left for our new life."

"I'm not going anywhere with you, Dillon." Katherine spoke quietly but firmly.

Confusion passed across his features as he looked at her. "Yes, we're going west. Don't you remember?"

"No. I'm not leaving the Circle A. But I think you should."

Jake drew his pistol from the holster, deciding the time had come to enter the exchange.

"You heard the lady, Swade. Get packing." He cocked the gun and pointed it at the former foreman.

"But you need me to help with the Circle A." Dillon's voice revealed his uncertainty.

"I can manage on my own now. The men trust me. I've let you stay this long out of gratitude, but no more. I want you off my place tonight."

## Second Chance

Swade shook his head in disbelief, but Jake moved forward, motioning toward the bunkhouse with the gun. Dillon preceded him, but stopped abruptly and turned to glare at Katherine.

"All right, I'll leave. But I know you'll come begging for help soon enough. We were meant to be together. I knew it the first time I saw you. Even if you are too uppity for your own good, I can fix that. You'll learn soon enough that you need me. And when you do, I'll be waiting."

Jake saw Katherine wince at the hateful tone behind Dillon's words. Wanting to spare her any further dealings with a man he believed was half-crazy, Jake moved forward and pressed the barrel of his gun against the former foreman's back.

"Get movin', Swade. The lady wants you gone and I mean to see that she gets what she wants."

"You've already given her what she wants as far as I can see," Swade sneered and made a move as though to turn around.

Katherine's gasp was almost muffled by the sound of Jake cocking the gun.

"Get inside, Katherine. You don't have to listen to him. I'll take care of it."

"I don't want him hurt, Jake. Just make him leave."

The weariness in her voice caught Jake's attention, and he hesitated. Usually she had a surplus of spirit and would not have allowed such a remark as Swade had just made to pass unchallenged. When she turned away and climbed the steps to the house slowly, entering without looking back, Jake grew even more worried.

"Move," he said and shoved Swade with the gun barrel.

"I won't let this pass, you know," Swade said conversationally as they crossed the distance to the bunkhouse.

"What?"

"This insult. I'll make you both pay."

"Hurt her and you're dead." Jake clenched his teeth against the fury pounding in his head at the thought of Swade paying Katherine back when he wasn't around to protect her. The desire to shoot the man was so strong he had to uncock the gun to remove some of the temptation.

"Who's gonna kill me?" Swade laughed. "You? I doubt you'll be alive long enough to manage that."

They entered the bunkhouse, and Jake stood by with his gun poised while Dillon packed his belongings.

"I'm not dead yet," Jake said.

Dillon looked up from his careless packing, and Jake frowned at the certainty in the man's eyes. "No, but you soon will be."

"Why's that?"

"Men like you always end up dead one way or another. If the law doesn't get you, someone else will. It's only a matter of time."

## Second Chance

Jake had to agree with him, for such was often the case in the life of an outlaw. He only hoped he would no longer be an outlaw when fate caught up with him.

Swade stood in the doorway holding his things. "Tell Katherine I'll be waiting."

"Over my dead body, Swade."

"I'm counting on it," he said, and then he was gone.

Jake remained in the bunkhouse alone for several moments after he heard Swade ride away. He hated to leave Katherine alone with that man out there somewhere, obsessed with her and the Circle A and what he believed was his by rights. But he had to get back to the Coltrains and finish what he had started. If he didn't, Katherine and Second Chance would never be safe again.

Katherine entered the kitchen and sat in her chair. Every bone in her body ached, and she was more tired than she'd ever been. The confrontation with Dillon had shaken her more than she wanted to admit. Though irritating, she had always believed Dillon Swade a capable hired man. But his parting words made her wonder about the stability of his mind.

She looked around the table and saw Mary and the crew staring at her questioningly over their half-eaten suppers. She would have to tell them something.

"Dillon will no longer be working with us." Katherine ignored the frowns on the men's faces and plunged on. "I caught him selling information to Charlie Coltrain the other night."

An outraged murmur arose from the crew, and Mary gasped. "Shouldn't we get the sheriff?"

Katherine waved her hand dismissively. "I just want to forget this ever happened. I've sent Dillon away and I'd rather not bring Jessup into it." The men nodded their agreement. They understood the unwritten code of the West—take care of your own problems whenever you can and leave the law out of it.

"Where've you been, girl, if you weren't with Banner?" Mary asked.

"I . . . I was out checking boundaries. Had a problem with my horse, and Jake helped me."

Mary stared at her hard. "Um, hmm," she muttered, obviously unconvinced.

Overpowered by weariness, Katherine didn't reply. A glance at the men told her they'd returned to their meals without further questions. She pushed away the plate of food Mary had set in front of her and stared out the window. When Jake stepped in the back door, her eyes met his and he nodded.

"I'd like to talk to Jake alone, please."

The others filed out quietly as Mary continued to clear the table.

"Go home, Mary. Leave that for tomorrow."

Mary hesitated, but seeing Katherine's determined look, she nodded and left the room. The front door closed, leaving them alone.

## Second Chance

"Is he gone?"

"Yes. I stayed with him until he rode away. I think you should make sure you have one of the men with you for the next few weeks and carry your gun. I don't trust Swade."

Katherine nodded. "Thank you for dealing with him. I would never have asked you, but I'm so exhausted. I don't think I could have coped with him tonight."

Jake sat down next to Katherine. His large hand reached out and covered hers where it lay listlessly on the table.

"I'm sure you can cope with anything life dishes out to you. You've dealt with a fire, been kidnapped, and taken part in a train robbery all in the space of a few days. I'd say you could use some peace and quiet."

Katherine turned her palm up and clasped his hand. "You're probably right. What will you do now?"

Jake turned his head to look out the window. When he turned back, he met her gaze squarely.

"I mean to give you some peace and quiet."

His soft southern tones touched a cord of memory in Katherine, and her melancholy increased. She looked into Jake's face and saw a matching regret. But she also recognized his determination. He was truly going to leave her alone.

"Will I ever see you again?"

"You can count on it, ma'am."

The thought occurred to her that she might see him in a pine box or at the end of a rope—if she saw him at all. Katherine stared at Jake long and hard, memorizing his strong, bronzed face. She would never forget the piercing green eyes, his lilting southern way with words, or the touch of his hands and mouth. Their time together would live on in her mind for the empty nights to come.

"Well." Katherine got up briskly, hoping he didn't notice the wetness at the corners of her eyes. "You'd best be getting on your way."

When Jake didn't answer, Katherine looked up. Before she could grasp his intent, Jake's mouth descended on hers. Her hands went up to rest on his shoulders as his arms went around her waist. He lifted her from the ground, and probed at her lips with his tongue. She opened her mouth and met the thrust fiercely with her own. The kiss held all the passion of the last few days, yet it was oddly gentle with the sorrow of parting. When he removed his lips from hers and set her gently on the floor, she could see he'd been as deeply affected by the embrace as she.

He reached out a hand to touch her cheek, and Katherine brought her own hand up to cup his. She pulled Jake's palm to her lips and kissed the rough center. Katherine heard him catch his breath, then he stepped back and headed for the door.

## Second Chance

"Believe that I'll be back, Katie."

Then he was gone.

Katherine continued to stare at the door long after Lucifer's hoofbeats retreated into the distance. She didn't care what Jake was or what he had done. She loved him. She would believe in that love and pray for his safe return.

She ascended the stairs slowly, the heaviness of her limbs threatening to overwhelm her before she reached the bedroom. Stumbling through the door, she dragged off her dust-encrusted clothes and left them in a heap on the floor. She fell into bed, pulling up the quilt to cover her naked form.

The men's shouting outside her window awakened Katherine the next morning. From the angle of the sun streaming brightly across her bed, the time must be midmorning. Katherine couldn't remember when she'd last slept past sunrise. Why hadn't Mary awakened her?

When she threw back the covers, her unclothed state confused her. Spying the pile of clothes on the floor, she remembered her exhaustion of the previous evening. She also recalled the parting with Jake and realized why her heart lay so heavily in her chest this morning, despite the promise of a bright new day.

Quickly donning her blue day dress, Katherine re-braided her hair and pinned it on top of her head. She reached for her husband's hat, hesitated, and picked up her nearly unused sunbonnet instead. She would have to venture into town today for the weekly supplies. After last week's trip, the thought held no appeal.

Mary's too loud voice greeted her as soon as she stepped foot in the kitchen. "I didn't want to wake you. Last night when you came in here you looked like you were at death's door." The housekeeper studied Katherine from head to toe, beaming approval. "The sleep must have done you good; the roses are back in your cheeks. And the dress does wonders for your figure."

Katherine knew Mary's low opinion of her usual choice of male attire and merely smiled at the compliment. "I'd better get into town for the supplies so I can get back and help. With Dillon and Jake both gone, we'll be short-handed."

Mary nodded. "Maybe you can look into hiring someone while you're there."

"I'll try," Katherine said, though she doubted her luck would come in on that score. Since the war it seemed as though every able-bodied man willing to work had gone farther west. Missouri was fast becoming settled—not wild enough for the younger crowd. Though with the Coltrain Gang running around, she couldn't understand how anyone could think the area too civilized.

Some of the men were breaking colts in the near corral. Katherine waved to them, thinking how easy Jake had made the task look. She walked to the pasture and sweet-talked two mares into joining her, then led the animals

## Second Chance

back to the yard and hitched them to the wagon.

Katherine's clothes were damp by the time she arrived in town, causing her to curse the humid Missouri heat as she did every day.

Second Chance seemed unusually quiet, even for a weekday. As she tied the horses in front of the general store, the sound of footsteps on the wooden walkway echoed in the still air. Katherine looked up to encounter the condescending gaze of Harrison Foley. He smiled humorlessly and held out his hand to assist her onto the walkway.

She ignored the gesture, lifting her skirts and stepping up next to him.

"I heard you left us."

Katherine narrowed her eyes, knowing where he'd gotten the information. "As you can see, I'm still here. You won't get your hands on the Circle A so easily."

Foley frowned at her bluntness. He liked to skirt around business issues politely, and her outspokenness made him uncomfortable. She loved making him uncomfortable.

"There was a train robbery yesterday."

Katherine had turned to enter the store but froze at his words. She attempted to answer in a steady tone. "How interesting. I suppose the Coltrains are responsible."

"Of course, my dear, who else? But there was a fascinating development you might like to hear. It seems they had a woman with them— a blonde woman who could shoot very well.

Unfortunately, no one saw her face." Foley smiled without humor. "Where did you say you were these past few days?"

"I didn't." Katherine's throat was thick with tension as she left Foley and entered the general store.

The place was deserted, and she wandered through the merchandise without seeing any of it. She'd known her hair would be like a beacon without a hat. At least no one had seen her face, so they had no proof. But she had no explanation for her whereabouts over the past few days. She wouldn't put it past Sheriff Jessup to throw her in jail to appease the town, which must certainly be in an uproar over the latest robbery. The sudden urge to take care of her purchases and get back to the Circle A before Jessup found out she was in town consumed her.

Returning to the front counter, she looked around the store for the owner. When he appeared several minutes later, his hostile stare told her that the news of the robbery was common knowledge.

"I've a list of supplies I need." Katherine held out the paper Mary had given her.

"We're all out."

"But you haven't even looked at it."

"We're out of everything you need."

Katherine sighed in exasperation. This was the only general store in town. If she couldn't get her supplies here, she'd have to go to another town. The day's trip was wasted.

## Second Chance

"I'd just like to conduct my business and leave. Then you won't be bothered with me again."

"We're all out." Since the man wouldn't even look her in the face but stared somewhere past her left shoulder, Katherine's pleading gaze had no effect. She drew in her breath to try one more time, when a voice from the doorway interrupted her.

"Mrs. Logan, could you step over to the jail for a few questions?"

Damn. Jessup had found her.

# Chapter Sixteen

Katherine straightened her back and took a deep breath. Perhaps she could throw Jessup off with a show of innocence. Turning slowly to face the sheriff, she smiled.

"I don't know what you'd want to ask me, Sheriff, but I'll be happy to come with you."

The storekeeper made a sound of derision, but Katherine ignored him and swept regally past Jessup, preceding the sheriff through the door and across the street to the jail. As she walked through the dry dirt, Katherine saw countless faces at store windows peering toward her in curiosity. The knowledge only made her back straighter and her steps more measured. Her days of cowering were over.

The sheriff reached past her to open the door, and Katherine entered the relative coolness of

## Second Chance

the darkened jail. The place was deserted, the rabble-rousers confined from the weekend having been released after a stern warning. Jessup indicated a chair in front of his desk, and Katherine inclined her head in thanks as she seated herself.

She would fare best if she was on the offensive, so Katherine opened the conversation immediately. "I hope you have a good reason for bringing me in here with the whole town watching." She looked him full in the face, struggling to keep her cool mask in place against the panic inside her. *Could he know something specific about the robbery?*

Jessup sat down and leaned back against the wall, observing her for a moment. Although she wanted desperately to move, Katherine forced herself not to squirm as he examined her.

"There was a train robbery yesterday."

"Yes, Mr. Foley told me. I hope no one was injured."

"A railroad employee was shot in the hand. But I guess you'd know about that, wouldn't you?" Sheriff Jessup's eyes never wavered from her own.

Katherine pretended confusion. "How could I? Foley didn't mention any shooting."

The two front legs of Jessup's chair hit the floor with a crash, and Katherine jumped despite herself.

"Come on now, Mrs. Logan. A light-haired woman was seen riding away with the gang after shooting the employee from her cover behind some brush. You aren't going to tell me that woman wasn't you. We both know better."

"Do we?" she drawled, doing her best imitation of Aunt Charlotte—the most southern, southern belle Katherine had ever encountered in Virginia. "I have no idea what you're talking about."

"Can you tell me where you've been the past few days?"

"Certainly. I was riding the boundaries of the Circle A, checking fence repairs and such."

"Was anyone with you?"

"No. I went alone."

Jessup sighed and leaned back in his chair. "Then you have no one to back up your story."

"I didn't think I'd need a witness when I rode on my own land."

The sheriff looked at her closely when he asked his next question. "Dillon said you ran off with that Banner fella."

Katherine stared back coldly, as if the very idea was too odd to be contemplated. "Mr. Banner left the day before I did. We did not leave together, as anyone on the Circle A can tell you."

"Why didn't anyone know where you'd gone?"

Katherine thought quickly, hesitating only a second before answering. "I decided to leave after everyone was asleep. I left a note but, obviously, it was misplaced."

## Second Chance

"None of this story you're telling me can be proved, ya know."

Katherine studied the sheriff long and hard, pleased when he began to squirm under her scrutiny. She smiled without humor.

"Can you disprove it?"

Jessup made an exasperated sound and got up to pace the room. He stopped abruptly next to Katherine's chair and glared down at her.

"I can get Swade in here. He'll swear you went with Banner."

"Mr. Swade has left town. When you find him, I'll be happy to answer any accusations he makes." Katherine thanked her guardian angel she'd sent Dillon away instead of turning him over to the law.

"I have a gut feeling you were at that train robbery," Jessup said angrily. "That's the word around town, too. If you think you had it rough here before, well, I wouldn't want to be in your shoes now."

"That's my worry, Sheriff. May I leave?"

"I suppose so."

Katherine headed for the door and Jessup opened it for her. "I'd appreciate it if you didn't go off on any more sudden inspections. I may need to find you again real soon."

"I'll do my best."

Katherine stepped into the bright sunshine, continuing to hold herself stiffly upright. The eyes of the town remained upon her. Returning to the wagon, she climbed in and clucked to the horses.

On the way out of town, Katherine impulsively turned into the schoolyard at the familiar sight of Ruth's buggy. She found Ruth at her desk; Matthew Rolland perched on its edge as he leaned over the blushing schoolteacher. Katherine hesitated in the doorway, feeling like an intruder.

Matt turned at that moment and saw her, a welcoming grin lighting his face.

"Look who's here." He got up and motioned for her to join them.

"Katherine, I was worried about you," Ruth cried, hugging her.

"You should know better than to worry about me. I always turn up eventually."

"Where were you?"

Katherine noticed Matt watching her intently, but when she looked at him he merely smiled and returned his attention to Ruth.

"Just checking fence repairs. I do it all the time. No one ever got so upset before."

"When Dillon came into town telling everyone you'd gone off with Jake Banner, I didn't know what to think."

Katherine rolled her eyes. She hadn't known Dillon would be so vocal with his news. It was no wonder the entire town believed her to be a train robber.

"Jake left long before I did. From what the sheriff just told me, the man's been busy."

"According to the sheriff, so have you," Matt said.

"Do you believe everything you hear?"

## Second Chance

"Not always. In this case, I wonder." Matt smiled at her slyly.

"Oh, Matt. If Katherine says she wasn't with Jake, she wasn't. Stop teasing."

Immediate guilt enveloped Katherine as Ruth defended her. The lies came so easily, she was beginning to believe them herself. In this case, Katherine rationalized, Ruth was better off ignorant of the truth. Jessup was sure to be nosing around, and it was only a matter of time before he decided to question Ruth. Katherine had no wish for her friend to have to lie.

"So what brought you to town?" Ruth asked.

"Supplies. But it looks as though I'll have to go to Danville for them tomorrow."

"Whatever for?"

"The townsfolk have decided an outlaw's money isn't good enough."

"Oh, no!"

Ruth sounded so distressed, Katherine smiled.

"Really, Ruth, it's not the end of the world."

"I hate the way everyone treats you. I get angry whenever I think of it." Ruth paused, an idea lighting her face. "Matt could go get your supplies and bring them out later. It would be fun to beat them at their own game."

"Sure, Katherine. Give me a list and I'd be happy to."

"Well, maybe just this once. I can't have you doing this every week, Matt."

"It's no trouble."

## Lori Handeland

He took the list from her outstretched hand, glanced over the scrap of paper, then placed it in his coat pocket. He really was a very nice man. Not dangerous or exciting like Jake. But nice. Pleasant. Dependable. Perfect in every way for Ruth. She stole a glance at her friend and found Ruth looking at Matt with an expression Katherine was now able to recognize. Ruth Sanderson was in love.

As Matt got up to leave, Katherine saw the same expression on his face when he looked at Ruth. It warmed her heart that her friend had found happiness.

"I'll bring your supplies out early this evening."

"Don't rush. I appreciate your help."

With a nod and a wave he disappeared out the door. Katherine turned to her friend with a knowing look.

"I see that you two have eyes only for each other."

"It's funny," Ruth answered, "I met him only last week, yet I feel as if I've known him for years."

"I know the feeling," Katherine replied softly, glancing out the window toward the hills.

"I heard Jake's gone back to the Coltrains."

"Yes. He felt he belonged with them."

"What do you feel?" Ruth asked.

Katherine sighed and turned to her friend. "I don't know. I offered to let him be a part of the ranch and my life. He turned me down. He would rather rob banks and get shot at than have an honest job. What can I do?"

"Will you see him again?"

"I don't know. When he left he told me to have faith in him. What does that mean?"

Ruth shook her head. "I'm sorry life's so complicated for you. I wish things could be as peaceful and joyous as they've been for me since Matt came into my life."

Katherine went over and placed her hand on Ruth's arm. "Don't worry about me. I'll see this through. But with this latest development in town, I must say I'm tempted to return east."

"No, Katherine, don't. Give Jake a chance to come around. You'll be wondering about him for the rest of your life if you leave now."

"The next time he comes into town might be in a pine box. I don't think I could stand that."

"Worry about that if it happens, not before. I've never known you to be a coward. Don't start now."

Katherine's spine straightened at the mention of the word "coward." The day Sam died she'd promised herself never to cringe or cower again. Ruth was right. She wouldn't slink away without a fight.

"Well, I'd better get back to the Circle A. With both Jake and Dillon gone, there'll be a lot of work to do."

Ruth frowned. "What happened to Dillon?"

"I fired him. He went too far when he told everyone I ran away with Jake. I hope I never see him again."

"I'll come out in a few days and see how you're doing," Ruth said, walking Katherine to the door.

Ruth waved as Katherine drove the wagon from the schoolyard. She envied Ruth's future. Her friend could look forward to a stable husband and children. Katherine's stomach tightened with want, but children were beyond her reach. She'd learned to live with that truth. The ranch would receive all her unused motherly instincts. Katherine had learned that by working hard she would drop into bed at night exhausted, shoving aside the longing for other things. The feelings were still there, but they became buried beneath the physical demands of life.

After arriving home, Katherine spent the rest of the day outside. As she worked side by side with the men, they teased her good-naturedly, accepting her as one of them. The lighthearted talk helped to keep her mind off her problems.

Shortly after supper, Matt Rolland drove a wagon of supplies to the front of the house. Katherine invited Matt into the parlor and set the men to work unloading the wagon.

She sat down in a chair across from Matt. "I can't thank you enough for helping me. Next week I'll send one of the men or go to Danville myself."

"No trouble. If you need anything else, let me know. A bachelor living in a boardinghouse has little to occupy his time after working hours."

## Second Chance

"I'm sure you find things to keep busy."

Matt's cheery face split with a grin. "When I came to Second Chance, I had no idea how busy things could be."

"Ruth's a lovely person."

"You won't get any argument from me."

"I'm glad she's found someone to appreciate her at last. I've always felt she deserved the best—someone straightforward, upstanding, honest."

Matt got to his feet abruptly. Startled, Katherine looked into his face. "Is something wrong?"

"No—no. I just realized how late it's getting. I'm supposed to have supper at Ruth's and, knowing her, she's already got the food on the table. I should be on my way."

Matt left without further conversation, but Katherine had the uneasy feeling she'd said or done something to upset him. For the life of her, she couldn't think what that could be.

Jake was not in a good mood. All evening he'd sat brooding by the cookfire, sipping a cold cup of coffee. Damn Dillon Swade. He'd planned to question the man about his involvement with the Coltrains, find out if Swade was the only contact, or merely a messenger boy, and if so, learn who called the shots. Jake had been looking forward to extracting the information from Dillon, by whatever means necessary. But when he'd tried to follow the man's tracks, the bastard had disappeared.

Jake stared into the flames, ignoring the other men's calls for him to join the gambling. He had no desire to be social. The one desire he did feel, for Katherine, was the second reason for his black mood.

His mind wandered back to the previous evening. Upon returning to the Coltrain camp, Charlie had met him at the entrance.

"Everything go all right?"

Jake looked at the outlaw oddly, wondering why Coltrain was so interested. Nodding, Jake attempted to walk toward his cave.

"Did you see anyone?"

Jake turned back and sighed. Obviously Charlie had his own reasons for the questions. He always did. If Jake wanted to get some sleep, his best bet would be to answer the questions now.

"Sure I saw people. I took her to the ranch."

"That Swade character still there?"

*So that's why he's so interested, he wants to see if his contact is still around.*

"He was there when we arrived," Jake said. "But not anymore."

Charlie's face turned dark with fury. "Why the hell not?"

"Mrs. Logan fired him. She didn't want a traitor on her ranch."

"Damn and blast the woman. I knew she'd be nothing but trouble the first time I saw her."

"Some of them are worth the trouble," Jake mumbled.

Charlie looked at him sharply. "Not to me. I should have shot her when I had the chance."

## Second Chance

"That wouldn't have been wise." Jake's voice was cold, deadly; his hand rested on the butt of his gun.

Charlie looked him in the eye for a long time. "Relax, Banner, she's fine and I won't touch her. I'm just hoppin' mad about Swade. Now that he's out of a job, he'll probably take off west and that's the end of my easy contact."

Jake was surprised Coltrain had admitted Swade's status outright. *Maybe he's beginning to trust me. Now is the time to see if I can discover more.*

"How did Swade find out about the railroad payroll anyway? He's just a ranch foreman."

Charlie answered as though he were talking to himself. "At least the one with the inside story is still in place. I'll have to meet with him directly. Whether he likes it or not."

Charlie strode away from Jake without another word or glance. Did the outlaw realize he'd spoken out loud?

Coltrain spoke with Jeff Soames, and the boy nodded his understanding, then saddled up and left the cavern.

Now, the following evening, Jake sat with his coffee, trying to figure out a way to learn the name of the other contact. Charlie would not volunteer the information on his own, and the outlaw was too clever to let anything slip even under subtle questioning. Jake would just have to follow Coltrain when he met the informant. That meant watching Charlie around the clock.

If Jake missed his chance, he would have to pose as an outlaw for who knew how long—an idea he did not find appealing. He wanted to end this mission so he could tell Katherine the truth.

A commotion at the entrance commanded Jake's attention, and he turned in time to see Dillon Swade lead his horse from the darkened opening. Jake's cup of coffee dropped to the dirt unnoticed as he jumped to his feet and headed in Swade's direction.

Charlie and several of the other men had already gathered around Dillon when Jake arrived.

"What's he doin' here?" Jake demanded.

"Good question." Charlie looked at Dillon expectantly. "Well, Swade, answer the man."

"I don't have no place else to go. Besides, you owe me money, Coltrain."

"I'll give you your money, then get out."

The surprise on Dillon's face gave Jake a measure of satisfaction. After the man had dealt with Coltrain right under Katherine's nose, Jake was happy to see him pay for his duplicity. Dillon would most likely head west to make his fortune—a very pleasant idea, to Jake's way of thinking.

"Why should I leave? I'm as good a rider and shot as the rest of the boys."

Swade walked close to Charlie, grabbing his arm to command attention. Jake drew in his breath sharply, as did several of the other men. Charlie didn't like to be touched.

## Second Chance

Coltrain looked down at the hand on his arm and then pointedly looked at Dillon. Unfortunately, Swade was too upset to heed the warning. Charlie was quick as a snake when he struck. Jake never saw him draw the knife until Dillon cried out and clutched his hand.

"Don't ever touch me." Charlie's ruined voice grated deeply in anger before he returned the knife to his belt.

Dillon wrapped his hand in a bandana. The wound was not serious; it was only meant as a warning.

Charlie gestured to his brother, and Bill Coltrain reached into his pocket to withdraw a small canvas bag. Charlie reached for the pouch, then threw it to the ground at Dillon's feet.

"Here's your share. Ride out tonight. I don't want your kind around."

"We've been dealing together for the past year and you never had no complaints. What's the matter now?"

"I need men who are loyal to their leader. Not someone who torches his boss's barn for money."

Dillon's face registered surprise at Charlie's knowledge. The expression was wiped off his face, however, when Jake knocked him to the ground.

The fury coursing through Jake at Charlie's revelation could not be contained. "You low-life traitor. She trusted you," he growled as he rolled in the dirt with Dillon, pummeling him unmercifully. The men moved back to allow the fight to continue.

Dillon weighed less, but his stocky figure packed work-hardened muscles. After the initial moment of surprise, he began to give as good as he was getting.

Their punches were vicious, all their suppressed hate at last finding a release. Before long, each sported a bloody nose, their knuckles torn and bruised. They clambered up from the ground and circled each other looking for a weak spot.

Dillon's hand wasn't badly hurt by the knife, but maybe he'd be a bit slower on that side. Jake feinted to the right and then the left. When he went right, Swade was somewhat slower. Jake circled again, then moved in to Swade's weak side with several hard and swift jabs to the man's face and body. Jake continued to take the advantage until his arms were grabbed from behind and someone pulled him away.

Jake continued to struggle against his captors until Charlie's voice broke sharply through the commotion. "I said, it's done. Banner, clean yourself up. Bill, throw Swade outside and make sure he's on his way."

Jake watched as Bill and another man dragged the nearly unconscious Dillon Swade out of the cavern. Jake shook off the men holding him and went to his cave to be alone.

Entering the small chamber, he sat down on his bedroll, beginning to feel the many aches that would become bruises by morning. He

## Second Chance

should have left Swade alone. Charlie was getting rid of him, and he would never have had to deal with the man again. But anger had outweighed common sense when he heard that Swade had burned Katherine's barn. Besides, it had felt so good to smash Swade senseless. He'd been dying to do just that from the first moment he met the man.

The blood from his nose had dried on his face. He'd have to go out to the stream and wash up. The men had returned to their gambling as Jake made his way down the path. He decided to take Lucifer and let the animal have some fresh grass for a change. No one paid him any attention as he walked to the entrance. The light in Charlie's cave told Jake the outlaw had retired to his own domain.

The night air was pleasant after the warm closeness of the cavern. Jake rode the short distance to the stream and let Lucifer graze in the prairie grass. Removing his clothes, Jake waded into the shallow water and sat down to relax. The cool, moving water soothed his bruises and washed away the blood.

His mind wandered back over the events of the evening. Suddenly he sat up, an idea searing his mind. If Dillon had burned the barn for money, who had paid him and why? Also, how had Charlie known of Dillon's actions? Dillon had obviously been surprised at Charlie's knowledge. That could only mean that Charlie's contact and the man who had paid Dillon were one and the same. Whoever had information about the railroad payroll was also interested in the Circle A.

*Harrison Foley. How could I have been so blind?*

Maybe because he'd been distracted by gray eyes and an alabaster complexion. Jake clenched his fists in frustration. Matt was right. He had no business falling in love with Katherine; it clouded his mind. As if he would have been able to stop himself.

Jake stepped out of the stream, drying himself with his shirt. As he dressed, the sound of approaching horse's hooves drifted to him on the night wind. Jake hurried to his horse and covered its nose so Lucifer wouldn't call to the approaching horse. The night rider did not slow as he passed the stream, but Jake could not help recognizing the shadowy figure. There was only one massive white stallion ridden by a man with golden hair.

Charlie was on the move.

# Chapter Seventeen

Jake followed Charlie, allowing the other man to get as far ahead as he dared without losing him. The outlaw was sharp and would be sure to spot him if followed carelessly. Charlie skirted the town of Second Chance and headed toward the site of the train robbery. There Jake saw him dismount.

Jake left Lucifer several hundred yards away from the familiar grove of trees and silently crept to the edge of the brush on the banks of the stream. Peering through, he observed Charlie at the water's edge, his hand resting on his horse's neck as the stallion drank deeply. Then, allowing the horse to graze, Charlie sat and leaned against a tree. The outlaw's eyes closed and he appeared to sleep.

Jake didn't know how long he lay on the hard

ground. He began to think Charlie had slipped away from the cavern for some solitude rather than to meet a contact when the sound of an approaching horse met his ears.

Charlie didn't move or open his eyes, and Jake drew his gun. It wouldn't do for the outlaw to be shot by a roving thief before Jake had the chance to turn him over for a hanging. To be honest, he'd begun to admire the way Coltrain commanded men, even if he did live on the wrong side of the law.

Spraying leaves and twigs in every direction, a horse and rider crashed through the brush on the far side of the stream. The moon was behind the horse and rider, so Jake could see nothing but a silhouette until they crossed the water and stopped in front of the reclining Coltrain.

Jake smothered an exclamation of disbelief as Matthew Rolland dismounted.

"Coltrain, I didn't ride all the way out here in the middle of the night to watch you sleep."

Charlie opened one eye, then the other. "I rarely sleep. What do you have for me?"

Matt walked forward and handed Coltrain an envelope. Then, without another word, Jake's partner remounted and rode away.

While Charlie read the missive, Jake's mind whirled with the implications of what he'd witnessed.

*Matt? Matt is Charlie's contact at the bank? Impossible.*

They'd been sent here to search out someone who had already been giving information to

## Second Chance

the Coltrains for a year. But maybe Matt had finally succumbed to the lure of money and joined ranks with the other side.

Jake shook his head. He'd known the man too long. But he had wondered why Matt was pushing him so hard to rejoin the gang, why his partner had been unable to uncover any information about the contact in the bank despite his years of experience at similar assignments. And most importantly, why he had been absent on the very day Jake was to hang.

Jake's attention returned to Charlie as the outlaw prepared to leave. Now was the time to make his move. He'd take him into Second Chance tonight, and Jessup could round up the rest of the gang tomorrow. Then he would confront Matt himself; he owed his friend that much.

Jake stepped through the concealing brush and cocked his pistol. The sound caused Charlie to turn; the outlaw's hand reached for his gun.

"Don't do it, Charlie."

The calm assurance of Jake's tone made Coltrain hesitate, then drop his hand. His black gaze bored into Jake's.

"What do you think you're doin', Banner?" Charlie asked.

"You'll have to come with me."

Charlie looked at him a moment, brow creased. "Who the hell are you?"

"Pinkerton sent me."

"You son of a bitch," Coltrain rasped.

"I agree."

A voice from the brush on the opposite bank of the stream made Jake spin toward the sound.

"You should have listened to me and kept your hands off Katherine. No one messes with what's mine," Dillon Swade sneered.

Time slowed as the sharp report of a gun echoed and a bullet slammed into the flesh around Jake's ribs. A dull thud against his side was followed by a piercing sting, and then warm blood trickled onto his skin. His Colt hit the ground, falling from suddenly nerveless fingers. He was surprised when another shot rang out.

Swade had stepped from the bushes only to meet a bullet from Charlie's gun. His eyes were sightless and staring before he fell to the ground, the dirt meeting his face with a crunch.

Jake slowly looked at Charlie, then his knees buckled and he followed Dillon to the ground.

"I hope there aren't any more surprises hiding in the trees."

Jake heard Charlie's wry comment as if from a long distance, then the world spun and blackness descended.

Dawn crept across the sky as Jake regained consciousness. He lifted his head, groaning when the pain sliced through his chest. Looking down, he saw his shirt soaked with blood. He had to get to Lucifer.

## Second Chance

Gritting his teeth, Jake forced himself to stand. The stream twirled in a dizzying spectacle before his eyes. He remained motionless for a moment as the water came into focus, then he began to lurch toward the spot where he'd left his horse.

The animal was still several yards away when Jake's legs collapsed. He lay in the cool grass, breathing heavily. Rest. If he could just rest awhile, then he would drag himself to Lucifer.

When Jake opened his eyes again, the sun was directly overhead. He must have blacked out for several hours, though he didn't remember losing consciousness. Jake tried to stand, then stumbled the rest of the way to Lucifer and attempted to mount. The horse, not trained well enough yet to ignore Jake's fumbling efforts, shied away from him. The movement rocked Jake's world, but he held on to the saddle and made another attempt. This time he succeeded in lifting himself into the stirrup before his stamina deserted him. He tried to throw his leg over the saddle, but the lurching movement was the last insult Lucifer deemed acceptable. The horse bucked, sending Jake flying backward to meet the unmerciful ground with a bone-shattering thud. The sound of Lucifer's hooves pounding into the distance echoed in his head, then unconsciousness swallowed awareness once again.

Working herself to exhaustion the day before had granted Katherine a night of sleep. But the thoughts she had been avoiding greeted her at daybreak.

After breakfast she joined the men working in the near corral. Katherine was engrossed in work when the sound of a horse galloping furiously toward the house caught her attention. She hurried to the wood fence and climbed up the two bottom rungs to see over the top.

Lucifer—riderless, his reins trailing—came to a stop in the empty yard. The horse was lathered and breathing hard. Katherine wasted no time in climbing the remainder of the fence and jumping to the ground. Hearing the men behind her, she motioned them away. "Stay back. I don't want him spooked any more than he is."

The horse's ears pricked forward at the sound of Katherine's voice, and he stamped impatiently. She approached him slowly, murmuring soft nonsense words to calm the animal. For a moment she feared he might bolt, but exhaustion won out and his head dipped toward the ground. Katherine caught the reins, scratching him between the ears when he lifted his head and turned toward her. Looking the animal over with a practiced eye, she found no injuries. But further examination revealed a streak of blood on the saddle, and Katherine's heart turned over. That could only mean one thing. Jake.

Turning abruptly, she surprised Joe standing close behind her. Katherine threw him the reins. "Cool him down carefully," she snapped. Her eyes swept the others nearby. "You," she

## Second Chance

said, pointing at the closest man, "saddle my horse." When the man hesitated, she shouted, "Now!" and he scurried away.

Shortly thereafter, Katherine mounted her mare and thundered toward Second Chance, intent on finding the one man who had shown kindness to both herself and Jake. She raced down the main street, ignoring the surprised faces of the townspeople, and stopped the horse in front of the bank. Dismounting, she threw her reins to a small boy nearby and made her way through the gathering crowd.

Matt Rolland glanced up in surprise as Katherine pushed aside his customer. When the woman started to complain, Katherine froze her with a look, and the woman backed away.

"Katherine, what's going on?"

She leaned forward, whispering so only Matt could hear. "It's Jake. His horse ran into the Circle A a while ago, all lathered and exhausted. But no Jake." She paused to swallow. "I found blood on the saddle."

Matt frowned, then slapped a Closed sign in front of her and left the window. He took Katherine's arm and led her toward the door.

"What's going on here?"

Katherine groaned when she recognized Harrison Foley's voice. An encounter with him was something she did not need right now. She was relieved when Matt squeezed her arm. "Let me do the talking," he whispered and turned to face his boss.

"There's an emergency at the Circle A, sir. I'll help Mrs. Logan and be back as soon as I can."

"Since the Circle A is legally the property of the bank, I'd like to know what's wrong." Katherine saw the small smile on his lips and gritted her teeth. He would love it if the ranch were in the midst of a back-breaking disaster.

"Sorry, no time. I'll explain later." Matt whisked Katherine through the door, and the crowd made way for them.

"You'd better be back soon with a good explanation." Foley's high, angry voice trailed after them as Matt mounted Katherine's mare. He held out his hand to help her up behind him, then kicked the horse into motion without acknowledging Foley's threat.

Matt pulled to a stop in front of the boardinghouse.

"I'll get my horse and come with you to the ranch."

Katherine merely nodded. The fear and sense of urgency that had spurred her into town had returned tenfold and she felt somewhat sick. Leaning over her mare, she rested her cheek against the animal's warm skin, trying to calm her churning stomach. By the time Matt returned with his roan gelding, she sat straight in the saddle, ready to return home.

As they rode, Katherine filled Matt in on the details of her time with the Coltrains. He needed as much information as possible to find Jake. Though surprised at the detailed and probing inquiry, Katherine pushed her doubts aside, grateful she had found the right person to help.

Upon reaching the Circle A, Matt inspected Jake's saddle and horse. The concerned frown on his face did not ease Katherine's mind.

"I need to find him before anyone else does," Matt muttered, then turned to Katherine. "I'll leave now. The fresher the tracks I have to follow, the better."

"You know how to track?" Katherine couldn't keep the surprise from her voice.

"Yes," Matt answered shortly, his attention returning to the bloodstained saddle. Suddenly he looked at her, his eyes bright with determination. "Could I get some supplies from you? Enough for a few days—better add some bandages and the like, too."

Katherine drew in her breath at Matt's implication. "Of course. Do you think it'll take us that long to find him?"

"Us?" Matt raised an eyebrow.

"I'm going with you."

"No," Matt said firmly, "you're not. I can move faster alone. You'll only slow me down."

"I can keep up with any pace you set."

"Katherine," Matt said softly and placed a hand on her arm. "If you really want to help him, let me go alone. I know what I'm doing."

As much as she wanted to be there when Matt found Jake, Katherine knew he was right. Matt could move faster without her, and the sooner Jake was found, the better. Finally, she nodded reluctantly and went to get the supplies.

A half hour later Matt was mounted on his gelding, the lead rope of a pack horse tied to the saddle. He had discarded his suit in the bunkhouse and changed into a borrowed pair of Levi's, cotton shirt, and hat. Looking at him, Katherine found it hard to believe she had accosted him in a bank earlier that day.

"I'll need your gun," he said.

"My gun?"

"Yes," he held out his hand for her weapon. "I don't know what I'll find out there."

"Of course," Katherine answered shakily as she handed over her Colt.

"I'll do what I can," Matt said and spurred his horse toward the road.

Katherine turned to see all the hands and Mary assembled behind her. When they noticed her looking at them they dispersed quickly, leaving her alone. The sudden silence made her realize how truly alone she was. Now came the waiting.

Matt found Lucifer's trail easily. In fact, it looked as though the horse had run straight for home at top speed.

Soon he approached a grove of trees. In the sky above, large black buzzards circled. Matt slowed and drew his gun. He had reached the site of the train robbery a few days previously. And the place he'd met Charlie Coltrain as well. The presence of the carnivorous birds made

## Second Chance

him uneasy, and he was too well trained not to suspect an ambush.

Leaving the horses, Matt approached the wooded area with caution. Several birds were picking at a dark object near the stream. Nervousness replacing discretion, he fired several shots into the ground near the scavengers. When they'd flown away, screeching in anger, Matt hurried over to the inert body and turned it over with his boot. Dillon Swade. What the hell had happened here?

Examination of the area revealed a man's stumbling tracks leading away from the grove and out through the waving grass.

So intent was he on following the tracks, Matt nearly tripped over Jake's still form. Muttering an oath, he dropped to his knees and searched for a sign of life in his partner. Not dead—yet. Hundreds of memories of Jake flooded his mind and Matt hesitated, uncertain of what to do.

Jake's skin had a gray tinge, and from the look of his shirt he'd lost a lot of blood. His hands were cold, and he did not respond when Matt shouted his name.

Suddenly Matt made his decision and ran back to where he'd left the horses, bringing the animals the few hundred yards to Jake. Hot water would be needed to cleanse the wound, then he could assess the damage. Getting to his feet, Matt froze as the sound of thunder rumbled ominously in the distance. Glancing at the horizon, he swore. Dark storm clouds billowed over the hills. He had to get Jake under cover quickly. A chill would be the death of him.

Returning to Jake's side, Matt ripped his friend's shirt open and bound strips of torn cloth tightly around Jake's chest to stanch the flow of blood. Quickly rearranging the supplies on the pack horse, Matt cleared a place for Jake. Then he hoisted his friend over his shoulder and, struggling with the man's weight and height, somehow managed to get him over the saddle and tied securely. Matt mounted his horse and turned toward the closest shelter available—the Circle A.

As he rode past the stream, Matt paused for a moment with the thought of giving Swade a decent burial. But a look at Jake's pallor made him spur his horse onward. Swade was very likely the one who had put Jake in the condition he was in. As far as Matt was concerned, the buzzards were too good for the man.

Another distant rumble caused Matt to look up as a streak of lightning split the indigo sky. Again he cursed. It hadn't rained for weeks and now, when he was out in the open with a wounded man, it looked as though the storm of the decade was approaching.

Warily Matt watched the sky grow darker as black clouds chased each other across the horizon. He could see the rain streaking from the sky as the wind swirled dust into his face. Glancing back at Jake, he was relieved to see his friend still securely on the saddle.

The rain reached them in a torrent, and the force of the wind drove stinging drops into

## Second Chance

Matt's face. He lowered his head, glancing up often to search the distance for a glimpse of the ranch. He was beginning to think he should stop and get Jake under some sort of improvised shelter, when he saw the hazy outline of the Circle A through the gloom.

No one was about as Matt rode to the house. The storm would work to their advantage if he could get Jake and himself inside without being seen.

Lifting Jake from the horse as gently as possible, he placed his friend over his shoulder. Jake still did not stir, and Matt feared the worst as he knocked on the front door.

He had scarcely withdrawn his hand when the door crashed open. Katherine stood in the doorway, pale and tight-lipped. Glancing at Jake, she drew a deep breath and motioned Matt to come in.

"He's been shot. Where can I put him?"

"Upstairs," Katherine said.

"No one should know we're here. He's a wanted man again after that train robbery."

"We'll put him in the attic. No one goes there except for spring cleaning."

Katherine picked up a lantern from the table and led the way upstairs. When they reached the second level, she continued to the end of the hall and opened another door. A staircase led upward.

Matt labored for breath from the exertion of carrying Jake up one flight of stairs. He squared his shoulders and followed Katherine up the second flight. When he reached the attic, Katherine pulled quilts and blankets out of a trunk and laid them on the floor to form a makeshift bed.

"Put him there. I'll get some clean cloths and water."

Matt complied, and together they looked down at the wounded man. Matt heard Katherine's sharp intake of breath at the sight of the blood. He put his hands on her shoulders and turned her toward the stairs.

"We won't know how bad he is until we clean him up. At least he's still breathing."

She nodded and hurried away.

Matt returned his attention to the man on the floor at his feet. The first step would be to remove the bloody shirt along with the rest of Jake's wet clothes.

By the time Katherine returned with warm water and cloths, Matt had Jake undressed and covered with a soft blanket. Looking up at her, Matt noticed she was silent and pale but not shaky. Good. He needed her help.

After the blood was cleaned away, the entrance wound was easy to find. A small, neat hole marred Jake's right side. Such a little hole for so much blood. Matt probed gingerly along Jake's ribs. As far as he could tell, only one rib was broken. It would cause some pain, but the broken rib was not the problem. Turning Jake's limp form to the side, Matt searched the broad expanse of skin for an exit wound.

"Damn," Matt swore.

## Second Chance

"What's wrong?"

Matt had forgotten about Katherine while he examined Jake. He looked up into her worried gaze.

"There's no exit wound, which means the bullet's still inside. I'll have to see if I can dig it out."

Katherine flinched at his words, then squared her shoulders. "What can I do?"

"I'll need whiskey, hot water, and a sharp knife."

Katherine reached out to tentatively touch Jake's face. After brushing back the hair from his forehead, she stood up. "I'll be right back."

Matt followed her to the stairs. "While you're doing that, I need to get those horses out of sight before someone sees them. I won't be long."

The rain had not abated, and the horses stood, heads bowed, in front of the house. Matt patted each animal's neck as he removed their saddles and the unused supplies. Then he led them to the pasture behind the house and turned them loose with the other horses. Struggling with the wet saddles and packs, he carried them into the kitchen, then hurried back to the attic room.

Jake had not stirred, and Matt felt his friend's forehead for fever.

"How is he?"

Matt turned at the sound of Katherine's voice. He tried to smile reassuringly.

"So far he's holding his own." He took the

supplies from Katherine's cool hands.

Matt had removed his share of bullets in the war, but he had never gotten used to the blood. More often than not the man died from infection anyway. He looked down at the unconscious face of his partner and gripped the knife tightly in a steady hand. That wouldn't happen in this case. Matt would make sure of it.

Kneeling, he placed the knife, a pan of hot water, and a full bottle of whiskey in a row on the floor. Then he moved closer to Jake's still form. Katherine continued to hover in the doorway, and Matt motioned for her to come closer.

"Kneel here." He pointed to the floor on his left. "I may need your help."

"I—I don't know how much help I can be. I've never done anything like this."

"I'll tell you what to do." Matt took her hand and pulled her down beside him. "He needs us now."

Matt was rewarded with a brisk, businesslike nod. He could count on Katherine to do her best.

"Hold out your hands," he said.

Katherine complied, and he poured whiskey over her hands as well as his own and the knife. Then he pulled the blanket back from Jake's chest and doused the wound in the same manner.

Matt hoped the bullet's progression had been slowed by glancing off a rib. Since Jake's rib was broken, there was a chance the bullet remained

## Second Chance

close to the surface. If it had gone in too far, he could do nothing for his friend.

Taking a deep breath, Matt explored the wound with the knife. Blood gushed from the opening, filling the air with a harsh, coppery smell. Matt swallowed hard but continued. He could feel Katherine's tension as she leaned closer to watch. Matt probed deeper, using his sense of touch since the blood made sight a useless tool. Jake shifted, muttering something unintelligible, but did not awaken. Just when Matt neared despair, the knife struck something hard. His attempt to maneuver the tiny piece of lead out of the hole was unsuccessful. Looking at the small hole, then at his large fingers, Matt knew he would only make the wound worse if he attempted to remove the bullet.

"You'll have to reach in there and get the bullet out."

"What?" Katherine paled further. "I—I don't think I can."

"You have to. My fingers are too big. I'll only make the wound worse, and he's lost enough blood already." Matt stared into her eyes for a moment before continuing. "The bullet's near the top. All you have to do is reach in and pull it out."

Matt continued to look at Katherine until she took a deep breath and reached her small, thin hand toward Jake. Leaning closer, Katherine peered into the wound, tensed, and inserted her fingers.

Almost immediately her face relaxed, and she

withdrew the tiny piece of lead, holding it out to Matt in triumph.

"Good girl," he said approvingly. "How does it feel to save a life?"

Katherine didn't answer, instead staring at Jake's face intently while Matt stitched the wound closed. When he began to use warm water to remove the fresh blood, she stirred.

"Let me do that. You need to get out of those wet clothes."

Nodding, Matt relinquished the soiled cloth and stood. "Pour whiskey over that wound again and then bind it. Do you have anything dry for me to wear?

Katherine answered without looking up from her task. "In the first room on the left you'll find some of my late husband's things. Take your pick. While you're down there, put the saddles and packs in Sam's room. No one goes there anymore."

As Matt walked down the stairs, he realized he would have to continue the charade both he and Jake played. Until Jake woke up and told him what had transpired and he informed Jake of his own discoveries, he could not be responsible for allowing Katherine to know their true identities, and their presence at the Circle A must remain a secret.

Jake lay still throughout the night. Matt and Katherine both fell asleep watching over him. Near dawn he began to mumble and thrash. Katherine awoke immediately and hurried to

## Second Chance

his side, placing her hand on his forehead. She frowned. He was burning up.

"Fever?" Matt asked at her side.

"Yes. I'll get some cold water." She hurried to the kitchen and returned with a bucket of well water.

As she climbed the stairs, Katherine heard Jake's voice.

"Damn that Swade. Why doesn't Katherine get rid of him?"

The rest of his words dissolved into a mumble.

"Is he awake?" she asked.

Matt turned and crossed the room to take the bucket from her.

"No, he's delirious." Matt paused, his brow furrowed in thought. "Listen, Katherine, I'll take care of him now. I need you to go downstairs and pretend that everything's normal."

"But I want to help."

"I know. But we can't let anyone know he's here or the sheriff will come and take him to jail. He'd never last there." Matt knelt and bathed Jake's body. The cool water quieted the injured man and the room became silent.

"I'm sure Mary can be trusted. Then I could stay with you."

Matt looked skeptical. "I don't think we can risk it. I didn't tell you last night, but I found Dillon Swade dead near where I found Jake. I'm sure Jake shot him in self-defense. But if someone finds the body and then finds Jake here, well, they'll draw their own conclusions. He'll be hung for murder with no second chances."

After a moment Katherine nodded in agreement. "All right. But what about Ruth?"

Matt frowned. "Tell her I'm fine. But don't let her know we're here. She'll want to come and help, and I don't want her involved."

"I hate to lie to her." Katherine paused and looked at Matt curiously. "Matt, why are you doing this?"

Matt didn't answer at first but continued in his attempt to cool Jake's body temperature. "He needs help. I can't turn my back on him. Can you?"

"No. But I'm sure my reasons are different from yours."

Katherine continued to stare at Matt, waiting for his answer. The silence in the room deepened. Suddenly the slam of the door downstairs made them both jump.

Matt looked at Katherine and nodded at the stairway. "You'd better get downstairs before someone comes looking for you."

Katherine nodded. "I'll bring more water when I can."

As she retreated to the second floor to greet Mary, Jake spoke again. Katherine could not make out the words, but she could have sworn she heard the name Pinkerton.

The day dragged endlessly. All of Katherine's attention focused on the small attic room. While Mary was outside hanging the laundry, Katherine made a trip upstairs with fresh water.

## Second Chance

But Matt practically pushed her out the door after taking the bucket from her hand. She could hear Jake raving inside, and her worry increased.

Early that morning she sent a message to Ruth telling her Matt was safe. She received no response, but near dusk, Ruth's buggy came to a stop in front of the house and Katherine left the barn to greet her.

It wasn't until she was next to the buggy that she saw Ruth had brought company. Sheriff Jessup unwound his tall, burly frame from the seat and turned to assist Ruth. Katherine's breath came in short gasps, and she fought to get her panic under control before anyone noticed.

"Katherine, what on earth is going on around here?" Ruth came forward and took her hands. "I've heard all sorts of nonsense in town."

Katherine glanced at the sheriff, fighting a nearly overwhelming urge to look up at the attic window. When he smiled and remained silent, she returned her attention to Ruth.

"Yesterday morning Jake's horse ran in winded and lathered with blood on the saddle—but no Jake." She looked at the sheriff again uneasily, but he remained silent. "I went into town to ask Matt what to do. He said he knew how to track and would find Jake himself."

Ruth wrinkled her brow in confusion. "I understood Matt's been a banker all his life. He never mentioned tracking."

Katherine shrugged. "He left here with two

horses and some supplies. Then a man came in last night with Matt's horse and a message that he was fine and would be back soon."

"What man?" Jessup finally spoke.

"I've never seen him before. He gave me the message, left the horse, and rode out." She gestured toward the hills.

"This man wouldn't be one of the Coltrain Gang, would he?" The sheriff stared at Katherine closely.

"How would I know, Sheriff? I'm not familiar with all the members," Katherine said coolly.

"Humph." Jessup glanced at the house, and Katherine tensed until he returned his gaze to her. "Seems mighty odd that this Rolland feller would be so concerned about Banner. Interestin' that he works at the bank, too. I've been wondering who the Coltrains' contact was there."

Ruth gasped. "Surely you can't be thinking . . ."

"Well, Miz Sanderson, things look mighty strange from my end."

"That's impossible." Ruth crossed her arms over her chest, her lips thinning in anger.

"If Rolland ever shows up again, I'll just ask him. Mind if I look around?" Jessup raised his brows at Katherine.

"Why?" The word burst from Katherine's stiff lips, and Jessup frowned.

"Got somethin', or someone, to hide?"

Katherine swallowed past the knot in her throat. "Of course not. Be my guest."

## Second Chance

Jessup nodded and walked toward the bunkhouse.

Katherine turned to Ruth and took her arm. "Jessup's always got a theory. He rarely knows what's truly happening. You know that, Ruth."

"I know. But this is so odd, like the sheriff said."

Katherine hesitated, hating to keep her friend in the dark. But she had promised Matt, and she would not break her word. Maybe if she explained to Matt what Jessup believed, he'd let her set Ruth's mind to rest.

Ruth remained silent until Jessup returned from his inspection of the bunkhouse. When he headed toward the main house, Katherine followed. She would not allow him to search her home unescorted.

Just as he neared the front door, Mary came onto the porch.

"Where do you think you're going?" Her voice echoed across the yard, and Jessup winced.

"I thought I'd have a look inside."

"Not today you won't. I just washed them floors. No one comes in tonight but Katherine."

"Mrs. Logan gave me permission to enter."

Katherine hurried forward. "That was before I knew Mary had washed the floors. Maybe you can come back tomorrow." Katherine worked hard to keep the pleasure from her face and voice.

"What d' ya need to go in for anyway?" Mary yelled.

Jessup grimaced and backed away from the

327

housekeeper a few paces before answering. "There's a man from town missing."

"And you think he's here? Harley, as usual, you couldn't find your own body in the dark. I worked in this house all day and there's no one here."

The sheriff frowned at Mary momentarily. "You willin' to swear to that?"

"I said no one was here and I meant it. You sayin' I lie?" Mary began to advance on the tall man.

Jessup took several swift steps backward and nearly tripped down the stairs. "No'm. I wasn't saying that." He turned and looked at Ruth. "You ready to head back to town, Miz Sanderson?"

Ruth nodded. Silently she hugged Katherine, then joined Jessup in the buggy.

Katherine watched until they disappeared from sight down the road. Turning toward the house, she saw Mary awaiting her on the porch.

"That man," Mary said in disgust.

"I take it he's not one of your favorites?"

"Harumph." Mary wrinkled her nose. "Never thought he'd be able to handle that job, but no one else wanted it. When we were kids he was nothin' but trouble."

Katherine smiled at the image of Mary and Harley Jessup as children. "I appreciate your keeping him out of the house."

Mary shrugged. "Floor's wet," she said as she returned to her work.

## Second Chance

\* \* \*

Throughout the night and the following day Matt tended to Jake in the sweltering heat of the enclosed attic. During that time he learned about Jake's deepest fears and secrets. But most of all he learned of Jake's love for Katherine.

Matt felt bad about keeping them apart. Katherine wanted to stay with Jake, and he understood her need. But in his delirium Jake could reveal any number of secrets relating to his and Matt's Pinkerton past and present—not to mention the loss of his accent when he was unconscious. For all their sakes, he had to keep Katherine away until Jake was lucid.

He had watched furtively from the small window when Ruth and the sheriff arrived. Although he was unable to hear what was said, Matt could tell from Katherine's rigid stance that she was not happy with the conversation. He breathed easier when Ruth and Sheriff Jessup rode away.

"Matt?"

The rasping whisper brought him to Jake's side. His friend's eyes were open and rational, though they seemed sunken in his pale face.

"It's me, you lucky dog. If anyone else had found you, you'd be a picnic for the buzzards like your buddy Swade." He lifted Jake's head and gave him water.

"Where are we?"

"In the attic at the Circle A."

At Jake's puzzled frown Matt said, "Your horse returned to the Circle A, and Katherine was smart enough to come and get me. I followed the tracks to the stream and found Swade dead and you near to joining him."

Jake put his hand over his eyes. When he removed it, he stared hard at Matt. "I remember now. You came to see Charlie. What the hell are you up to, Matt?"

Matt frowned at the accusation in his partner's voice. "My job, what do you think?"

"I think you sold me out for a share of blood money."

Matt stood and turned away from Jake, anger flooding him. "I think you should hear all the facts before you decide to condemn a man."

When the silence continued, Matt looked closely at Jake. His friend had slipped into unconsciousness again.

# Chapter Eighteen

"Banner, you'd better come out of this soon."

Matt's voice came to Jake through the fog surrounding him. He struggled to surface and hold on to consciousness.

"Can't a man get any rest around here?" Jake mumbled, opening his eyes.

Matt, who sat against the wall close by, jumped up and moved to Jake's side. A delighted grin lit his features.

"Well, it's about time. I'd begun to think you were meant for a Missouri dirt grave after all."

Jake frowned. "How long have I been out?"

"Two days since you woke up the first time. Three since I brought you here."

Jake groaned. "I feel like hell."

"You should. You've got at least one broken rib, and we had to do a bit of fancy digging to get that bullet out. Not to mention the fever."

Jake looked Matt in the eye and nodded a silent thank you, which Matt acknowledged with a shrug. They had saved each other's lives so many times in the past that gratitude was understood and easily accepted.

"Do you think we could finish the fascinating conversation we were having before you lost consciousness?" Matt asked.

Jake frowned, his mind hazy. "Refresh my memory."

"I'd be delighted," Matt replied, sounding anything but. "You were accusing me of being a double agent."

Jake suddenly remembered everything in painful clarity. His eyebrows drew together as he stared at Matt. "Care to explain what you've been up to?"

"My job. If I remember correctly, I was supposed to find the contact at the bank."

"That doesn't mean you're supposed to *be* the contact at the bank, Matt." Jake struggled to get up, falling back with a groan at the slash of pain through his midsection.

Matt pushed Jake back onto the bedroll. "Who said I was the contact?"

"What were you doing giving information to Coltrain? I saw you, Matt. I also picked up your favorite hat laying outside the bunkhouse where Dillon Swade slept. You know, the go-between to Charlie? Don't try to lie."

"Did you ever stop to think I was just the new messenger boy in this situation? That maybe my

## Second Chance

hat fell off in a cursed Missouri dust storm?"

Jake rubbed his eyes with the back of his hand. His lids felt as if they'd been scraped raw with sand. "Let's quit dancin' around the truth here, Matt. Spit it out."

"I'm a better actor than you give me credit for, Jake. When Dillon disappeared, the contact had no one to carry messages. And this person is not the type to meet Charlie on his own, alone. Since I'd been seen around town being friendly with you, Katherine, and Katherine's best friend, the contact figured I would be open to some easy money." Matt grinned. "Of course, I couldn't resist."

"Matt," Jake said warningly. "Just tell me who the hell it is so we can get out of here."

"Foley, of course."

"Foley. That's how I had it figured, until you showed up instead." Jake frowned. "But he hates the Coltrains. They robbed his bank, for cryin' out loud. He spouts his love of everything Yankee all over Second Chance."

"The only thing he loves more than a Yankee is the money he makes by cheating one," Matt replied.

"But Pinkerton said no one in town knows how the money is shipped here until it arrives."

"Someone slipped up, Jake. After Foley hired me to work for him, I got in his safe." Matt cracked his knuckles. "One of my better skills. Anyway, inside I found the name of Foley's contact with the folks who distribute the payroll—the Addler Express Company."

"I wouldn't want to be the agent who checked out Addler. There'll be hell to pay with the boss over this." Jake sighed. "Have you contacted the sheriff and had Foley arrested?"

"Well, there's a little problem with that."

"What now?"

"The sheriff thinks I'm the contact at the bank, and you're a wanted man again after that little stunt with the train."

"So tell him the truth."

"I don't trust the man, Jake. You've seen how he is. I'm afraid he'll shoot first and ask questions later. The people of this town are hot for the blood of the Coltrains. If Jessup doesn't take care of us, someone else will."

"What's the plan?" Jake asked.

Matt grinned. "Who said I have a plan?"

"You always have a plan."

"Right again. The way I see things, we're the ones who'll have to stop the Coltrain Gang from stealing the next payroll. Then we can march them into town and turn them over to Sheriff Jessup. He might believe our story long enough to contact Pinkerton and confirm it if we show up with Charlie and the boys."

"Nice plan, Matt. There's only one problem."

Matt raised his brows. "Oh? What's that?"

"I'm no longer with the gang, and Charlie knows who I work for. I don't think I'll be able to find out where the next job is."

"Jake." Matt shook his head sadly. "Think, man, think. Who brought the information to Charlie about the last job?"

## Second Chance

"You brought him a note."

Matt nodded, smiling.

"You read the note."

"What do you think? I'm a spy, remember? Reading sealed missives is my job. The railroad payroll will be leaving Second Chance on Wednesday's stage."

Jake smiled despite the ache in his side and the throbbing from his head. "Let's plan us an ambush."

"You've got to start eating something."

Mary's voice next to her ear caused Katherine to flinch. She raised her head from her hands and looked around the kitchen. The men had finished their supper and gone to the bunkhouse. She hadn't noticed. As she looked up at Mary, the concern on the woman's wide face made Katherine bite back the snappish words rising to her lips. Mary was one of the few people who truly cared about her in this world. Maybe she was too overbearing and nosy at times, but she acted that way out of love.

Katherine attempted to soothe the woman. "I'm sorry, but I'm just not hungry lately."

"Pining away for someone who was no good in the first place won't help. Forget him."

Katherine sighed. If things were only that simple. It had been three days since Matt rode in with Jake. During that time the tension of pretending nothing was wrong had become greater and greater. Maybe if she'd been able to spend some time with Jake she would feel better. But Matt steadfastly refused to let her in the room when she brought food, water, and medical supplies. Jake remained unconscious and she could do nothing for him, he said. He had pointedly ignored her revelation that Jessup believed him to be the bank contact, but allowed her to tell Ruth what was going on, though Katherine had to make her friend swear not to come to the Circle A until Matt gave the word. Ruth's mind was at rest, but every night Katherine lay awake, staring at the ceiling, worrying that Jake might not survive.

"What kind of life would you have with him, girl?" Mary sat down at the table, pressing a conversation.

Katherine stared into space and considered the question—riding for days on end, hiding in caves or worse, always on the run. Mary was right. That kind of life couldn't last. Eventually one of them would be dead. Since Jake had turned down her offer of a normal life, there was nothing more to think about. When he got well, he would slip away again. She must forget him; just as he would forget her.

Katherine got up from the table without answering Mary. Ignoring the woman's concerned look, she went upstairs to her room. Once clothed in a nightdress, Katherine lay on her bed. Weariness weighted her body, but sleep eluded her. She listened as Mary finished her work in the kitchen and left for home. Darkness became complete as Katherine continued to stare at the ceiling.

## Second Chance

Time passed and Katherine heard the hollow sound of footsteps on the attic stairs. Matt came downstairs each night after Mary left. He returned upstairs in less than an hour, and Katherine assumed he needed time away from the stuffy attic room. She turned on her side and closed her eyes. Sleep did not come. Finally she made a disgusted sound and swung her feet onto the floor.

This was her house, after all, she reasoned. If she wanted to go in the attic, no one could stop her—short of force. Well, tonight Matt would have to do just that. She meant to see Jake.

The decision made, Katherine didn't hesitate. She hurried down the hall in bare feet, her nightdress streaming behind her. As quietly as possible, she opened the door and crept up the stairs.

The room was still. Katherine's eyes went directly to where Jake lay on the floor. He slept peacefully, a lantern burning low on the table next to him. She only wanted to look at him for a minute, then she would go back to her room before Matt returned.

Katherine crossed the room quickly and knelt next to Jake's sleeping form. He slept deeply, long lashes resting on his cheeks. Katherine cocked her head to study him. He looked so much younger and more approachable when asleep. The slight thrill of sexual excitement that had always struck Katherine whenever Jake looked at her was not present—just the overwhelming need to reach out and touch him.

Before she realized what she was doing, Katherine laid her palm against his cheek. He was cool. The fever was gone. She sighed and suddenly she was looking into wide-awake green eyes.

Jake smiled, and Katherine relaxed. His hand came up to catch hers where it lay against his face. He brought her palm to his lips and kissed the center.

"What are you doing here?" he asked.

"Shh," Katherine whispered, darting a glance at the door. "He'll send me packing if he hears us."

Jake chuckled. "Matt's being overprotective of his patient. He's been hovering over me day and night like my mama."

"Matt's a good man."

"I owe you my life again, I hear."

Katherine looked down at their joined hands, suddenly feeling shy. "Matt's the one who saved you."

"But you helped, and I'm relying on your hospitality again. Matt told me how you never flinched taking the bullet out of me. Thank you."

Katherine nodded, unable to say more.

"Katie." Jake's voice whispered against her skin. His soft, southern tones would haunt her in the night for years to come. He tugged on her hand, and she looked into his eyes.

"Come closer so I can thank you properly."

## *Second Chance*

Mesmerized by his heated gaze, Katherine allowed herself to be pulled forward. She leaned over Jake and touched her lips to his.

He made a noise deep in his throat and reached up to draw her down next to him. As he raised the blanket covering him, Katherine slipped underneath and pressed herself to his naked form, careful not to touch his wounded side. The heat from his body seemed to melt through her summer nightdress, and Katherine's body tingled wherever it touched his. Jake's mouth opened and she took the invitation, slipping her tongue inside to stroke his slowly.

Jake drew away to nuzzle at Katherine's neck. "I've missed you," he said.

"And I've missed you." She gasped when Jake's fingers slipped inside the bodice of her nightdress and began to tease her nipple. "Should you be doing this?"

"Best medicine I can think of," Jake murmured against her neck.

"More sleep and less exertion would work wonders." Matt's voice from the stairway caused Katherine to scramble away from Jake guiltily.

"Matt, why don't you go for a walk?" Jake asked.

"I'm not supposed to be here, remember? What if someone saw me?"

"Go back downstairs then." Jake's voice faded to a sleepy mumble.

"I don't think that'll be necessary." Matt walked over and looked down at the now sleeping man, then he looked at Katherine with raised eyebrows.

Her face flamed, and she was grateful the dim light would hide the redness. Katherine rose and headed for the stairs.

"He needs rest."

She paused at the doorway, not turning. "I know. I'll stay away until you think he's well enough."

"Good girl. It won't be long now and this will all be a memory."

Katherine returned to her room, Matt's words echoing in her head. He was right. Very soon, Jake Banner would only be a memory.

After two days of rest Jake felt able to sit a horse and use his gun. Though stiff, he could function.

He and Matt had spent their time planning an ambush for the Coltrains. Before first light they would be on their way so they could hide in the hills overlooking the area where the stage robbery would take place.

Matt had gotten them clothes from Sam Logan's room. Though Jake hated to wear the man's things, he had no choice.

They crept from the house at the darkest point of night and saddled the roan and Lucifer. Leading the animals to the road, they mounted and rode for the hills. Jake winced

## Second Chance

at the thought of Katherine's disappointment when she found them and the horses missing the next morning. He had considered telling her the truth, then decided to wait. After the incident with the train robbery, he didn't trust her not to ride after them in an attempt to help. But he hoped that before another night had passed he could end all the lies between them.

When dawn crept over the hills, Jake and Matt lay on opposite sides of a rock incline framing a narrow road. From their vantage points they could observe anyone who ventured onto the path below.

The summer sun reached its zenith, and the heat along with it, when Jake heard the sound of several horses approaching. He waved at Matt and received an excited grin in return. Matt loved a good ambush.

A group of riders came into view, coming to a halt below them. Jake easily recognized Charlie on his white horse. Bill rode next to him. Jake swore under his breath at the sight of Jeff Soames in the rear. He could only hope Jeff survived the next few minutes.

They waited until the outlaws dismounted and turned their horses over to Jeff and a companion. The two men led the horses through the passageway to the other side. Before the outlaws could hide in the brush lining the road, Jake fired off a shot that spit into the dirt at Charlie's feet.

"Surrender or die!" he shouted.

Jake stifled his unease as Charlie looked up calmly. The man's cold eyes searched the high rocks. Seeing no one, he turned to Bill and shrugged.

"Who the hell are you?" Bill shouted.

Jake didn't answer. Instead, he put a bullet into the dirt at the second outlaw's feet.

The rest of the gang looked up at the rocks warily, but no one made a move to give up. Jake had expected as much.

"You have one minute," he called.

Charlie and Bill glanced at each other, then Charlie nodded. The two moved quickly, rolling into the brush before Jake realized what had happened. The other men followed their lead. As the air rang with the sound of gunshots, Jake heard several bullets ricochet off the rock he crouched behind.

Matt got off quite a few shots before the gang could find his concealed location. The men on the ground had a disadvantage. Jake and Matt could easily see them from their vantage points, but the same was not true of the view from below. Less than an hour later, Jake counted five dead outlaws.

"Throw down your guns now before anyone else gets killed," Jake yelled.

Further gunfire met his demand. Jake returned the fire, but something about the sound of the blasts pricked his attention and he peered downward. Immediately he saw the cause of his unease. The gunfire was coming from farther away. The outlaws had moved under cover of

## Second Chance

the gunshots toward the end of the road and the safety of their horses.

"They're going for the horses," Jake shouted to Matt as he jumped up and ran along the cliff.

A bullet whistled past Jake's ear as he dove behind a rock, wincing with pain as his wounded side burned from the impact with a rock. Both he and Matt returned the shots and another outlaw went down. When Charlie and Bill reached the horses and mounted, Jake fired his Colt repeatedly. Bill flinched when a bullet plowed into his arm, but the outlaw kept his seat and spurred the horse into a gallop with Charlie on his heels. Jeff and the other man who'd been with the horses grabbed their mounts and rode after the departing outlaws. The commotion scattered the remaining animals. The two gang members left behind threw down their guns, raising their arms in defeat.

"Cover 'em, Matt."

Jake descended the rocky incline. After retrieving the discarded guns, he tied the two men. By the time Matt joined him, Jake had caught two horses and mounted one.

Matt glanced at the two bound gang members. "Pretty sorry performance on our part, Jake."

"It won't be if we can catch up to Charlie and Bill. If they get away they'll just start another gang down the road, not to mention lessening our bargaining power in town. We can pick up these two later." Jake kicked his horse into a run and Matt followed.

Charlie pulled his white stallion to a stop at the foot of a sheer expanse of red and orange rock rising from the ground. He scanned the horizon behind him. No sign of pursuit. Yet. But they would come soon. Now was the time to split up and hope they could confuse the men following them.

He pointed at the other two outlaws. "You two head for Texas. Lay low there a few months. We'll find you when it's time to come back."

The two nodded, galloping away without a farewell.

Bill tied a strip from his shirt around his bleeding arm.

"How bad are you hit?" Charlie asked.

"Just a nick. I'm fine," Bill growled.

Charlie frowned at his brother. Even though they were blood kin, he'd never been able to like the man. Bill possessed a streak of mean that had been there since they were kids, even before their Yankee stepfather had beaten hate into them. The war had brought even more changes in Charlie. And he regretted them. But Bill had always been mad at the world and would remain that way.

"We'll separate too. You go west and then turn south in a few days. I'll head north. We can spend the winter in San Antonio."

Bill grimaced and shook his head. "I've got some business to take care of in town first."

## Second Chance

Charlie stared at his brother in amazement. "Are you crazy? There's someone on our tails. Must be some Pinkerton friends of that Banner character."

"You should have let me kill him in the beginning. There was always somethin' strange about that Georgia boy."

Charlie sighed. He'd been hearing this litany ever since he'd returned from the meeting with Rolland to report Banner's true identity and subsequent death. His error in judgment would haunt him for months to come.

"Let's get out of here, Bill."

"No. I mean to take care of that snitch Foley and his new messenger boy."

"What're you talkin' about?"

"I figured it out. One or the other must have tipped off the law about the stage robbery. Both Banner and Swade are dead, and it sure wasn't one of the boys. I mean to make sure their lyin' tongues never move again."

Before Charlie could argue, Bill spurred his horse and headed toward Second Chance.

Charlie debated following his brother, but a glance at the horizon revealed there was no more time. Two riders had appeared in the distance, and they were closing in fast. He recognized the massive black horse as Banner's mount. The damned Pinkerton agent had not died after all. But the lawmen would have to follow Bill back to town to save the miserable folks of Second Chance. This time his brother was on his own.

At a signal, the well-trained horse reared. Charlie removed his hat and threw back his head, letting his golden hair stream out behind him in the wind. After a long look at the softly waving grasses of Missouri, Charlie and the white stallion were Texas bound.

Bill had nearly reached town when his horse pulled up lame. Swearing violently, he dismounted and walked the remaining distance.

As he entered town, people stared and pointed. He must look out of place with his long hair, guns, and bloody arm.

Bill pulled out one of his pistols and cocked it. No one in this two-bit town was going to stop him from taking care of a snitch.

He left his horse untied in front of the bank. His glance swept the area and noted several other mounts he could chose from once he completed his business.

When he entered the darkened structure, a woman screamed. The customers hurriedly backed away from him.

"Where's Foley?" Bill aimed his gun at the nearest clerk.

The terrified man pointed a shaking finger toward an office at the back of the bank.

"Obliged." Bill nodded and continued on his way.

Wasting no time with the closed door, Coltrain kicked it open and sauntered in. Foley glanced up, the look of anger on his

## Second Chance

face replaced quickly by wariness.

"What the hell..."

"You're a traitor, Foley, and it's time you met the devil."

"What are you talking about? I've done nothing but help you since you came here. I'm on your side, remember?"

Bill laughed. "Not anymore. Where's your new messenger boy? I'll take care of him too while I'm at it."

Foley watched Bill warily. "If you mean Rolland, he left with that Logan woman and never came back. He's the one you're looking for, not me." Foley licked his lips, eyes darting toward the door. "Yes, that must be why he left, to turn you in. I'm sure if you hurry, you'll find him at the Circle A."

"I'll get to him later."

"But I can still help you." Foley spoke faster, his words running together with fear. "If we eliminate Rolland, no one knows I'm your contact. We can even go to another town and start over."

"No good."

"Why? We'll be rich beyond our wildest hopes. I joined up with the Coltrains because we were the same kind of people, willing to do anything for money." He stood up straighter, attempting to look Bill bravely in the eye. "Don't tell me now I picked the wrong gang."

Harrison continued to stare at Bill for a few minutes, and Bill enjoyed the cornered look on the man's face. Suddenly Foley reached under his desk.

A gunshot sounded. Foley started, then looked down in surprise as a red stain spread across his white shirt.

"Big mistake," Bill said as the banker slid to the floor. He walked calmly through the bank and out the door, his gun visible and ready.

"You want to drop that gun, Bill?" a voice asked.

Coltrain froze just beyond the doorway. Jake Banner and Rolland, the other stinking traitor, stood in the street with guns drawn. The townspeople had retreated a safe distance, and Bill heard the door of the bank close and lock behind him. The only way out was past the men in front of him.

"Thought you were dead, Banner."

"Sorry, Bill, can't oblige you there."

"That's all right, I wanted to do it myself anyway. Nice of you to bring Rolland along. I can take care of you both at once."

As his finger tightened on the trigger, two shots rent the air. Bill gripped his chest, then fell to the wooden platform.

Matt approached cautiously, gun drawn, and checked the fallen outlaw for signs of life. He shook his head and withdrew.

People crept closer to examine the body. A group stood around Bill's lifeless form and stared. Several of them glanced at Jake, frowning.

"Gang shootout," a few murmured.

## Second Chance

"Where's Jessup?" someone yelled.

The door of the bank opened and those inside streamed out.

"Foley's dead," a clerk said.

"Damn." Jake strode into the building.

He found Foley, indeed dead, on the floor of his office. Jake pulled the gun from the banker's fingers and held the weapon up to Matt. "He almost got off a shot."

"Hold it right there, Banner, Rolland. Drop them guns or you're dead."

# Chapter Nineteen

Katherine had gone about her normal routine upon waking. As usual, she waited until Mary left the house before taking fresh water to the attic.

The minute she opened the door to the stairs, she sensed a difference. The room above was quiet—but unnaturally so, the quiet of emptiness. Katherine ran up the stairs, and her gaze swept the vacant room. They were gone—without a word, without a warning. She wanted to throw herself down on the floor and pound the wood with her fists.

But what had she expected? Jake had never meant to stay. Would another night of passion between them have eased the ache that had already started between her breasts?

Returning to the kitchen, Katherine sat at the table. Where was Matt? Could he really be

## Second Chance

the Coltrain contact? She found that hard to believe, yet he was gone without a word. She would have to check with Ruth and see if she'd heard from him.

Early afternoon had arrived before Katherine left the Circle A. As she pulled her mare to a stop in front of Ruth's house, the sound of gunfire drew her attention.

Ruth ran onto the porch. "What's that?"

Katherine nudged her horse back to the street and looked in the direction of the sound.

"There's a crowd in front of the bank," she told Ruth. "I'm going down to see what happened."

Katherine kicked her mare into a trot before Ruth could reply. Her mind repeated a litany. *Not Jake, please not Jake.*

When she reached the bank, Katherine saw a body on the sidewalk in front of the building, and a chill passed over her.

"What happened?" she asked the nearest bystander.

The man answered without looking up, his gaze still intent on the door. "Coltrain Gang had a shootout. Seems Foley was feedin' the Coltrains their information. So far, he's dead and Bill Coltrain too."

Surprise flooded Katherine at the news that Foley was the Coltrains' contact. She had dismissed him as an arrogant nuisance, never dreaming he could be so bold. She didn't think the proper Bostonian had the gumption to aid a gang of southern thieves. Besides the fact that he was the richest man in Second Chance. What could possibly have been his motive?

The voice of the man next to her stopped Katherine's thoughts. "Don't know how many more outlaws are dead inside. Jessup just went in."

The man's observation, spoken in a tone of ghoulish curiosity, caused the chill that Katherine had first felt in her fear for Jake to settle deep in her bones.

Ruth arrived, and Katherine related what she'd heard.

"Where's Jessup?" Ruth asked.

"Inside," the same man answered over his shoulder.

Ruth and Katherine stood tensely waiting with the crowd. All eyes were focused on the bank as time passed. Finally, three figures emerged from the building. Katherine and Ruth gave a simultaneous sigh of relief when they recognized Jessup, Jake, and Matt. But after the relief passed, Katherine looked at the three men in confusion. Jessup smiled broadly at Jake and clapped him on the back. What was going on?

The sheriff held up his hand for silence to address the crowd.

"I guess this is as good a time as any to let you all in on a little secret. I've just learned that these men here—" he gestured at Matt and Jake "—are from the Pinkerton Agency in Chicago. They were hired by the railroad to put the Coltrain Gang out of business. We owe them our thanks."

## Second Chance

Silence greeted his words, then the crowd erupted into whistles and cheers. Jake and Matt looked sheepish at all the attention, nodding and waving to acknowledge the crowd's enthusiasm.

Katherine looked down at Ruth and saw the same stunned expression on her friend's face as she was certain graced her own.

Jake gestured for silence.

"I'd just like to say that I could never have accomplished my mission if it hadn't been for the unselfish help of Mrs. Logan. If it weren't for her, the Coltrains would still be roaming your streets."

A sea of faces turned to stare at Katherine, hesitating before they again broke into cheers. Katherine's eyes met Jake's, and he smiled.

Fury, deep and wild, filled her mind, and Katherine's only desire was to get away before she broke down and howled tears or curses. Yanking hard on the mare's reins, she turned and raced for home.

Jake watched Katherine disappear into the distance. He had expected her to be happy about his true identity. Well, he'd ride to the Circle A as soon as things were cleared up in town. Jake smiled to himself at the thought of the night to come. He would tell Katherine everything; they would make love and plan their future. A weight of guilt had been lifted from his chest now that all his lies could be explained.

"Matt?"

Jake glanced down to see Katherine's schoolteacher friend at the foot of the stairs. She looked at Matt timidly. Jake glanced at his partner and saw the look on his face at the sight of the woman. He laughed to himself.

*Matt's in love.* At least Jake wouldn't have to worry about leaving his friend without a partner. If he didn't miss his guess, Matt would be retiring from the detective business as well.

Jake leaned over and spoke softly to Matt. "Go on. I'll handle things here."

Matt looked surprised. "You sure?"

Jake nodded. "You've got a lot of explaining to do. Best get to it."

Matt's gaze swung in the direction of the Circle A. "From the looks of things, you'll be doing more explaining than me. Maybe you should go."

"No. I'll give her a chance to cool down before I make my appearance." Jake nodded and smiled at Ruth. "Go on, Matt, the lady's waiting."

Neither Matt nor Ruth spoke on the short walk to her house. Various people lining the streets slapped Matt on the back and expressed their thanks, but he merely smiled and nodded. His mind raced in an effort to remember all the lies he had told Ruth. Jake's brush with death had made him realize the depth of his feelings for the auburn-haired schoolteacher. He had one chance to make things right between them

## Second Chance

and he meant to use his silver tongue to its best advantage.

Matt followed Ruth into her parlor and took the seat she indicated.

"Should I make some coffee?" she asked, not looking at him.

"No."

"Tea?"

"No!" Matt pressed his palms together and took a deep breath. "Nothing, thank you."

Ruth nodded and drifted around the room, lighting a lamp against the coming shadows, then stopping to gaze out the window pensively.

"Come and sit down," Matt said gently.

Ruth didn't move at first, and Matt feared she would continue to ignore him. Suddenly she turned and sat gracefully in the chair facing his.

Looking into her face, Matt was at a loss. He could read nothing in her eyes beyond calm curiosity. Maybe he had misread her feelings for him. He almost wished she would scream abuse so he would know she cared.

"Go ahead, Matthew. Explain yourself."

Matt felt as though he'd been caught putting a frog on Ruth's chair. Taking a deep breath, he reached for her hand.

Ruth didn't acknowledge the contact, but neither did she draw away. Her fingers were ice cold, and Matt grasped them more tightly, attempting to impart some of his warmth into her fragile bones.

"I don't know where to start," he admitted. "I've never had to explain to anyone before."

"Why don't we start with something simple? Like your name."

"Matthew Ward."

"Well, at least you were partially honest, Mr. Ward."

Matt had the sudden urge to pull on the collar of his shirt. The garment was much too tight.

"Ruth, I'm sorry for the lies. But they were necessary. I had a job to do and I did it. Now I can tell you anything you want to know."

Ruth stared deeply into his eyes for several moments. Finally she seemed to make a decision and smiled. Though the smile was somewhat strained, the rest of her body relaxed.

"I think I understand most of the deceptions you practiced. But there is one question I need to ask."

"Anything you want, Ruth."

"Did you court me for information about the townsfolk, or were you truly interested in me?" Ruth's voice faded near the end of the question and her gaze fell to their joined hands.

Matt hesitated for a moment, then sighed and told her the truth. "I have to be honest with you. I followed you that first night for the express purpose of meeting you." Ruth attempted to pull her hand from his grasp. "No, wait, I'm not finished. As I spent more time with you, something happened to me. I don't know . . . I began to care for you. When we were together

## Second Chance

I forgot I wasn't the person you believed me to be. I was just a man with a woman. A woman I loved."

Ruth's head snapped up and her eyes widened as they met his. Matt smiled and pulled her to her feet. As they stood toe to toe they were the same height. He didn't mind. That was perfect for what he had in mind.

Matt placed his hands on Ruth's shoulders and drew her toward him. As their lips touched she sighed, and he watched her lashes flutter shut before he closed his own eyes and surrendered to the sensations of their first kiss.

A long while later, Matt reclined in a chair with Ruth on his lap. He had unbound her hair, and his fingers played with the long, fine strands. Placing a kiss on the tip of her nose, he said, "I love you, Ruth. Will you marry me?"

Ruth seemed to consider his question as she traced the scar along his jaw with the tip of her finger. Then she smiled. "That was my plan all along."

After several hours at the jail and several re-tellings of the truth, Jessup was finally satisfied he'd heard the entire story. Jake had wired Pinkerton in Chicago to inform him the mission was over. He would report in person later and give his boss the details he craved.

Jake stepped from the hot, stuffy building and breathed deeply of the night air. The sky, clear and studded with stars, spread out in a peaceful curtain above him. He was bone-weary, his side on fire, but he could think of nothing else except riding to the Circle A and straightening things out with Katherine.

A short time later he tied his horse in front of the house. A light burned in Katherine's office, and Jake smiled. He wondered if she was getting any work done.

Letting himself in the front door without a sound, Jake crossed the few feet to her office. He looked in and found the room deserted. The sound of a gun being cocked behind him made Jake freeze. Turning slowly, he met Katherine's icy gaze.

"I've been expecting you," she said.

Jake looked at the gun. "Is that necessary?"

"Yes. I don't want you anywhere near me or I won't be able to think straight."

Katherine motioned for him to precede her into the office. After Jake seated himself, she took a chair, the gun never wavering from his chest.

Jake made a sound of exasperation. "Katherine, this is ridiculous. Put that thing away. I want to explain."

"Oh, so now you're ready to explain. Where was all this honesty when we were lying in each other's arms? Didn't I deserve the truth then?"

"I wanted to tell you, but everything was so confusing. Between Dillon's insinuations that you were a contact for the Coltrains and . . ."

"That was a lie." Katherine glared at him.

## Second Chance

"I know. But I couldn't take a chance until I was sure."

"I told you about Sam. My life was hell because I trusted, because I cared for a man who purposely lied to me. A man who pretended to be something he wasn't then showed me his true self only when it was too late. I can't believe the same thing has happened to me twice in one lifetime. God, I feel like such a fool."

Jake could hear the hurt in her voice, and he knew no other defense but the truth.

"Katherine, I've seen too many agents who've gotten themselves and others killed because they trusted the wrong people. I was so close to being through with this assignment, I just wanted to get my proof and then I could tell you the truth."

"And what is the truth? Who are you? Is everything you've told me a lie?"

"Not everything."

"What then? Is your name even Jake Banner?"

"It's Jake Parker."

"Well, at least I called out the right name as we made love." Her voice was bitter with pain. "You'd best get on with the rest of your explanation."

"Well, you know I'm not from the South?"

"It's obvious now that you've dropped the accent. You're quite good. I'm sure that makes you proud of yourself." Katherine's face reflected her sarcasm.

"I learned a lot about the South during the war and afterward." Jake's voice was low, his distaste of the subject obvious.

"I'm supposed to believe your nightmares were real? More than likely you used your supposed fear of the dark to gain my sympathy."

"I couldn't pretend that, Katherine. I fought in the battle of Antietam. I got shot." He touched the small scar at his temple, remembering. "When I came around, I was buried under Confederate bodies in the sunken road. You've heard of that, I'm sure— Bloody Lane they call the place now. And it was. Because of that place, Antietam was the bloodiest single day of the war. Ever since, I can't stand to be in a dark, closed place."

Katherine didn't speak, but Jake could feel her gaze on him as he tried to dispel the memories he'd just brought forth.

"It's too late." Katherine's voice was cold, emotionless.

Jake stared at her in amazement. He was limp with the emotions that came upon him whenever he talked about Antietam. Not that he mentioned such an experience to many. Until now, only his family knew of what had happened to him there. Jake leaned forward and stared into Katherine's face.

"What are you talking about, 'too late'? I can answer any question you have. I want you to know everything, Katherine. We can plan a future."

## Second Chance

"Not together. I can't live with someone I don't trust. Too much of my life has been spent that way."

Jake was beginning to get angry. He had opened up the darkest horror inside him, and she said it was too late. How could she love him as an outlaw, then turn him away when he revealed he was an honest man? He'd never understand women.

"There won't be any more lies. We can live here and work the ranch. You won't have any problems with the townspeople now."

"No, now that you're a hero I'm suddenly acceptable. But that's all a lie. You and I both know the truth. I did harbor a Confederate outlaw. I saved your life. I helped you rob a train. I meant to do every one of those things. I wasn't acting a part."

"You aren't thinking rationally. Maybe I should come back when you've calmed down."

"I'll never be any calmer than I am at this moment. I'm sorry for what you endured in the war, Jake, really I am. But it doesn't change what I'm feeling. I want you to go back to wherever it is you came from. Don't ever come on my land again. I'll have a guard on the house until you've left town."

Jake stared at Katherine in the flickering light of the lantern. Though her face looked drawn, her eyes never wavered.

She meant what she said. Uttering an expletive, Jake pushed himself out of the chair. Katherine's gun remained on him.

"All right, I'm leaving. You won't need a guard to keep me away. You may not believe me now, but I love you. Throwing away our love is something you'll regret every day of your life."

Before he realized it, Jake was back on his horse and riding toward town. The breeze cooled his anger-flushed skin and cleared his head.

She wanted nothing to do with him. Well, he'd oblige her—for the time being. Tomorrow he'd take the first train to Chicago and make his report to Pinkerton. Then he'd go home to St. Louis and see his parents for a while. From what he'd seen earlier, Matt would be staying in Second Chance and could keep an eye on Katherine. In a few months, Jake believed she would feel differently about him.

Katherine retained her rigid stance even after the front door slammed and she heard the pounding of hooves fading into the distance. Finally she uncocked the pistol and laid the weapon carefully on top of the desk. Only then did she allow herself the luxury of tears.

From the moment she'd heard Jake's true identity, she had felt torn and betrayed inside. She had trusted him with her love, her body, her life. Even when she believed Jake Banner, or Jake Parker as he'd said, to be a thief and a murderer, she had gone on trusting him. But he could not trust her with the truth about himself.

## Second Chance

Well, she thought as she dried her eyes on the sleeve of her dress, he was gone as she'd asked. Time to get on with her life. Katherine made her way slowly up the stairs, walking as though she were suddenly a very old woman.

The next day Ruth and Matt came to see her. From Ruth's beaming face and Matt's wide grin, Katherine could tell they'd resolved whatever differences were between them. She put on her best false smile and greeted them.

"Katherine, I'm so happy." Ruth hugged her as soon as she stepped from the buggy. "Matt's explained everything, and we're going to be married in the fall. He's going to stop all this spying nonsense and take over the bank."

Katherine glanced at Matt, and he shrugged. "Someone has to. I was a banker before the war. Looks like it's time to be one again."

"I guess I'll be turning my mortgage payments over to you now, Mr. Rolland."

"My name's Matt Ward, Katherine. But please don't be formal with me after all we've been through."

"All right then. Matt."

He smiled. "I have some good news for you. Further payments won't be necessary. I looked over Foley's private records this morning and he loaned your husband the money personally, not through the bank. Since Foley has no living kin and left no will, the Circle A is out of debt."

Katherine was stunned. After all the months of scrimping and worrying, suddenly her biggest problem disappeared as though it had never existed.

"I don't understand. Why did he lie?" Katherine asked.

"I don't know for sure, but Foley enjoyed having power over people," Matt explained. "He held notes on several ranches connected to his spread. My guess is that he planned to create an empire for himself in Second Chance through foreclosures. He sold information to the Coltrains for the money, not for any political leanings or lack of them. I doubt if the idea of right and wrong ever entered his mind; he only cared about getting what he wanted."

Ruth hugged her again. "Now you don't have to worry about going back east. Isn't that wonderful? The Circle A will be making a profit in no time."

Katherine returned her friend's embrace and asked the pair inside. For the next hour Ruth attempted to interest her in plans for the wedding. Katherine participated in the conversation as well as she could, having no desire to dampen Ruth's spirits with her own grief.

As they were leaving, Ruth remarked, "Matt will be able to stay here until the wedding thanks to Jake."

"Why's that?" Katherine asked.

"Jake has gone to Chicago to make the final report to Pinkerton." Ruth hesitated when she saw the look on Katherine's face. "I thought

## Second Chance

you knew. Jake said you two had come to an agreement on your future."

He had already left. Katherine couldn't understand why she felt such pain, as though she'd been punched in the stomach. After all, she had insisted he leave. Just because he chose to race out of town with no regrets should mean nothing to her.

"I'm sorry," she said, catching only the last word of what Ruth had just said. "What was that?"

"I said, I'm sure he'll be back when he's done. Didn't you two talk?"

"Yes. We talked." Katherine looked her friend directly in the eye. "He won't be coming back."

Ruth looked at Matt in confusion. "But, but, I thought . . ."

When Katherine didn't answer, Matt took Ruth's arm and led her to the buggy. "We have to be going now," he said. "We'll come by in a few days."

Katherine nodded at him gratefully. She had no desire to repeat what had transpired between her and Jake, even to Ruth. Perhaps in a few days, when the shock of all the deceptions wore off, she would feel more like talking.

For the next several days, Katherine threw herself into life at the Circle A. She worked from dawn until dark every day, sometimes dropping into bed fully clothed, only to rise the next morning and repeat the same behavior. No one mentioned her frantic energy, although Mary followed her around urging food at regular intervals.

Matt had returned Lucifer along with some money that Jake had given him.

"For the use of the horse," Matt told her.

Katherine refused the money but accepted the horse. She had taken to riding the animal herself and had to admit that Jake's talent for training horses was an exceptional one.

With the burden of the mortgage lifted, Katherine found she had sufficient funds to rebuild the barn. She ordered the lumber immediately, gritting her teeth as the merchants and townspeople went out of their way to be friendly. Although Katherine found their behavior irritating because of the source of the goodwill, she accepted the treatment and forced herself to be civil.

Despite the changed attitude of the town, she was still surprised when one Saturday in late July wagons full of people and materials pulled into the yard. She walked out to meet them, bewildered.

As the men unloaded the wagons, Katherine spotted Ruth and waved her over.

"What's going on?" Katherine asked.

"Your barn raising." Ruth smiled happily.

"Whose idea was this?"

"Why, everyone's. They want to make things up to you, Katherine." Ruth looked intently into her face. "Let them. It can't hurt."

## Second Chance

Forgiving and trust had come hard to her since her life with Sam. Then the callous treatment of these very people had hardened her heart. She had opened it to Jake, only to have her life filled with lies and deceptions. But as Katherine watched the men work industriously on the barn and the women unload food from their wagons, something inside her began to thaw.

She could fill her life with work, but she'd always be alone. Or she could open up and allow herself the friendship these people were offering. True, she might be hurt again. But isolation was a coward's way of life, and if there was one thing she would never be again, it was a coward.

"We'd better let Mary know there's company or we'll never hear the end of it." Katherine pulled Ruth toward the house and the waiting women.

Jake found the trip to Chicago long and lonely. He had chosen to ride there by horse, hoping that some time alone would help calm his frustration over Katherine. But when he reached the sprawling city, he was still tense and short-tempered.

Alan Pinkerton was not happy to be losing two of his most trusted agents and made several attempts to talk Jake out of the decision. But Jake remained adamant. He had no heart for the task anymore, he told the agitated man. Jake had hoped to make his report and be on his way in a few days, but the added paperwork associated with his withdrawal from the agency extended his stay to a week.

Deciding he'd had enough time with himself, Jake sold his horse and purchased a train ticket to Illinoistown. There he could board a ferry to cross the Mississippi into St. Louis. It had been over a year since he'd seen his parents, and a visit would be expected by now.

He informed no one of his arrival, planning to surprise his family. But when he walked into his parents' house, the silence made him think he should have wired ahead.

"Mother?" he called.

A slight figure appeared at the top of the stairs. "Jake! I can't believe you got here so quickly," his mother cried.

Jake frowned. "What do you mean? I just came for a visit on my way through town. I can't stay long."

His mother walked slowly down the stairs shaking her head. Jake noticed the lines of fatigue on her face and moved quickly to take her hands in his.

"I sent a message to Chicago yesterday. It's your father."

Jake looked up the stairs and then took them two at a time, not stopping until he stood at his father's bedside.

Looking down at the sleeping figure, Jake was struck by the whiteness and transparency of his father's skin. *When had he become so old?* Jake heard his mother enter the room.

## Second Chance

"What happened?"

"Consumption." Her voice was flat with despair.

Jake's heart plummeted at the word. It was a death knell. Some of those with the disease lived on for several years, but for most the end came quickly.

"What do the doctors say?" he whispered.

"What can they say? Make him comfortable." She smiled sadly. "You know how he hates to sit still."

Jake thought of his father—energetic, loudly enthusiastic about everything, always in the midst of a task or planning a new one. The image in Jake's mind did not fit the shrunken figure in front of him.

Jake sighed and stared out the window. It was not the homecoming he'd expected. He would have to send a message to Matt. He doubted he would be able to attend his friend's wedding.

As July melted into August, Katherine wondered if she was working too hard. While previously she'd been able to work all day, becoming tired only when she stopped at nightfall, now she felt as though her limbs were weighted with stone about midafternoon. The past few days she'd even had to sit a spell or she would have fallen.

It wasn't until she tried on her gown for Ruth's wedding that suspicions formed in her mind. As the seamstress attempted to close the back of the dress, the fabric ripped.

"Ma'am, this dress doesn't seem to fit. Pardon me for asking, but have you put on weight?"

Katherine frowned at the woman. Since she'd been working day and night outside, her attire had consisted of men's blue jeans and shirts, which were always too big. She hadn't worn a dress for over a month. Maybe she had put on weight.

Katherine shrugged. "Are you sure the measurements are correct?"

"Yes, ma'am. We've checked you twice before this. You know how nervous Miss Ruth is about this wedding."

Katherine nodded. Her friend had decided to make the wedding a huge event. She attended to every detail herself and drove everyone involved in the production to distraction. This was the first time Ruth had allowed Katherine to go to the dressmaker alone. And then only because the gown was nearly done.

"Can you fix it?" Katherine asked.

"Certainly, ma'am."

Katherine looked the young woman in the eye. "Let's not mention this to Miss Ruth. You know how upset she'll get."

The dressmaker nodded in agreement, and Katherine smiled at the look of relief on the woman's face. She would be as glad to see the day of the wedding as Katherine.

It wasn't until she was on her way home that Katherine began to piece things together. She became increasingly tired and winded when working. Her measurements had increased.

## Second Chance

And her monthly flow had not come since...

Katherine's heart fluttered with the tiny beginnings of hope. Since before Jake arrived in Second Chance.

But how could such a miracle be possible? Sam had told her over and over that she was responsible for their childless state. He had children all over the West. If that was a fact, then how could what she hoped be so? She was barren.

Wasn't she?

# *Chapter Twenty*

Ruth's wedding had been lovely, but Katherine was never so glad to see the end of anything in her life. Her dress was too tight and the corset she'd worn to be able to squeeze into the ensemble pushed all the breath from her lungs. Although Katherine thought her pregnancy must be obvious to all who saw her, she received no strange looks. Nothing but pleasant conversation followed her throughout the day.

After all the guests had left, Katherine helped Ruth escape from the elaborate wedding gown ordered from Chicago. Both Ruth's dress and her own had been fashioned with a bustle, a style now fashionable in the East.

"This is so lovely, Ruth," Katherine said, fingering the ivory silk bodice trimmed with lace.

"We'll have to save it for you then."

## Second Chance

"I won't be needing it."

Ruth frowned. "I'm sure Jake will be back, especially now."

Katherine's hands froze in the act of stroking the smooth, soft underskirt. "What do you mean, especially now?"

Ruth sighed and fixed Katherine with a stare usually reserved for lying students. "It's obvious to me that you're going to have a baby. Marriage usually comes before that event, or haven't you noticed?"

"Not in this case."

"I'm sure if you get in touch with Jake, everything will work out."

"I won't be getting in touch with him."

"Why ever not?" Ruth asked.

"I haven't heard a word from him since he left, not even a letter. Obviously he's gone back to his real life. I wouldn't want him to come back to Second Chance just for the baby. I need someone to want me just for me, not for any other reason."

"We'll probably see him when we take the train to St. Louis," Ruth ventured.

"If you mention one word, Ruth Ward, I'll never forgive you. I will not be the object of anyone's pity. I want this baby, more than you'll ever know. I can raise it alone and I mean to. Don't interfere. Promise me."

Ruth hesitated, looking deep into Katherine's eyes. Finally she sighed. "If that's the way you want things, all right. Remember that you can count on Matt and me for anything you need."

Katherine took her friend's outstretched hand. "I know and I'm grateful. I'm grateful for a lot of things, Ruth, especially this wonderful chance I've been given to have a child. You can't know how happy I am about my life."

Even to Katherine's ears, the words sounded forced and overly cheerful. But Ruth's skeptical look told her she wasn't the only one who could hear the falseness of her tone.

"Let's get you into your beautiful new nightdress." Katherine changed the subject. "I'm sure Matt is pacing the parlor downstairs waiting for me to leave."

Instead of returning to Second Chance after a short visit home as planned, Jake had remained in St. Louis. He worked in his parents' mercantile and helped take care of his father. Jake urged them to move west where the air was said to be better for those with his father's condition. But they refused. They had been born in St. Louis, met, married, and raised a family there, and in St. Louis they would die. As the days turned into months, Jake's father faded gradually. The move west would never have been in time.

Jake kept in touch with Matt and learned that Katherine fared well and the Circle A was out of danger. He was happy her life had improved, but he ached to be near her and touch her once more. Matt never mentioned if Katherine asked after him, and Jake refused to inquire.

## Second Chance

Sometimes he worried that she had forgotten him. But at night, when he lay awake in his childhood room, he remembered their love and believed they were meant to be together. It was just taking longer than he'd hoped to achieve that togetherness.

The summer passed quickly and autumn arrived. Jake's impatience mounted. Matt and Ruth were married by now, yet he remained in St. Louis.

On a warm day in mid-September Jake was at work in the store. He heard a buggy pull up in front and waited patiently behind the counter for a customer.

"Never thought I'd see the great Jake Parker working at a job like regular folks."

"Matt!" Jake grinned and stepped out to greet his friend. "And Ruth. Marriage agrees with you."

Ruth blushed and smiled. She looked into Jake's eyes as if trying to read his mind. After a few moments of the intense scrutiny, Jake began to feel uncomfortable. He turned to Matt with a questioning glance.

"Um, aah." Matt shuffled his feet. "Jake, are you planning on returning to Second Chance soon?"

Jake looked at Matt and Ruth closely. Something was wrong; he could smell it.

"Why?"

"Well, we were just wondering," Matt said. "Aaah, um, Katherine would be happy to see you, I'm sure."

Jake saw the glare that Ruth sent in Matt's direction and frowned.

"What's goin' on back there? Someone giving her trouble again?"

"No, nothing like that. It's just, you told me you'd be going back when Katherine had a chance to cool off. Have you changed your mind?"

"Of course not." Jake didn't miss the look of relief that passed over Ruth's face at his words. "My father isn't getting any better, and I've been working here. To be honest with you both, I'm impatient to see her. Maybe I'll take a weekend off and ride down there so we can work things out."

Matt and Ruth beamed at him, and a trickle of unease ran through Jake.

"I think that would be best." Matt slapped Jake on the back heartily.

"You're sure there's nothing wrong?" Jake asked again.

Ruth and Matt looked at each other, and Ruth gave a slight shake of her head.

"No, partner," Matt said. "Nothing that a trip to Second Chance won't fix."

Jake closed the store and took Ruth and Matt home to see his parents. They could only stay for two hours before their train left for Chicago. After a final meeting with Pinkerton, the newly-weds would spend a two-week honeymoon in the city, then Ruth must return to Second Chance and open school at the end of the month.

## Second Chance

At the ferry, Jake shook hands with his friend and embraced Ruth.

"Have a great time," Jake said.

"We will." Ruth smiled and put her hand on his arm. "You'll go to Second Chance then?"

"This weekend, I think." Jake covered Ruth's hand with his own and squeezed.

As the ferry drifted across the great Mississippi, Jake heard his name being called. He turned around and saw his parents' hired man running toward him.

"Mr. Jake, come quick. It's your father."

As time passed, Katherine's pregnancy became visible to everyone. Her hired men never commented on her condition, beyond forbidding her to lift anything or remain outside for too long. With the coming winter, the amount of work lessened and she was able to get by without hiring any more help. She appointed Joe the new foreman, and he proved adept at the job.

The townsfolk remained civil, though their exaggerated friendliness diminished as the size of her belly increased. Katherine stayed at the Circle A and sent others to town to avoid the curious stares and whispers. She had Mary and the Wards for company, which was all she needed. Or so she told herself.

As Mary left for home one evening, she stopped at the door to Katherine's office. Katherine looked up from her book and smiled.

"Leaving now?"

"In a minute. Girl, I've been thinkin'."

Katherine suppressed a groan. She had been waiting for her housekeeper's lecture, but the woman had remained unnaturally silent. That situation was about to change.

"Raisin' a baby's not easy, ya know?"

"I'm sure it's not."

"Especially for a woman alone."

"I won't be alone. I have you and the men." Katherine smiled. "Not to mention Ruth and Matt."

"That's not the same. A child should have a mother and a father."

"I'll manage."

Mary came into the room and lowered her bulk into a chair. "The townsfolk have been mighty tolerant of this situation."

"My life is none of their concern." Katherine's voice was low with anger.

"You may not care, but think about the child. It's common knowledge you don't have a husband. The little 'un will be labeled a bastard from the first in this town."

Katherine was silent. She had sat up many nights trying to think of a solution to her situation. She had found no answers.

"What do you suggest I do?" Katherine asked.

"Sell the Circle A." At Katherine's gasp Mary waved her into silence. "Hear me out, now. If you went farther west you could say you were a widow lady. No one would know any different. You could have a whole new life. You've got to think of the baby."

## Second Chance

Katherine didn't answer. The thought of selling the Circle A made her ache deep inside. But . . . maybe Mary was right. Would it be fair to make her child bear the stigma of its birth? Katherine pressed her fingertips to her temples, feeling the strain of another decision press upon her.

"I don't want to upset you, girl," Mary said gently, even quietly for once. "I figured you should be thinkin' on it leastways."

Katherine looked up into the wide, caring face of her housekeeper and smiled. "I know you mean to help, Mary. I'll think about what you've said."

"And don't think you're gettin' away from here without me either." Mary returned to her bluff manner, though Katherine saw the telltale shine in the housekeeper's eyes. "I aim to take care of that baby and won't hear no sass from you about it."

Katherine nodded her head but was unable to speak, warmed by the love and the loyalty of her friend.

Once Mary had left, Katherine remained in her office well into the night. The more she thought about Mary's words, the more they made sense. She had an obligation to her child, and that had to come first. Yes, giving up the ranch would tear her apart. But she must think of the baby. Once, not very long ago, the Circle A had meant everything to her. She had finally found the home she had always desired and couldn't imagine ever letting the place go. But now she knew that wherever her child resided would be her home. Home wasn't a place; home was a feeling in your soul.

She stared out the window for a long time, her palm resting on her swollen abdomen as the child struggled within her. It was times like these, when she was alone with the wonder of their child, that Katherine ached for Jake the most. She still looked for him at odd times of the day and night, though she tried not to. Whenever she heard a rider coming up the main road she held her breath and hoped— always in vain.

Katherine reached out her hand and traced a fingertip down the cold windowpane. If she hadn't been pregnant, would she have swallowed her pride and gotten in touch with Jake to try to resolve their differences?

Ruth and Mary both believed that Jake had a right to know about the baby, and maybe he did. But she couldn't bring herself to tell him. She had nearly ruined her life once by marrying a man who only wanted her for a child; she would not ruin her precious child's life by making the same mistake twice.

Katherine turned away from the window with a tired sigh. Her back ached. For that matter so did her hips and her legs and her feet. Thinking of Jake had made her melancholy, and she sniffed against the sudden tickle in her nose. She would not cry again over that man. She would miss him every day of her life, probably more so when she had the child to remind her of their time together, but it was that child she must think of now.

As she wearily climbed the stairs to her room, Katherine made her decision. As soon as the baby arrived and the snows ceased, her small family would be on their way west.

"There's gonna be 'n ice sterm, mister."

The stooped old man peered at Jake through the freezing rain. His isolated farmstead was the first Jake had seen since riding out from St. Louis early that morning.

"You'd best hole up here a spell."

Jake didn't have to glance at the evil-looking clouds to realize the oldtimer was right. The rain, which had turned to sleet, stung his face. Within the next hour travel would become impossible. From the look of the sky, a blizzard would follow on the heels of the ice.

"If you don't mind the company, sir, I'd be much obliged," Jake said.

The old man motioned for him to put his horse in the barn, then retreated to the warmth of his cabin.

As Jake rubbed down the wet horse, his mind went back over the past three months.

His father had taken a turn for the worse that day in September, remaining unconscious through the last days of his life. Jake had organized the funeral and stayed on to find a manager for the mercantile. His mother had taken the death hard. Jake couldn't in good conscience leave her until after the Christmas holiday, though his impatience to be back in Second Chance ate at him day after day.

When he could finally leave with a clear conscience, a break in the rail line headed south toward Second Chance forced him to ride in the dead of winter.

He had sent one letter to Katherine explaining the situation but received no response. With the uncertainty of the mail system, Jake didn't know if Katherine ever received the letter, or had chosen to ignore it. Either way, an increasing urgency to reach Second Chance plagued him. This storm would slow him up by several days at least. He swore violently, and his horse shied at the anger in his voice.

The old man proved to be good company. A soldier in the Mexican War, he regaled Jake with tales of days past. The ice storm lasted three days, followed by the anticipated blizzard. When the sun finally shone again, over a week had passed.

Jake's impatience mounted during the forced confinement. An increasing need for haste tickled at the back of his neck day and night.

"I'm thankful for the shelter, sir." Jake attempted to pay the man for his trouble.

"No, son, I'm grateful for the company. If you ever get this way again, stop by."

"I'll do that."

Throughout the day Jake's horse picked its way through the deep drifts of snow. By nightfall, Jake knew he would have to travel another week to reach Second Chance, barring any other unforeseen difficulties.

Six days later, thoroughly tired of sleeping in the freezing snow, Jake hoped he had seen his last day in the open. By that evening he would be at the Circle A, and if things went well he would sleep in a warm bed—preferably with the warm body he'd been dreaming of for months.

As the day wore on, Jake watched the sky carefully. What had begun as a typical gray winter day was fast becoming a dark, storm-filled horizon. Carbon-colored clouds rolled over the distant hills. He urged his horse to move faster, but the animal ignored his command. The stallion could only do so much against the knee-deep whiteness, and he patted the animal's neck in sympathy.

"Not much longer now, boy. You've worked hard this trip and I appreciate it."

Jake scanned the distance for a sign of the town. He should be getting close. If his luck held out he might reach the Circle A before the storm reached him. Glancing at the sky again, his spirits sank. The clouds had moved closer and were gaining speed.

The wind picked up, but Jake kept to the trudging pace. He would keep going as long as possible, and he might stumble across a shelter. Ducking his head against the wind, Jake glanced up every few minutes and scanned the horizon with tearing eyes for a sight of civilization.

The icy rain blew at them in a fierce gust, and Jake's horse stopped and whinnied in anger. Jake squinted into the painful onslaught. Was that a light ahead? Yes, thank God. Jake sighed with relief and kicked the horse. It refused to move.

"Come on, boy, only a little farther."

No amount of encouragement could move the animal. Finally Jake slid to the ground and tugged the horse in the direction of the light.

He kept his eyes focused on the small pinpoint as the storm swirled about him. Ice and snow mixed together and blurred his vision. His two-weeks' growth of beard was frozen solid. Glancing back at the horse, Jake saw the animal was covered with white froth.

It seemed to take hours, but gradually the light grew bigger and finally materialized into the window of a house.

Jake stopped in amazement, and the horse bumped into him, its face frozen over with ice. Maybe he was dreaming, but he had run smack into the Circle A.

Jake began to chuckle. Maybe God was on his side after all and this was a good omen. He looked around for a place to leave the horse out of the wind, and his eyes lit on a newly constructed barn. Life on the Circle A must be improving. He smiled as he led the animal into the shelter.

The air, warmed by the bodies of the horses, hit him like a blow after the icy sharpness outdoors. He led his horse into an empty stall,

## Second Chance

rubbing him with thick cloths until the ice melted or fell to the ground. After feeding the animal, Jake rubbed its nose a moment, then exited the barn.

The storm had not abated, and the sting of the wind battered his damp cheeks. Jake climbed the steps of the porch and knocked loudly on the front door. He held his breath as a shadow passed in front of the office window, and a second later the door opened.

Every word he'd planned to say to Katherine over the months they'd been separated fled from his brain at the sight of her in the doorway. Jake's eyes focused on hers, and he saw surprise, replaced by happiness and then a flash of anger. He caught the door with his foot as she attempted to swing it closed and pushed his way into the house.

"What do you think you're doing?" Katherine demanded, pulling her voluminous wrapper close about her neck.

"I've come to talk some sense into you."

"I've always had plenty of sense, thank you."

Jake stared at her, drinking in the sight of her loose hair and the fire in her eyes. But as his gaze drifted lower, Katherine began to back away toward the office. Something was not right.

Though the gown attempted to erase the shape of her body, Jake could see the ripe fullness of her breasts and the exaggerated rounding of her middle. A single step brought him close to her, and he pulled the material from her clutching fingers to reveal the form beneath.

"What is this?"

Katherine grimaced. "What does it look like?"

"My baby is what it looks like. When were you planning on telling me?"

"Never."

Jake attempted to speak, but his anger made the words stick in his throat. Instead, he picked Katherine up bodily and stalked into her office. Placing her feet back on the floor, he pointed to the chair behind her desk.

"Sit," he growled.

"I don't take orders . . . aah."

Katherine's legs crumpled and she sat obediently—on the floor at Jake's feet.

"What's the matter?"

Breathing heavily, Katherine ground out between clenched teeth, "Baby's coming."

Jake's face drained of blood. "Where's Mary? The doctor?"

When the pain had passed, Katherine looked up at him. "I've been having pains since yesterday. I sent Joe for both Mary and the doctor before the storm hit. I don't think they'll make it back now." She glanced at the swirling whiteness hitting the windows.

"What will we do?"

"Boil water."

"Very funny. Katherine, the only babies I've delivered are horses."

"Well, you're about to move up to people. Can't be much different from what I've heard.

## Second Chance

You stand there and I push. Ow!"

Jake watched helplessly as Katherine's face reflected her inner struggle. Suddenly a gush of fluid wet the floor.

"What's that?"

Katherine gave him a look of disgust. "It's supposed to happen. Help me upstairs to bed and quit panicking. This baby's coming and there's nothing we can do but greet the child when it gets here."

Jake helped her to her feet, pushing back the rising tide of nervousness inside him. When they were halfway up the staircase, Katherine doubled over with pain, and Jake carried her the rest of the way to her bed. He stood looking down at her, uncertain of what to do next.

When the pain passed, Katherine looked at him and sighed. "There's a basket of things Mary put together for when the time came," she told him. "They're in the kitchen." When he hesitated, she hissed between clenched teeth, "Go!"

As Jake hurried down the stairs, Katherine groaned with another pain. They were coming closer together. His pace increased along with his fear.

The pressure came and went in waves, but she always knew it would be back. Katherine felt the sweat on her neck and in her hair. Why hadn't she put up her hair? At least her neck would feel cooler. She realized she was naked, covered only by a thin sheet, and wondered momentarily who had removed her clothes. But her mind refused to focus on anything but the pain. Life had become an endless river of agony. Either the pain was there or hovering past her next labored breath. Would this never end?

A cold cloth met the damp skin of her forehead, and she smiled with pleasure.

"Feels good," Katherine mumbled.

The cloth moved over her face and neck. Hands lifted her hair and tied the tangled mass back from her face.

Katherine opened her eyes to see Jake hovering over her, concern evident on his features.

"How long has it been?" she asked.

Jake squeezed her hand as he stared into her eyes. "A few hours. You're doing fine. Can't be much longer now."

He sounded more hopeful than knowledgeable, and she attempted a smile. The attempt became a grimace as the familiar pressure began to rise and build inside her.

"It's coming again," she whispered.

"Squeeze my hand and bear down."

Straining with all her might, Katherine pushed until she thought her head would explode. A loud groan echoed in the room, the sound coming from her own parched throat. Jake pulled his hand from hers and moved to the end of the bed.

"I can see the baby's head. Push harder, Katie."

Drawing on strength she hadn't known existed, Katherine bore down again. After

## Second Chance

several similar efforts, the child slipped from her body into Jake's waiting hands. She fell back onto the bed breathing freely and deeply, her ears filled with the angry squalling of her child.

Exhausted, she closed her eyes and listened while Jake bathed the baby in the water she'd instructed him to heat for that purpose. When several moments passed and he didn't speak, Katherine struggled up onto her elbows.

"Is everything all right?" she cried. "Give it to me."

Jake turned. He had wrapped the baby in a clean blanket. When he looked at her and Katherine saw the wonder on his face, she relaxed.

Holding out her arms, she asked, "Do I have a son or a daughter?"

Jake sat on the edge of the bed. He seemed reluctant to hand over the tiny bundle in his arms. But when a cry erupted from the blanket, he quickly relinquished the baby to Katherine.

"We have a son." Jake reached out to touch the black down on the baby's head as Katherine put the child to her breast.

She stared at the large, brown hand where it rested on the small head. The baby made quiet sounds of contentment as he suckled.

Katherine glanced up and the warmth of Jake's gaze answered the warmth lighting her heart. She smiled tentatively. Why hadn't she realized that second chances were a rare and beautiful gift?

"Why did you come back?" she asked.

"I always planned to. I wanted to give you time to get over your anger."

"You nearly waited too long."

"Your timing has always been off," he said.

"I'd say my timing has always been perfect."

The baby lost the nipple and began to cry and beat the air with tiny fists. Jake laughed. "He has your temperament, I see."

Katherine guided the tiny mouth back to its destination, then reached over their son to trace the small scar at Jake's temple.

"No more lies," she whispered.

Jake reached to turn out the lamp, plunging the room into darkness.

"No more lies, no more fears. We've been given a second chance, Katie, and I won't let you down."

# LEIGH GREENWOOD'S
# SEVEN BRIDES *Rose*

For penniless Rose Thorton, the advertisement for a housekeeper to cook and clean for seven brothers seems like the answer to her prayers, and the incredibly handsome man who hires her like a dream come true. But when she sets her eyes on her hero's ramshackle ranch in the wilds of Texas brush country and meets his utterly impossible brothers, even George's earth-shattering kisses aren't compensation for the job ahead of her. The Randolph brothers are a wild bunch—carving an empire out of the rugged land—and they aren't about to let any female change their ways...until George lays down the law and then loses his heart to the beguiling spitfire who has turned all their lives upside down.

_3499-9 $4.99 US/$5.99 CAN

**LEISURE BOOKS**
**ATTN: Order Department**
**276 5th Avenue, New York, NY 10001**

Please add $1.50 for shipping and handling for the first book and $.35 for each book thereafter. PA., N.Y.S. and N.Y.C. residents, please add appropriate sales tax. No cash, stamps, or C.O.D.s. All orders shipped within 6 weeks via postal service book rate. Canadian orders require $2.00 extra postage and must be paid in U.S. dollars through a U.S. banking facility.

Name _____
Address _____
City _____ State _____ Zip _____
I have enclosed $_____ in payment for the checked book(s).
Payment <u>must</u> accompany all orders. ☐ Please send a free catalog.

# SENSATIONAL HISTORICAL ROMANCE BY LEISURE'S LEADING LADY OF LOVE!

*"Catherine Hart writes thrilling adventure ...beautiful and memorable romance!"*
—*Romantic Times*

## SWEET FURY
## CATHERINE HART

She was exasperating, infuriating, unbelievably tantalizing; a little hellcat with flashing eyes and red-gold tangles: a virgin with barnyard morals. If anyone was to make a lady of the girl it would have to be Marshal Travis Kincaid, and with his town overrun by outlaws, it was going to be an uphill battle all the way. She might fight him tooth and nail, but Travis swore he would coax her into his strong arms, silence her sassy mouth with his lips, and then unleash all her wild, sweet fury.

\_3562-6  $4.99 US/$5.99 CAN

**LEISURE BOOKS**
**ATTN: Order Department**
**276 5th Avenue, New York, NY 10001**

Please add $1.50 for shipping and handling for the first book and $.35 for each book thereafter. PA., N.Y.S. and N.Y.C. residents, please add appropriate sales tax. No cash, stamps, or C.O.D.s. All orders shipped within 6 weeks via postal service book rate. Canadian orders require $2.00 extra postage and must be paid in U.S. dollars through a U.S. banking facility.

Name _____
Address _____
City _____ State _____ Zip _____
I have enclosed $_____in payment for the checked book(s).
Payment <u>must</u> accompany all orders. ☐ Please send a free catalog.

# Don't miss the first title in the brand-new
## *Americana Series!*

# Where The Heart Is
# ROBIN LEE HATCHER

## Bestselling author of *The Magic*

"*Where the Heart Is* is a warm, tender, compelling historical romance!" —Jayne Ann Krentz

For spinster Addie Sherwood, a position as the first schoolteacher in the frontier town of Homestead also means a chance to escape a loveless marriage of convenience. But within days of her arrival in Idaho, she receives another proposal, this time from handsome rancher Will Rider. But Addie vows she will not accept his offer until she is sure he really loves her. For her dream of a new life will turn to ashes unless Will believes, as she does, that home is where the heart is.

_3527-8                                            $4.99 US/$5.99 CAN

**LEISURE BOOKS**
**ATTN: Order Department**
**276 5th Avenue, New York, NY 10001**

Please add $1.50 for shipping and handling for the first book and $.35 for each book thereafter. PA., N.Y.S. and N.Y.C. residents, please add appropriate sales tax. No cash, stamps, or C.O.D.s. All orders shipped within 6 weeks via postal service book rate. Canadian orders require $2.00 extra postage and must be paid in U.S. dollars through a U.S. banking facility.

Name _____
Address _____
City _____ State _____ Zip _____
I have enclosed $_____ in payment for the checked book(s).
Payment <u>must</u> accompany all orders. ☐ Please send a free catalog.

# "HISTORICAL ROMANCE AT ITS BEST!"
## —*Romantic Times*

*Discover the real world of romance with Leisure's leading lady of love!*

# SHIRL HENKE
## Winner of 6 *Romantic Times* Awards

**Terms of Surrender.** Although gambler Rhys Davies owns half of Starlight, Colorado, within weeks of riding into town, there is one "property" he'd give all the rest to possess—the glacially beautiful daughter of Starlight's first family. To win the lady, the gambler will wager his very life—and hope that the devil does, indeed, look after his own.
\_3424-7                               $4.99 US/$5.99 CAN

**Terms of Love.** Cassandra Clayton doesn't need any man to help her run her father's freighting empire, but without one she can't produce a male heir. When she saves Steve Loring from a hangman's noose, she thinks she has what she needs—a stud who will perform on command. But from the first, Steve makes it clear that he wants more than silver dollars—he wants Cass's heart and soul too.
\_3345-3                               $4.99 US/$5.99 CAN

**LEISURE BOOKS**
**ATTN: Order Department**
**276 5th Avenue, New York, NY 10001**

Please add $1.50 for shipping and handling for the first book and $.35 for each book thereafter. PA., N.Y.S. and N.Y.C. residents, please add appropriate sales tax. No cash, stamps, or C.O.D.s. All orders shipped within 6 weeks via postal service book rate. Canadian orders require $2.00 extra postage and must be paid in U.S. dollars through a U.S. banking facility.

Name_____
Address_____
City _____ State _____ Zip _____
I have enclosed $_____in payment for the checked book(s).
Payment <u>must</u> accompany all orders. ☐ Please send a free catalog.

# Wild and Wonderful Frontier Romance
## by Norah Hess
## Winner of the *Romantic Times*
## Lifetime Achievement Award

***Kentucky Woman.*** Spencer Atkins wants no part of a wife and children while he can live in his pa's backwoods cabin as a carefree bachelor. And Gretchen Ames will marry no man refusing her a home and a family. Although they are the unlikeliest couple, Spencer and Gretchen find themselves grudgingly sharing a cabin, working side by side, and fighting an attraction neither can deny.
_3518-9                                    $4.99 US/$5.99 CAN

***Mountain Rose.*** Chase Donlin doesn't hesitate before agreeing to care for his dying stepsister's daughter, his niece in all but blood. But Chase never dreams that "little" Raegan will be a blooming young woman. How is he to act the part of guardian when every glimpse of her sweet-scented flesh sets off a storm of desire in his blood?
_3413-1                                    $4.99 US/$5.99 CAN

***Kentucky Bride.*** Fleeing her abusive uncle, D'lise Alexander trusts no man...until she is rescued by virile trapper Kane Devlin. His rugged strength and tender concern make D'lise forget everything except her longing to become his sweetest Kentucky bride.
_3253-8                                    $4.99 US/$5.99 CAN

**LEISURE BOOKS**
**ATTN: Order Department**
**276 5th Avenue, New York, NY 10001**

Please add $1.50 for shipping and handling for the first book and $.35 for each book thereafter. PA., N.Y.S. and N.Y.C. residents, please add appropriate sales tax. No cash, stamps, or C.O.D.s. All orders shipped within 6 weeks via postal service book rate. Canadian orders require $2.00 extra postage and must be paid in U.S. dollars through a U.S. banking facility.

Name_____
Address_____
City _____ State_____Zip_____
I have enclosed $_____in payment for the checked book(s).
Payment <u>must</u> accompany all orders.☐ Please send a free catalog.

"The stuff fantasies are made of!" —*Romantic Times*

# Tempestuous Historical Romance
## by Connie Mason

Winner of the *Romantic Times* Storyteller of the Year Award!

***Treasure of the Heart.*** When Cody Carter and Cassie Fenmore learn they are to share the inheritance of the Rocking C Ranch, they have no doubt a tempest of trouble is brewing. But neither can guess that, when the dust has settled, all their assumptions will be gone with the wind—replaced by a love more precious than gold.
\_3539-1                                  $4.99 US/$5.99 CAN

***A Promise of Thunder.*** Storm Kennedy has lost her land to Grady Stryker, a handsome Cheyenne half-breed, and finds herself forced to marry him in order to get her claim back. She may be his legal wife, but Storm vows she'll deny him access to her last asset—the lush body Grady thinks is his for the asking.
\_3444-1                                  $4.99 US/$5.99 CAN

***Caress and Conquer.*** Caught stealing to support her invalid mother, Amanda Prescott is horrified to learn she will be transported to the American Colonies to serve a term as an indentured servant. And worse, her master turns out to be none other than Tony Brandt, the very man who has unwittingly caused her downfall—the only man whose consuming love can win her freedom.
\_3532-4                                  $4.99 US/$5.99 CAN

**LEISURE BOOKS**
**ATTN: Order Department**
**276 5th Avenue, New York, NY 10001**

Please add $1.50 for shipping and handling for the first book and $.35 for each book thereafter. PA., N.Y.S. and N.Y.C. residents, please add appropriate sales tax. No cash, stamps, or C.O.D.s. All orders shipped within 6 weeks via postal service book rate. Canadian orders require $2.00 extra postage and must be paid in U.S. dollars through a U.S. banking facility.

Name_____
Address_____
City _____ State_____ Zip_____
I have enclosed $_____in payment for the checked book(s).
Payment <u>must</u> accompany all orders. ☐ Please send a free catalog.

## HISTORICAL ROMANCE
### *BITTERSWEET PROMISES*
### By Trana Mae Simmons

Cody Garret likes everything in its place: his horse in its stable, his six-gun in its holster, his money in the bank. But the rugged cowpoke's life is turned head over heels when a robbery throws Shanna Van Alystyne into his arms. With a spirit as fiery as the blazing sun, and a temper to match, Shanna is the most downright thrilling woman ever to set foot in Liberty, Missouri. No matter what it takes, Cody will besiege Shanna's hesitant heart and claim her heavenly love.

\_51934-8     $4.99 US/$5.99 CAN

## CONTEMPORARY ROMANCE
### *SNOWBOUND WEEKEND/GAMBLER'S LOVE*
### By Amii Lorin

In *Snowbound Weekend,* romance is the last thing on Jennifer Lengle's mind when she sets off for a ski trip. But trapped by a blizzard in a roadside inn, Jen finds herself drawn to sophisticated Adam Banner, with his seductive words and his outrageous promises...promises that can be broken as easily as her innocent heart.

And in *Gambler's Love,* Vichy Sweigart's heart soars when she meets handsome Ben Larkin in Atlantic City. But Ben is a gambler, and Vichy knows from experience that such a man can hurt her badly. She is willing to risk everything she has for love, but the odds are high—and her heart is at stake.

\_51935-6     (two unforgettable romances in one volume) Only $4.99

**LOVE SPELL**
**ATTN: Order Department**
**Dorchester Publishing Co., Inc.**
**276 5th Avenue, New York, NY 10001**

Please add $1.50 for shipping and handling for the first book and $.35 for each book thereafter. PA., N.Y.S. and N.Y.C. residents, please add appropriate sales tax. No cash, stamps, or C.O.D.s. All orders shipped within 6 weeks via postal service book rate. Canadian orders require $2.00 extra postage and must be paid in U.S. dollars through a U.S. banking facility.

Name_____
Address_____
City _____ State_____ Zip_____
I have enclosed $_____in payment for the checked book(s).
Payment <u>must</u> accompany all orders. ☐ Please send a free catalog.

# Don't miss these fabulous historical romances by Leisure's leading ladies of love!

*Savage Illusion* by Cassie Edwards. A Blackfoot Indian raised by white settlers, Jolena Edmonds dreams of a hard-bodied brave who fills her with a fiery longing. But when at last she meets the bold warrior Spotted Eagle, a secret enemy threatens to separate them forever.

\_3480-8 $4.99 US/$5.99 CAN

*Exiled Heart* by Susan Tanner. As wild as the windswept Highlands, Cecile Lotharing never dreams her parents will arrange a match to save her from ill fortune. Torn from all that she cherishes, Cecile faces a bleak future and a joyless marriage unless she can win the love of her intended's exiled heart.

\_3481-6 $4.99 US/$5.99 CAN

*Montana Surrender* by Trana Mae Simmons. Although a mysterious horseman has Jessica's ranch hands convinced they are seeing spirits, the sable-haired beauty vows to unmask the sexy master of disguises. But when solving the mystery leads to a night of unbelievable ecstasy, Jessica has to decide if discovering the cold truth is worth shattering the passionate fantasy.

\_3472-2 $4.50 US/$5.50 CAN

**LEISURE BOOKS**
**ATTN: Order Department**
**276 5th Avenue, New York, NY 10001**

Please add $1.50 for shipping and handling for the first book and $.35 for each book thereafter. PA., N.Y.S. and N.Y.C. residents, please add appropriate sales tax. No cash, stamps, or C.O.D.s. All orders shipped within 6 weeks via postal service book rate. Canadian orders require $2.00 extra postage and must be paid in U.S. dollars through a U.S. banking facility.

Name_____
Address_____
City _____ State_____ Zip_____
I have enclosed $_____in payment for the checked book(s). Payment <u>must</u> accompany all orders.☐ Please send a free catalog.

# Passionate, Unforgettable Historical Romance
## By Charlotte McPherren

***Love & Fortune.*** Everything was perfect—the moonlight, the swirling red veil she wore to disguise her face, the sizzling sensuality she felt as she stared into the Confederate officer's eyes. Yes, Fortune Landry is certain the sultry Gypsy dance irrevocably bonded her to Grady MacNair. But it had also led to a terrible betrayal on that long-ago night. When they meet again years later, the instant attraction between them is proof that the Gypsy spell still holds strong. But Fortune fears that, if Grady learns her true identity, his hatred will burn with the same passion that now brings her such ecstasy in his masterful embrace.

\_3560-X                                   $4.50 US/$5.50 CAN

***Song Of The Willow.*** Ladies don't wear men's pants or herd cattle, nor do they curse or sneak whiskey, but Willie Vaughn does. Growing up in a household of five men, Willie can steal a base, rope a cow and hold her own in a brawl. But she never thinks she'll have to learn to seduce a man—until she meets the handsome and dangerous Rider Sinclair. He is determined to teach the winsome tomboy a thing or two about love—but he doesn't expect to learn a thing or two in the process.

\_3483-2                                   $4.50 US/$5.50 CAN

**LEISURE BOOKS**
**ATTN: Order Department**
**276 5th Avenue, New York, NY 10001**

Please add $1.50 for shipping and handling for the first book and $.35 for each book thereafter. PA., N.Y.S. and N.Y.C. residents, please add appropriate sales tax. No cash, stamps, or C.O.D.s. All orders shipped within 6 weeks via postal service book rate. Canadian orders require $2.00 extra postage and must be paid in U.S. dollars through a U.S. banking facility.

Name _____
Address _____
City _____ State _____ Zip _____
I have enclosed $_____ in payment for the checked book(s).
Payment <u>must</u> accompany all orders. ☐ Please send a free catalog.

# JESSIE'S OUTLAW
## Cheryl Anne Porter

A lonely orphan, Jessie Stewart never imagines that her dreams of happiness will be fulfilled until a wounded man appears in her root cellar. Exasperating, infuriating, and unbelievably handsome, the stranger has secrets to hide and enemies to flee. Whoever he is, whatever he has done, Jessie longs to help him, no matter how great the danger to her life or her virtue. As deadly gunrunners pursue the desperate pair across the scorching New Mexican desert, the sassy girl will have to dodge bullets and the law and silence the desperado's protests with her sweet lips if she ever hopes to unleash the wild, tantalizing ecstasy of their love.

_3541-3                                                      $4.50 US/$5.50 CAN

**LEISURE BOOKS**
**ATTN: Order Department**
**276 5th Avenue, New York, NY 10001**

Please add $1.50 for shipping and handling for the first book and $.35 for each book thereafter. PA., N.Y.S. and N.Y.C. residents, please add appropriate sales tax. No cash, stamps, or C.O.D.s. All orders shipped within 6 weeks via postal service book rate. Canadian orders require $2.00 extra postage and must be paid in U.S. dollars through a U.S. banking facility.

Name_____
Address_____
City _____ State_____ Zip_____
I have enclosed $_____in payment for the checked book(s).
Payment <u>must</u> accompany all orders.☐ Please send a free catalog.